Praise for *On Harrow Hill*

"A truly ingenious play-fair mystery novel that's police procedural adjacent while still being able to bend the rules of the latter by featuring an unconventional sleuth and his unconventional friends . . . A thrilling mystery with a smart, sympathetic detective that will puzzle you every step of the way."

—DOREEN SHERIDAN, *Criminal Element*

"Verdon's brilliant seventh mystery featuring retired NYPD homicide detective Dave Gurney (after 2018's *White River Burning*) showcases a nifty impossible crime variant . . . The surprises keep coming as the plot builds to an impressive reveal. Verdon has never been better at crafting a bizarre setup and resolving it in a satisfactory way." —*Publishers Weekly* (starred review)

"A glorious explosion of detective fireworks." —*Booklist*

"I believe John Verdon to be the finest mystery writer working today . . . Verdon does not crank out his stories using a formula. Each and every mystery is a gift to readers who love to play along and try to identify the culprit with no tricks used at all."

—RICHARD KLINZMAN, *The Florida Times-Union*

"Clever, cerebral . . . Part puzzle, part police procedural and all entertainment. Verdon has a knack for creating outlandish, almost unbelievable, situations that reach logical, realistic conclusions . . . No matter how weird the circumstances of *On Harrow Hill* become, Verdon retains tight control of his plot."

—OLINE H. COGDILL, *Shelf Awareness*

"Sure to impress . . . The best Verdon piece I have read, though I have loved them all a great deal. The flow of the story is perfect, revealing much as the narrative builds.

Verdon has done well to develop this quirky, layered story that is not a simple A to Z crime thriller . . . A book I could not stop reading."

—MATT PECHEY, *Mystery and Suspense Magazine*

"John Verdon has written another tightly wound, intelligent mystery that keeps you guessing until the very end. Retired NYPD detective Dave Gurney, a sharp-minded, Sherlockian sleuth with an old soul, is drawn into a murder investigation in a seemingly idyllic small town that has been corrupted by one family's manipulative power. When the family's patriarch is brutally killed, the list of suspects with motives rooted in betrayal, loss, and toxic social inequality seems endless, but all evidence points to the one man with the perfect alibi: he died two days before the murder. Or did he? As the plot's precisely calibrated gears move from one revelation to the next with sure-handed finesse, *On Harrow Hill* engages the mind and heart in equal measure."

—HEATHER YOUNG, author of *The Lost Girls* and *The Distant Dead*

"*On Harrow Hill* is the latest airtight mystery only ex–NYPD detective Dave Gurney can solve. Drawn into another seemingly impossible murder case in a small town with far too many secrets—and suspects—Gurney's keen skills and almost preternatural insights are once again on dazzling display. John Verdon is a master at crafting these Sherlockian stories, each more mind-bending than the last, and *On Harrow Hill* is destined to be the next hit in the series."

—J. TODD SCOTT, author of *Lost River*

Praise for the Dave Gurney series

"John Verdon writes grown-up detective novels, by which I mean stories with intelligent plots, well-developed characters and crimes that have social consequences . . . The author's brainy gumshoe-for-hire, Dave Gurney, checks all these boxes."

—MARILYN STASIO, *The New York Times Book Review*

"The hard-edged characters . . . recall Chandler's 'mean streets,' but the ornate

puzzles laid before Verdon's detective might have challenged the 'little grey cells' of Hercule Poirot."
—DANIEL STASHOWER, *The Washington Post*

"Outstanding . . . The twisty plot builds up to a logical and satisfying reveal. Verdon expertly combines a baffling whodunit with thoughtfully drawn characters."
—*Publishers Weekly* (starred and boxed review)

"Verdon is a gifted writer and storyteller." —*Booklist*

ALSO BY JOHN VERDON

Think of a Number
Shut Your Eyes Tight
Let the Devil Sleep
Peter Pan Must Die
Wolf Lake
White River Burning

ON HARROW HILL

A DAVE GURNEY NOVEL

JOHN VERDON

COUNTERPOINT
Berkeley, California

On Harrow Hill

First hardcover edition: 2021
First paperback edition: 2022

The Library of Congress has cataloged the hardcover edition as follows:
Names: Verdon, John, author.
Title: On Harrow Hill / John Verdon.
Description: First hardcover edition. | Berkeley, California : Counterpoint, 2021. | Series: A Dave Gurney novel
Identifiers: LCCN 2020012064 | ISBN 9781640093102 (hardcover) | ISBN 9781640093119 (ebook)
Subjects: GSAFD: Mystery fiction.
Classification: LCC PS3622.E736 O5 2021 | DDC 813/.6—dc23
LC record available at https://lccn.loc.gov/2020012064

Paperback ISBN: 978-1-64009-510-6

Cover design by Jarrod Taylor
Book design by Jordan Koluch

COUNTERPOINT
2560 Ninth Street, Suite 318
Berkeley, CA 94710
www.counterpointpress.com

Printed in the United States of America

10 9 8 7 6 5 4 3 2 1

For Naomi

The deadliest flaw in human nature
is the ability to hold an unshakable opinion
based on inadequate evidence.

—ANONYMOUS

PART ONE

RESURRECTION

1

Listen carefully," said Dave Gurney, "to this eyewitness description of a murder."

He was standing at the podium in a lecture hall at the state police training academy, conducting a seminar titled "Evaluation of Eyewitness Statements." There was a projection screen on a low stage behind him. He held a one-page form in his hand. Some eager cadets were leaning forward. All watching him.

"This recorded statement was given to an NYPD transit officer by Maria Santiago, a twenty-two-year-old teacher's aide at a Bronx public school:

> 'I was on the northbound platform at the 138th Street subway station. I was coming home from work, so it was around four o'clock. Not very crowded. There was this skinny, dark teenager, trying to look cool. Crazy clothes, like kids wear now. Near him there were these four older Anglo guys. Like construction guys. They started looking at the kid. Bad looks. One of them, big guy in a black leather jacket, dirty black jeans, said something about the kid's clothes. Kid said something back. I'm not sure what, but in a Puerto Rican accent, like mine. Big guy suddenly pulled a gun out of his jacket pocket, shot the kid. People were running, shouting, everyone going nuts. Then the cops came.'

"Ms. Santiago's full statement is longer than that," said Gurney, looking up from the witness report, "but those are the main details. Anyone want me to go through it one more time?"

A female cadet in the front row raised her hand. "Could you, please?"

He read it again. "Anyone want to hear it a third time?"

No one said anything. He picked up a second report from the podium.

"This next example also comes from the NYPD transit division. It, too, describes a platform homicide. The statement was given by John McIntyre, a forty-five-year-old gas station owner:

> 'It was rush hour, crowded, loads of people on the platform. I hate the subway, but once in a while I have to take it. It's filthy. It stinks. People spit on the floor. So there was this fellow, coming home from work. Tired, stressed like. He was standing there, waiting for the train, minding his own business. And there was this bunch of black gangsta-rap assholes watching him. Scum of the earth. Puffy jackets. Stupid sneakers with the laces hanging off them. Stupid hats with hoodies over them. The leader of the pack has his eye on the guy who's coming home from work. Evil eye, you could see it, looking for trouble. They say something back and forth. Then the black guy pulls out a gun, they get into a struggle, black guy gets shot with his own gun. Goes down on the platform. Ugly thing. But he asked for it. They call that karma, right? High on some shit. Meth makes them fuckers crazy.'

"Like the other statement," said Gurney, "this one was edited down to a few essential points. Anyone want to hear it again?"

The same cadet asked for a repeat reading, and Gurney obliged. When he finished, he looked around the room and asked if anyone had any reaction to either statement.

At first the class remained silent. Then someone in the back row said, "Yeah, my reaction is stay the hell away from New York City."

A few more comments followed from around the room.

Gurney waited. "Anyone have any idea why I chose those two statements?"

Eventually, a blond cadet with an earnest farm-boy face spoke up. "To make us glad we're not transit cops?"

That was greeted by a few loud laughs.

Gurney waited.

The female cadet in the first row cocked her head and looked at him with a glint of suspicion in her eyes. "Because the two statements are from witnesses to the same homicide?"

Gurney smiled. A student's leap of intuition always brightened his day.

In a scan of the room he saw expressions of disbelief, confusion, curiosity. A few cadets seemed to be practicing the police art of the neutral stare. He waited for the objections.

The first came from a wiry young man with small eyes and a sour mouth. "So, which one of them was lying?"

"They both took voluntary polygraphs, and the test expert concluded they were both telling the truth."

"That's impossible. There are direct contradictions—who had the gun, who was alone, who was part of a group, ethnicity, initial provocation, everything. They can't both have been right."

"True," said Gurney mildly.

"But you said—"

"I said they were both *telling the truth*—not that they were both *right*."

"The hell does that mean?" There was an angry vibe in the wiry young man that went beyond challenging an assertion—a vibe that did not bode well for a positive career in law enforcement. Gurney didn't want to derail the lesson by confronting that issue now.

He addressed the whole class. "I'll give you some more information. Then maybe someone can tell me what it means. Altogether, six witnesses to the incident were interviewed and submitted signed statements. According to those statements, one participant in the confrontation had a gun, the other had the gun, they both had guns. The individual who was shot was a dark-skinned African American in his twenties, or a light-skinned Hispanic teenager. He was solid-looking, he was thin, he was medium height, he was short. The other participant was wearing a black leather jacket, a dark shirt with no jacket, a brown windbreaker. The confrontation prior to the gunshot lasted five seconds, thirty seconds, more than a minute. They argued with each other, or they didn't speak at all." He paused. "What do you make of all that?"

"Jeez," muttered the farm-boy cadet. "Sounds like the witnesses were on something."

Gurney shrugged. “In the opinion of the officer conducting the interviews, all six witnesses were sober and credible.”

“Yeah, but . . . somebody got shot, so somebody had a gun. So, which one had it?”

Gurney smiled. “Right statement, wrong question.”

That resulted in a baffled silence, broken by a big bodybuilder with a shaved head in the back row. “Asking which one had the gun is the wrong question?”

“Right.”

The bodybuilder cadet squinted thoughtfully before replying. “Because they both had guns?”

“Or . . . ?” prompted Gurney.

“Neither one had a gun?”

“And if that were the case . . . ?”

The silence was broken this time by a voice from the middle of the room. “Someone else fired the shot!”

“That’s exactly what was confirmed by the only objective witness,” said Gurney.

That last phrase prompted some puzzled looks.

He waited to see if anyone would catch on.

The cadet in the first row who had asked for repeated readings was the first to speak up. “Was ‘the only objective witness’ a transit surveillance video?”

Gurney gave her an appreciative nod. “The video established the position of the victim at the moment he was hit. During autopsy a reconstruction of the path of the bullet indicated the probable position of the shooter relative to the victim’s entry wound. Transferring that trajectory back to the video revealed a young man in the crowd taking a small pistol-shaped object from his pocket and pointing it toward the victim. Immediately after the moment of impact, he returned the object to his pocket and walked quickly toward the platform exit, where he—”

The angry cadet interrupted. “You’re telling us that *none* of the witnesses could hear what direction the shot came from?”

“The brain’s greatest strength, the ability to create instant connections, can be its greatest weakness. All the witnesses thought they saw a gun in the hand of at least one of the participants in the confrontation. A moment later they heard a gunshot. They all connected the sound with the visual image. Their brains discounted the directional component of their hearing in favor of visual logic: you see what you think is a gun, you hear a gunshot, your brain automatically puts them together. And your brain is *almost* always right."

The bodybuilder was frowning. "But didn't you say that neither one of them actually had a gun? So . . . the witnesses who claimed they saw one . . . what did they actually see?"

"A cell phone."

That led to the longest silence so far—no doubt reminding many in the room of the tragic news stories involving that very mistake being made by stressed police officers.

The farm-boy cadet looked appalled. "So, the witnesses were wrong about everything?"

"It happens," said Gurney.

A cadet directly in front of him raised his hand. "What's the bottom line on this? It sounds like we shouldn't even bother taking eyewitness statements."

"Statements can be helpful," said Gurney. "But the bottom line is caution. Keep an open mind. Remember that eyewitnesses can be very credible—and very inaccurate. And the problem carries over into courtrooms. Eyewitness testimony, which is actually the least reliable evidence, is the most persuasive. And it's not because anyone is lying. The fact is, people often see things that aren't really there."

The angry cadet piped up. "Mental cases, maybe. Idiots who don't pay attention. Trust me—when I look at something, I see what's there."

"I'm glad to hear that," said Gurney with a pleasant smile. "It's a perfect introduction to a pair of animations I think you'll enjoy." He opened a laptop computer on the podium and switched on the projector.

"The first ten-second animation you'll see shows a large blue ball bouncing across the screen. There are some numbers printed on the ball. The other animation will show a large green ball, also with numbers on it. Apart from those numbers, the balls may have other differences between them in size, surface texture, and the way they bounce. Pay close attention and see how many differences you're able to notice."

Gurney tapped a key on the laptop, and what looked like a large beach ball bounced slowly across the screen behind him.

"Next, the green ball," said Gurney, again tapping a key.

After it completed its passage across the screen, he switched off the projector.

"Okay, now tell me about the differences you noticed. I want to hear from everyone, but first from you," said Gurney, turning toward his challenger.

There was a new uncertainty in his eyes. "Some of the numbers on the balls might have been different."

Gurney nodded encouragingly. "Anything else?"

"The green one bounced a little faster than the blue one."

"What else?"

The angry cadet responded with a shrug.

"So," persisted Gurney, "different numbers, different bouncing speeds. Any other differences between the balls?"

"Obviously, the colors."

Gurney then addressed the same question to the other cadets and listened to their descriptions of the differences in the speeds, sizes, surface textures, and numbers on each ball.

He waited until they'd all offered their opinions.

"Now, I have an apology to make. I misled you—in the same way that I was misled when I was first shown the animation of the bouncing ball."

He paused again. "Did anyone notice what I just said?"

At first no one responded. Then the bodybuilder's eyes widened. "You said *animation* this time. Not *animations*."

"Correct."

In response to the perplexed faces around the room, he continued, "There was only one bouncing ball. I showed you the same animation twice."

His challenger with the sour mouth said, "But you obviously messed with the color to make the ball look blue the first time and green the second. So it doesn't prove anything, except that you lied."

The room got very quiet. Gurney smiled. "I messed with your brain, not the color. The color of the animated ball occupies the midpoint between blue and green on the color spectrum. Because of what I told you at the beginning, you expected the first ball to be blue and the second to be green. And because that's what you expected, you saw it the first time as bluer than it was and the next time as greener than it was. If you took a polygraph test on the two colors you saw, you would have passed. You would have been telling the truth, *as you saw it*. That's my point. Witnesses may be telling you the truth about what they saw, but that truth may exist only in their own heads. And a polygraph test only measures the *honesty* of someone's recollection, not its *accuracy*."

A raspy-voiced question came from the back of the room. "So what kind of evidence are we supposed to trust?"

"DNA. Fingerprints. Credit card and bank records. Phone records, especially those with GPS data. Emails, texts, and social media posts can also be useful in establishing motives, relationships, and states of mind."

"How about surveillance videos?" someone asked.

"Absolutely," said Gurney. "The fact is, I'd take one high-quality video over a dozen eyewitness reports anytime. Cameras are basically pure optic nerves. They have no prejudices, no imagination, no desire to fill in the blanks. Unlike humans, they only see what's actually there. But be careful when you view those videos."

"Careful of what?" someone else asked.

"Careful that your own brain doesn't screw up what the camera got right."

2

After giving a reading assignment on the subject of his next lecture, Gurney ended the class and made his way along a colorless, fluorescent-lit corridor to the office of Harris Schneider, the academy's part-time psychologist and occasional trauma counselor.

He was a small, middle-aged man with a large salt-and-pepper mustache never quite free of crumbs, a brown tweed jacket with elbow patches, and a briar pipe, overflowing with tobacco, that he always seemed on the verge of lighting. He listened as Gurney expressed his concern about the angry cadet in his seminar—the fact that he was already exhibiting the reflexive hostility characteristic of a mid-career burnout.

Schneider cleared his throat. "Yes, I know. Unfortunate. Already on our radar. Not good." He nodded, as if agreeing with himself. "Appropriate action will be taken at the appropriate time." He flashed a quick smile, as if pleased with his command of the situation. He glanced at the full bowl of his pipe, took a vintage chrome lighter out of his jacket pocket, and placed it on the desk in front of him—a gesture that, along with a sniffle and another clearing of his throat, signified that the meeting was concluded.

Gurney was tempted to restate his concern in more vivid terms—describing the consequences he'd witnessed when guns and badges had been given to angry men. But surely Schneider knew what could happen as well as he did. He thanked the man for his time, perhaps a bit too brusquely, and headed for the parking lot.

Emerging onto the windy tarmac, he was struck by the bizarre changeability of spring weather in the mountains of upstate New York. In the first chilly hour after dawn there was a bleak overcast, which was replaced two hours later by a perfect blue sky and warming bath of sunlight, which had now given way to racing clouds and swirling gusts of snowflakes.

He zipped up his nylon windbreaker, lowered his head, and hurried to his car, an aging but still functional Outback. He switched on the ignition and the heater, then checked his phone for messages. There was one, from Madeleine.

> "Hi. Just got in from the clinic. There's a message on our landline from a Mike Morgan, I assume the same Mike Morgan who used to be your partner? He wants you to call him back as soon as you can. If I'm not here when you get home, I'll be at Deirdre Winkler's. They have two baby alpacas I'm dying to see. I'll be home for dinner. If you can, pick up some milk."

Mike Morgan. Among the memories the name brought up, most were less than positive. One was indelible. It involved an event that created a unique link between them and resulted in Morgan being viewed as an NYPD hero—until the halo of heroism was overshadowed by the discovery of less commendable behavior.

The one time Madeleine had met him, she was less than charmed. And she'd expressed no regrets when Morgan, after partnering with Gurney for less than a year, was quietly forced out of the department.

His recollections were raising an uncomfortable question: *What might Morgan want?* He wondered about it for much of the fifty-minute trip home to Walnut Crossing.

As he drove up the two-mile-long dirt road from the county route to the hilltop property where he and Madeleine had been living since they moved from the city, he noted that the wind had abated and the snowflakes were falling more slowly. They coated the branches of the old apple trees along the road, the forsythia bushes between the pond and the barn, and the overgrown pasture between the barn and their farmhouse.

He parked in his usual spot by the mudroom door. As he was getting out of the car, a flock of yellow finches burst out of a snow-laden lilac bush by the feeders and flew across the pasture to the cherry copse. He walked quickly into the house, hung his windbreaker in the mudroom, passed through the big kitchen, and headed straight for the landline in the den.

He played Morgan's message, making a note of the number. The man's tone was tense, perhaps even fearful.

With more curiosity than appetite, he returned the call.

Morgan answered on the first ring.

"Dave! Thanks so much for getting back to me. I appreciate it. God, it's good to hear your voice. How are you doing?"

"No significant problems. How about you?"

"Right now things are a little crazy. Actually, more than a little. That's why I need to talk to you. Are you aware of my situation here?"

"I don't even know where *here* is."

"Right. Of course not. Ages since we spoke. I'm up in Larchfield. In fact, I'm the village police chief. Hard to believe, right?"

Gurney silently agreed. "Where's Larchfield?"

"Just an hour north of Walnut Crossing, but I'm not surprised you never heard of it. Quiet little place. Serious felony rate close to zero. In fact, we've never had a murder here. Not until last night."

"I'm listening."

"I was hoping I could sit down with you."

"You can't tell me about it on the phone?"

"It's a bizarre situation. Too many angles. I can't afford to screw it up. Can I come and explain it to you?"

Gurney hesitated. "When did you want to do this?"

"I could be at your house in an hour."

Gurney checked the time on his phone—2:58 p.m. Although he had no desire for a reunion with the man, there was a piece of their history together that put the option of refusing out of reach.

"You have my address?"

The excitement in Morgan's voice was palpable. "Of course. You're famous. You know that, right? You were featured in all the upstate newscasts last year—'Retired Cop from City Solves White River Murders.' You weren't hard to find, thank God!"

Gurney said nothing.

"Okay, then. See you in an hour."

3

Although their partnership had lasted only ten months, Gurney knew more about the personal life of Mike Morgan than that of anyone else he'd worked with in his twenty-five years in the NYPD. From the day he was assigned to replace Gurney's retiring partner in the homicide division, Morgan had treated him as a confidant—with the result that Gurney had learned more than he wanted to know about the man's longing for approval from his revered cop father, his reckless relationships with women, his waves of paranoia.

He'd also witnessed Morgan's obsession with superficial orderliness, especially punctuality. So it was no surprise when, at exactly 3:59 p.m., a black Chevy Tahoe began making its way up through the low pasture toward the house.

Gurney went out through the mudroom and opened the side door. The cool air carried the mixed scent of wet snow and spring grass. He watched as the big SUV with a circular LARCHFIELD POLICE DEPARTMENT emblem on the door pulled in beside his Outback.

Morgan got out, looking around anxiously at the fields and hills, then walked the path between the house and the raised asparagus bed. He was wearing neatly creased black pants and a gray dress shirt with a three-star chief's insignia on the starched collar. Although the man still had the trim body of an athlete, his stride was stiffer than Gurney remembered, and the worry lines on his face seemed to have deepened.

As he reached Gurney, he extended his hand, smiling a little wildly. "David!

Wow! So good to see you. Long time, eh?" His grip was unpleasantly tight, then suddenly looser, as if he'd caught himself in a bad habit.

"Hello, Mike."

Morgan took a deep breath and blew it out gradually through puffed cheeks, stepping back and looking around again at the hills and fields. "You're really out here, aren't you? Not another house in sight. You okay with that?"

"*Okay*?"

"I mean, this is like the backwoods. Not a soul around. How much land do you have?"

"About fifty acres. It was a farm once. Mostly old pastures. Some small quarries. Cherry and maple thickets. Lots of trails."

Morgan nodded, not really listening, looking around yet again. "You have any snakes?"

"Not really. Nothing poisonous."

"I hate snakes. Always have. I read once about a guy putting a rattlesnake in his neighbor's mailbox. Can you imagine?"

Gurney stepped back from the doorway with a half-hearted welcoming gesture. "You want to come in?"

"Thanks."

Gurney led him past the mudroom into the kitchen and over to the round pine table by the French doors. He gathered up his notes for the academy lecture and put them aside.

"Have a seat. Coffee? Tea?"

Morgan shrugged. "Whatever you're having."

While Gurney busied himself with the coffee machine, Morgan remained standing, looking first around the room, then out through the glass doors.

"I appreciate this. Letting me come here on such short notice."

When the coffee was ready, Gurney filled two mugs and brought them to the table. "Milk? Sugar?"

"Nothing. Thank you."

Gurney sat in the chair he usually occupied for breakfast and Morgan sat opposite him. Gurney took a sip of his coffee and waited.

Morgan grinned nervously and shook his head. "I thought about this all the way here, but now . . . I'm not sure where to begin."

Gurney noted that the man's fingernails were still bitten to the quick. They had always looked like that, the swollen fingertips overlapping the stubs of the gnawed nails. Unlike most people afflicted with that compulsion, however, Morgan had never engaged in it in public. It reminded Gurney of his mother's combination of public dieting and seemingly inexplicable obesity.

Morgan wrapped his hands around his coffee mug. "I guess the last thing you knew about my situation was that I left the department." He hesitated, making it sound like a question.

"I heard you'd moved upstate."

"That all came together nicely. You know that Bartley let me hang in until I hit twenty years and could get my pension, right?"

Gurney nodded. Considering the mess he'd gotten himself into, Morgan was fortunate to have been given such a gentle exit.

"That gave me a little breathing time to look around. I heard through the grapevine there was an opening for a head of security at a small upstate school, Russell College, in Larchfield. I applied, I interviewed, I got the job."

"Nothing negative reached them about your NYPD problem?"

"Apparently not. But that's understandable. There hadn't been any official disciplinary action. On the record, I'd simply retired. Twenty and out." Morgan stared down into his coffee for a moment, as though it contained some image from his past, before continuing.

"The college job was fine. Respectable, decent salary, et cetera. But a year later the Larchfield police chief resigned. It was suggested that I'd be a logical replacement." A flicker of pride appeared in his eyes. "I went through an interview process with the village board, and two weeks later I had gold stars on my collar."

"Simple as that?"

The pride gave way to uncertainty. "Sounds kind of unusual, right?"

"More than *kind of*." Gurney considered which of the questions that came to mind to ask first. He chose the mildest. "What does the job entail?"

Morgan paused, staring again at his coffee. "It's a strange place, Larchfield. Crime-free, tons of money, not a single wilted petal in the village flower beds. A living, breathing painting of upscale perfection."

"But . . . ?"

Morgan's mouth stretched into a sour expression. "Larchfield has always been under the thumb of a super-wealthy family. The Russells. Three generations ago they owned all the land in the area, which they gradually sold off with deed restrictions that allowed them to control everything from the styles and colors of the houses to the composition of the tarmac in the streets. There was a struggling college nearby—which the Russells saved and expanded with big endowments, with strings that ensured their control of it in perpetuity. And that isn't the half of it. For over a century all the public institutions of Larchfield—from the library to the local theater to the two-hundred-acre park—have prospered through the benevolent dictatorship of that family." He paused. "There isn't much that happens in Larchfield without Russell involvement . . . and Russell approval."

"Sounds like a private kingdom. Who's the current king?"

"Ah, well, that's the thing. Until last night, it was Angus Russell."

"He's your murder victim?"

Morgan nodded. "All hell is breaking loose."

"How was he was murdered?"

"His right carotid artery and right jugular vein were both severed—with one cut. As he was coming out of his bathroom."

"One cut?"

"A single slash. Clean and deep. Probably between three and five in the morning, according to the ME."

"Who found the body?"

"The wife and the housekeeper—but in different ways. The wife, Lorinda Russell, says she came down to breakfast around eight. She made herself some tea in the kitchen, then brought it into the breakfast alcove at the end of the main dining room. She sits down and starts checking her phone. Then she hears this sound. A little *ptt*, is the way she described it. Then she hears it again. Then again. She looks around and sees a dark red spot on the beige carpet next to her. As she's watching, another drop falls on the same spot. She looks up. There's a pendant light fixture in the ceiling on the end of a gold chain, and there's some kind of liquid dripping down the chain from a dark red spot on the ceiling. At first, she has no idea what she's looking at. Then she realizes what it is. And she starts screaming."

"She told you that she realized it was blood?"

Morgan nodded. "She seemed to have trouble saying the word. Claims the sight of blood, even the thought of it, has made her sick ever since her father fell off a tractor and got ripped up by a hay baler. The housekeeper, Helen Stone, was outside the alcove window, giving instructions to one of the gardeners. Stone hears the screaming and comes dashing into the house. She sees the blood coming through the ceiling, and she runs up the staircase to Angus Russell's bedroom, which is directly above that breakfast alcove."

"Angus and Lorinda have separate bedrooms?"

"Unusual marriage. Major age gap. Seventy-eight to twenty-eight."

Gurney shrugged. "Magical power of money. So the housekeeper went into the bedroom and found the body? What about the wife?"

"She went up behind the housekeeper. Went as far as the bedroom door, took a look inside, and collapsed. Stone went right in. She found the body, along with 'more damn blood than you could imagine having been in one old man'—is the way she put it."

"All from the neck wound?"

"With one exception. His left forefinger had been cut off, so there was a separate puddle of blood around that hand. No idea yet what its significance might be. I'd say Angus got up in the middle of the night to use the shared bathroom between the two bedrooms. When he came back into his room, someone was waiting for him. One hard slash across the right side of the neck with a super-sharp blade. Best guess is that Angus made a half-turn away from the attacker and toppled headfirst over a chair. He ended up in a strange position, forehead on the floor, stomach and thighs slanting down across the seat of the chair, legs angled up in the air behind him. Like a sick joke."

The comment reminded Gurney of a macabre moment in the White River murder case—when a severed head, with one eye closed as if it were winking, came rolling out of a crime scene, sending an on-site TV reporter into a state of catatonia. But he had no taste for dwelling on gruesome deaths. He preferred to focus on practical steps.

"So the lord of the manor got his throat cut and a finger amputated, assailant unknown. Were you able to lift any useful prints?"

Morgan shifted in his chair, still gripping his coffee mug. "The only clear prints our tech found—other than those of the victim, his wife, and the housekeeper—were ID'd by AFIS as belonging to a local named Billy Tate. If this were a normal case, he'd be our prime suspect. He and Angus hated each other, had a bad history together, including death threats. But none of that matters now."

"Why not?"

"Tate was killed in a freak accident the night before last."

"And his fingerprints at the scene . . . ?"

"We're trying to sort that out. If this isn't some kind of a screwup, then Tate must have been in Angus Russell's bedroom at some point. Exactly when, we can't be sure. No precise way to date the prints. But we know it couldn't have been last night, because last night Tate was laid out in a coffin in the local mortuary."

Gurney knew that determining when and why an enemy of the victim had been in his bedroom would be an investigative priority, probably the key to solving the murder. At the moment, however, there was a simpler question on his mind.

Oddly, it was Morgan who put it into words first. "At this point, you're probably asking yourself what made me so desperate to see you."

4

Twenty minutes later Morgan concluded a dire description of how, given the prominent family involved, the case was likely to turn into a political minefield that could make or break his career—and how Gurney's investigative talents, strongest in the areas where his own were weakest, could save the day. He had only one request—that Gurney come to Larchfield at 9:00 a.m. the next morning to examine the crime scene. After that, he could decide whether he was willing to get involved.

With some reluctance, Gurney agreed, and with a sigh of relief, Morgan departed.

After watching the man's SUV disappear around the barn onto the dirt-and-gravel road, Gurney returned to the kitchen. He remembered suddenly that he hadn't stopped for the milk Madeleine asked him to pick up on his way home from the academy. So he picked up his wallet, got in the Outback, and drove through five miles of old farmland to the village of Walnut Crossing.

"Village" was a word that brought to his mind the antique charm of places he and Madeleine had visited on their honeymoon in the English countryside. But "village" had become a misnomer for Walnut Crossing, which each year had been sinking deeper into the economic and social malaise of upstate New York, with its spreading blight of empty storefronts and expanding populations of the unemployed and unemployable.

He pulled into one of the main street's two "convenience" stores and went to the small dairy section of the wall-length cooler devoted almost entirely to beers, soft drinks, and strangely flavored waters. He took a half gallon of nonfat milk to the cashier's counter, where he waited while a toothless woman in a housedress and green rubber boots purchased a handful of brightly colored lottery tickets.

As soon as he got home, he put the milk in the fridge and took out an onion, a pepper, a stalk of celery, and a large zucchini. He chopped the vegetables and put them near the wok. He filled a pot of water for pasta and placed it on the stove. He set the pasta water on high and went for a quick shower and change of clothes.

The relaxing effect of the warm water streaming down over his back kept him in the shower twice as long as he'd planned, and when he finally returned to the kitchen to finish preparing dinner, he found Madeleine at the stove with her back to him, stirring the vegetables in the wok. The pasta was boiling, and the table by the French doors was set for dinner.

"Hi," she said without turning. "Thanks for getting things started. I see you remembered the milk."

"You didn't think I would?"

"I figured it was a toss-up."

He saw no need to reveal how true that was. He went over and kissed the back of her neck. Her tousled brown hair had a sweet outdoor scent. "How was your day?"

She turned off the gas under the wok and stirred the pasta. "The part I spent at the clinic had its ups and downs. Eight intakes referred by the drug court. Two of them were scared to death, possibly scared enough to embrace the program. The other six were in denial. I could see the little wheels turning in their heads, trying to guess what I wanted to hear, trying to beat the system—anything rather than face their addiction."

Gurney shrugged. "Liars and manipulators. Your typical clinic clientele."

"But the few who do want help and end up turning their lives around—they make what I'm doing there feel worthwhile." She turned off the gas under the pasta, carried the big pot to the sink, and emptied it into a waiting colander.

He realized his tone had been needlessly negative. "Of course what you're doing is worthwhile. I didn't mean to suggest it wasn't. All I was saying—"

She cut him off. "You don't like addicts. You had your share of difficult experiences with them in the city. I understand."

He smiled, having read somewhere that smiling makes your voice sound warmer. “So the intakes were the mixed-blessing part of your day. How was the other part?”

“Very interesting. I’ll tell you about it in a minute.”

She shook the pasta-filled colander gently until it stopped dripping, carried it to the stove, tilted its contents into the wok with the sautéed vegetables, and stirred everything together with a long wooden spoon.

Once they’d served themselves from the wok and were seated at the table, Madeleine removed a folded sheet of paper from under her napkin and passed it across to him.

“This could be a little project for us.” Her face was bright with excitement.

He unfolded the paper and saw what appeared to be a structural diagram for some sort of shed.

“Dennis printed that out from a farm website,” she added.

He frowned at the man’s name. “What is it?”

“An alpaca shelter.”

“We don’t have any alpacas.”

“Not right now.”

He looked up from the paper.

“But we could get one,” she said. “Or two. Two would be better. They’re very social. One would get lonely.”

“How long have you been thinking about this?”

“I guess I started when I was helping the Winklers with their alpacas two years ago at the fair.” She fell silent, perhaps at the memory of how the fair had ended in disaster—the culminating horror of the Peter Pan murder case.

After a moment, she looked at him with a wistful smile. “It’s not something we need to do right away. We’d have to build that house for them first. And that could be a fun thing to do together.”

Gurney looked again at the design, then laid it in the middle of the table. “Alpacas are expensive, aren’t they?”

“That’s what everyone thinks, but when you take the pluses and minuses into consideration, they cost very little. Almost nothing.”

“The pluses and minuses?”

“I’ll let Dennis explain all that.”

“What?”

"I invited the Winklers for dinner."

"When?"

"Tomorrow night."

"To give us an alpaca sales pitch?"

"I wouldn't call it that. It's ages since we've gotten together. If they want to tell us about their alpacas, that's fine with me."

They ate for several minutes before she laid down her fork and waited for him to meet her gaze. "The alpaca idea isn't as crazy as it sounds. And the Winklers aren't as awful as you think. Try to keep an open mind."

He nodded. "I'll do my best."

She picked up her fork. "Did you return that call from Mike Morgan?"

"I did."

"His message sounded terribly anxious."

"Some of that is just the way he is, but he does seem to be in an unusual situation. He actually came to the house to talk about it."

"What does he want?"

"Help with a murder investigation in a village up north. Larchfield. Peculiar place. Peculiar crime scene. Most peculiar thing of all is that Morgan's the police chief."

"You don't think he's up to it?"

"Intellectually he may be up to it. But emotionally he's a wreck." He paused. "How much more do you want to know?"

"Enough so I can understand what you decide."

"Decide?"

"About whether to get involved with his murder case."

He didn't respond to that.

She turned and gazed out through the French doors. "Look at the grass."

He looked out past the little bluestone patio toward the henhouse and the old apple tree. The wet grass was glistening in the slanting evening sunlight. The only trace of the earlier snow was a cottony white patch at the base of the apple tree.

"Amazing," she said, the expression on her face reflecting the radiance of the scene. She sighed and turned back to Gurney. "Tell me as much as you like."

He took a moment to figure out where to begin.

"Morgan's father was near the top of the ladder at the NYPD, and his twin brothers were both precinct commanders. There was an eight-year gap between them and Morgan, and he claimed they called him 'the mistake.' His father alternated between ignoring him and pointing out his deficiencies. Morgan was hell-bent on winning his family's approval. He was great on paper, aced his promotion exams. But he had all kinds of fears, along with a disastrous way of dealing with them."

"Drugs?"

"Women. Sometimes women who were involved in cases he was investigating. Even a potential suspect or two. Those mistakes could have put him in prison. But apparently the rush blinded him to the risk."

"Sounds like he was fixing a low self-esteem problem by doing something that would make it worse. Like the addicts I see at the clinic. How did he get away with it?"

"No one wanted to get on the wrong side of his father, so there was a tendency to let things slide, as long as they weren't too obvious or didn't screw up a prosecution. But eventually one of the captains got fed up and told Morgan he needed to resign or the issue would go to the professional standards unit, with the possibility of criminal prosecution. In the end, he was allowed to stay a few more months to get to his pension-vesting date. A quiet exit."

"Zero consequences for his actions?"

"Right."

"And the Larchfield authorities concluded that this law-enforcement paragon would make an ideal police chief?"

"Not immediately. He told me he was hired first to head up security at their local college. A year later they chose him to replace the departing police chief. The first job seems a bit of a stretch. The second seems inconceivable. Coincidentally, the man who was just murdered was the main interviewer and decision-maker for both of Morgan's positions."

"Do you have a sense of why he wants you involved in the investigation?"

Gurney gazed far out through the French doors as though the answer might lie somewhere in the low pasture. "He spent his last half hour here making my involvement sound like the most reasonable thing in the world."

She raised a quizzical eyebrow.

"He claims that this murder is the kind of case that would benefit from our combined strengths. He sees himself as a 'possibility' thinker and me as a 'probability' thinker."

"Meaning what?"

"That he's good at coming up with multiple scenarios for how and why a crime was committed, but lousy at estimating likelihoods and prioritizing investigative efforts."

"Isn't that 'lousy' part what a police chief ought to be good at?"

"Nothing about this situation is what it *ought* to be."

"Then just say *no*. His inability to do his job isn't your problem."

"It's not that simple." His gaze drifted out the glass doors toward the low pasture. "The thing is . . . there's an unspoken debt involved. About six years ago, right after Morgan and I got teamed up, we were doing follow-up interviews on a bodega homicide in the South Bronx projects. As we were leaving the apartment of a witness, we came face-to-face with three gangbangers coming out of the apartment directly across the hall—their meth factory, it turned out. They figured we'd come for them, and things got instantly insane—their Uzis against our Glocks. Morgan jumped back into the apartment we'd come out of, and I dove into the stairwell for cover. My wrist smashed against the railing, my weapon went flying down the stairs, with three Uzi maniacs coming at me. That's when Morgan came charging out into the hall, between me and them. He had his Glock in one hand, his backup Sig in the other, and everybody starting shooting at once. Over a hundred shots fired in no time at all. Complete mayhem. When it got quiet, the three gangbangers were spread all over the tile floor, and Morgan was standing there, untouched." He paused, looking pained. "I never told you about this because—"

"Because you never wanted to bring the frightening facts of your job into our home." She paused. "So, the way you see it, he risked his life to save yours?"

"All I know is, he did what he did, the guys who were coming at me are dead, and I'm alive."

She picked up her fork and began moving strands of her leftover pasta toward the center of her plate. "I'm wondering . . . do you see him as a self-absorbed, anxiety-driven womanizer? Or a fearless, self-sacrificing hero?"

"Couldn't he be both? Fearless when confronted by a clear and present danger, but otherwise in a self-absorbed flight from his demons?"

"Or maybe the man you thought turned into a hero that day was still the same emotional mess—making a suicide attempt. One that happened to fail, fortunately for you."

Gurney's gaze settled on the shed diagram in the middle of the table. "That thought did occur to me. Maybe I just don't want it to be true."

"So your bottom line is that you're alive because of what he did—regardless of what his motive may have been—and you owe him something in return?"

"I'm not sure what. But something, yes." He turned up his palms, in lieu of an answer. "Anyway, I've agreed to go to Larchfield tomorrow morning. Maybe things will be clearer after that."

He looked out toward the henhouse, then back at Madeleine. "I don't particularly like Morgan. Never did. But I can't just walk away. It's not just about that shoot-out in the projects. There was a . . . an awful thing . . . that happened at the promotion ceremony where he got his gold detective's shield. That's a big moment in a cop's life. It was for me, and I suspect it was ten times that for him. But then, at the end of the ceremony, his father came up to him. His big-deal father he was desperate to please. His father looks him in the eye, like he was a perp. No handshake, no congratulations. All the son of a bitch said was, 'That gold shield is a family tradition. Don't disgrace us.'"

Gurney felt a mixture of anger and sadness whenever that moment came to mind. That father, hard and cold. That son, longing for something he would never get.

Madeleine was watching him. When he met her gaze, he saw in it an understanding of what he was feeling, an understanding perhaps deeper than his own.

5

In keeping with the unpredictability of springtime in the mountains, the next morning was strangely balmy, the air soft and humid in the hazy early sunlight. As Gurney headed for his Outback, the sweet scent of the damp pasture grass jogged a childhood memory of the Bronx park where he'd spent so many summer hours, away from the tensions that had locked his parents' marriage into a permanent state of unhappiness.

He entered the address of the Larchfield Police Department in his GPS and set out, leaving thoughts of that park and that marriage behind him.

His route took him through a landscape that was by turns picturesque and depressing. There were expanses of bucolic countryside—glorious green fields and red silos, meandering streams and century-old fieldstone walls, hillsides covered with wildflowers. And there were sad emblems of economic decline—the broken windows and creeper-covered walls of once-thriving dairy plants, barns and farmhouses gone to ruin, bleak villages where even the FOR SALE signs were disintegrating.

As he approached the foothills of the Adirondacks, the old pastures and maple groves were overtaken by thickets of pine and hemlock, the land gradually becoming more forested. The scattered businesses included small motels, campgrounds, gun stores, rod-and-bait stores. All appeared in need of refurbishing.

Eventually his GPS directed him off the state route onto Skeel Swamp Road, a winding byway through a lowland of tree trunks standing in the shallow beaver ponds that had rotted their roots. A little beyond the beaver ponds a faded sign announced that he was entering Cemetery Flats. The only visible structure in the next mile was Dick & Della's Place—an old-time diner, surrounded by pickup trucks. A mile past that a sign welcomed him to Bastenburg.

Where it entered the town's commercial strip, Skeel Swamp Road was renamed Center Street, and its speed limit was reduced to twenty-five, giving Gurney ample time to observe the defining elements of the place.

In addition to two fast-food franchises, he passed a Quick Cash soda-can redemption center, a Hardly Used clothing store, a Thirsty Boys Beer Emporium, Maria's Pizza and Laundromat, Smoker's Heaven, Dark Moon Potions and Lotions, Golden Dragon Takeout, Iron Man Martial Arts, a pawn shop, a bail bondsman, a no-name gas station, two tattoo parlors, and a hair and nail salon.

There was a memorable sign in the window of the last storefront he passed on the strip.

CHURCH OF THE PATRIARCHS

FOR GOD, COUNTRY, AND THE RIGHT TO BEAR ARMS

Leaving the commercial area, the road rose gradually toward a distant ridge. When he was about halfway to the top, a dark blue BMW sped past him, going at least twice the speed limit, despite the poor condition of the road surface and the presence of a Bastenburg police cruiser parked on the shoulder. The BMW flew by it, but the police vehicle stayed where it was. As Gurney drove by, he noted that the officer appeared alert but showed no indication of initiating a pursuit.

When Gurney finally arrived at the crest of the hill and could see down into the next valley, he was amazed at how different it was from the one he'd just driven through. In place of the desolate beaver ponds, a glistening stream meandered through emerald meadows. In the middle of the valley the stream widened into a sky-blue lake with chartreuse willows on its banks. The end of the lake was bordered by a postcard fantasy of a New England village, complete with a white church spire.

Halfway through the gentle descent into this postcard world, a small sign on the mowed grass verge of the road bore the word LARCHFIELD in polished copper letters on a dark blue background. Even the surface of the road was different here—smoother, quieter, free of the cracks and patched potholes on the Bastenburg side of the hill.

As he was passing through an intersection at the near end of the lake, Gurney noted that Skeel Swamp Road was now called Waterview Drive. It led him along the manicured edge of the lake, past the willows he'd observed from the rise, to the edge of the village square. His GPS directed him onto Cotswold Lane—and announced immediately that he'd reached his destination. His dashboard clock read 8:59 a.m.

He pulled over to the curb under a giant maple just coming into leaf. Looking around, he thought perhaps there'd been a mapping error or that Morgan had given him the wrong address. On his left was the square itself—a parklike rectangle of perfect grass, gravel paths, stone benches, and flower beds with boxwood borders. On his right was a shaded sidewalk and a row of three large Victorian homes whose wide porches were surrounded by lilacs. Nowhere was there anything resembling a police station.

He could just make out the address on the porch post of the home he was closest to. He recognized it as the number he'd entered in his GPS. He headed up the bluestone path that led to the porch steps. There was a discreet plaque mounted on the clapboard siding beside the front door. Just as he got close enough to read the words on it—LARCHFIELD POLICE HQ—the door opened and Mike Morgan stepped out.

"You're here! I was starting to worry!"

Gurney gestured toward the house. "This is your police station?"

"Yes. I'll explain later. Right now we need to get to the Russell estate." He pointed to a driveway beside the house. "Bring your car around back. We'll go together in mine."

Gurney drove the Outback around to a parking area behind the house, where he noted three Larchfield police cruisers, two unmarked Dodge Chargers, and Morgan's Tahoe. As he was getting out of his own vehicle and into Morgan's, he saw that the areas behind the two adjacent Victorians were also paved parking areas. The vehicles in one were civilian and generally upscale. In the other, there was a metallic-silver Lexus with a rear wheel elevated on a jack.

Morgan explained, "The house on the left is the village hall—mayor's office, justice of the peace, village board, code enforcement, et cetera. The one on the right is the Peale Funeral Home. The one in the middle is our headquarters. There's a peculiarity in the village zoning ordinance—an architectural clause that requires public and commercial buildings to conform to residential design standards—part of the historic Russell grip on everything in Larchfield."

Gurney took a moment to absorb that before changing the subject. "Any developments at the crime scene?"

"Couple of things. One of our guys discovered a surgical scalpel on the floor under some shelving—in a greenhouse-conservatory type of structure on the back of the house. Same area where the break-in took place. There was blood on the scalpel, probably the murder weapon. Looks like the killer stumbled and fell on his way out, and the scalpel got away from him."

"Prints?"

"Smudged but maybe recoverable. Lab's doing what they can." He pressed the start-engine button.

"You said there were a *couple* of things."

"The Russells' dog. It was found in back of the house, out by the woods, dead. Head appeared to have been hit with a hammer. The ME agreed to take a look, but he wasn't happy about it. Said we should be sending the animal to a *veterinary* pathologist. Very touchy about his status." Morgan backed out of his space and headed down the driveway.

Before he got to the end, a dark blue BMW turned sharply into the same narrow passage from the street side, coming to a stop nose-to-nose with the Tahoe.

"Jesus!" Morgan grimaced. He put the big SUV into reverse and slowly backed up into the parking area. The BMW came up the driveway and stopped beside him. Morgan lowered his window. The other driver did the same.

He had close-cropped dark hair, small unblinking eyes, and a downturned mouth. He peered at Gurney for a long moment before turning his attention to Morgan.

"We need to talk." His tone was emotionless, but his eyes were insistent.

"Definitely," said Morgan. There was a tic at the corner of his mouth. "But right now I need to get out to Harrow Hill. Do you have any specific information about—"

The man interrupted. "Not about what happened to Russell. But we need to talk. There's a lot at stake. I'm sure you understand. So, call me. Before noon." Giving Gurney another once-over, he turned his car around and disappeared down the driveway.

"Jesus," said Morgan a second time. He exhaled slowly, his hands on the steering wheel.

Gurney stared at him. "Who the hell was that?"

"Chandler Aspern," said Morgan, as though the name had a sour taste. He put the Tahoe back in drive and drove slowly out of the parking area.

It wasn't until they reached Waterview Drive, the road encircling the lake, that he spoke again. The tic was still working at the corner of his mouth. "He's the mayor of Larchfield. For years the sharpest thorn in Angus Russell's side. They both have enormous manor houses on Harrow Hill. All the land is technically owned by the Russell family, but Aspern has a hundred-year lease on half of it—a lease that Angus Russell was desperate to break."

"Why?"

"Because the land has quadrupled in value since the terms were negotiated."

"How much money is involved?"

"It's conceivable that Aspern could sell the lease to his half of Harrow Hill, with development rights, for somewhere in the neighborhood of sixty million dollars. If Russell could have gotten the lease invalidated, those development rights would have reverted to him. But there was a larger issue than the money. It was about control. Russell was always fiercely determined to get his own way. On top of that, he despised Aspern. And the feeling was mutual."

"Why did he lease him the land to begin with?"

"He didn't. The deal was worked out years ago between their fathers, who were business partners, and both of whom died soon after the deal was finalized."

"So, your victim had at least one serious enemy."

Morgan burst out in a nervous laugh. "Be nice if it was only one. Control freaks like Angus Russell collect enemies by the dozen."

"I assume there's a will. What do you know about his beneficiaries?"

"Best guess is that everything will be funneled through private trusts and there won't be any significant assets to go through public probate. Maybe none at all. I wouldn't be surprised to see the bulk of his wealth going to his wife and his sister."

"He had no children?"

"No."

"Charities?"

"He considered them all frauds."

"How about close friends? Local institutions?"

"I don't think he had *any* friends. As for institutions, one possibility would be his sister's church. Hilda Russell is the Episcopal pastor of St. Giles—the church on the square with the white spire. And there's Russell College, endowed by Angus's grandfather. It overlooks the lake."

"Is that where you were head of security?"

"Yes."

"Angus hired you for that job?"

"Yes."

"Then hired you again as village police chief?"

"Yes."

"He was empowered to do that?"

"Officially, I was appointed by the village board."

"But Angus unofficially controlled the board?"

"Angus unofficially controlled a lot of things. Some key people owed him a lot—money, favors, his willingness to keep secret the embarrassing facts he'd discovered about them, et cetera. He had enormous power, and he enjoyed using it."

"How do you think his death will affect your position?"

Morgan's jaw muscles tightened visibly, as did his hands on the steering wheel. He started to speak, stopped, then began again. "A lot will depend on how this case turns out . . . how smoothly it's managed . . . how clear the outcome is."

"How do you see Aspern in that process?"

"I'm not sure what you're getting at."

"Do you see him as a friend or an enemy?"

"Definitely not as a friend. That's not how he relates to people. He sees everything in terms of transactional allies and enemies—what people can do *for* him or *to* him."

Gurney nodded, trying to organize everything Morgan had told him. But he realized it was way too soon to start pigeonholing information, with so much more to be learned, and he turned his attention to the area they were driving through.

Waterview Drive followed the outline of the lake, which Gurney estimated to be about two miles long and half a mile wide. The homes along it were set on large verdant lots that ran from the shoulder of the road down to the edge of the lake. The properties were separated from each other by lush plantings of laurel and rhododendrons. The homes were mostly big traditional colonials—painted in a muted palette of olives, grays, tans, and deep reddish-browns that reminded him of dried blood.

The cars were as conspicuously upmarket as the real estate. He turned to Morgan, who was chewing obsessively on his lip.

"What sort of people live in Larchfield?"

"Their common denominators are wealth, entitlement, and the willingness to pay a ridiculous amount of money for a house in order to live next to someone else who was willing to pay a ridiculous amount of money for a house. As usual, the ones who consider themselves the cream of the crop tend to be the scum of the earth."

Gurney was surprised by the bitterness. "Sounds like you hate living here."

"Carol and I don't live *here*. There's no way we could afford it, even when she was working. We're out in the wilderness between here and Bastenburg. Land is cheaper in the middle of nowhere."

The *poor-me* attitude was familiar to Gurney from their days in the NYPD. It was getting on his nerves all over again. A mile or so later, with the shimmering blue lake on their left and a dense forested rise on their right, Morgan slowed and turned up into the woods on a dirt-and-gravel lane marked PRIVATE ROAD.

"This is the foot of Harrow Hill—the Russell side of it."

Gurney peered ahead to where the lane began to climb more steeply through the dark woods. The gloomy greens of ragged hemlocks and ledges of flinty black rock set the hillside far apart from the nearby picture-book world of Waterview Drive.

"Seems a rather cheerless approach for a grand estate," said Gurney.

Morgan flashed a humorless smile. "Cheerfulness has never been a Russell virtue."

After ascending through a sequence of sunless switchbacks, they arrived at a gateway in a high stone wall. The ornamental iron gate was open, but a length of yellow police tape was taking its place. Beyond the tape there was a long allée of tall beech trees arching over a beige gravel driveway. Gurney could see, centered at the end of the driveway, the portico of a massive, rectangular stone building. He couldn't help feeling there was something cold, almost inhuman, in the perfect geometry of it all.

A young officer with a Larchfield PD badge on his sleeve appeared from nowhere with a clipboard, eyeing Gurney through the windshield. Morgan lowered his side window.

"Morning, Scotty."

"Morning, sir. If you don't mind, sir, for the crime-scene log, I'll need the name of your passenger."

Morgan spelled it out. The officer entered it on his clipboard, lowered the yellow tape, and waved them through.

The arrow-straight driveway split at the end into two matching arcs that met under the portico. A smaller driveway led from the far side of the portico to a six-bay carriage house with a slate roof. Morgan parked in front of the main house behind six other police vehicles: four black-and-white cruisers, an unmarked Dodge Charger, and a gray tech van. Wide cream-colored stone steps led to an entrance door of polished mahogany.

"Quite the palace, eh?" said Morgan. "Built with Cotswold stone that Angus's grandfather had shipped over from England."

Gurney noted Morgan's alternating awe and contempt in the face of Larchfield wealth, but responded only with a noncommittal grunt.

Morgan opened his door. "Where do you want to start? Inside the house or outside?"

"First, I need to understand the personnel situation—who's on-site, what their responsibilities are."

"The two main people you'll meet are Brad Slovak and Kyra Barstow. Brad's a detective, acting as case CIO and scene coordinator. Kyra's our main evidence tech and an instructor in the forensic sciences program at the college. We have four patrol officers on-site to assist Brad and Kyra."

"The medical examiner was here yesterday?"

"Dr. Ronald Fallow. Lives locally, so he got here quickly. He examined the body in situ, transported it to his office in Clarksburg, and scheduled the autopsy for this morning. We might get preliminary findings by the end of the day. Or we might not. Fallow's not easy to deal with."

"What did you tell your people about my coming here?"

Morgan ran his tongue across his lips, his gaze fixed on the dashboard. "Basically, I told them that you're a former NYPD homicide detective, a very successful one, retired, teaching investigative techniques at the academy. And since most of your police experience was in the city, it would be interesting for you to observe how an upstate department like ours approaches a major crime."

"That's what you told them?"

"It's essentially true."

"You mean, it's not totally untrue."

Morgan shrugged off the distinction. His aptitude for using true statements to create misleading impressions had always been one of his dubious talents. In fact, it was a significant ingredient in Gurney's mixed feelings about getting involved.

"Okay," he said, "let's start with a walk around the perimeter."

6

Since the evidence team had not yet completed their examination of the site, Gurney and Morgan donned regulation sets of white Tyvek coveralls, shoe covers, and nitrile gloves before entering the restricted area.

Gurney, with Morgan following, began his examination on the right side of the huge house, where a lawn sloped away from daffodil beds toward a line of shrubbery at the edge of the natural woodland beyond. He could hear the chirping of birds and the distant *ratatatat* of a woodpecker. The morning sun was turning the ground-floor windows of the house into gleaming rectangles of light.

A movement at the bottom of one of the windows caught Gurney's eye. There was a window box full of red tulips, and he thought they might have swayed in a passing breeze. Then he realized what he'd seen moving was actually inside one of the large glass panes. A black cat on the sill had raised its head and was watching him through narrowed amber eyes.

He moved on, seeing nothing unusual on that side of the house, apart from the fact that it looked more like a grand museum than a private home. The back was equally impressive. That was where the conservatory was appended to the main part of the building. Nearly the full height and width of the house, it consisted of an ornate dome-like structure of glass panels set in a framework of intricate arches. A verdigris patina on the metalwork, along with the overall design, gave it a distinctly Victorian look.

Double lines of yellow police tape extended in a widening pattern from the sides of the conservatory out to the woods at least a hundred yards away, enclosing a broad fan-shaped area of the lawn. Lengths of string were laid out in a crisscross search pattern within the enclosure. Two figures in crime-scene coveralls, heads down, were making their way along the outer edge.

Morgan lifted the tape for Gurney to pass under, then followed him. Gurney saw two other Tyvek-suited individuals just inside the glass door—a short, stocky, ruddy-faced man and a tall, dark-skinned woman, engaged in a discussion. The man's gestures appeared argumentative.

Morgan gestured for them to come outside.

The man came first. His reddish hair was cut in the prevalent law-enforcement style—shaved on the sides, close-cropped on top. His bull neck made his round, cheeky face look small. He acknowledged Morgan in a terse military style. "Sir."

The woman followed, looking lean and athletic even in her coveralls. Her expression was mildly questioning.

Morgan introduced them. "Brad Slovak, Kyra Barstow . . . Dave Gurney."

"Sir," said Slovak again, this time with a deferential nod.

Barstow extended her hand. Gurney shook it. Her grip was strong.

"Any developments?" asked Morgan.

Slovak ran his hand back through the sandy-red stubble on the top of his head and glanced at Barstow before answering. "We've been trying to get to the bottom of the problem with the fingerprints."

Barstow shot a sideways glance at him. "There is no problem with the prints." There was a West Indian lilt in her voice.

Slovak tilted his head from side to side, the movement of someone trying to loosen tight neck muscles. "The suggestion that the prints in the bedroom belong to Billy Tate?" He shook his head. "There has to be another—"

She cut him off. "The man's prints are the man's prints. A fact. Not a *suggestion*. They're clear, clean, and recent. And there's the AFIS ID—"

Now he cut her off. "The system isn't perfect. Mistakes are made. Human error. AFIS has been known to screw up. Their search algorithms depend on human judgment. Nothing in the system is perfect. Point is, everyone we've spoken to says Tate was never in the house—and that Angus would have put a bullet in him if he even set foot on the property. Plus, coming anywhere near Angus would have violated the terms of his parole—"

"I've been doing this for a long time," interrupted Barstow. "Nineteen years. Thousands of prints, thousands of IDs. Never has there been the kind of screwup you're talking about. Not by me. Not by AFIS."

A timely *ratatatat* from the woodpecker in the forest punctuated her assertion.

Slovak repeated his neck-stretching exercise. "I'm just saying—"

Morgan spoke over him, to Gurney. "You were always fascinated by odd little discrepancies. This one make any sense to you?"

"Not yet. But it could be significant."

"Why?" Slovak's tone was more curious than challenging.

"Things that make no sense at first often tell you the most in the end."

Morgan asked Barstow if she had run the prints through the system a second time.

"I did."

"Same result?"

"The same."

"Anything come back yet on the bloodstained scalpel?"

"We should hear momentarily if the prints on it are of any use. And maybe get data on the blood by noon."

"Bloodwork being done at the college lab?"

"With a sample to Albany for confirmation."

"How about the dog?"

"Dr. Fallow found a piece of fabric in its mouth."

"That fabric," interjected Slovak, "could be a major break. The dog probably got his teeth into the intruder's sleeve or pants leg before getting whacked on the head. Good chance of recovering his DNA from it."

"Or *her* DNA," added Barstow.

Morgan nodded with a tense smile and turned to Gurney. "As long as we're here at the attacker's entry point, do you want to go inside and see the murder site?"

"Might as well."

As they headed for the conservatory door, Morgan's phone rang. He peered at the screen, grimaced, and took a few steps away. After saying something into the phone—Gurney thought he heard the name "Chandler"—Morgan looked back at Slovak.

"Take Dave through the house. I'll catch up with you."

"Yes, sir." Slovak sounded pleased with the assignment. He strode over to the conservatory door, gesturing to Gurney to join him. He pointed to where a glass pane had been smashed out of its frame. Pulverized remnants were strewn on the concrete floor. Gurney recognized the distinctive shatter pattern of break-resistant glass.

"Was the security system activated?"

"Actually, sir, there isn't any security system."

"On an estate like this? Nothing at all?"

"Strange, right?"

Strange indeed, thought Gurney, as he examined the metal frame by the door handle. Every bit of the pane had been pounded out of it.

"Very thorough," he said, as much to himself as to Slovak. "Almost obsessively so."

"And well planned," said Barstow, who had joined them.

"I don't know about planning," said Slovak, giving her a testy look, "but this isn't the work of a burglar with a brick. According to the housekeeper, nothing's been disturbed and nothing's missing."

"Whoever did this knew *exactly* what they were doing," said Barstow, pointing at the glass on the conservatory floor. "I'd say that shatter pattern resulted from the use of just the right kind of tool for that kind of glass."

That got Gurney's attention. "Describe it."

"A heavy hammer with a small head to concentrate the impact. The injury to the dog's head looks to have been caused by the same kind of implement."

Slovak shifted impatiently on his feet. "We'll get the real answer from Dr. Fallow."

Barstow's gaze remained on Gurney. "Unless there's anything else you want from me, I need to catch up with my team and see how the second perimeter search is going."

"The second?"

"I like to go through a crime scene at least twice. If you have any questions about on-site evidence, you can reach me anytime through Chief Morgan." She exchanged nods with Gurney, ignored Slovak, and headed with long elegant strides across the lawn toward the two Tyvek-clad figures at the edge of the woods.

"Okay!" said Slovak with the irritation of a man delayed at a traffic light that had finally turned green. "Let's get started."

7

Gurney had been in botanical-garden conservatories before, but never in anything quite like this. A tropical world of trees, shrubs, and flowers was cosseted in the decor of a grand English manor. The planting bed enclosures resembled fine furniture. The little pathways winding among them were of polished yellow stone, edged with satin-finished hardwood.

He followed Slovak under the arch of a wood-framed device with wheels on each of its four corners and a system of overhead pulleys—presumably designed for lifting and moving the heavier plants in their large earth-filled urns.

As they passed through a sliding door into the house itself, the loamy scents of the conservatory were replaced by something equally distinctive—the smell of money enshrined in polished chestnut floors and antique Persian carpets; in paneled mahogany walls and hand-carved balustrades; in fireplaces the size of alcoves; in alcoves the size of living rooms.

Having led Gurney to an alcove off the main dining room, Slovak explained that this was where the discovery had been made—where the blood from the victim's slashed throat, seeping down through the floorboards, had stained the ceiling and then dripped onto the rug beneath it, next to the chair where Mrs. Russell had been seated. "If she'd been just a couple of feet to the left, it would've dripped right on her." He sounded both excited and appalled.

Gurney peered up at the stain on the high ceiling.

"If you want a closer look," said Slovak, "I can have a ladder brought in."

"No need. I'd rather see it from the top side."

Slovak led the way through the dining room into a hallway lined with life-size portraits of old men in elaborate gilt frames and up a staircase. Gurney noted that segments of the carpeting on several stair treads had been neatly cut out and removed.

The stairs led to a second-floor hallway, from whose carpet two similar excisions had been made. There were several doors along one side of the hallway. One was open, and a plastic crime-scene-containment curtain was hanging in front of it. Slovak held it aside.

"You can go right in, sir. The tech team's already been through here. Twice. This is the husband's bedroom. The next one down the hall is the wife's."

Gurney pointed to the carpet. "I'm curious about those cutouts."

"Bloodstains. One was obvious. Others showed up under luminol—partial shoe-prints, like the attacker had stepped in the victim's blood and tracked it out here. Also a couple of drops, maybe off the scalpel. Barstow cut the carpet pieces out and sent them to the lab. Hopefully, what we get back will answer questions, not just raise more. That business about Tate's prints . . ." Slovak shook his head, his voice trailing off.

"You sound like you might have . . . some difficulty . . . with your tech officer?"

"I don't have any difficulty. It's just that she's got this attitude thing going."

"Oh?"

"The superior tone. '*I've been doing this for nineteen years.*' That kind of crap."

"Has she ever been wrong?"

"Who knows? She pretends to be perfect. But people cover things up, right?"

Gurney decided that this was not the best time to pursue what was likely a routine problem of personal chemistry. He stepped past the plastic curtain into the bedroom.

Everything in there was big—a king-size four-poster bed, a chest of drawers twice the size of his own, and two seven-foot-high armoires on one side of the room; a massive Queen Anne table on a Persian carpet in the middle; and a ceiling-high stone fireplace on the other side. There were three large windows along the wall opposite the doorway.

He went to the nearest window. It overlooked the carriage house, which placed the bedroom on the opposite side of the house from the conservatory—perhaps sufficiently isolated from the breaking of the glass that it might not have been heard.

He turned back to the room, letting his gaze wander around it. Noting dusting powder on most of the hard surfaces, he asked where Barstow had found Billy Tate's fingerprints.

Slovak pointed at the doorway. "Two of the prints she claims are his were lifted from the doorknobs. And there were some partials on the floor by the bathroom, just outside that area where the blood is."

Exactly where someone might have knelt to cut off the victim's finger, thought Gurney, as he made his way to that end of the room.

The size of the bloodstain surprised him. A good six feet in diameter, it filled the area between the side of the bed and the bathroom doorway. The chair Russell had toppled over was in the middle of it. On the wall to Gurney's right there was a line of dried droplets, which he recognized as the spatter that occurs when a blade is slashed through an artery and specks of blood are sent flying onto nearby surfaces.

"If you want to see what this place looked like when we got here yesterday, I can show you," said Slovak, taking out his phone and starting to tap icons.

Gurney didn't answer. He was busy reconstructing the basic elements of the attack in his mind. Angus Russell getting up, half-asleep, going to the bathroom; then stepping out of the bathroom, heading for his bed. His attacker stepping in front of him, scalpel in hand. A sudden backhand slash across the side of the neck—a fatal incision severing both right carotid and right jugular. Russell falling headfirst over the chair.

"Were the lights on when you arrived?" asked Gurney.

"Not the regular lights. Just a small nightlight in a baseboard socket next to the bed. I asked the housekeeper if she'd touched anything when she found the body. She was positive she hadn't. And the wife was in no condition to touch anything. She passed out in the doorway and was still in a state of shock when we got here."

Gurney nodded. "So, if Russell had turned on the bathroom light when he went in there, which he must have done, then turned it off as he came out, his eyes probably wouldn't have adjusted to the semidarkness in the bedroom. He probably never saw his assailant."

"Right," said Slovak, nodding. "He comes out of the bathroom. Assailant steps in front of him. One quick, deep slash. Assailant exits the way he entered."

"But then, on the way out, the assailant dropped what you believe is the murder weapon. Then got attacked by the dog."

"And killed it."

"What kind of dog was it?"

"German shepherd. Big male. Even dead it looked scary."

"They let it out at night?"

"So the housekeeper told us. They had one of those invisible electric dog fences, enclosing about six acres around the house."

"Do you know where the dog was killed?"

"I assume where we found it. At the edge of the woods, not far from the conservatory."

"Why do you assume that's where it was killed?"

Slovak blinked in confusion and ran his hand back over his stubbly hair, as if to aerate a sweating scalp. "Why kill it and move it? That dog weighed over a hundred pounds. You think it matters?"

"It might."

"I'll see what we can do to pin it down."

"Probably a good idea," said Gurney. "But you're the CIO on this. You run the case any way you want. It's your turf, Brad. I'm just an observer, asking questions."

Slovak gave him a knowing look. "You're not just *any* observer."

"Meaning?"

"When Chief Morgan told us you were coming, I did some research. I found an article in *New York* magazine from six years ago. Titled 'Supercop.'"

"Jesus," muttered Gurney.

"The article said you had the highest percentage of cleared homicide cases in the history of the NYPD, and that you'd worked hundreds of homicides. *Hundreds.* You know how many I've worked? *Two*—both when I was on loan to the Bastenburg department—and they were both domestics. I also found newspaper articles about cases you solved since you moved upstate—the White River murders and those killings up in Wolf Lake. So, any advice you have for me, I'm ready to listen."

Gurney's allergy to flattery led to an awkward silence.

He noted that Slovak was still holding his phone, which he'd taken out when he offered to show Gurney the photos he'd taken of the scene. It seemed like a good path back to the reality of the moment.

Gurney pointed to it. "Let's see what you've got."

Slovak tapped an icon, bringing up a series of photos that showed Russell's body tilted down over the chair in the grotesque face-on-the-floor, legs-in-the-air position Morgan had described. But *seeing* the body on the phone screen, stripped of every iota of dignity, was different from just hearing about it.

"These are the ones I took," said Slovak. "Our photographer took a lot more, different angles, plus a video. I can get those for you if you—" He was interrupted by the ringtone of the phone. He took the call. It lasted less than a minute.

"That was Chief Morgan. He wants me to interview the three gardeners, find out if they saw anything, et cetera. Freddy Martinez, our only Spanish-speaking officer, can translate. You can stay up here and get a closer look at things. Chief said he'd join you in a few minutes."

When Slovak had departed, Gurney's attention returned to the bloodstained area in front of the bathroom door, but now he was visualizing the revolting images he'd seen on Slovak's phone.

Over the course of his career, he'd come to accept these disturbing experiences as a natural part of dealing with violent deaths. But being horrified, disgusted, or touched by the details of a brutal crime didn't help in solving it. For some detectives, those emotions did seem to provide extra motivation, a willingness to go the extra mile. Gurney had never lacked motivation. But his personal motivation to get to the bottom of things—to expose the lies and find the truth—had little to do with empathy for the victim. It came from a colder place in his psyche. It arose from his desire to *know*.

He could picture himself trying to explain this to Madeleine. And he could imagine her asking, with a skeptical tilt of her head, what had compelled him that morning to get into his car and drive to Larchfield. "Didn't it have something to do with your feelings about the way Mike Morgan was treated by his father? And your feelings about being alive because of what he did in that South Bronx hallway?"

He could picture himself replying that although his feelings had influenced his decision to be present that morning, they wouldn't drive his pursuit of the truth. If that pursuit was to begin in earnest, it would be for another reason altogether.

He could picture Madeleine's likely response—a patient smile.

His phone rang.

He was too logical a man to believe that coincidences were driven by unseen forces, but it gave him a tiny frisson to see Madeleine's name on the screen.

"Just wanted to let you know," she said, "our dinner has been moved to tomorrow evening."

He had no idea what she was talking about.

"With the Winklers," she added. "You might want to put a reminder on your phone." She paused. "How are things in Larchfield?"

"Hard to say. There's an odd—" He stopped speaking at the sound of footsteps coming up the stairs.

A moment later, Morgan pushed aside the containment curtain and came into the room, his expression more strained than usual.

"Sorry, Maddie, got to go. Talk to you later."

Morgan was shaking his head. "Damn! As if the situation wasn't bad enough by itself, now I've got Aspern to deal with. That's who was on the phone. Expressing his 'concerns' about the investigation, the media, the negative impact on the precious image of Larchfield." His gaze rose to the ceiling, as if searching for an escape hatch.

"What's his concern about the investigation?"

"That my department may not be up to handling it. Or, more to the point, handling it quickly enough to avoid the town's reputation being shredded."

"A reputation he's heavily invested in?"

"Not just heavily. Totally. Apart from the long-term Harrow Hill lease he inherited from his father, he's acquired most of the old farms in the immediate area—which he's been subdividing into ten-acre parcels and advertising as 'Serene Country Estates Nestled Around a Picture-Book Village.' Larchfield's most prominent resident getting his throat sliced open in the middle of the night is not the picture Aspern is trying to promote."

Gurney glanced toward the gruesome stain on the floor. "Inconvenient facts are still facts. What does he expect you to do?"

"God only knows. Identify the killer this afternoon? Arrest him tonight? Use my magic powers to keep the story out of the news?"

"If Aspern is concerned about your department, why don't you just turn the case over to the state police? That's what their Bureau of Criminal Investigation is there for."

Morgan began pacing around the room, uttering little sounds of misery and indecision. Finally, he stopped and shook his head. "I can't do that. It would be giving up too soon." There was something pleading in his tone. "If we could manage it ourselves, that would be ideal. If we can't, we can't. But to give up before we've hardly gotten started . . ." He shook his head in a way that resembled a shiver.

"Small-town departments 'give up' all the time," said Gurney. "They deal with drug arrests, burglaries, assaults—you know the drill—and hand homicides over to BCI. Simple matter of resources."

"We have resources. We have an arrangement with the college's forensic sciences department that gives us access to their state-of-the-art lab. We can get results here faster than BCI can get them from their lab in Albany. Admittedly, our people don't have much major crime experience—except for Kyra Barstow—but they're not stupid. They just need some direction."

Gurney saw in Morgan's eyes an obstinacy that would make further suggestions to transfer the investigation useless.

"So, your lead guy will be Brad Slovak?"

"You think that's a mistake?"

"Hard to say, not knowing what your options are."

Morgan turned toward one of the windows, gazing out at nothing in particular, and sighed. "Brad's okay. Obviously not in your league. But we've got good support from Kyra on the tech side. In any event, it's the best we can do at the moment."

Gurney felt uncomfortable with the man's far-from-subtle plea for help. He walked over to one of the windows and changed the subject. "Have you checked out the other buildings on the property?"

"Of course. Automatic part of securing the site."

"Find anything of interest?"

"The carriage house was an eye-opener—Angus's Mercedes, his wife's Porsche, a big Mercedes SUV, and three vintage Bugattis. I'm guessing a million bucks' worth of transportation. There are two apartments on the second floor—for the housekeeper and the groundskeeper."

"Either of them hear or see anything?"

"Zip. We got a lot of detail on what they did that evening—TV shows they watched, when they went to bed, et cetera. But nothing useful. Questions about recent visitors, disputes, problems didn't produce anything specific. We didn't hear anything we didn't already know. Which is that Angus had more than his share of enemies, and his wife is an icy self-centered bitch. But those interviews were limited. We plan to continue them."

"Slovak handled them?"

"Yes. He also took Mrs. Russell's statement."

"While you were making the trip to my house?"

"Right."

Gurney wasn't thrilled that Morgan had absented himself from the critical early hours of the case in order to pull him into it. "Besides the main house, conservatory, and carriage house, what else is on the property?"

"A barn for the maintenance equipment, a utility garage for a pickup truck and a couple of four-by-fours, a gardening shed, and Mrs. Russell's meditation studio. That's where we'll meet with her. Let me confirm that she's up to it."

He checked the time on his phone and placed a call, which was picked up right away.

"Hi, Glenda . . . How is she? . . . We'll see her first, Helen Stone second . . . When she comes out of the shower, tell her we'll be there at 11:15 . . . Right . . . No, Brad's with the three gardeners. I'm bringing another detective with me . . . No, no need to tell her . . . Any problems, call me."

He slipped the phone back in his pocket. "You got the gist of that?"

Gurney nodded. "But the gist didn't include the purpose."

"The purpose is to amplify the statement she already gave—with any details that might not have occurred to her yesterday."

"I gather she was in bad shape?"

"It took her a couple of hours to recover from the initial shock. After that she was coherent enough. Her doctor claimed she'd suffered an acute PTSD reaction to the sight of the blood. Rapid onset, rapid recovery."

"Her doctor was here?"

"He was. A participant in the Russells' superelite medical plan. Instant house calls—any reason, any time. Premium is seventy-five grand a year to start. Anyway, she didn't want to stay in the main house, which was fine with us, so she moved out to the cottage. That's when Brad took her statement. Then her doctor gave her a pill to help her sleep. For the past twenty-four hours we've kept a female officer with her."

"And you want me to sit in on this follow-up interview?"

"Or be an active part of it. I think you'll find it interesting."

"Any special reason?"

The tic returned to the corner of Morgan's mouth.

"The lady is quite . . . unusual."

8

Lorinda Russell's personal cottage stood in the center of a lush lawn bordered by mountain laurels at the end of a mowed trail through the woods. The slate roof had a stone chimney at either end. Bright green ivy softened the edges of the door and window openings, giving the facade a fairytale quality.

As Morgan and Gurney were approaching the front door, it opened, and a female officer came out to meet them. She was unsmiling, with hard eyes that had seen too many bad things.

"Mrs. Russell okay?" Morgan asked.

"She's on her feet, speaking clearly." The officer hesitated, glancing at Gurney.

"Detective Gurney is joining me for the interview," said Morgan. "You can speak freely."

"She's gone from basket case to boss of the world. No signs of grief. Nothing. There's a strange brain behind that movie-star face. Hope I'm not talking out of turn."

"No problem, Officer. Good time for a break. Come back in half an hour."

"Yes, sir." She stepped away, heading in the direction of the main house.

Morgan took a deep breath and led the way through the ivy-framed doorway.

Gurney's first glance around the interior brought to mind English cottages he'd seen in design magazines in his dentist's waiting room. With antique oak beams, armchairs in flowery chintz fabric, and a potbellied woodstove set inside a stone fireplace, the place radiated country gentility. But his attention soon shifted from the furnishings to the tall, dark-haired woman standing next to the hearth.

She had the classic features and unblemished skin of a young model. Her beige slacks and white blouse were form-fitting. She was holding a phone, speaking in a calm voice.

"It needs to happen now . . . That's not my concern . . . Good . . . Correct . . ."

Seeing Morgan and Gurney waiting in the room's timbered archway, she waved them in without expression, pointing them toward the couch as she concluded her call. "You have the address . . . Tomorrow at nine, no later."

She tapped an icon on her phone, then greeted Gurney with a perfunctory smile. "I'm Lorinda Russell. Who are you?"

Morgan answered for him. "This is Detective Dave Gurney. My former partner in the NYPD. He's a homicide expert—the best. I've asked for his input on the situation here."

Her gaze remained on Gurney. "Is Dave a deaf mute?"

Morgan reddened.

Gurney smiled. "Rarely deaf."

"Good." She pointed again at the couch. "Have a seat. I need to make another call."

"I'm sorry for your loss," said Gurney, still standing.

She had no reaction. As she was swiping through several screens, she asked Morgan, "How soon will your people be finished?"

"Finished?"

"In the house." She tapped an icon and raised the phone to her ear.

Morgan looked uncertain. "I hope by the end of the day. Why?"

She didn't answer, speaking into the phone instead. "This is Lorinda Russell. Call me to set a time for the arrival of your crew." She tapped another icon, laid the phone on the coffee table, waited pointedly for Morgan and Gurney to settle themselves on the couch, then sat in an armchair facing them.

"Did you know that blood is considered a form of hazardous waste?"

Morgan blinked in apparent confusion.

"Finding a competent cleaning company has been a challenge," she said, her eyes on Gurney. "Some don't want to deal with bloodstains at all, and only one was willing to deal with this amount of blood. But I'm sure you're more familiar with the problem than I am."

In his two-plus decades in the NYPD's busy homicide division, Gurney had encountered many reactions to the murder of a spouse, but never one like this.

She went on in an even voice. "The blood needs to be removed completely, without a trace, before I can go back in that house." Her gaze lingered another few seconds on Gurney. There was a flicker of something challenging in her expression—something he'd observed in individuals who enjoyed competition.

She switched her attention to Morgan. "Where do things stand with your investigation?"

"At the moment we're processing evidence. Lab work is underway. We're gathering video files from private and municipal security cameras in the area. Officers are canvassing nearby residents. Everything possible is being done, and we hope—"

She cut him off. "In other words, right now you know nothing."

Morgan looked embarrassed. "Lorinda, everything is being done that can—"

"How about you, Detective Gurney? Any *input*?"

"Just questions."

"Ask them." Her fingers began to tap quietly on the arm of her chair.

"In the period leading up to the attack, were there—"

"The *murder*."

He raised a curious eyebrow.

"I prefer clarity. It wasn't just an attack."

"Okay. The murder. Were you aware of any conflicts in your husband's business or personal life that could be connected to what happened here?"

She uttered a sharp sound that could have been a cough or a laugh. "Angus's life was nothing but conflict. He was a warrior. His most endearing trait. But it creates enemies."

"Any that might be willing to kill him?"

"I'm sure quite a few."

"Anyone in particular?"

"If you mean anyone that leaps to mind immediately, that would be our wretched neighbor, Chandler Aspern. But I'd be more concerned about the ones that don't come to mind, wouldn't you?"

"Aspern comes to mind because of the lease disagreement?"

"That, and because he and Angus hated each other. Quite openly. If it was Chandler who'd been murdered, Angus would be everyone's favorite suspect. I went through all of this with Detective Slovak yesterday. You should read his report." She looked with some annoyance at Morgan, then back at Gurney. "Let me ask you something. How much danger do you think I'm in?"

"The killer was in the bedroom next to yours. If you were a target, you'd be dead."

"So you think I'm safe?"

"Probably."

"But I shouldn't bet my life on it?"

"I wouldn't if I were you."

Her fingers stopped tapping. She was regarding Gurney now as if he were a mystery to be solved. "There's something bothering you. What is it?"

"I find it interesting that you have no security cameras, no alarms."

"That's being rectified. I was on the phone this morning arranging for the installation of a state-of-the-art system."

"Good idea."

"Are you being sarcastic—implying it would have been a good idea *before* Angus was murdered?"

"It certainly would have been a good idea," said Gurney blandly. "But I'm guessing it was never seriously considered. What I've been told about Angus makes me think of someone I knew a long time ago—a powerful man with a lot of enemies and no alarm system. He regarded an alarm as a sign of fear, and fear was an emotion he'd never acknowledge in himself. Fear was the emotion he inspired in *others*."

She was looking at him with real interest. "What happened?"

"He underestimated one of his enemies."

She smiled but said nothing.

Gurney switched gears. "When was the last time Billy Tate was in your house?"

"Four years ago, not long before he was incarcerated. But he wasn't actually *in* the house. He was at the front door, demanding payment for some job Angus had hired him to do, but which he didn't do very well. Angus refused to pay him. That's what led to the threats and the assault conviction that put him in prison."

"When was he released?"

She looked at Morgan.

"A year and four months ago."

Gurney asked her if she'd seen Tate since his release.

She said she hadn't.

He decided to switch gears again. "Did Angus have a regular time each night when he got up to go to the bathroom?"

"I have no idea."

"His being up, moving around in the bathroom, that wouldn't wake you?"

"No."

"You're a sound sleeper?"

"Yes."

"Do you know if he was in the habit of getting up more than once?"

"I wouldn't be surprised, considering his age." Looking suddenly bored, she picked up her phone from the coffee table and glanced at the time. "I have calls to make. Is there anything else you need from me right now?"

"One last thing," said Gurney, standing up from the couch. "It would be helpful if you could put together a list of people who might welcome your husband's death."

"Detective Slovak already asked for that, and I'll tell you what I told him. If you mean people who'd be glad Angus is dead, the list is endless. If you mean people getting a significant financial benefit from his death, the list is short."

"Okay. Start with the short list."

"Hilda Russell. Chandler Aspern. And Angus's conniving, gold-digging wife."

Morgan stared at her, his expression frozen.

Gurney asked, "Are those the words people use to describe you?"

"Those, and a lot worse." She brushed a hair back from her perfect face. There was a combative glint in her dark eyes.

As they were heading back along the path to the main house, there was a jittery edge to Morgan's chronic anxiety. "What did you think of that?"

Gurney didn't answer right away. He was unsettled as much by the attitude of the new widow as by his active involvement in a meeting he had intended to simply observe.

"You mean, what did I think of her short list?"

"I mean, what did you think of Lorinda herself?"

Gurney waited for the woodpecker in the forest to conclude a long series of *ratatatats* before answering. "Conniving and gold-digging might be close to the truth. Also, controlling and smart. But I have the feeling there's another quality in her, something I can't put my finger on. How much do you know about her?"

"Larchfield is as gossipy as any small town. People like Angus and Lorinda figure in a lot of stories. People say she was a wild teenager, brought up in a crazy family over in Bastenburg. There's a unified school district here, so she went to the same high school as the Larchfield kids. The rumor was that there was an inappropriate relationship between her and the school principal, Hanley Bullock, when she was fifteen. She never said anything publicly about it, nothing was ever proven, and it never became a police matter. But in the end Bullock resigned, his wife divorced him, and he moved out of the area."

"And Lorinda?"

"When she graduated and turned eighteen, she married Angus, who was sixty-eight at the time and had recently dumped his third wife. That was ten years ago, and people are still talking about it."

Morgan stumbled forward on a rough spot in the path, just managing to catch his balance. He didn't speak again until they emerged onto the lawn in front of the conservatory. "We're going to meet with Helen Stone over in the carriage house."

"Okay."

"What about the other two names on her cui bono list?" asked Morgan, as they proceeded across the lawn. "Any thoughts?"

"I'm not sure what I think. What can you tell me about Hilda Russell?"

"Not much more than I told you on our drive over here. She's Angus's younger sister, the Episcopal rector of St. Giles on the village square. She and Lorinda are as different as two human beings can be. Except for willfulness. They both have a ton of it."

"What about her relationship with Angus?"

"They seemed close enough, at least on the surface. In the community, Hilda was better liked than Angus. She didn't antagonize people the way he did. Although . . ." Morgan slowed his pace, then stopped. "At least one person had a problem with her. Or with her church."

"What do you mean?"

"I told you Billy Tate was killed in an accident the night before Angus's murder—which is why his fingerprints being at the crime scene is so problematic. I didn't go into the details of his death, because they didn't seem relevant. He couldn't have killed Russell. Dead is dead. End of story. But the fact is, the accident that killed Billy Tate occurred at Hilda's church. On the roof." He paused. "Tate, as you may have gathered by now, was a bit of a lunatic. A wild child who got wilder as an adult. He was on the roof of St. Giles, spray-painting graffiti on the steeple, with a thunderstorm blowing in. He was struck by lightning, knocked off the roof, fell a good twenty-five feet onto a hard gravel path. Stone-cold dead."

"This was witnessed by someone?"

"Two patrol officers, a dog-walking couple, Brad Slovak, and yours truly. In fact, we have it all on a phone video, taken by one of the dog walkers. I'll show it to you back at headquarters—after we talk to Helen Stone."

9

As they were heading to the carriage house, Slovak approached them. He didn't look happy.

"Sir," he said, giving Gurney a crisp nod, then speaking mainly to Morgan. "Martinez and I just finished interviewing the three gardeners. Bottom line, they didn't see anything, didn't hear anything, don't know anything. I showed each of them our file photo of Tate, asked if they'd ever seen him here, or anywhere near here. All said no."

Morgan was chewing on the inside of his lower lip. "Talk to Tate's parole officer, find out if he was making his weekly appointments, if there was anything about him that—"

"Excuse me, sir, I already did that. Tate's parole period concluded a month ago. The PO told me he came close a couple of times to violating Tate for erratic behavior. But he kept his appointments and didn't get too far over the line. The PO said he'd heard about the accident. The craziness of Tate being up on that roof in a thunderstorm didn't surprise him."

Morgan checked his watch. "This would be a good time to follow up with the guys doing the door-to-doors, see if they've discovered anything."

"Make sure they're checking for any exterior security cameras," added Gurney.

"Yes, sir." With a parting nod, Slovak strode off toward the row of police vehicles under the front portico.

"Well," said Morgan. "It would be nice if Tate's print ID is a simple algorithm screwup. If it's not that, I don't know what the hell it is. You have any ideas?"

"I'm thinking an algorithm screwup wouldn't work that way. Let's say those prints belong to Person X, and the system parameters are set in a way that the prints are mistakenly identified as belonging to someone other than Person X. Doesn't it seem unlikely that the person the algorithm mistakenly settled on would just happen to be a local resident with a history of conflict with the victim?"

Morgan looked pained. "Okay, but if the prints *are* Tate's, where does that leave us? There's no way around the fact that Tate died at least twenty-four hours before Angus was murdered."

As Morgan's voice was rising, he was looking helplessly at Gurney—whose reaction to agitation in others was a countervailing calmness.

Gurney shrugged. "I believe Helen Stone is waiting for us."

The side of the carriage house, like the cottage, was covered with bright green ivy. An entry door led to a staircase that rose to a small landing and a second door.

The door was opened by a gray-haired, square-jawed woman in a sweatshirt and jeans. Her combative gaze seemed to convey great confidence in her own convictions.

Morgan spoke first. "How are you doing, Helen?"

She stared at him. "Never better."

"I guess that was a stupid question. Can we come in?"

"If you don't mind standing. The chairs are being used."

She stood back out of the doorway, and they stepped into an entry foyer. Straight ahead was a large living room with stacked boxes everywhere and piles of clothing on the chairs and sofa. A window as wide as the room looked out on the lawn and woods.

"This is Dave Gurney," said Morgan, "a homicide detective I worked with in the city."

She looked at him without interest, then back at Morgan. "What can I do for you?"

He eyed the boxes in the living room. "Are you going somewhere?"

"With Angus gone, I have no desire to stay here."

"You don't get along with Lorinda?"

"You could say that."

"What's the problem?"

"I'm not going to talk about her. I don't want her name in my mouth. I worked here as long as I did because Angus wanted me to. He's gone, so I'm going."

"Where to?"

"My sister in Richmond."

"When?"

"Tomorrow afternoon. I'd leave now if I could get a flight."

Morgan shot a glance at Gurney, who saw it as a request for assistance.

He smiled at Stone. "You've made me curious. What's the single worst thing you can tell me about the relationship between Angus and Lorinda?"

He could tell that she was thinking about it. That "single worst thing" approach usually worked.

"The worst thing was his inability to see her for what she was. He was brilliant, the smartest man I ever met, except when it came to her. With her, he was a drug addict. In total denial. He treated her like a *queen*, for God's sake."

"It must have been difficult for you, working here under those conditions."

"Life is difficult. Some can handle it, some can't."

A movement behind her in the living room caught Gurney's attention. Perched atop a china cabinet was a black cat with gleaming yellow eyes, like the one he'd seen watching him from a window in the main house.

He pointed. "Is that yours?"

She looked back over her shoulder. Her voice softened. "That's Prince. Short for Prince of Darkness. He follows me everywhere."

"Interesting name for a cat."

"Appropriate," she said, then added, looking at Morgan, "Was there anything else?"

He blinked, as if his mind had been elsewhere. "I was wondering if anything occurred to you since yesterday."

"I went over everything with your detective."

Morgan seemed about to ask another question when he was stopped by a sharp rapping.

Stone stepped around him and pulled the door open. "Yes?"

It was Kyra Barstow. She looked past Stone at Morgan. "Sir, we need to talk."

He excused himself and went out onto the landing, closing the door behind him.

Stone stared impatiently at Gurney.

"Tell me something," he said. "You knew Angus pretty well, right?"

"Probably better than anyone."

"So you probably have a better idea than anyone who his enemies were."

"That Slivovak person asked me to make a list. I told him he should go make a copy of the county phone book."

"Angus generated that much animosity?"

"He was a strong, determined man. He lived by a code that's gone out of style. Old Testament morality. Eye for an eye. Our so-called 'society' has gotten away from that, and we're paying the price. Angus didn't suffer fools gladly. He spoke his mind. The plain truth. People don't like the truth."

The apartment door opened abruptly and Morgan stepped in, agitated and apologetic. "Something's come up. Dave, I need you to come with me. Helen, we'll talk again before you leave."

Gurney followed Morgan down the staircase and out onto the lawn.

"We have to get back to town," Morgan said as he strode toward the police vehicles under the portico.

Kyra Barstow was already there, by the tech van, tapping the screen of her phone. Morgan got into the driver's seat of the Tahoe, motioning Gurney to the passenger seat.

"The lab results are in," he said, starting the engine. He didn't say anything more until they'd driven through the allée and past the uniformed officer at the gate.

"The scalpel that Slovak found in the conservatory? The blood on it is Angus's. And the bloody prints on it? They belong to Billy Tate. That piece of fabric in the dog's mouth? The trace of blood on it belongs to Billy Tate. And there were micro-particles of glass in the fabric that match the smashed pane from the conservatory door. As for the blood traces on the staircase and hall carpets? The blood on the shoe prints is Angus's—probably from being stepped in. But one of the droplets on the carpet is Tate's."

"Tate is definitely dead, right?" asked Gurney.

"I saw it happen. I saw the lightning hit him. I saw him fall. I saw the ME pronounce him dead. I saw the body get wheeled into the mortuary."

"Sounds pretty definite. You have a next step in mind?"

"I told Kyra to call Brad, fill him in on the lab findings, then meet us at headquarters. I called Peale, asked him to check the mortuary."

"To make sure your dead suspect is still dead?"

Morgan's eyes widened in desperation. "I guess. I don't know. Dead is dead, right? It's not a temporary condition." His phone rang. He pushed the speaker button on his steering wheel.

"Chief Morgan here."

"This is Danforth Peale."

"Thanks for getting back so quickly. You checked?"

"Where are you?" There was a harsh note in the man's patrician accent.

"On Waterview Drive. On my way into the village. Is everything . . . all right?"

"You wouldn't have sent me on this peculiar errand if you expected everything to be *all right*, would you? You knew damn well something was wrong."

Morgan's mouth was slightly open—the look of a man staring at calamity.

The waspy voice went on, ragged at the edge. "The body is gone."

"Say that again?"

"Gone. Somebody stole Tate's goddamn body."

10

Morgan pulled into the parking area behind the big Victorian funeral home, stopping next to the silver Lexus with the jacked-up rear axle.

After he made calls to Slovak and Barstow, giving them the missing-body news and telling them to come directly to the mortuary, he turned to Gurney. "What do you think's happening here?"

"Hard to say. But it's an interesting development."

"Why the hell would someone steal the body?"

Gurney didn't answer him.

Morgan got out of the Tahoe, lit a cigarette, and began sucking on it as though the smoke were oxygen. Slovak came barreling up the driveway in an unmarked Dodge Charger, followed by Barstow's tech van.

Morgan ground out his cigarette on the pavement. Barstow opened the back doors of her van and produced four sets of crime-scene coveralls—which would have been overkill at a normal burglary, but was appropriate here, given the missing body's connection to a murder.

Slovak was the first to speak. "So, what's the theory? Somebody snatched Tate's corpse and dragged it into Russell's house to leave trace evidence? Doesn't make much sense to me."

"Not necessarily the whole corpse," said Barstow lightly. "All the killer needed to bring was a little blood for the carpet, maybe some for the fabric in the dog's mouth, plus a finger or two to make the prints. We know from the mutilation of the victim's hand that the killer was adept at cutting off fingers."

Slovak winced. "Then why go to the trouble of carrying the whole body away?"

"Good question." She looked at Gurney. "Any ideas?"

"Too soon for ideas. We need more information."

On cue, the back door of the funeral home opened, and a man stepped into the parking area. His pink cashmere sweater and green slacks struck Gurney as being more suited to a golf course than a funeral home.

"Morgan! Get in here."

It was the same arrogant voice Gurney had heard on the speaker in the Tahoe. The man who'd called himself Danforth Peale looked to be in his late twenties. He had neatly combed blond hair, a pale complexion, and a pouty mouth.

Morgan offered a brittle smile. "Be with you in a second, Dan. Just getting prepared."

With everyone in coveralls, shoe covers, and nitrile gloves, they followed Peale into a hall that smelled of antiseptic. At the end of it was a closed door.

Peale turned to Morgan, his voice tight with anger. "That's the embalming room with the cadaver-storage unit. When you called, I came down from my office and discovered the damn mess in there. I didn't touch a thing."

He led them into a large clinical-looking space, similar to an ME's autopsy room. The disinfectant odor was stronger here. In the center was a gleaming white embalming table, hooked up to specialized plumbing equipment for irrigation and draining. An operating-room lighting fixture was suspended from the ceiling above it. Glass cabinets lined the walls. The glass door on one of them had been smashed.

What captured Gurney's attention, however, was the cadaver-storage unit on the other side of the embalming table. Seven feet high and at least that wide and as deep, it resembled a giant safe or industrial walk-in closet. Its door, nearly the full width of the unit, was wide open. Inside, a casket with its lid raised rested on a mortuary trolley, similar to the rolling stretchers used in hospitals. Inside the casket was a bloodstained fabric liner. Gurney could see an area on the edge of the lid where the wood was splintered.

"Damned idiots did that," said Peale, following Gurney's gaze. "There's a latch under the side rail, but they didn't take the time to find it. They just pried open the lid."

"*They*?" said Gurney. "You have reason to believe it was more than one person?"

"That's obvious, isn't it? Tate's body weighed at least a hundred fifty pounds. And the trolley is still where I left it in the unit. Meaning the body was lifted out of the casket and carried out of the building. Damn near impossible for one person."

Slovak was stroking his chin in a near-parody of thoughtfulness. "Unless he, or she, rolled the casket out to the back door on that trolley thing, pried the top off, dragged the corpse into the trunk of their car, then rolled the trolley back in here."

Barstow was staring at him. "Why would they take the time to replace the trolley?"

Morgan, who Gurney knew abhorred any conflict he might be called on to resolve, interrupted with a raised hand. "Let's debate the scenarios later." He turned to Peale. "Have you seen any signs of forced entry?"

Peale pointed to a doorway off the main room. His sweater sleeve rode up a few inches on his wrist, revealing what appeared to be a gold Cartier watch. "The window in there is open. It was closed the last time I was down here."

"Closed and locked?"

"Maybe not locked. I'm not sure."

"Apart from the broken casket and open window, has anything else been disturbed?

"Obviously that," Peale said, pointing to the smashed glass door of the case on the wall.

"Was something taken?"

For the first time, the haughtiness in Peale's voice was diluted with something that sounded like fear. "Five surgical scalpels and one bone mallet."

Barstow spoke up. "Could you describe the mallet?"

"My largest. Ten-inch handle. Lead-weighted head. Narrow-diameter striking surface. Why do you ask?"

"Long story."

Morgan returned to his own line of questions. "Are you aware of anything else that's been taken or disturbed?"

Peale pointed to an area on the bare wall between two cabinets. "There are some peculiar scratches over there."

Morgan and Barstow stepped closer, peering at a horizontal number eight with a vertical line through the middle of it. It appeared to have been scraped into the paint with a sharp-pointed instrument. Barstow pulled out her phone and took a photo.

"Anything else?" asked Morgan.

"No, apart from that, everything is wonderful!"

Morgan's mouth tightened. He spoke with the forced evenness of a man defusing a bomb. "This would be a good time to turn the room over to Kyra. Her crime-scene team will go over it with a fine-tooth comb. If the intruders left any evidence behind, they'll find it. In the meantime, I'd like to get a broader picture of the situation—especially the time period between the arrival of Tate's body and its removal. You mentioned having an office upstairs. That might be a good place to talk, unless you'd rather come next door to headquarters."

Peale stared at him for a long moment before answering, as if anger at the desecration of his workplace was getting in the way of his ability to think. "My office . . . is fine."

Gurney, meanwhile, had noted what he suspected was the lens of a discreet security camera mounted atop the hinge bracket of one of the wall cabinets.

He pointed to it. "Is that what I think it is?"

Peale looked up, reluctantly, it seemed. "I'm afraid so."

11

Danforth Peale's "office" had little in common with the image the term brought to mind. With the exception of a handsome walnut file cabinet and a laptop computer on a small Hepplewhite table, there was no hint of it being a place where business was conducted, even the genteel business of burying the wealthy dead.

The old-money look of the furnishings evoked the cozy den of an Ivy League dean. One wall was covered with sepia prints of what Gurney guessed were the winning boats in various yacht races, another with old botanical prints. Four damask-covered Queen Anne chairs were grouped around an oval coffee table. In the center of the table stood a Chinese vase.

Peale gestured to the chairs as he chose one for himself. Once they were all seated, he spent a few seconds flicking invisible specks off his sweater before looking up with a strained smile.

Morgan cleared his throat. "I'd like to hear more about that security camera in the embalming room—and your whole security setup."

Peale sat back and crossed his legs. The preppy loafers visible below the cuffs of his green pants looked expensive. He steepled his fingers thoughtfully in front of his chin. "Three or four years ago, some vandals from Bastenburg broke into the embalming room. They were observed by a neighbor and apprehended almost immediately. No damage was incurred beyond a forced lock on the back door. But it did raise a concern, and I brought in a security expert who installed a state-of-the-art system. Supersensitive to sound and motion, audio-tropic, video-tropic, hi-def, full color."

Slovak interrupted. "Sorry, sir? Audio-tropic? Video-tropic? Could you—?"

Peale cut him off. "The camera lens pivots automatically in the direction of any detected sound or motion, follows it, and transmits it—to be recorded on that computer." Peale pointed to the laptop on the Hepplewhite table. "Wonderful theory. Horrible reality."

"Sir?"

Peale addressed his answer to Morgan and Gurney. "The damn system's strength is its weakness. Its level of sensitivity makes it a waste of my time. There's a street that runs in back of my parking area. Every damn vehicle that passed set off the system's functions. Every single morning, on that computer, I would have a series of videos of the rear wall of the embalming room—which, as far as the camera was concerned, was the source of the sound of the passing cars. All those hi-def files ate up the computer memory."

"So you turned it off?" asked Morgan.

"Not entirely." Peale flicked another invisible speck off his sweater and re-steepled his fingers. "I left the search and transmit functions on, since I'm often here in the evening and I can glance at that computer screen to see if anything problematical is occurring. In fact, nothing ever is. But I did turn off the record function."

"So, the basic monitoring function is on all the time?"

"Just from nine in the evening till six in the morning. To my knowledge, Larchfield's never had any daytime crime at all."

"So," said Morgan with a summarizing frown, "if you were in this office the night of the body's removal, you would have witnessed it happening on that computer?"

"Correct."

"But no recording was made."

Peale's voice hardened. "Also correct. Infuriatingly so."

"It would be helpful if you could take us through everything that happened between the time you took possession of the body and the last moment you saw it."

Peale raised his hands in objection. "Let's be clear about that 'possession' term. I was told that the deceased's next of kin, Darlene Tate, had requested that the body be brought here, pending a decision regarding its final disposition. I complied with that request as a courtesy, not as a legal transfer of possession. I agreed purely as a temporary matter of accommodation to the bereaved."

Morgan looked at Slovak, as if for confirmation.

Slovak nodded his assent to Peale's account and added some details, seemingly for Gurney's benefit. "During my call to Billy's stepmother, she asked that the body be taken here. She said she'd come as soon as she could to discuss arrangements. Since the fatal accident had been witnessed by Chief Morgan, myself, and the couple who photographed it happening, Dr. Fallow waived the need for an autopsy."

Perhaps in response to a look of surprise on Gurney's face, Slovak added, "In addition to being a local physician, Dr. Fallow is the county's part-time medical examiner—so he gets to make the autopsy decisions."

"He signed a preliminary death certificate?"

"Yes, sir, he did," said Slovak. "Right after we brought the body in on the trolley."

"He arrived that quickly?"

"Yes, sir. He lives right here in the village. As soon as we saw Tate fall, we called him—in his capacity as a regular medical doctor. When he examined Tate on the ground, he pronounced him dead, then signed the certificate in the embalming room."

Peale resumed his narrative, again addressing himself to Morgan. "As I was saying, I was informed that Darlene Tate would be arriving with further instructions."

"Did she show up as promised?"

"Sooner than I'd expected. Around four thirty that morning. I was still here in the office."

Morgan asked, "Did she give you specific instructions at that time?"

"Indeed she did. Specific and unnatural."

"Unnatural in what way?"

"First of all, she insisted on conducting our meeting down in the embalming room rather than my office. She asked to see the body. I cautioned her concerning the brutal effect of the lightning strike on the side of his face. It was a burnt vertical gouge, with some of the bone over the eye and cheekbone exposed. But she insisted that I wheel the body out of the storage unit so she could see it. Reluctantly, I complied—fully prepared for a shocked reaction. The shock was my own, when I saw the look on her face."

He paused before adding, "She was smiling."

Morgan grimaced. "*Smiling*?"

"Radiantly."

"Did she say anything?"

"She asked if Billy was really dead."

"And you told her he was?"

"Of course."

"How did she react to that?"

"She said, 'Let's hope he stays that way.' Honestly, it gave me the shivers."

"God," muttered Morgan. "Did she provide you with funeral instructions?"

"Only that there was to be no embalming, no obituary, no visitation hours, no service of any kind."

"Did she make any other requests?"

"She said she needed a couple of days to decide on a location for the burial, and she asked me to keep the body here until then."

"And that was it?"

"Not quite. She wanted to pick out a casket immediately. I keep a limited selection in a display room downstairs. She picked the cheapest one. Then she insisted that I place the body in it, at that moment, while she watched. I would normally refuse such a request. But I was desperate to be rid of her, so I did. It was awkward, unsanitary, and unprofessional. The clothing of the deceased was still wet in places where there'd been bleeding." Peale sighed and shook his head.

Slovak looked appalled.

Morgan leaned forward in his chair. "What happened then?"

"I had removed some personal effects from the pockets of the deceased's jeans and sweatshirt—a nearly empty wallet, a phone, a car key—and I suggested that she take them. But she said no. *Absolutely not.* She demanded that her stepson's body be left just as it was. She was adamant."

Slovak looked confused. "Did she say why?"

Peale continued to speak directly to Morgan, as if underscoring a preference for addressing only the highest-ranking person in the room. "She said she wanted everything he had to rot in his grave with him. *Rot in his grave.* Her exact words."

Morgan asked Peale if he put those belongings in the casket with the body.

"Yes. I laid them on the body, dressed just as it was—in the bloodstained hoodie, jeans, and sneakers. I closed the casket. I latched it. I rolled it into the refrigerated storage unit. I shut the door. And finally, thank God, I was able to bid farewell to that woman."

"And the next time you visited the embalming room? When was that?"

"When you called me an hour ago and asked me to check on Tate's body."

Morgan appeared to be struggling to assimilate everything Peale had said. Eventually, he turned to Gurney. "You have any questions?"

About a dozen, he thought. But this was not the best time to ask them.

12

After leaving Peale, Gurney, Morgan, and Slovak went down to the embalming room, where Kyra Barstow was supervising the work of the two Tyvek-clad evidence techs Gurney had observed that morning on the lawn of the Russell estate.

Morgan asked if Barstow could come next door for a meeting at headquarters. She said that she'd join them in a minute; first, she needed to give her team some additional instructions for the examination of the casket.

True to her word, she arrived in the conference room just as Gurney, Morgan, and Slovak were taking their seats. Morgan ran his fingers over the satiny tabletop and gestured at the room's thick carpeting and mahogany paneling. "Just like our old precinct house," he said, making an obvious joke.

Gurney forced a smile at the memory of the stained floor tiles, cheap plastic chairs, and scarred tabletop in the detectives' meeting room in the converted tenement building with its noisy pipes, temperamental heating system, and ubiquitous mice. He might have smiled more easily if he didn't interpret the comment as an attempt to remind him yet again of their history together, its inescapable debt.

Morgan turned to Barstow. "Anything of interest in Peale's embalming room?"

She nodded enthusiastically. "Plenty of fingerprints, shoe prints, fibers, hairs, bloodstains. I'll get the lab to work through the night. By tomorrow morning we should have some results in hand."

Morgan looked pleased, or at least less worried. "Let's take a few minutes to assess what we learned from Peale and prioritize next steps. Who wants to start?"

Slovak raised his hand like a schoolboy. "Detective Gurney has been really quiet. I'd love to hear his thoughts."

"You and me both," said Morgan. "Dave?"

"You mentioned there's a video of Tate's accident, taken by a witness."

Morgan nodded. "It's been downloaded to our evidence archive. You want to see it?"

"Very much so."

Morgan began manipulating an app on his phone. A burnished wood panel in the conference room wall slid open, revealing a large monitor. After a few more swipes and taps on his phone, the big screen came to life, showing a nighttime image of a white church facade, illuminated by a streetlamp at the edge of what Gurney recognized as the village square. The steeple of the church was framed by a black sky.

Gurney's attention was attracted by a shadowy figure on the sharply pitched roof next to the base of the steeple. The camera began to zoom in slowly. The shadowy figure—in black pants and a gray hooded sweatshirt—moved closer to the edge of the roof and became illuminated by the streetlamps below.

Slovak leaned toward Gurney. "That's Billy Tate."

Gurney could see that Tate was holding a can of something in one hand and grasping the corner of the steeple with the other.

Three flashes lit up the sky in rapid succession, followed by a long rumble of thunder.

Tate began moving the can in a curving motion along the side of the steeple.

Two blue-white flashes lit the sky, more brightly this time, followed by louder thunder.

A still-brighter flash created an eerie silhouette of the steeple and the hooded figure next to it. The flash was followed almost immediately by the crashing of thunder, and a few seconds later by another flash and another crash.

Slovak pointed at the screen. "It's coming now . . . right after this next wind gust."

Bits of debris, leaves, and dust were roiled up into the air and whirled past the front of the church. Tate stepped in closer to the steeple, bracing his body against it.

"Watch," said Slovak excitedly. "Here it comes . . ."

A blinding lightning bolt blasted Tate away from the steeple and over the edge of the roof. With a fast downward sweep, the camera followed the body's fall to the ground.

Gurney flinched, not just at the sight of the impact but at a sound embedded in his memory—as vivid at that moment as the day he heard it, while he was still a probationary officer in the NYPD. An addict had jumped from a sixth-floor apartment window and struck the pavement less than ten feet from where Gurney was standing. The stomach-turning sound of the body hitting the ground had stayed with him for three decades.

While the camera remained on Tate's inert form, two uniformed officers rushed into the scene, followed by Slovak, followed by Morgan—both in civilian clothes. Slovak knelt next to the body and went through an extended check for vitals. One of the uniformed officers initiated CPR, shouting at the same time for a defibrillator. Slovak could be seen taking out his phone.

Morgan fast-forwarded the video to a later point where a man in chinos and a loose cardigan entered the area with a small leather bag. He squatted by the body and applied a stethoscope to the chest and carotid artery. Because of the position of the camera it was difficult for Gurney to be sure, but the man seemed to be palpating the neck area, then checking the eyes. After a while, he stood up and spoke to Slovak and Morgan and a third officer, all of whom had been closely observing the examination.

Morgan stopped the video and turned to Gurney. "The guy you just saw examining Tate is Dr. Fallow."

After another fast-forwarding, the video showed a rolling stretcher being guided toward the body. Gurney recognized the man pushing it as Peale. There was some discussion between him and the doctor, after which Peale, Morgan, Slovak, and one of the uniformed officers lifted the body onto the stretcher. With Peale leading the way, Morgan rolled the stretcher out of the frame.

At that point he stopped the video again.

"Any questions?"

"From the point at which the video begins, until the body is removed, how much time elapses?" asked Gurney. "With the fast-forwarding, I couldn't tell."

"There's an embedded time code, which I disabled for this viewing, since it's a bit of a distraction. The total time from start to finish is a little less than an hour. The first twenty minutes or so is devoted to Tate on the roof. What I showed you starts at the end of that portion. The full version includes the defibrillation efforts, the arrival of the EMTs in an ambulance, along with two police cars from Bastenburg."

"How did Tate get up on the roof?"

"There's an interior ladder that goes up into the steeple, and a door in the back of the steeple that opens onto the roof."

Gurney turned to Slovak. "Is graffiti the reason Tate was up there?"

"*Reason* doesn't mean much when you're talking about Billy Tate."

"Tate hated Angus, and the pastor of St. Giles is Angus's sister," said Morgan. "So, it could have been a way of lashing out at him."

Barstow was frowning. "There's something I'd like to see again. Could you take the video back to the point just before the final lightning bolt?"

Morgan did as she asked.

"There!" she said, peering intently at the screen. "On the side of the steeple, about waist-high where Tate is standing. Can you enlarge that area?"

Morgan went through a series of taps and swipes on his phone, and that portion of the scene expanded to fill the frame.

"It's not very clear," said Barstow, "because of the angle of the camera and the limited lighting from the streetlamp, but you can make out the graffiti. See the curving, intersecting lines?"

They all leaned forward, studying the area she was pointing at.

"Now look at this," she said, holding up her own phone.

On the screen was the photo she'd taken in the embalming room of the figure scratched into the wall paint—a horizontal number eight with a rough line bisecting it.

The murky graffiti on the steeple had the same shape.

Morgan's worry lines deepened. "Any idea what that thing is supposed to be?"

"While you guys were up in Peale's office, I checked the internet to see if I could find anything like the figure on the wall," said Barstow. "It might be just a coincidence, but it resembles the ancient alchemy symbol for sulfur."

"*Sulfur*?" Slovak uttered a dismissive grunt. "What's sulfur got to do with anything?"

"Maybe nothing," said Barstow. "Except that the site where I found it said that sulfur was once believed to be the main ingredient in hellfire. Because of that connection, some people who called themselves Satanists adopted the symbol as their emblem."

Her explanation produced a fraught silence.

"Am I missing something here?" asked Gurney.

Morgan shifted uneasily in his chair. "Billy Tate's girlfriend, a woman by the name of Selena Cursen, is supposedly involved in witchcraft—whatever that means."

"The Rich Witch," said Barstow.

Gurney stared at her. "The what?"

"The Rich Witch. Her parents set her up with a fat trust fund, probably because they knew she was unemployable. Dabbles in all sorts of occult nonsense. Big spooky house in the woods. Soulmate of Billy Tate, ever since he got out of prison. Dresses in black. Silver studs in her lips. Very intense gaze—like she's imagining a plan she has for you. Makes a lot of people uncomfortable."

"She's a loner?" asked Gurney. "Or is there a local group she's part of?"

"I've never heard of any group," said Barstow. "You, Chief?"

Morgan shook his head. "Far as I know, the only creepy group around here consisted of her and Tate." He paused for moment, then spoke to Slovak. "Brad, you need to pay Selena Cursen a visit. The symbol scratched on Peale's wall is enough to make her a person of interest in the theft of the body. But go easy. Offer your condolences. Tell her you're just following up on the accident. Try to get a sense of how she reacts to questions about Tate. Don't say anything that might trigger her to clam up or call a lawyer."

Slovak looked less than happy. He rotated his shoulders like a weightlifter working out a cramp. "If that figure eight thing suggests she's involved, how about we get a search warrant for her house, go in there and tear it apart?"

Morgan shook his head. "The figure eight may not mean what we think it does. Too loose a connection for a judge to issue a warrant. We need more."

"I have a question," said Gurney. "The video of the accident shows you and Brad helping to lift Tate onto the stretcher. Did you get a clear view of his face?"

Morgan nodded. "Perfectly clear."

"So, you have no doubt that the person who fell off that roof was, in fact, Billy Tate?"

"No doubt at all. You, Brad?"

Slovak shook his head emphatically. "Zero doubt."

"Even with the lightning damage to his face?" asked Gurney.

"The damage was awful," explained Morgan, "but only to the left side. The right side was untouched. No one at the scene had any doubt about his identity. It's one of the few things about the case I *am* sure of." He gave Gurney a questioning look. "You seem puzzled."

"I'm trying to understand the connection between the theft of Tate's body and the murder of Angus Russell. I don't see the purpose of putting a dead man's fingerprints on the murder weapon. Stealing the body involved a major risk, but I don't see a payoff that would justify it. If Tate was dead before Russell was killed, we're obviously not going to believe he was the perp. So what was the point of leaving that phony evidence in Russell's house?"

"Maybe the killer has a really twisted sense of humor," suggested Slovak.

Gurney shook his head. "If it was just the killer's macabre idea of a joke, the trouble he took to pull it off seems way out of proportion. And as a form of misdirection, it makes no sense. It makes me wonder what I'm missing."

Morgan flashed a rare smile. "That gives me hope. Back in the city, every time you zeroed in on an odd fact in a case, it led to the solution."

"Speaking of oddities," said Gurney, "that meeting Peale described with Darlene Tate was hardly normal. Did something happen between her and her stepson that explains it?"

Slovak spoke first. "Billy Tate and I were in high school at the same time, a year apart. There was a rumor circulating about him and his stepmother. Pretty X-rated stuff."

"They were having sex?"

"It was just a rumor at first, but when his father shot him, that seemed to seal the deal."

"His father shot him?"

"Five times. EMTs thought at first he was dead. But he recovered. His father's doing a minimum twenty in Attica for attempted murder."

"When did this happen?"

"Ten, twelve years ago. Billy was a junior at Larchfield Academy."

"The relationship between Billy and Darlene—did that situation continue after high school?"

"I don't know. For a while, people got tired of talking about it. But it came back to life when Billy got involved with Selena Cursen. When that started up, somebody fired a few shotgun blasts into Selena's house. We got an anonymous call that it was Darlene, but there was no way to make the case." Slovak looked at Morgan for confirmation.

Morgan shrugged. "No witnesses. No evidence. But plenty of bad feelings all around."

"Your idyllic part of the world sounds remarkably messy," said Gurney.

Slovak nodded. "The thing is, the guys on the village board made sure the media reported that the Tates lived in Bastenburg, not Larchfield. I bet they'd love to say Angus got killed in Bastenburg, if they could."

Morgan's fingers were tapping restlessly on the table. "Okay. Time for next steps. Dave, any thoughts on priorities?"

"Only the obvious ones. The body theft probably required more than one person. A vehicle must have been used to transport it. Someone may have seen it being loaded in back of the funeral home, or unloaded at its destination—possibly the Cursen property? Assuming this happened after dark, the body theft would have occurred after eight the evening following the accident, and it, or parts of it, would have been brought to the Russell house in the time window the ME estimated for Angus's death—3:00 a.m. to 5:00 a.m. It would make sense to focus your door-to-door inquiries on what people may have seen roughly between nightfall and dawn."

Morgan nodded his agreement. "Brad, I want you to get on that ASAP."

Slovak grimaced. "I have all the guys doing door-to-doors around Harrow Hill. I don't have anyone left to do the same thing around the funeral home or out by Selena's place."

"Split your people up. Or borrow officers from Bastenburg. Your choice."

Morgan turned to Barstow. "Kyra, you stay on top of the crime-scene processing at Peale's and the overnight lab work. Call me as soon as you get results. Is there anything I'm missing?"

She smiled. "You heard Peale's description of his stolen bone mallet?"

He nodded. "It sounded like your description of the sort of hammer used to break into the conservatory."

"And to kill the dog."

"Right. The hammer does seem to link the body thief directly to the Russell break-in. Brad, when the scalpel comes back from the lab, show it to Peale. See if he can confirm it's one of the five taken from the embalming room. Dave, any other ideas?"

"Peale said he left Tate's phone in the casket. The body thief may have taken it. If it's turned on and the battery is still alive, it can be pinged and located. You should also get a warrant for Tate's recent call records and text messages."

Morgan asked Slovak to follow up immediately on both suggestions. Then he took the sort of deep breath that precedes a difficult topic.

"There's one final issue. The media situation. So far, it's been manageable. Tate's death was covered as a freak accident, with no mention of the lurid stories surrounding his background or his hostility toward Russell. Angus's murder received broader attention in the upstate media markets—Albany, Syracuse, Rochester—and we're getting some pressure from reporters for updates. But that's nothing compared to the tornado that's going to hit us when word gets out that there may be a connection between the two deaths. What I'm saying is, be ready for a god-awful storm. Give out *no* information. Refer all questions to me."

13

After Slovak and Barstow left to pursue their assignments, Morgan leaned back in his chair and let a slow exhalation puff out his cheeks. His gaze moved slowly around the conference room, stopping at the big recessed screen. He picked up his phone and tapped a series of icons, and a wood panel slid across the opening. He ran a finger lightly along the polished tabletop.

"An example of Angus's largesse. The man was hell-bent on everything in Larchfield being first class."

After a silence, he spoke again without looking at Gurney. "I remember you once saying that asking for help wasn't a sign of weakness, it was a sign of sanity. You still believe that?"

"I do."

"I'm glad you came here today."

Gurney said nothing.

"You've been a huge help. Huge. The situation here is turning into . . . I don't know what, but I know it's the kind of thing you're better at than I am. And it's obvious that Brad and Kyra have tremendous respect for you." His gaze met Gurney's. "How are you feeling about your involvement?"

"Honestly? Like a fifth wheel. I know you want help, but an outsider in an undefined position with no legal standing doesn't strike me as the kind of help you need. You and your people know Larchfield better than any outsider ever could."

The tic was back at the corner of Morgan's mouth. "There's something I haven't told you. About my personal situation here. A complication. When I was heading up security at Russell College, I did some extra jobs for the Russells. Private investigations. Background checks on people Angus was doing business with. Things like that."

"For which you were paid?"

"Generously. Which is part of the problem."

"Oh?"

"What I mean is, a previous relationship like that . . ."

His voice trailed off. He started over, addressing his comment to the ceiling as if it were a softening filter between himself and Gurney. "In a high-profile case like this, a previous relationship can bite you in the ass. So, I'm trying to insert some distance. Establish a framework of objectivity. You get what I'm saying?"

"I get that things here are more tangled up than you told me."

Morgan nodded, now looking at the floor. "I don't know why I didn't mention it before. Compared to everything else going on . . . I guess it didn't seem that urgent. And there's something else—I might as well lay it all out. A situation with my wife is occupying a lot of my brain. I didn't want to dump this on you. But I guess you have a right to know. So there are no secrets between us."

Gurney waited for him to go on.

"After the city, the job at Russell College felt like a gift. It headed off any speculation or questions about my exit, because 'Director of Security' at a classy private college sounded like a step up. I didn't just land on my feet, I landed in Shangri-La. I barely noticed that Carol wasn't all that thrilled. I figured with her social work and nursing degrees she could find a job up here, no problem. The only thing that mattered to me was *my* opportunity. *My* career." He paused, shaking his head.

When he continued, his voice was thick with regret. "So we made the move. But once we got here, reality set in. Things weren't as perfect as I'd imagined. We couldn't afford to live in the village, so we ended up out in the sticks, where we discovered all the rural pleasures—poison sumac, snakes, carpenter ants, septic-system backups. It took Carol longer to get a job than I'd imagined. When she finally did, it was for half of what she got paid in the city. And right off the bat she got involved in a battle with a pack of fundamentalist fanatics in Bastenburg—lunatics living in an armed camp they called a church—with rumors of polygamy, child marriage, sex abuse, violence. Carol became a thorn in their side. She used every criminal and civil lever to drag the leader into court and make his life miserable. But, as vile as he was—and still is—he had money and connections. When I was made police chief, her activism started making things dicey for me." He rubbed his hands hard on his thighs, as if trying to warm them.

"I've had to bend over backward to avoid creating any impression that I was involved in her private war. In my paranoia, I even avoided having conversations with her about it. She was totally obsessed, and I stopped listening to her. I became *extremely* protective of my job. I was turning my back on everything that mattered to her. That crusade of hers had become her life, and I was ignoring her life to protect my job. I was acting as if she didn't exist." Morgan was leaning over the table, his forehead in his hands, staring into a private abyss.

Gurney wondered if that was the end of his story. Was the estrangement from his wife occupying his mind so completely that he'd become unable to do his job?

"Carol is dying," Morgan said softly.

Gurney blinked. "What?"

"She has terminal cancer. Brain, heart, lung. Treatment has been discontinued."

"Jesus, Mike. I'm sorry."

"So, that's it. That's my situation."

In the silence that followed, Gurney had the disquieting feeling that Morgan's marriage was, in its own way, a darker echo of his own. There were major differences, certainly, but the similarities were clear enough to bring to mind that time-worn saying:

There, but for the grace of God . . .

And clear enough to soften his antipathy to Morgan's neediness.

It was in this frame of mind that he found himself listening more openly when, a little while later, Morgan proposed an arrangement for Gurney's continuing involvement in the case.

And it was in this frame of mind that he accepted.

With the privileged enclave of Larchfield in his rearview mirror, Gurney passed over the crest of the ridge that separated the emerald valley behind him from the grim expanse of Bastenburg in the flatlands ahead of him.

As he passed through Bastenburg's main street, it seemed that even the sunlight was duller here; he suspected this had less to do with the quality of the light than with the town's aura of depression, its vacant storefronts and vacant-eyed loiterers.

For the rest of his hour-long drive home he tried to focus on the beauties of the countryside rather than the perplexing questions surrounding the Harrow Hill murder. But it was only at the end of the trip—when he rounded the barn and headed up through the low pasture and saw Madeleine tossing handfuls of feed corn to the chickens—that he was able to relax in the present moment and see what was right there in front of him.

For better or worse, Gurney was hard-wired for rational endeavors, but happiness, he'd learned repeatedly, was not the fruit of a logical pursuit, not something to be captured. It was a gift. It arrived suddenly, surprisingly—as it did now in his glimpse of Madeleine, smiling in her pink windbreaker, with the hens scurrying around her, pecking at the tossed corn. He parked the Outback by the asparagus patch and got out, inhaling the scent of the moist grass.

After shaking the last few grains out of her feed can, she came over and gave him a welcome-home kiss. "The little door between the chicken run and the coop is stuck. Maybe you can get it open while I get dinner started."

It turned out that problem was not easily solved. It involved considerable thumping and yanking, as well as the use of a silicone lubricant and a pry bar, both of which he had to fetch from the barn. But there were upsides to the endeavor. In the half hour it consumed, his mind didn't sink even once into the Morgan-Larchfield morass; and by the time he entered the house, Madeleine had prepared one of his favorite dinners: baked salmon, steamed asparagus, and basmati rice with a sweet pepper sauce.

He changed his shirt and washed his hands, and they sat down to eat at the little round table that looked out over the patio.

"Thank you," she said. "I tried to do it myself, but I wasn't able to budge that door."

Madeleine put more sauce on her salmon. "How is the situation in Larchfield?"

"Everything there is odd. And the longer I was there, the odder it got."

She ate a forkful of rice and waited for him to go on.

"It appears that someone stole the body of a local idiot from a mortuary and used it to plant evidence suggesting that the idiot committed a murder the day after he died. The CIO on the case is a young guy with virtually no relevant experience who spent half his time ingratiating himself with me and the other half antagonizing the crime-scene tech. At the end of the day, Morgan told me his wife is dying and offered me a blank check to take over the investigation."

Madeleine put down her fork. "His wife is dying?"

"That's what he told me."

"You believe him?"

"Yes. I mean, he'd have to be completely warped to lie about something like that. Don't you think?"

She shrugged. "You know him better than I do."

"Well . . . I have to assume he's telling the truth."

She picked up her fork again. "You've accepted the blank check?"

"I told him I'd do what I could. No guarantees."

"You don't sound very happy about it."

"I'm not."

"Then why—"

"Because I'd be less happy if I turned him down."

She gave him one of those looks that made him feel like she was seeing his motives more clearly than he was.

His gaze settled on the alpaca shed design, which was still on the table, although now partly covered by the salt and pepper shakers. He wondered when Madeleine would bring the subject up again. Surely it would be a topic at the upcoming dinner with the Winklers, a thought that contributed to his lack of enthusiasm for their visit.

"Look," said Madeleine, pointing to the sunset's wash of amber light on the hillside.

"Very nice," he said, looking out through the glass door.

Madeleine reheated the pepper sauce, and they consumed their remaining salmon, rice, and asparagus without much further conversation. She insisted, as usual, on clearing the table and washing the dishes by herself. He stayed in his chair. His eyes were on the softly glowing hillside, but his mind was in Larchfield.

When Madeleine finished the dishes, she wiped off the sink island, folded the dishtowel, and went upstairs to practice her cello. Gurney's thoughts, meanwhile, were proceeding by a winding route through the odd aspects of Billy Tate's absurd death, the theft of his body, and its seemingly senseless implication in the murder of Angus Russell.

These peculiarities alone would make the case a serious challenge for any homicide department—even without the elements of rumored incest, witchcraft, and a mayor with an apparent financial motive for murder. And then there was the matter of the police chief's refusal to refer the case to the State Police Bureau of Criminal Investigation.

That thought reminded Gurney that Larchfield was within the NYSP zone where Jack Hardwick had been stationed when he was a BCI investigator.

Despite Hardwick's compulsive vulgarity and combative personality—a combination that had finally ended his state police career—Gurney had always felt that the man's fearlessness and no-nonsense intellect more than made up for his outrageous manners and attitude.

He decided to give him a call to see if he knew anything useful about Larchfield. The call went to voicemail, and he left a message.

Since no immediate next step came to mind, he decided to relax in one of the chairs out on the patio. Although the sun had disappeared below the western ridge, the chair was still warm. He settled into it and watched the hues of the clouds changing from peaches and corals to pinks and purples. From inside the house the strains of a Bach cello piece drifted out, lulling him into a rare state of peace.

When, sometime later, Madeleine came out and perched on the arm of the Adirondack chair across from him, he opened his eyes. The air was cooler now, and the color was gone from the sky.

"So," she said, "while I was trying to focus on my music, I kept feeling there are things you haven't told me."

"About Larchfield?"

"About your willingness to help Morgan."

He was about to say there wasn't anything he hadn't told her, but that wasn't true.

He sighed. "This is going to sound ridiculous."

"So?"

"I mean, really ridiculous. In addition to the rational issues giving me pause, there's the fact that Morgan reminds me of my mother."

"Why?"

"There's a plaintiveness in his attitude that I have a hard-wired resistance to. My mother was always trying to get me to pay attention to her, solve her problems with my father, fix the sad mess of her life. When she praised me, it was always for something I'd done *for her*. When she criticized me, it was always for something I hadn't done *for her*. The constant message was that I owed her something."

"You hear that in Morgan's voice?"

"I do. I'm sane enough not to let an echo make my decisions. But I hear it."

"We all deal with echoes."

"Maybe so. But that's one of the things that makes me want to back away. But one of the things that makes me want to help him is even more ridiculous." He hesitated.

She smiled. "I like ridiculous motives."

"We had mice in our precinct house. A contract exterminator would come in every three months, but what he did would only last a couple of weeks. Then the mice would come back. Morgan started bringing in traps. Catch-and-release traps. He went to a lot of trouble to do this. Setting them every night with peanut butter. Gathering them up every morning. Taking them to a local park on his lunch break. Letting the mice go. Enduring a hell of a lot of abuse."

"So you figure there's some good in him? An adulterer who likes mice can't be all bad?"

Gurney shrugged.

Madeleine smiled. "Maybe all your pros and cons have nothing to do with your decision. Maybe it's the challenge of the case itself."

They stayed on the patio, listening in silence to the chirping of the birds returning to their roosts, until the deepening dusk and the chill in the air persuaded them to go into the house.

The wearying effect of Gurney's long day soon overtook him and he decided to go to bed. His sleep, however, was troubled by weird dreams that persisted through the night. In the last one, he found himself in a cavernous building, standing in a long line of Black Angus cattle. The air smelled of raw hamburger. Blue and green balls were floating down from the ceiling. A voice on a loudspeaker demanded that he guess what color the balls were. A bell was tolling for a funeral he was supposed to attend. There was an elegant sign on the wall in italic lettering: *MORGAN'S SLAUGHTERHOUSE.*

The bell became the ringing of his phone on the bedside table. Half-awake, he picked it up.

"Gurney here."

"Dave?" It was Morgan's voice, its stress level ratcheted up a few notches.

He blinked a few times to clear his vision and peered at the time on his phone. "It's six o'clock in the morning. What's wrong?"

"The case just got turned upside down. Nobody stole Tate's body. The son of a bitch got up and walked out of there."

"What?!" Gurney sat up, instantly awake.

"He's not dead. He walked out of that embalming room. Nobody *put* his fingerprints in Russell's bedroom. He left them there himself."

"How do you know this?"

"The casket. The lab did a microanalysis of the splintered edge. The casket wasn't broken *into*. It was broken *out of*."

PART TWO

THE WALKING DEAD

14

During the drive to Larchfield, Gurney was only minimally aware of his surroundings—the sparkling of the dew in the early-morning sunlight, the pure green of the fields, the swaths of yellow wildflowers. The Larchfield scenarios forming in his mind were collapsing one after another under the weight of improbability.

More disturbing were his visualizations of Billy Tate in that tightly closed casket. Having miraculously survived that dreadful fall, he was surely in great physical pain as he regained consciousness. And the terror of finding himself in that dark, constricted place—it was awful even to imagine it. Gurney felt the grip of fear in his own stomach as he pictured Tate desperately struggling in the panic of his confinement before the latch screws finally gave way.

Immersed in this horror, Gurney came within inches of hitting a cow that had escaped from its pasture. It was the nudge he needed to keep his mind on the road.

He arrived in Larchfield at 7:55 a.m. He parked, switched off his phone to avoid interruptions, and headed into the incongruously genteel police headquarters. The classic Victorian building appeared more suited to tea parties than criminal investigations.

A uniformed officer met him inside the front door and led him along a carpeted hall to the conference room. Brad Slovak was standing in front of an urn with a coffee mug in one hand and a large donut in the other. Several paces away, Kyra Barstow was speaking to a wiry woman with a knifelike nose and vigilant eyes. Morgan was standing by himself at the head of the long table, an anxious frown creasing his forehead, a phone to his ear.

When he saw Gurney he ended his call and lowered the phone. He turned to the others. "We're all here. Let's get started."

He took the chair at the head of the table. Barstow and the wiry woman sat on one side of the table, Gurney on the opposite side. Slovak brought the remainder of his donut over on a napkin and took the chair next to Gurney.

"We obviously have a monster of a case on our hands," said Morgan.

Morgan sounded so tense that Gurney expected to see beads of sweat on his forehead at any moment. He took a deep breath and continued, "Because Tate's survival comes as such a shock, especially to those of us who saw him fall, I've asked Kyra to present the forensic data—to remove any doubt about the facts. We can't afford any more false starts." He gestured toward Barstow. "Lay it out for us."

She glanced around the table, her gaze settling on Gurney.

"The evidence is consistent with Tate's revival inside the casket, followed by his emergence from it," she began. "So, it makes sense to look first at the evidence of what happened inside the casket, prior to its being broken open; then the evidence of his emergence from the casket and from the storage unit; then the evidence of his movements around the embalming room and his departure from the building."

With obvious confidence in the logic of this approach, she continued. "Beginning inside the casket, we found ample blood and print evidence of Tate's being placed there, as Peale reported. The inside of the casket lid has scratch marks and microscopic residues of his fingernails, as well as complete handprints consistent with an effort to push up against the closed lid—an effort that succeeded, due in part to the casket's cheap construction. Greta here will describe the evidence of that success."

She gestured toward the woman seated next to her. "A word of explanation for Detective Gurney. Dr. Greta Vickerz is a professor of mechanical engineering at Russell College and a consultant to the forensic sciences department. She has particular expertise in stress fractures in wood."

Barstow tapped an icon on her phone. The sliding panel in the wall opened, revealing the large monitor screen. A moment later a photo appeared that showed the splintered area on the edge of the casket.

Vickerz spoke with an Eastern European accent. "This splintered part that you are seeing, it is where the screws were pulled out of the wood as a result of upward force being exerted against the inside of the lid. The bad splintering you are seeing is due to flimsy construction of the casket. Ironic that shoddy materials get some credit for saving a life. If it was better made, the man inside would eventually have died from hypoxia or carbon dioxide toxicity."

She paused, and Gurney asked, "Are you sure the force that broke open the casket came from inside it?"

"Absolutely. There is no indication of a pry bar, which would leave definite marks. There's no way a force sufficient to splinter the wood could have been applied from outside the casket without leaving tool traces. If you wish, I can show our microphotos of the torn fibers and explain exactly how the fracturing process occurred."

Morgan intervened. "I don't think that will be necessary." He glanced at Gurney, as if seeking agreement, but got no reaction.

Barstow thanked Vickerz, who excused herself from the room, and continued her evidence narrative.

"We found traces of Tate's blood on the inside wall of the storage unit, which would have occurred naturally as he climbed out of the casket. We found his handprints on the inside of the storage unit door and on the small emergency handle. We found sneaker prints on the floor of the unit that match the sneakers on Tate's feet in the video segment showing him on the mortuary trolley. Following his likely path, we found his fingerprints at several locations in the room—in the glass cabinet that was broken into, by the symbol scratched on the wall, on the edge of the embalming table, on the window sash in the adjoining equipment room, on the wall of the hallway leading to the back door, and on the doorknob."

Morgan looked impressed. "Thank you, Kyra. Very credible reconstruction." He sent another approval-seeking glance in Gurney's direction before he continued. "There's no doubt that Tate survived. So now we're looking for him as a murder suspect, not a stolen corpse. You agree, Dave?"

Gurney was silent for a moment. "I'm having a hard time reconciling the trauma of the lightning impact and the fall with his forcing his way out of the casket and walking away."

Morgan nodded nervously. "I know what you mean. But this scenario explains evidence that otherwise makes no sense." He paused. "Brad, anything yet from computer forensics?"

"They said they'd get back to us later this morning." He turned to Gurney. "Even though the recording function on Peale's computer was turned off, the camera data was still being transmitted to it. I got the computer last night from Peale. It's a long shot, but I thought a digital remnant of the data might have been retained, and maybe they could do something with it."

"Definitely worth checking on."

"I figured if we had video, it would end any doubt about what happened. *Seeing* beats *reconstructing*."

Barstow's eyes narrowed. She seemed on the verge of responding to the apparent devaluing of her presentation when Slovak's phone rang.

He peered at the screen. "I better take this."

The growing alarm in his terse questions and exclamations during the call held everyone's attention. When he put down his phone, he sat for a moment in a kind of adrenaline-jazzed distress before speaking.

"One of the guys doing door-to-doors found another body. A woman. In a drainage swale on Waterview Drive, by the turnoff for Harrow Hill. He figures she's been dead for a couple of days. Her throat was cut."

After Morgan sent Slovak and Barstow to the new crime scene—with instructions to report back ASAP—he slumped back in his chair. "Christ. What the hell is going on?"

Gurney shrugged. "On his way to or from the Russell house on the night of Angus's murder, Tate may have encountered the victim and saw her as a problem to be eliminated. We'll know more when we get an ID and a more precise time-of-death estimate. Will Slovak contact the medical examiner?"

"That's the procedure."

"He's the one who pronounced Tate dead. When do you plan to bring him up to date?"

"God, so much has been happening so fast—"

"Sir?" An obese gray-haired officer was standing at the conference room door.

"What?" Morgan's voice was strained.

"Someone here to see you. From that computer group at the college."

"*Computer forensics.*" The precisely articulated correction came from behind the officer. A slim young man with a fashionable three-day beard stepped into view. He was wearing pencil jeans and a tightly fitted white shirt. "Brad Slovak asked me to give this information directly to you."

The officer departed and the young man entered. "I'm Ronan Ives. I've been working on the Peale computer matter. Shall I explain our findings?"

"Go ahead."

"So, we began by double-checking to make sure that the camera output wasn't being encoded somewhere in computer memory, despite the record option being deselected. There was no trace. Next step was to analyze the specs for the software controlling the behavior of the system. That's where we made an interesting discovery. The camera output that's transmitted to the laptop can be recorded on that device, or not, simply by clicking on the preferred option in a clearly displayed box. However . . ."

He smiled, obviously pleased with what he was about to reveal.

"There's a secondary system that's *always on*, unless it's actively deselected through a process buried in a series of technical menus. That automatic secondary system transmits the camera data to a cloud-based storage field, where it's retained for seven days. It's a safeguard—in case the user's own computer fails to record the data due to an oversight or hardware glitch. Bottom line, the camera data for your period of interest is retrievable."

Morgan's eyes widened. "Have you seen it?"

"No. It's password-protected."

"So how do we get access?"

"Get permission from the licensed user, along with his registered ID and password. Otherwise, you'll need a warrant."

Morgan took a few moments to absorb this. "I'm pretty sure we can get permission."

"So, I'll wait to hear from you."

As soon as the young man departed, Morgan picked up his phone.

"I'll give Peale a call."

"Might be better to drop in on him," Gurney suggested. "Face-to-face is always a plus."

Morgan nodded.

They found Peale in the rear parking area, looking as preppy as the day before in a teal sweater, yellow Bermuda shorts, and tan moccasins. He was coiling a power cord attached to a tire jack that was no longer supporting the rear wheel of the Lexus.

"Returning this to my neighbor. Convenient having someone next door who's a car enthusiast and tool junkie. Something I can do for you?"

Morgan smiled. "We may have a breakthrough in the missing-body case. We need the ID and password for your security camera software, so we can access its backup storage."

"Am I hearing you right? Are you saying there's a video of the break-in and theft of the body?"

"A video of what actually occurred that night."

Morgan's answer struck Gurney as a truthful evasion of the issue.

If Peale noted the equivocation, he didn't react to it. Looking excited at the prospect of the video, he gave Morgan his ID and password.

Morgan phoned the information to Ronan Ives, then he and Gurney headed back to headquarters. After asking Gurney to wait in the conference room, Morgan went to his office to get the agreement formalizing Gurney's temporary role in the department.

Sitting at the conference room table reminded Gurney that he'd turned off his phone to avoid any distraction during the earlier meeting. Now he turned it back on and checked his voicemail. He found three new messages.

The first was from Madeleine.

> "Hi. Just a reminder that the Winklers are coming for dinner at six. Love you."

The second was from Jack Hardwick.

> "Larchfield? Why the fuck do you want to know about Larchfield? Rich lizards living next door to other rich lizards. Medieval fiefdom, lorded over by Angus the Scottish Scumbag. Classy veneer over rotten wood. You want to know more, buy me a coffee tomorrow morning at Abelard's. Eight sharp. Call if you can't make it."

The third was another from Madeleine.

"Hi, again. Could you pick up some flowers for the table? Maybe tulips from Snook's Nursery? See you later."

A moment later Morgan appeared with some papers tucked under his arm and a mug of coffee in each hand. He placed one in front of Gurney, took the seat across from him, and laid the papers in the middle of the table.

"You won't find any surprises there," said Morgan. "I just spelled out what we talked about yesterday afternoon. The terms of your involvement. One copy for you, two copies for the department. Before you leave today, we'll take your photo, laminate it into an official ID." Morgan was sounding breezy, but his tic was working overtime.

"So long as we understand that I'll be taking my own path. I'll keep you and your people informed. But I need to follow my instincts."

"Wouldn't want it any other way. I'll send out a memo to the department, so there's no confusion about your authority."

Morgan's phone rang. He took the call. After listening for half a minute, he said, "Got it. Thank you." He put the phone down on the table.

"That was Ives at forensics. He accessed the last seven days of Peale's camera data and downloaded it to our internal system. He coded the segments separately, so we can go directly to the night in question. You want to see it now?"

15

Once Morgan had located the downloaded video segments in the system, he proceeded to the one tagged with the date of Tate's disappearance from the mortuary and tapped the PLAY icon.

A sound, nearly inaudible at first, took the form of a muffled groan, and the screen came to life with a shot of the embalming room. Gurney assumed that it was this sound that had activated the camera, as well as one of the room's lighting circuits. As the groan was repeated, building in intensity to a kind of teeth-clenched roar, the camera's field of view moved to the right, toward the cadaver storage unit. Seemingly responding to a series of dull thumps from the unit, the panning motion was followed by a slow zoom in, until the side of the unit nearly filled the frame. The time code in the corner of the screen was changing from 9:03 p.m. to 9:04 p.m.

The next sounds were more frantic—a combination of growling shouts, grunts, and dull scraping sounds. Gurney pictured, with a twinge of claustrophobia, the scratches and fingernail residues Kyra Barstow had found on the inside of the casket lid.

Pounding continued intermittently for the next quarter of an hour. Then, a different sound—the straining, tearing, and snapping of wood fibers. The time-code display read 9:29 p.m.

What he heard next brought to mind the image of someone stumbling and bumping into something inside the storage unit, followed by a cry of pain and another silence. Soon a new series of thumps and knocks began, louder and more immediate than the earlier ones, suggesting that Tate was moving around and testing the solidity of the walls that surrounded him.

At 9:44 p.m. Gurney heard the distinctive metallic clunk of an exit lever. The door of the unit swung open.

The camera position offered only a side view of the unit, and its occupant only became visible when he finally staggered into the room. His hooded sweatshirt appeared blood-soaked.

The motion-sensitive camera followed him as he moved unsteadily toward the embalming table. He leaned forward, grasping the edge of it. His breathing sounded labored and raspy.

Gradually he straightened himself and began to make his way around the room. The bloody hood concealed his face and allowed only animal sounds of pain and rage to emerge. He might as well not have been human at all. Thinking of this feral creature as "Billy" seemed incongruous.

When he reached the doorway to the equipment room, he hesitated, then went inside. Soon there was the sound of a window being opened. Gurney wondered whether his purpose was to get more air or a clearer view of his surroundings. *Where am I?* would have to have been one of the top questions in his mind.

A minute later he came back into the main room—at an angle that provided a passing glimpse of the damaged side of his face.

"Holy Christ," muttered Morgan.

Even shadowed as it was by the sweatshirt's hood, the vertical gouge down through red and black charred flesh was so appalling that it was a relief when he turned away in the direction of the cabinet on the wall next to the doorway.

The cabinet appeared to interest him. He remained there for some time before making an effort to open it. Discovering that the glass door was locked, he smashed it with his elbow, which triggered another yowl of pain. He reached through the shattered opening, removed two handfuls of shiny implements, and stuffed them into the pockets of his sweatshirt.

He pulled a phone out of one of those pockets. For a while he just stood there, as if trying to make up his mind about something. Then his fingers moved as if he were sending someone a text message. He started to put the phone back in his pocket, then stopped and sent what appeared to be a second message. The time code on the video indicated that it was 10:01 p.m.

He started moving in the direction of the hallway that led to the back door, then stopped and faced a section of the wall next to the smashed cabinet. He remained in that position, rocking almost imperceptibly from side to side, for several minutes. Then he took one of the shiny instruments out of his pocket and stepped closer to the wall. He scratched a looping figure eight design into the white paint, added a vertical slash, and put the instrument back in his pocket. He stepped back, as if to admire what he'd done, then turned and walked with new determination into the dark hallway. Moments later there was the sound of a door being opened, a few seconds of silence, and the sound of it being firmly closed.

The time-code display read 10:19 p.m.

Five minutes later, in the absence of any further sounds or movements to activate it, the camera stopped operating.

The screen in the conference room went blank.

The untouched coffee in Gurney's mug was cold.

Morgan's expression conveyed a sense of overload.

Gurney provided a low-key counterpoint. "Interesting video. Intense, but no surprises. Entirely consistent with Kyra's evidence narrative."

"She did describe it like it happened," said Morgan, as if the consistency were reassuring.

"And the time code tells us when it happened," said Gurney, "which gives us a reliable window for tracing Tate's movements."

Morgan picked up his coffee mug, took a sip, made a disgusted face, and put it down. His gaze fell on the papers in the middle of the table. "You should take a look at your contract. And sign it. As soon as you do, you'll be covered."

Gurney picked up one of the copies and gave it a once-over. It was basically the same as the agreement he'd had the previous year with Sheridan Kline as an adjunct investigator on the White River multiple-murder case. "This is fine."

Morgan slid a pen across the table. "I should give Barstow a call and tell her the video confirms her version of events."

"Let her and Slovak both know that Tate exited Peale's premises at ten nineteen that night. That could be important," said Gurney.

"Will do."

Morgan made the call, gave Barstow the news, and asked her to pass it along to Slovak.

As Gurney was signing the agreement, there was a knock at the open conference room door. A uniformed cop, the one who showed Gurney in that morning, was standing there. "That funeral director from next door wants to see you. He sounds pissed off."

"Dan Peale?"

"*Mister Danforth Peale* was the way he put it. Angry like."

"Did he say what the problem was?"

"No, sir."

Morgan's tic reappeared. "Bring him in."

Peale appeared at the conference room door as the cop was stepping away to get him. There was a disconnect between his cheery yellow Bermuda shorts and the fury in his eyes. He slammed the door behind him and strode over to the conference table.

"Fallow's a bloody idiot!"

Morgan recoiled.

"That son of a bitch's addled judgment is about to destroy three generations of family tradition! I want him arrested and prosecuted for criminal malpractice!"

"I'm not sure I—"

Peale cut him off. "The video. The software company told me how to access it. Tate wasn't dead after all. I'm telling you, I want Fallow prosecuted! I want the bastard in prison!"

"For mistakenly pronouncing Tate dead?"

"For recklessly doing so while under the influence."

"You're suggesting he was drunk?"

"Damn right he was drunk!"

"That's a serious accusation."

"Do you realize the seriousness of what he's done to *me*? What people will say when it gets around that Danforth Peale put a living human being inside a closed casket? My professional life will be destroyed—as a direct result of Fallow's gross incompetence!"

Peale's rage left Morgan at a loss for words.

Gurney asked mildly, "Did your observation of the body give you any reason to doubt that Tate was dead?"

"Absolutely not. But I certainly didn't perform a rigorous examination. It's not the responsibility of a funeral director to second-guess a medical examiner."

"How do you know that the doctor had been drinking when he examined Tate?"

"He smelled of alcohol. I assume he'd been drinking it, not spraying it on his clothes."

"Was anyone else aware of the odor?"

"How the hell should I know? I wasn't conducting a goddamn survey."

"Did you mention your observation to anyone at the time?"

Peale shook his head. "I didn't want to create any problems for him, given his sketchy history. It didn't occur to me that he might be creating a worse problem for *me*." He turned toward Morgan. "What do you plan to do about this mess?"

Morgan's arms were crossed in a near-parody of defensiveness. "Everything is already being done that can be done. I understand your frustration. I share it. The damage. The potential damage. All the unknowns. Believe me, I know. Our number-one priority is getting this under control."

Peale was nodding in a way that looked more like impatience than agreement.

Morgan's phone rang. He looked at it, then at Peale. "Sorry, I have to take this."

Peale waved his hand in the air, as if to signify that he had no more to say. He turned on his heel and strode out of the room.

From Morgan's half of the phone conversation, Gurney gathered that the call was from a reporter by the name of Carly who wanted an update on the Russell investigation, and that Morgan was trying to put her off by promising significant news later that day.

As soon as he put his phone down, it rang again. This time Gurney could tell little from Morgan's responses, other than the fact that the news was good.

When he ended the call, he sounded excited. "Looks like we have an ID on the homicide victim in the drainage ditch. Plus, a woman told one of Brad's guys that she saw someone out on Waterview Drive, not far from Harrow Hill, around 2:00 a.m. the night Angus was killed. Feel like taking a ride?"

16

Once they were underway in the Tahoe, Gurney raised a question about Peale's rant. "That comment he made about Fallow having a 'sketchy history'—do you know what he was referring to?"

"Three years ago Fallow came close to losing his medical license—in connection with a DUI conviction."

"Any difficulties since then?"

"Not that I know of."

"Any history of conflict between him and Peale?"

"Why do you ask?"

"Peale's level of anger seemed . . . extreme."

"I guess there could be some bad blood between them, but nothing that's ever come out publicly."

They fell silent. Soon they were on Waterview Drive, passing the manicured grounds of one mansion after another. Through occasional breaks in the lush greenery, Gurney caught glimpses of the azure lake. Then, directly ahead, he saw a pair of police vehicles parked on the side of the road—a black Dodge Charger and a Larchfield patrol car. Brad Slovak and a uniformed cop were standing on the grass verge as Morgan pulled in behind the patrol car. Gurney noted that they'd stopped at the only overgrown property by the lake.

Slovak approached Morgan as he and Gurney got out of the Tahoe. "Woman's name is Ruby-June Hooper. Sound familiar?"

Morgan looked blank. “Should it?”

“She pops up in the news every couple of years, whenever she’s offered another million for these four acres of hers. Always says the same thing—she was born here and she’s gonna die here. She wouldn’t tell me or Dwayne who she saw out here the other night. Insisted on talking to you.”

“Where is she?”

“In her house. Behind them trees.” Slovak pointed at a path that led into a thicket.

Morgan motioned to Gurney to come along. The path through the trees brought them to a narrow lawn that separated the house from the woods around it. It was full of crabgrass, dandelions, and wandering, clucking, pecking chickens.

The house, a smallish clapboard colonial whose white paint needed refreshing, would have been unremarkable in virtually any other upstate locality. On Larchfield’s Waterview Drive, however, its mild shabbiness was startling. The unkempt land on which it sat might have been considered pleasantly natural elsewhere, but here, adjacent to the genteel grounds of its neighbors, it seemed to radiate aggression.

The woman waiting for them in the doorway was wearing a shapeless dress. Her straight gray hair covered her forehead and ears like a loose hat. Her dark eyes peered first at Gurney, then at Morgan.

“You’re the one took Tucker to the hospital. You’re the one I want to talk to.” She pointed at Gurney without looking at him. “Who’s that?”

“The best detective I know,” said Morgan with an awkward smile.

“Which of you is the boss?”

“He is,” said Gurney.

“That’s all right, then. He took Tucker to the hospital. I don’t ever forget a kindness.”

“Tucker . . . ?” said Morgan.

“When he got passed out in the pansies with the heatstroke.”

“Yes!” said Morgan with obvious relief. “In the village square.”

“Hottest day of the summer it was.”

“I remember.” His moment of relief gave way to his perennial unease. “You wanted to talk to me?”

“Better we talk inside.” She stepped back and gestured them into an unfurnished hallway. On the right side of it there was a door to a small dining room and a stairway up to the second floor. On the left side there was a wide opening into a living room.

"You go right on in. Don't pay no mind to Vaughn," she said, tilting her head toward a man in full hunting camos sitting in a wheelchair in front of a picture window at the far end of the room, "and he won't pay no mind to you." The window provided a panoramic view of the lake.

"Vaughn," she added, "is a lifelong duck hunter."

She led them to the other end of the room, where four armchairs formed a loose semicircle in front of a three-cushion couch. The center cushion was occupied by a sleeping gray dog whose little legs seemed inadequate for his large body. Ruby-June sat next to him and rested her arm on him as if he were part of the couch.

Morgan took the chair farthest from her, Gurney the one closest.

"So." Morgan put on a smile. "What did you want to tell me?"

"I spoke to a man the other night, a man who I've since been told is dead. Not just dead now, but dead when I spoke to him."

"Do you know who this man was?"

"Course I do. Otherwise, how would I know he was dead?"

"Can you give me his name?"

"That's what I'm wanting to tell you. It was Billy Tate."

"And when exactly did you see him?"

"It was just about twenty-four hours after he fell off Hilda's roof and died. Course, I didn't know that when I spoke to him, or I can't think that I would have done so."

"What time was it? Do you recall?"

"I'd say two in the morning."

"Where was this?"

"Out on the road. Tucker here wanted to take care of business." She scratched the head of the dog on the cushion next to her. "We were on our side of the road, but Tucker can be particular, and he wanted to go to the other side. We was making our way across—Tucker's not so quick on his feet these days—when Billy come driving along. He slowed way down, letting us pass."

"You say you spoke to him?"

"I did. I said, 'Good morning, Billy.' 'Cause it was rightly morning, being after midnight. He passed by real slow, almost stopped. 'Ruby-June,' he said, kinda hoarse like. Something wrong with his throat, like he was sick."

"And then, after he said your name . . . ?"

"He drove on down the road."

Morgan looked at Gurney.

Gurney asked, "What direction was he going?"

"Toward Harrow Hill."

"What kind of car was he driving?"

"I don't know cars. Kind of square like. Some kind of Jeep, I think? Used to drive around town in it. Orange color."

"Billy's window was open?"

"Course it was. We wasn't shouting at each other through the glass."

Gurney smiled. "Sounds like you've known him a long time."

"Since he was being raised up. Crazy boy from the beginning, which you can't blame him for being. You'd be plenty crazy, too, if your stepmama was Darlene Tate."

"What was the problem with Darlene?"

"I'd rather not say. To talk about it, I'd have to think about it, wouldn't I? And thinking about it would dirty my mind."

"Fair enough. You said that Billy sounded hoarse. Do you remember how he looked?"

"Same as always. Wearing that thing on his head. Like he'd been wearing it for years. I venture he did it because it made him look like, you know what I'm saying, like a bad boy. Which most folks hereabouts would say he was. But maybe he was just hiding, you know what I mean?"

"Tell me."

"Hiding from the prying eyes of the world. Hiding from the judgment of them that's always judging. Hiding what he done with Darlene."

Gurney nodded. "So you don't think Billy Tate was a bad person?"

"Not deep-down bad. Marched to his own drummer, for sure. And he did have a temper. Didn't take crap, that's a fact. A fierce streak in that boy. And now everyone's saying he died the night before I saw him out on that road—just thinking that in my mind gives me a cold feeling. Right now, sir, I feel a shiver right through me."

"I can understand that," said Gurney. "Have you told anyone you saw him that night?"

"No, sir! Folks already think Vaughn and I are long gone around the bend. No way I'm handing them more ammunition."

Gurney nodded sympathetically. "Is there anything else you want to tell us?"

"Yes, sir. More like a question, though. I'm talking here with a troubling notion in my mind—that the Billy Tate I saw was what they call on the TV shows 'the walking dead.' Like the horror movies, which is not what I truly believe. But I've been told by reputable people with their heads on straight that Billy Tate is dead. So, that's my question to you. Is that boy dead, alive, or somewhere in between?"

Gurney sat back in his chair and looked over at Morgan. It was up to him to decide how much to reveal.

"Well, Ruby, I'd say we're currently of the opinion that he may be alive."

Ruby-June Hooper smiled broadly for the first time since they arrived. "Thank you, sir! That's a trouble off my mind." She gave the dog an enthusiastic scratching behind the ears. "You hear that, Tucker? Mama's still got her marbles. Ain't nobody carting us off to the loony bin. Not just yet."

Morgan handed her his card. "If you see him again, Ruby, let us know as fast as you can. That's my personal number. Day or night."

"I thank you. If Vaughn had the slightest idea about anything, he'd thank you, too."

On their way out through the thicket, Morgan wondered aloud if he'd revealed too much to Ruby. Too little? Should he have asked her to keep the information to herself? Gurney said that it probably didn't matter—which seemed neither to surprise nor reassure Morgan. Back at the road, while Morgan remained absorbed in second-guessing his response, Gurney filled Slovak in on what Ruby-June had told them.

Slovak's eyes filled with speculative excitement. "So, Tate has a friendly exchange with her, then drives another mile down the road, runs into another local lady who just happens to be out, doing God knows what, at two in the morning. This time he gets out of his car, cuts her throat, and dumps her in a drainage ditch—on his way to kill Angus Russell!"

"That's one way of putting it together. What information do you have on this new victim?"

"Mary Kane, age seventy, retired school librarian. Lived in a small cottage, across from the first turnoff to Harrow Hill. Former gatehouse of the lakeside estate behind it."

"Any estimated time of death?"

Slovak ran his hand back over the bristly red hair on the top of his head. "I'd guess at least two days. Classic signs of early-stage decomp. Fallow passed by a couple of minutes ago on his way there. He'll probably give us a tighter time window. If it's between two and three days, that would line up with the Russell murder—and be consistent with what the Hooper woman just told you."

Classic signs of early-stage decomp sounded to Gurney like Slovak's jargony effort to sound more inured to this sort of thing than he actually was. The sight of a two-day-old corpse in a ditch would leave any young detective unnerved. The odor alone was gut-wrenching.

Emerging finally from his tangle of second thoughts, Morgan spoke up. "Brad, assuming that Kyra now has control of the homicide scene, this would be a good time for you to take a run out to Selena Cursen's place. Take Dwayne Wolman with you, in case there's any difficulty. Remember, go in easy and see what you can get. If we need to go in hard later, that's an option. The video of Tate walking out of the mortuary gives us proof that he's alive, so we have reasonable grounds for a search warrant at his girlfriend's place, if necessary."

"You think Tate might be there now?"

"I'm guessing he'd head for someplace less obvious. But if you get a hint of his presence, call for backup."

"Yes, sir."

As Slovak was turning to leave, Gurney asked, "How are your people doing on the search for security cameras in the area?"

"Three so far that seem to be in position to capture vehicle traffic to or from Harrow Hill. We're tracking down the property owners to get access to the files, assuming they've been saved. I'll keep you informed."

Morgan turned to Gurney. "You ready to go to the murder site?"

Their destination was a two-minute drive along the same road. A barricade was set up a hundred yards or so before the site to divert civilian traffic. The cop manning it moved it out of the way to let the Tahoe through.

A perimeter of yellow police tape demarcated the site itself—approximately an acre that extended from a small cottage on one side of the road to a grassy, shrubbery-bordered swale on the opposite side.

Morgan parked between the evidence van and the body-transport van, just outside the tape. He got out and called to Barstow, who was conferring with her two techs next to a search grid that ran from the cottage across the road to the far side of the swale.

"You want us in coveralls?" Morgan asked.

"Just shoe covers and gloves, as long as you don't kneel or sit anywhere inside the tape."

"You go ahead," said Morgan to Gurney. "The gloves and booties are in the back of her van. I'll wait here for Fallow. When he finishes with the body, I'll fill him in on the Tate situation."

Gurney went to the van, put on the protective items, and ducked under the tape. It didn't surprise him that Morgan had come up with a reason to remain where he was. Back in the NYPD, the man always managed to minimize his exposure to the ugly starting point of every homicide investigation, the body of the victim. Never having become used to it, it was one more reason his career was an endless source of stress—all in the fruitless pursuit of his father's approval—an emotional trap with no way out.

Barstow's voice interrupted Gurney's train of thought. "Would now be a good time for me to give you a tour of the highlights?"

"Now would be ideal."

"We start over here," she said, leading him toward the cottage.

It was a small, cream-colored clapboard house with a brass knocker in the center of a green door. There were red geraniums in boxes under the two front windows. The bright colors gave the place a playful appearance. An open porch faced the road. There was a lavender ladder-back chair on the porch and next to it a small wooden table. On the table was a cup with a desiccated residue of coffee in the bottom of it, a blank index card, a pen, and a flashlight. It appeared that everything had been dusted for prints. What held Gurney's attention longest was the line of dried blood droplets that began on the table and extended eight or ten feet across the porch.

"Appears that the victim's throat was cut while she was sitting in that chair," said Barstow. "Bloodstains look like a typical throw-off pattern from a blade slashed through a large artery."

Like the pattern on Angus's bedroom wall, thought Gurney.

"There was also a phone on that table," she added. "Battery was dead. It's being recharged now, so we can check for any calls or text records around the time of the attack." She turned and pointed at a rough line of brownish smears on the macadam surface of the road. "Attacker dragged the bleeding body across the road, through the shrubbery on the other side, and left it in the drainage ditch."

Gurney nodded. "I know one of Slovak's people was doing door-to-doors on this road this morning. But there are no houses on that side. How did he happen to find the body down behind the bushes?"

She thought about it for a moment. "The stink would be hard to miss if the breeze was right. Want to see the body?"

"After I take a look through the house. Your people finished in there?"

Barstow nodded. "It's all yours."

The front door opened into a small living room. She followed him in. At the back of the room a doorway led to a small kitchen with a table with two wooden chairs. Off the side of the living room there was a hallway with three doors—a bathroom and two small bedrooms.

"We didn't find any evidence of disturbance in the house," said Barstow.

"Was the front door open?" he asked.

"Closed but unlocked."

"Did you find her house keys?"

"Yes. In the back of a kitchen drawer. Doesn't appear that she bothered much with them. With virtually no crime, lot of folks around here leave their doors unlocked."

"Is there a basement or accessible attic?"

"Both, but there's nothing in them but dust."

"Any security cameras on the property?"

"None that we found."

He took another slow walk through the house, noting that Mary Kane had a fondness for birds, evident in the many amateur watercolors hanging on the walls. It touched him in a way that was obvious to Barstow.

"You okay?"

"Fine."

"Ready to take a look at the body?"

Gurney followed her across the road and through a break in the barrier of bushes a few yards from the Harrow Hill turnoff.

Stepping down into the broad drainage swale, his gaze went immediately to the body on the ground—a thin, gray-haired woman. Her white slacks and tan sweater were stained with dirt and blood. The skin on her hands and face showed early signs of putrefaction. A gentle breeze was carrying the odors away from where Gurney was standing, allowing him to move closer without the nausea they would have induced.

The contour of the ground under the body had tilted the head back, so that the neck wound was open and had become a magnet for flies. Even so, it was clear that the fatal damage had been a single deep cut inflicted by a very sharp blade.

Four other individuals were present in the swale. A young patrol officer was standing with his arms folded and his mouth drawn down in disgust. An obese fellow was taking a series of photos, sidling in a slow semicircle around the upwind side of the body. A gaunt man was pushing a mortuary trolley, like the one in Peale's embalming room, toward the body. The fourth individual, whom Gurney assumed was Dr. Fallow, was speaking loudly into his phone, his back to the body. He had an athlete's physique gone soft and a large head with receding hair. The hair, neatly combed straight back, was incongruously brown above a white mustache. His blue blazer appeared to have been purchased when he was twenty pounds slimmer.

The man pushing the trolley brought it to a stop near the body. He unfolded a black plastic transport bag and laid it on the ground, then called to the young cop to help him slide the body into the open bag. The cop approached with reluctance, checked the integrity of his gloves, and did as he was asked. After the gaunt fellow zipped up the bag, they lifted it onto the trolley, which they pushed along the swale in the direction of the parked vehicles.

The big man in the blue blazer ended his phone call and, after a curious glance at Gurney, set out after the trolley. The photographer took a few more shots of the site, then climbed up out of the swale, nodded to Barstow, and headed for the break in the bushes.

Gurney went over to the spot where the body had been resting. Bright green elsewhere, the grass there was dull, matted down, bloodstained.

He gazed at the surprisingly small indentation her body had made—as though she were a child. "Mary Kane," he said softly.

Barstow gave him a quizzical look.

"It's a habit I have. Saying the name aloud. It moves my focus from the corpse to the person who was once alive—where it belongs—the person whose life was stolen from them.

"Sounds painful."

"It should be painful. Otherwise, this is nothing but a game."

Hearing himself, he was taken aback by his sententious tone. Hadn't his own investigations been powered more by intellectual challenge than by empathy for the victim? Hadn't he often found the "game" intriguing, motivating, all-consuming?

Barstow's voice brought him back to the moment. "Do you have any scenario yet for what happened here?"

"You've been here longer than I have. You tell me."

"Well, we know from the mortuary video that Tate walked out of there about twenty after ten that night. So, sometime between then and the Russell murder, he drove out here. You can see the turnoff to Harrow Hill is pretty sharp, so he must have come to a near-stop in front of her house, with her sitting on the porch. She may have recognized him—under that streetlight."

She pointed at the arching arm of the light pole across the road from the cottage. It was one of the first things Gurney had noted when he arrived at the scene. He was pleased that its significance hadn't escaped her.

"So," she continued, "if Tate realized he'd been recognized, he may have decided to deal with it."

Gurney nodded. "The proximity to Harrow Hill, the timing, and the neck wound point to Tate being the killer. But there's a problem with motive. I just spoke to a woman a mile down the road who saw Tate driving this way shortly before the Russell murder and spoke to him. With no consequences. Why would Tate let one person who recognized him stay alive, but not another? Maybe we're making the wrong assumption about the motive here. Maybe it had nothing to do with being recognized."

Barstow was watching him with increasing interest.

He went on, "I'd like to know what this woman was doing on her porch—with an index card and a pen and a phone—in the middle of the night."

"You love this, don't you?"

"Sorry?"

"It's written on your face. Baffling questions excite you."

Gurney didn't respond.

"So, when will you be taking over the investigation?" There was a sparkle of amusement in her gray eyes.

"*Taking over* is not what I do."

"It would be an improvement."

"You have a problem with Brad?"

She shrugged. "Brad and I have a history."

"Oh?"

She let out a burst of laughter. "Lord, no, it's not what you're thinking. Back when Brad was taking criminal justice courses at Russell College, I was one of his instructors. We had no problem then, but ever since he got promoted to detective, he's been trying very hard to prove that we're equals."

That explained a lot. After a pause, he asked, "How long have you been up here? Your accent sounds West Indian."

"It's Jamaican."

"Were you born there?"

"In Albany, actually. My mother was Jamaican. She took me there after she divorced my father, when I was three. I came back when I was seventeen."

He nodded with interest, then looked at his watch. "Time to get back to business. I need to check on a conversation your chief is having with the medical examiner."

He started toward the parking area, then stopped. "You said that the phone you found on the porch is being charged. Can you let me know as soon as you can what you find on it?"

17

As he reached the yellow perimeter tape, he was surprised to see the ME's body-transport van pulling out onto the road, followed by a black Mercedes with an MD plate. It seemed impossible that Morgan could have shared the bombshell news of Tate's survival without it provoking a longer discussion.

Morgan waved to Gurney from window of his Tahoe, gesturing for him to get in.

"New plan," he announced as they headed back toward the village. "The situation with Fallow is delicate. The thing is, in addition to being the county ME, he's a member of the village board—the board I report to. And he's not likely to be pleased by an accusation that he pronounced a living person dead."

"Accusations are never pleasing. What's the problem?"

"He's a difficult person. Always was, and that doubled after the drunk-driving incident."

Gurney could see where this was going. "Since the message will be unwelcome, he'll want to shoot the messenger, and you'd rather it be me than you."

Morgan looked pained, but kept his eyes on the road ahead. "You're an outsider with a golden reputation. He can't do you any harm. Besides, you're better at these things than I am."

"Have you told him anything so far?"

"I just told him that because the Russell investigation was so important, I'd brought in one of the country's top homicide detectives."

Gurney grimaced at the characterization. "You didn't mention Tate at all?"

"I told him we'd made a disturbing discovery about the Russell murder, and it would be best to discuss it back at headquarters. He's meeting us there, while his assistant takes the Kane body in for autopsy."

Fallow was already in the conference room when they arrived. He was intent on the screen of his phone and didn't look up, even when they both took seats across from him.

This close, Fallow looked ten years older than he had in the swale. Gurney noted a drinker's web of capillaries on his pudgy nose. Several more seconds passed before he put aside his phone and acknowledged their presence.

"Before I forget," he said rather officiously, "the Russell autopsy report is available. The digital version has been entered in your system, hard copy is available on request." He eyed Gurney. "I assume that you're the hired gun."

"Good assumption."

Morgan broke the ensuing silence. "Any autopsy surprises?"

Fallow smoothed his white mustache before answering. "Two points of interest. The neck wound contained a trace of white paint dust, likely left behind by the incising blade."

Gurney recalled the segment of the video that showed Tate scraping the figure eight symbol onto the white wall of the embalming room.

"And we located the missing forefinger." Fallow paused, straightening the cuffs of his blazer. "It was inserted in the victim's anus."

Morgan recoiled. "Jesus."

Fallow checked his watch. "You said there was a development in the Russell case you wanted to discuss?"

Morgan cleared his throat. "Because of Dave's key involvement in the investigation, I'd like him to explain the situation."

Gurney hid his annoyance. "You're a busy man, Doctor, so I'll get through this as quickly as I can. You were the pronouncer of death at the Tate accident scene, is that right?"

"It's a matter of record. What's that got to do with the Russell case?"

"You checked his vitals and overall condition?"

"Of course."

"What did you discover?"

"What's the point of this?" Fallow's voice was rising.

"Please, Doctor, just tell me what you observed."

"Absence of circulatory and respiratory function. High-voltage electrical burns exposing a narrow vertical area of forehead and cheek bones. The angle of the head and digital manipulation of the neck indicated a cervical break. There was bleeding from the ears. There was evidence for a reasonable inference of spinal injuries, as well as catastrophic neurological damage related to electrocution. Most conclusively, CPR and defibrillation efforts had been initiated without success and discontinued prior to my arrival."

Gurney nodded slowly. "So, even if the subject were not already dead at the time of your examination, death would have been imminent and inevitable?"

"The subject *was* dead at the time of my examination. Imminence and inevitability are irrelevant."

"What if I told you that Billy Tate walked out of Peale's Funeral Home?"

Fallow erupted in a sharp burst of laughter. "I'd say you were misinformed."

"What if I told you we have a witness who spoke to Billy Tate nearly twenty-four hours after you pronounced him dead?"

"I'd say it doesn't matter how many delusional witnesses might claim to have spoken to him. It wouldn't change the fact that the young man was struck by lightning, fell off the roof of St. Giles Church, and was killed instantly. If you've managed to lose his body, I suggest you find it. If you're claiming that the man I pronounced dead is wandering around Larchfield, you're making a serious mistake." He checked his watch again. "If you have no other questions . . ."

"Just one," said Gurney. "Did you by any chance have anything to drink the night Tate fell off the roof?"

Fallow stared at him. His voice tightened. "If you're suggesting my professional judgment was in any way impaired—"

"I'm not suggesting anything. I'm asking a simple question."

Fallow stood up from the conference table and glared at Morgan. "If this absurd confrontation was your idea, you'll live to regret it."

"Before you leave, Doctor," said Gurney in a matter-of-fact way, "we have a security camera video you might be interested in."

"Video of what?"

"Billy Tate's resurrection in Peale's embalming room."

18

The video, which Fallow watched with increasing distress, deflated him. He insisted that what he'd witnessed on the screen was impossible, but the strength of his conviction was gone.

"There was no doubt whatever in my mind that he was dead. I don't understand. There's no way he could have been alive."

"I understand what you're saying, Doctor, but there's another piece of the puzzle that supports the likelihood of Tate's survival. Two pieces, in fact. Two murders."

Before Gurney could go on to explain it, he saw the connection suddenly dawning on Fallow—beginning, no doubt, with the neatly sliced throats of Mary Kane and Angus Russell.

"The scalpels . . . Oh, my God . . . the scalpels he took from the mortuary cabinet."

"We also have Tate's fingerprints and DNA at the Russell murder scene."

Fallow swallowed hard.

Gurney continued. "We'll be issuing an APB today for Billy Tate, followed by a public statement, which will trigger a media explosion—including the inevitable *Dead Man Rises* stories. Things may get ugly, especially for you personally. Be prepared for that."

"Can't you control what details go to the media?"

"To some extent. But it's public knowledge that Tate was declared dead. Now it will be public knowledge that he's wanted for questioning in connection with two new murders. That's not something we can conceal."

Gurney didn't need to mention that Fallow's alcohol-related arrest was also a matter of public record. He could almost see the panic wheels turning in the man's brain as he imagined the career-smashing way that fact was likely to be covered by the media: MEDICAL EXAMINER WITH HISTORY OF ALCOHOL ABUSE DECLARES UNCONSCIOUS MAN DEAD.

Fallow turned to Morgan. "You were there. You saw him. How could anyone in that condition have survived?"

Morgan said nothing.

Fallow began shaking his head. "Newspapers, television ... God, what a horror!"

Gurney spoke calmly. "I'd suggest you refer any media inquiries you get to the Larchfield Police Department. It will be better for everyone if that function is centralized."

After a long moment, Fallow departed, still shaking his head.

Morgan gave Gurney a deer-in-the-headlights look. "When you say Larchfield Police Department, you mean me?"

"Unless you've got a spokesman on staff that I don't know about."

Morgan sighed. "I'd better get working on a statement."

"If I were you, I'd get the APB on Tate out first. The Mary Kane murder suggests he has no qualms about killing anyone who could be a threat to him."

Morgan nodded. "I'll get right on it."

"Sir?" Slovak was in the conference room doorway. "Sorry to interrupt, sir, but I just got back from Selena Cursen's. Should I fill you in now?"

"Fill Dave in. I'll catch up with him." He hurried out.

Slovak joined Gurney at the table and starting talking. "It was totally weird. She kept smiling and saying weird shit. *He's the Dark Angel who rose from the dead. Beware the Dark Angel who rose from the dead.*"

"Did she let you into the house?"

"No. She must have been outside and heard my car coming. You approach her place on this long, narrow dirt road through the woods. You have to drive real slow, with all the ruts. It's like a tunnel, with thick pine branches meeting over the top, so there's hardly any light. Then you come to this black iron gate that separates the woods from the grounds around the house. You look at that house, you can't help thinking bad shit goes on in there. When I got to the gate, she was standing there, all in black. With those shiny stud things in her lips. Smiling, like she was waiting for me. I had to force myself to get out of the car. I told her we were trying to get a better understanding of Billy Tate's accident, and would she mind if I asked her some questions."

"What did she say?"

"That's when she started with the weird shit. She knows that Tate's alive. But she seems to believe he actually died and came back from the other side. The way she was looking at me, the way she sounded, gave me the shivers."

"Any evidence that she was high on something?"

"Not really. Selena's always been strange. Harmless-strange. But today she was scary-strange. The look in her eyes almost made me think she was right."

"Right?"

"About Billy being dead and coming back to life. I know that's nuts, but . . . that look, like she knew something no one else did."

"Does she have any family?"

Slovak shook his head. "Her parents and sister died in a fire about ten years ago. The family house burned to the ground in the middle of the night. The fire marshal never came up with the reason. He suspected arson, but couldn't prove it. Selena was the only one of the Cursens who didn't die in the fire—because she was sleeping in a tent in the woods that night, or that's what she said. There were whispers going around, but no solid facts, just a feeling people had that Selena might be capable of anything. And there was the fact that she ended up with a huge inheritance. And went to live by herself in that haunted house out by the swamp."

"How old is she?"

"Around my age, I guess. Late twenties?"

"Was she in high school with you?"

"Her parents sent her to a school near Albany. For kids with emotional problems. Right after she came home, the family house burned down."

"And her relationship with Billy Tate began when?"

"Right after he got out of prison. At least that's when Darlene went batshit over it."

"Okay. Let's move ahead to the night Tate fell off the roof. You got a good look at the body. Was it your impression that he was dead?"

"My impression?" Slovak ran his hand back over his bristly scalp. "I'm not sure. His head was twisted to the side, and there was a burn line on the side of his face. Jimmy Clapper, one of our patrol guys, tried doing CPR, but that just seemed to increase the bleeding. They used the defib unit, too. Multiple times. Nothing worked. And Fallow making the official pronouncement kind of sealed the deal."

Gurney decided it was time to talk to Tate's stepmother.

Following the directions he got from Slovak, he took the two-lane state road up the long hill from the lush Larchfield valley and down into dreary Bastenburg. At the town's single traffic light, he turned onto Stickle Road and was soon driving through a scruffy area where abandoned pastures, overrun with thorn bushes, alternated with dilapidated trailers and collapsed barns.

Gurney was keeping an eye on his odometer, since Slovak's directions were based on distances rather than on the often illegible addresses on the tilting mailboxes. At 2.4 miles from the commercial center of Bastenburg, he arrived at the incongruously named Paradise Inn—Darlene Tate's place of business, as well as her residence—a ramshackle two-story structure with a tavern on the ground floor and an apartment upstairs. According to Slovak, access to her apartment was through the barroom.

Gurney parked in the weedy lot at the side of the building. Two other vehicles were present, both pickup trucks. Inside the rear window of one was a Confederate flag decal. A rifle was on display inside the other.

He got out and walked around to the front entrance. Above the sagging overhang, the words PARADISE INN were stenciled in red letters on a yellow background. A looping garland of blinking Christmas lights hung from the overhang. Rather than adding an element of cheer, the effect in the glare of the midday sun was repellent. He opened the glass-paneled door and stepped inside.

It took a few seconds for his eyes to adjust to the low light level. There were no windows. Apart from the glass door, the only sources of illumination were a widescreen TV on the wall at the end of the bar and a few low-wattage light fixtures in the ceiling.

Only one of the barstools was occupied—by a shapeless woman in an oversized flannel shirt and a John Deere cap on backward. Straggly gray hair reached her shoulders. She was leaning forward, elbows on the bar, hands wrapped around an empty glass. She glanced over at Gurney, then up at the TV, where colorfully dressed contestants were shrieking and dashing back and forth in a frenetic game show.

A young man with a shaved head and a bodybuilder's physique was perched on a stool behind the bar, cleaning his nails with the tip of a narrow-bladed hunting knife. He eyed Gurney with the quiet calculation common to ex-cons.

Gurney spoke with the steely politeness common to cops. "Good afternoon, sir. I'd like to speak to Darlene Tate."

"And you are . . . ?"

"Detective Gurney, Larchfield Police."

The young man slipped his knife slowly into a sheath on the side of his belt, picked up a phone from under the bar, and tapped a few icons. He put the phone to his ear and turned away. When he spoke, it was in a low voice.

All Gurney could make out was the word "police."

The young man lowered the phone. "Mrs. Tate would like to know the subject of your inquiry."

"Tell her I have some questions about her stepson."

He turned away and spoke into the phone in as low a voice as before. A few seconds later, he turned back to Gurney.

"Mrs. Tate does not wish to discuss her stepson. She says if you dropped dead, you could talk to him yourself in hell. No offense intended."

The shapeless woman with the straggly hair was taking an interest in this back-and-forth. Or maybe that was just an impression created by the fact that her mouth was hanging open.

Gurney motioned to the young man to follow him to the end of the bar.

"Tell Mrs. Tate that I'm investigating a murder that her stepson may have been involved in. I'd like to close the case, and she may be able to help me."

The young man raised his phone and passed along Gurney's message. The response this time was evidently positive. He pointed down a row of high-backed booths running along the wall parallel to the bar.

"Last one."

The six booths Gurney walked past were dingy, unlit, unoccupied. In the seventh, a small lamp produced just enough light to give him his first impression of Darlene Tate—a battle-scarred version of Lorinda.

She licked her lips. "Murder? For real?"

"Very real."

"Wouldn't put it past him. Wouldn't put nothing past him. Who'd he kill?"

"Mind if I sit down?"

She licked her lips again. There was a glass in her hand and a bottle of tequila on the table. "You want a drink?"

"Maybe later." He slid into the seat opposite her and smiled. "I appreciate your willingness to speak to me."

"Nice face. You sure you're a cop?"

"You have a nice face, too, Darlene." Actually, it wasn't a nice face at all. The bone structure was strong, but there was a sourness around the corners of the mouth and a reptilian coldness in her eyes. "Mind if I ask you some questions about Billy?"

She squinted at him sideways as though an odd thought had occurred to her. "What do you care what he did, now that the little bastard's dead?"

Gurney followed that opening. "You saw him at the mortuary that day, am I right, after he was struck by lightning and fell off that church roof?"

"People always look smaller when they're dead. You ever notice that?" She didn't wait for an answer. "I seen a lot of dead people, but never one I was happier to see dead."

She gave Gurney a hard look, as if daring him to say a good word about her stepson.

"Did he have any friends?"

"*Friends*?" She made it sound as if he'd asked whether Billy knew any Martians.

"Billy was a user. A filthy, lying user. A psychiatrist told us he was a sociopathical psychopath. When he was ten years old. You ever know anyone like that, evil like that from their childhood?"

"Did he get in trouble a lot?"

"He was never *out of* trouble. He had that impulsive control disorderly thing."

"How did he end up with Selena Cursen?"

She shook her head, picked up the tequila bottle, and poured a large shot into her glass. She drank it down slowly, then laid her glass back on the table. "Fucking bitch."

"If Billy were still alive, and I wanted to find him, where should I look?"

She frowned at her empty glass, blinking, as though she couldn't quite parse what he'd asked her. "He's dead," she said finally, picking up the bottle and pouring herself a generous double shot. "Ask Greg Mason."

"Who is Greg Mason?"

"His gym teacher, coach, who the fuck knows what else." She downed her tequila in one long swallow. "Ask him." Her voice trailed off, her eyes half closed.

"One last question, Darlene. Do you think Billy is capable of premeditated murder?"

Her eyes opened and she gazed at him with a drunk's sudden shrewdness. "He's dead. Not capable of anything. Why are you asking me that?"

"You did see him at Peale's Funeral Home, right?"

"You telling me he's not dead?"

"If he were alive, do you have any idea where he might be?"

She shook her head violently. "Find him! Go find him! Find him and KILL HIM!"

The muscular young man appeared beside the booth, eyes bright with animal alertness. "Everything okay?"

She picked up the tequila bottle. "Fine. Fucking fine!" She slid out of her seat and stumbled against the table. "How can he not be fucking dead?"

As she was guided unsteadily to a door in the room's rear wall, she cried out without turning, "If he's with that witch bitch, kill them both!"

19

Sitting in his car outside the Paradise Inn, Gurney called headquarters and asked for Slovak.

He came on almost immediately. "Hey, Detective Gurney, I was just about to call you. We have new information. Video files from security cameras in the village and out near Harrow Hill. A couple of the cameras were covering the streets around Peale's place, including the access to his parking lot, the night Tate disappeared. At the time Peale's video shows him leaving the embalming room, there's no vehicular traffic at all in that area."

"So he walked to his own car? Do we know where it was parked?"

"A woman who lives near the town square says she remembers it clearly—an orange-colored Jeep on a side street in back of her house."

"Did she see Tate?"

"No, but we have a clip from a stockbroker's security camera in that area, showing Tate walking toward the side street where she saw the Jeep."

"You reviewed the clip?"

"Yes, sir."

"How did Tate look?"

"Unsteady. Head down. Like he was keeping a careful eye on the ground in front of him."

"Interesting. What else do you have?"

"We have videos from cameras out by Waterview Drive that show Tate driving in the direction of the Harrow Hill turnoff around the time Ruby-June Hooper claims she saw him go by, which squares up with our guesstimate for the Kane murder, and the later Russell murder."

"All very consistent."

"There's more. A local stoner and his girlfriend came in a while ago to report another Tate sighting, more recent. They were freaked out, because they'd heard he was dead."

"Where and when did they see him?"

"Out past the far side of Harrow Hill, the side facing away from the lake. There's an old picnic area there by a pond where teenagers go to smoke weed and make out. They were there last evening, sometime after sunset. They hear a car coming, so they sit up and pay attention. It's Billy Tate in his orange Jeep. Stoner boy says he almost had a heart attack. Dead man driving. Felt like he was in a zombie movie."

"This was yesterday?"

"Right."

"Any security camera images confirming this?"

"That area has very few houses. It's mainly back roads. We haven't checked yet, but I doubt we'll find anything."

"You find these kids credible?"

"Yes and no. He's an obvious druggie, but she seems straight enough. She's the one who insisted they report it."

"Peculiar."

"That they bothered to report it?"

"No. That Tate would drive around locally, two days after the Russell and Kane murders. He must have had a good reason to take a chance like that. Are you making any progress tracking down the phone we saw Tate using in the mortuary video?"

"The carrier says there's no phone registered to him. Could be an untraceable prepaid."

"Check for phones registered to Selena Cursen—he may have gotten it through her. Also, we know exactly when he made the call from the time code on the video. Ask the carrier to check for any call originating at that time through the Larchfield cell tower. And get the receiving name and phone number."

"You think I'll need a warrant?"

"Make the request to the carrier on an emergency basis. Get the process moving, then get a warrant for the file."

"Yes, sir. I'll get on it right now."

"Before you go . . . is there a Greg Mason at the high school?"

"Sure. Been there for years. He's head of the Phys Ed department. Why?"

"I was told he may know something useful about Billy Tate. I'm going there now. And one more thing. Have Selena Cursen's house staked out, in case Tate shows up."

The sprawling campus of Larchfield Academy occupied a grassy rise just outside the village. The entrance, just like the Russell estate, was through a pillared gateway in a drystone wall. The main school building was an ivy-covered neoclassical structure more suited to a grand old university than a rural high school. Perhaps another demonstration of Russell largesse.

Gurney parked near the marble front steps in a shaded area demarcated by a sign reading FOR THE CONVENIENCE OF OUR VISITORS.

The school's massive front door opened with surprising ease into an entry area that was cordoned off from the rest of the marble-floored lobby. A uniformed security guard was manning a desk next to a walk-through metal detector.

Gurney identified himself, explaining he was with the Larchfield PD, and asked to see Greg Mason.

The man who came striding across the lobby two minutes later was conspicuously neat. There wasn't a hint of a wrinkle in his fitted blue dress shirt or sharply cuffed gray slacks. He had the physique of a man who believed in staying in shape. His salt-and-pepper crew cut was as carefully managed as the rest of his appearance.

He stopped on his side of the metal detector with a puzzled look.

"Why did you come here?"

"To speak with you, if you can spare me a few minutes."

"It's my wife—my ex-wife—you should be talking to. She's the one who discovered the problem."

"What problem?"

"The vandalism. Isn't that why you're here?"

"No, sir. I'm here to ask about a former student."

"Oh." He looked confused, then curious. "Which student?"

"Perhaps we could speak in your office."

Mason checked his watch. "How long will this take?"

"Not long. Just a few questions."

"All right. Follow me."

From the lobby, he led Gurney down a high-ceilinged corridor to a corner office. Its oak door had a smoky glass panel and a brass knob. Gurney felt like he was walking into the dean's office back at his college. The furniture inside was simple in an old-fashioned, classy way. There was a mahogany desk in the center of the room. Mason motioned Gurney to a chair in front of it. Gurney sat. Mason remained standing. Perhaps, thought Gurney, he'd read an article on power dynamics.

"So," said Mason with a less-than-warm smile, "what's this all about?"

"Billy Tate."

The smile vanished in a flash of revulsion. "Is this about the accident at the church?"

"I'd like to know whatever you can tell me about him."

"I wouldn't know where to begin."

"You could begin by telling me why you had such a negative reaction to his name."

Mason folded his arms. "You won't find many people here with positive reactions."

Gurney waited for him to go on.

"Billy Tate was the most troubling—and most troubled—student we've ever had in this school. At least, during the thirty years I've been here."

"What was your worst experience with him?"

"Lord, so many to choose from. You mind telling me why you're asking?"

"Some questions have been raised by the incident at St. Giles. I'm trying to find out as much as I can about him. Your name was mentioned as someone who could be helpful."

Mason hesitated, appearing less than satisfied by Gurney's answer, but in the end, he sighed and sat down in his desk chair.

"The striking thing about Tate was the combination of his God-given ability and the evil way he chose to use it. He was a natural athlete. Wiry, fast, incredibly strong. Fifty, sixty push-ups without breaking a sweat. Impervious to pain. I persuaded him to try out for the school wrestling program. I sensed there was too much ego in him, so I paired him up with a bigger, more experienced wrestler. The star of the team. The challenge brought out something frightening in Tate. He broke the bigger kid's arm. And it wasn't an accident. He knew what he was doing. He seemed to think it was funny." Mason's mouth tightened in an expression of contempt. "That's partly what led to his detour into the juvenile justice system."

"Partly?"

"There was an initial intervention by our guidance counselor, who happened to be a skilled therapist and, in the interest of full disclosure, my wife." Mason produced an awkward smile. "Now my ex-wife."

He straightened a stack of index cards on his desk before continuing. "Tate made what Linda considered to be threats on her life. They were vivid, detailed, and disgusting. She did not take that lightly. She had recordings of her sessions with him and filed an official complaint. Appropriate hearings were held, and Tate ended up spending six months in a juvenile detention facility. All this happened when he was barely fourteen years old."

Gurney found nothing surprising in the age factor. He had no illusions about the so-called "innocence" of childhood. In his NYPD days, he'd investigated premeditated murders committed by kids a lot younger than fourteen. One gruesome assassination of five family members was carried out by an eight-year-old, whose calm stare—coming from an otherwise cherubic face—was more unnerving than that of any mob hit man.

"Was he close to anyone in school?"

Mason shook his head. "Tate's evil streak was pretty near the surface. Even the rough kids kept their distance. The only one who seemed comfortable around him—odd as it may seem now—was Lori Strane, legal name Lorinda, now Mrs. Angus Russell."

That got Gurney's attention. "How do you mean, 'comfortable'?"

"I'd see her talking to him, sometimes smiling. She definitely wasn't afraid of him, not like everyone else was."

"Interesting. What else can you tell me about her?"

"Nothing."

"You said that very quickly."

"Rumors are a form of social poison. I refuse to repeat them. Whatever I may have heard about her would fall in that category."

"Like her relationship with your former principal?"

"No comment."

"Okay. Just tell me what she was like, the way you might describe any other student. I'm not recording this, and I won't quote you."

Mason gazed off into the middle distance, as though he might be evaluating a tricky bit of terrain. He cleared his throat. "She was an astonishingly beautiful young woman. The boys were obsessed with her. I think half the men in Larchfield would have left their wives for her, if they thought they had a chance."

Gurney smiled. "So, everyone was in love with the unique Lori Strane and scared to death of the unique Billy Tate."

"That's a reasonable summary."

"Did Tate have any redeeming qualities?"

"None that I was aware of. I may be prejudiced due to the threats he made to my wife, but I can't recall ever hearing a good word about his character or behavior."

Mason joined his hands together on the desk in front of him, interlocking his fingers tightly. "I suppose his upbringing played a role in how he turned out. Are you aware of his family situation?"

"His father shooting him five times?"

"That, and the man himself. Elroy 'Smoky' Tate. A mob-connected arsonist, or so the news stories intimated. And Billy's birth mother was no prize, either—an 'exotic dancer' who OD'd on heroin when he was in kindergarten. Maybe it's understandable how he turned out."

Mason's tone was about as understanding as a hammer.

"I was told Billy recovered completely from the shooting. Is that right?"

"Physically, yes. But mentally and emotionally, no. He was worse than ever. I hate to say this about another human being, but I thank God he's no longer among us."

Mason unclasped his hands, stretching his fingers, then slapped his palms lightly on the desktop, as if to suggest that there was no more to be said.

Gurney had no objection. Letting the man end the interview on his own terms would make it easier to meet with him again if the need arose.

They both stood up. Gurney extended his hand, and Mason reached across the desk and shook it. "Will someone be getting in touch with my ex-wife regarding the vandalism?"

"I'll check when I get back to headquarters. What sort of vandalism are we talking about?"

"I'm not exactly sure. Linda lives in the house. I live in a condo out at the end of the lake. I still take care of the property, mowing and so forth, but that's just once a week. She no longer works here, but we stay in touch, particularly with any issues concerning the house."

"Like this incident of vandalism?"

"She has a private therapy practice in the village, and when she arrived home last evening, she called to say that the front door of the house had been defaced. I told her to report it to you folks. That's what I thought you were responding to."

"Did she say what she meant by 'defaced'?"

"Some kind of design scratched into the paint. Hopefully not into the wood."

"Design?"

"That's all she said."

"Could you call her, please?"

"Now?"

"It could be important."

Sighing impatiently, Mason took out his phone and placed the call. After a long moment, he looked at Gurney. "It's going to her voicemail. Shall I leave a message?"

Gurney ignored the question. "Where's the house located?"

"At the end of Skinner Hollow."

"Where's that?"

"Out past the north side of Harrow Hill. Middle of nowhere, really."

"Is that the side of the hill facing away from the lake?"

"Yes."

"Did your wife call you before or after she entered the house?"

"I have no idea. Why does it matter?"

"It may not matter at all. I'm going to drive out there now and take a look. I'll let you know what I find, okay?"

Skinner Hollow consisted of a narrow, two-mile-long dirt road running by a stream in a ravine with sides too steep to accommodate any structures. At the end the ravine broadened suddenly into a pine forest, which in turn gave way to a mowed field. In the middle of the field stood a white farmhouse with blue shutters and a blue door. Behind it was a classic red barn. Unlike Ruby-June Hooper's house on the lake, to which it was similar in size and structure, this house was as neat and crisp as Greg Mason. Even the gravel driveway was spotless.

The driveway widened to form a parking area in front of the house, partly occupied by a dusty white Corolla. As soon as Gurney pulled in next to it, he could see the nature of the "vandalism" on the front door. A chillingly familiar figure eight with a vertical slash through the middle had been scraped into the door's blue paint by something with a very sharp point.

He lowered the Outback windows and listened. He peered at the windows of the house, then scanned as much of the surrounding field as he could see from the car. He opened his glove compartment and took out his ankle holster and 9mm Beretta. He strapped on the ankle holster. Beretta in hand, he stepped out of the car. His level of alertness amplified the crunch of the gravel underfoot.

As he approached the defaced door, he noticed that it was slightly ajar. That, even more than the scratched symbol, was disturbing.

He called out, "Mrs. Mason!"

A flock of yellow finches took flight from a large viburnum at the corner of the house. He called out her name two more times.

Silence.

He stepped up to the door and rapped on it sharply, calling out her name one more time.

Silence.

Clicking off the Beretta's safety, he pushed the door open with his foot.

Silence.

He stepped inside and found himself at the front end of a center hall that ran back to a glass-paneled rear door. Through the rear door he could see a stretch of bright green lawn and the corner of the red barn. On his right was a small dining room; on his left a living room.

From an abundance of caution, he announced his presence loudly one more time. "Larchfield police! Anyone in the house, show yourself now!"

Silence.

He stepped into the living room.

The interior wasn't disorderly. It just wasn't compulsively orderly. A small plate with crumbs on it had been left on an end table along with an empty glass. A copy of *The New Yorker* was open on the floor next to one of the armchairs. A tilting pile of books stood in the middle of the coffee table. A bunched-up lap blanket was hanging off one arm of the sofa.

Gurney continued along the hall to the modest kitchen. This, too, showed the signs of normal use. Several dishes were propped in a drying rack on the countertop. A few others remained in the sink, along with a used tea bag and some yet-to-be-washed silverware. Several kitchen drawers were not quite closed. There was a small breakfast table by a side window, and the afternoon sun flooding over it magnified a scattering of crumbs.

He was about to take a look upstairs when something caught his eye.

In the middle of a small oval rug beside the breakfast table, there was a nickel-sized stain that looked like day-old blood.

He got down on his knees and gently raised the side of the rug nearest the stain. Peering under it, he could see that it had penetrated the rug fibers and was visible on the underside. Using the flashlight on his phone, he saw that the spot where the seepage had occurred had not completely dried. He lowered the rug back in place and began an examination of the rest of the floor.

He soon found what appeared to be long scuff marks, of the sort that might be made by dragging something heavy across the floor. He followed the marks out of the kitchen and down the hall to the rear door. Rather than opening and passing through it, risking further contamination of the scene, he retreated back along the hall and out the front door. From there he walked around to the back door to see if the trail continued outside it.

It did—taking the form of a body-wide depression in the grass, continuing across the lawn in the direction of the barn.

He followed it, discovering that it led around the corner of the barn and stopped at the barn's sliding door. The concavity in the grass was more obvious there, as though the dragged body had rested there. A brown bloodstain in the grass a few inches from the door seemed to confirm this.

To avoid interfering with possible prints on the steel handle, Gurney instead gripped the edge of the heavy door and pulled it sideways along the top-rollers that supported it. As it slid open, the buzzing whine of flies grew louder. The sound was a warning of what he was likely to find, but it hardly prepared him for the sight.

A farm tractor was facing the open doorway. It was fitted with the sort of front-loader that might be used to move large amounts of gravel or manure. The loading bucket was positioned about four feet above the barn floor. It was supporting a woman's body at a downward angle—her legs and feet higher than her torso, her head hanging down to within a foot of the concrete floor. Her hair was pulled back into a single long braid. The end of the braid was just touching the floor. Flies were swarming around her eyes and a gaping wound in her throat.

The tilt of the body was reminiscent of the photos Gurney had seen of Angus's body. But there was a significant difference.

The floor under Angus's throat had been soaked with blood. But there was no blood on the barn floor. Not a single drop.

Gurney took out his phone and called headquarters.

20

Within half an hour of his call, all the key individuals had arrived—two patrol officers to secure the area and maintain an entry and exit log; Kyra Barstow with her crime-scene processing team; Dr. Fallow with his gaunt assistant; the rotund crime-scene photographer who earlier that morning had been documenting Mary Kane's body in the drainage swale; and, with his facial tic more noticeable than usual, Mike Morgan.

The patrol officers set up a yellow-tape perimeter, enclosing a rectangular acre or so, with the house and its parking area at one end and the barn at the other. Everyone whose functions required them to be within the perimeter donned the standard protective clothing.

Gurney gave Morgan and Barstow a detailed description of his movements and observations at the scene. He also reported what Slovak had told him about the local stoner and his girlfriend seeing Billy Tate in his Jeep passing in the direction of the Mason house the previous evening. He concluded by explaining to the photographer the areas of the house, lawn, and barn that required documentation—in addition to the standard shots of the body in situ.

He then accompanied Fallow across the lawn to the barn, giving him an abbreviated summary of the facts he'd just shared with Morgan and Barstow.

Fallow's only response was a tight-lipped nod.

At the open barn door, after gazing for a long moment at the body, he asked Gurney if it was in the exact position in which he'd found it.

Gurney assured him that it was, and Fallow began his examination.

"David?"

Barstow had followed him. "I'm thinking we should start our site processing inside the house, then work our way out here. That okay with you?"

He nodded his assent. "The blood spot on the kitchen rug suggests the killer made initial contact with the victim inside the house, knocked her unconscious, then dragged her out here. So it would make sense to start there."

"You just referred to 'the killer.' Does that mean you're not sure it was Billy Tate?"

"I'm not *sure* of anything. I've discovered that being sure this early in a murder case is a sure way of being wrong."

Gurney then heard sharply raised voices and noticed men jostling out by the opening in the perimeter tape. Heading that way, he could see that the two patrol officers charged with securing the restricted area were struggling to restrain a man trying to enter. He got a clear line of sight to the man's face.

Greg Mason, eyes wide and voice ragged, demanded to be allowed onto his property. Behind him on the lawn, alongside the official vehicles, was the car Gurney assumed he'd arrived in—a blue Prius, with its driver's-side door hanging open.

One of the cops barring Mason's entry was repeating, like an automatic tape loop, "Just calm down, sir. Just calm down, sir. Everything will be explained. Just calm down."

"Mr. Mason," said Gurney, walking up to him.

Mason blinked several times and stared at him. "You said you'd call me as soon as you got here. That was a goddamn hour ago. What the hell is going on here?"

"Can we sit down?"

"What?"

"Let's go sit in your car."

Apparently content to let Gurney deal with the problem, the two cops backed away.

Gurney led Mason toward the Prius. Gurney directed him to the car's passenger side and took the driver's seat himself. This seemed to confuse Mason, but he made no objection.

"A hard day," said Gurney softly.

Mason stared at him. "What is it? What happened?"

The fear in the man's voice told Gurney that he might be guessing at the truth.

"We found the body of a woman on your property."

Mason blinked, his mouth opening slowly. "A woman?"

"Yes."

Mason's lips moved for a few seconds before he spoke and his voice contracted to little more than a whisper. "Do you mean my wife?"

"Can you describe her to me?"

Mason looked lost.

"Her age?"

"Fifty . . . fifty-one. Yes. Fifty-one."

"Her hair?"

He sounded as if his mouth had gone dry. "Brown. Mostly brown. A little gray. Here and there."

"Long or short?"

"Long. She . . . likes it long."

"Did she ever braid it?"

"Sometimes. A single braid. Down the back." He began breathing heavily. "Oh, God. What happened to her?"

"We're trying to find out."

"Where is she?"

"In the barn."

"She never went into the barn."

Gurney hesitated. "She may have been placed there."

"*Placed* there?"

"That's the way it looks."

"Are you saying she was killed?"

"I'm sorry, sir, but it appears that way."

"She was *killed*? You mean *murdered*?"

"It appears that way."

"How? Why?"

"Those are the questions we hope to find answers to."

"You're positive that the . . . the body you found . . . is Linda?"

"We'll be asking you to confirm the identification, when you feel able."

A silence fell between them, broken finally by Mason.

"Do you know things . . . things that you're not telling me?"

"I'm afraid, sir, that right now we don't know very much at all."

Mason nodded in a way that appeared more like a mindless rocking motion than a cogent response. "Can I see her?"

"Soon. The medical examiner is . . . here now."

"Where?"

"In the barn."

"Where in the barn?"

Gurney wanted to be reasonably truthful, without being too specific. "By your tractor. I assume it's your tractor?"

"That's where you found her?"

"Yes."

Mason let out a sharp little sound, halfway between a stifled whimper and a laugh.

"She hated that tractor." He closed his eyes. When he opened them, they were full of tears. He lowered his head and slowly bent forward, his hands clasped between his knees.

Gurney was tempted to reach out and put a consoling hand on the man's shoulder but instead maintained, as he normally did in situations of crime-scene grief, a professional distance. It wasn't a difficult decision, since he found emotional detachment in general to be a comfortable state of mind.

Mason straightened himself in the seat, gazing blankly for a while in the direction of the barn, then turning to Gurney with a look of perplexity.

"Why were you asking about Billy Tate?"

When Gurney didn't answer, Mason's eyes widened. "Tate is dead . . . isn't he?"

Again Gurney said nothing.

"My God! He's not alive, is he? How could he be alive?"

"Good question."

"Do you . . . are you saying . . . my God, is he involved in this?"

"It's a possibility."

"I don't understand. He was struck by lightning. It was in the news."

"Some new evidence has come to light. It's possible that Tate survived."

"What? How could that—"

"Mr. Mason?" Mike Morgan had come to the side of the car. "Mr. Mason, I'm sorry, I know how difficult this is, but would you feel able at this point to look at the victim's face and tell us whether or not the victim is your wife?"

Gurney was beginning to wonder if Mason had understood the question when he finally responded, distractedly. "Yes, I . . . I'll do that."

"The medical examiner will be bringing the victim's body over this way in just a moment."

A rolling stretcher emerged from the barn, guided by Fallow and pushed by his assistant.

Gurney and Mason exited the Prius. A cool breeze had come up, the sun was gone, and small dark clouds were scudding across the sky. The green of the lawn had lost some of its vibrancy.

"Dave?" Kyra Barstow was calling to him from the front porch of the house, her hand raised to get his attention. "There's something here you need to see."

He glanced at the approaching stretcher, which he now saw was bearing a dark plastic body bag. He hoped that Fallow would have the delicacy to open the zipper just far enough to show the woman's face without revealing the god-awful wound to her throat, and he knew that Morgan was quite capable of handling the formality of the identification process.

He made his way around the official vehicles and followed Barstow into the house. The front door, the newel post and banister of the staircase leading to the second floor, and several spots along the hallway had already been dusted for prints. In the living room, one of her Tyvek-suited assistants was going over the rug with a noisy trace-evidence collection vac.

"Up there," she said, indicating the staircase.

He'd only climbed a few steps when he saw it.

On the wall of the landing at the top, illuminated only by weak window light reaching it from the adjacent bedrooms, there was a message painted in large dripping letters.

I AM

THE DARK ANGEL

WHO ROSE

FROM THE DEAD

Whether it was the meaning of the message, or the likelihood that it had been written in the blood of the dead woman in the barn, or the suggestion it conveyed that the dreadful work of this "angel" might not be over, the sight of it on that dim-lit wall gave Gurney gooseflesh.

He went back down the stairs and out onto the porch. Barstow followed him out.

"We need to know more about Tate. I can't tell whether he's psychotic—or trying to create that impression—or whether something else is going on."

"Something else . . . like what?"

"I wish I knew. Most homicide cases, your first hypothesis is often pretty close to the truth. But this Tate thing is a whole other animal."

She seemed fascinated by this. "The guys who leave messages at murder sites, they do tend to be the crazy ones, right?"

"They're the ones with a hunger for recognition, justification, admiration. The messages are directed at an imagined audience. The wording sometimes reveals mental deficits, delusions, emotional disorders. But once in a while, all that craziness is being faked. I've had cases with perps who came across as total maniacs, when in fact—"

A sound not far away stopped him—a small, wavering moan—barely audible, yet as full of pain as a scream.

Greg Mason was standing in front of his car, between Fallow and Morgan, looking down at the face in the open end of the body bag. His own face was contorted with misery.

"Poor man," said Barstow softly.

Gurney watched as Morgan helped Mason back into the passenger seat of the Prius. He remained there, bent over, speaking to him, while Fallow zipped up the body bag and, with the help of his assistant, rolled the stretcher over to their cadaver-transport van.

Gurney followed them.

"Dr. Fallow?"

Fallow turned and regarded Gurney with an unblinking lack of expression.

"Doctor, if there's anything you can share with me at this point, even if it's just a guess, it could be extremely helpful. The time factor in this case—"

Fallow cut him off. "There's always a time factor. Everything is always needed immediately."

Gurney was starting to back away when Fallow surprised him with a rapid-fire recitation of facts.

"Slight blue paint residue on the lower edge of the neck wound. Multiple hair follicles torn from the scalp, consistent with the body being dragged by the hair to its final location. Right carotid and right jugular severed. Substantial quantity of blood had been drained from the body and removed from the site. Evidence of a sharp blow to the upper parietal bone of the cranium, consistent with the use of a tool similar to the one used to kill the Russell dog."

"Upper parietal?" said Gurney. "Does that mean she was struck on the top of the head?"

"Yes." Without another word, Fallow strode away to his Mercedes, while his assistant loaded the stretcher and body bag into the van.

Soon both vehicles, Mercedes first, were heading along the gravel driveway, out of the grassy clearing, and into the shadows of the pine woods.

As Gurney was watching their departure, Morgan came over. He looked around and lowered his voice. "Did you detect any odor?"

"Odor?"

"From Fallow. Alcohol."

"No."

"Good." He checked his watch and added, "I need to get back to headquarters and start preparing a statement. Press conference this evening at seven o'clock. I don't suppose you'd be willing to—"

"Don't even think of it."

Morgan nodded. "Right. So . . . what are your thoughts about this business here?"

"Apart from its being horrendous, I'd say it adds at least three troubling data points to the puzzle. First, the timing. Unlike the Kane murder, this one isn't a direct by-product of the Russell murder, with Tate eliminating someone who recognized him on his way to Harrow Hill. This is about something else. Second, the missing blood. It seems to have been drained from the body and taken away. One wonders for what purpose. And finally, something you haven't seen yet—a message in blood inside the house. It gives the impression of something beginning rather than ending. On the wall at the top of the stairs."

Morgan hesitated, then made his way reluctantly across the parking area toward the house.

Gurney went to his Outback, took out his phone, and called Madeleine.

He was half hoping that the call would go to voicemail, but she answered it.

"Let me guess," she said. "Something's come up, and you won't be home for dinner."

"I have a difficult situation here."

She waited for him to go on.

"Two more bodies were found today. Women whose throats were cut."

She let out a sharp little groan.

"And it may not be over."

"What do you mean?"

"The killer left a message, but I don't want to get into that now—"

"You don't need to explain. I'll talk to the Winklers. Call me when you can."

"I will."

"Be careful."

"I will."

"I love you."

"I love you, too."

He checked the time on his phone, took a long, slow breath, leaned back in his seat, and closed his eyes—to withdraw, if just for a moment, into a place of peace—before what he was sure would be an emotionally draining conversation with Greg Mason.

A rapping on the window next to his head jarred Gurney back into the world. He opened the window and found Morgan staring down at him.

"You all right?"

"Fine," said Gurney. His mouth was dry. He hadn't eaten anything since the coffee and toast he'd had for breakfast.

"A hell of a thing, that writing on the wall," said Morgan.

"Yes, a hell of a thing."

"Look, I've got to get back to headquarters and get ready for that damn press conference. Situation here seems under control. Barstow's got the evidence-collection process moving along. Body's gone for autopsy. Patrol team's keeping an eye on the perimeter. You plan on spending some time with Mason?"

"Yes."

"Good. If you need to reach me . . ." He ended the sentence with a vague gesture and headed for his Tahoe.

Gurney rooted through the storage compartment between his front seats. He came up with a small bottle of water. He drank it all and tossed the plastic bottle on the floor behind his seat.

He got out of the car and made his way over to the Prius. As soon as he got in next to Mason, he could see that the man's earlier expression of desolation had tightened into something more like anger. He was nodding to himself, as if affirming some private conviction.

Gurney watched and waited.

"It's the only explanation. What you said. About Tate being alive. The evil son of a bitch is alive!"

"What makes you so sure?"

"No one else would do such a thing. Everyone loved her. Everyone in that school loved her. Everyone except Billy Tate."

"Because she reported his behavior to the police?"

Mason seemed not to hear the question. "When they graduated, kids kept in touch with her. They adored her. And not just kids. She had a way with people." He made *a way with people* sound like a mysterious gift. "She was an amazing person. Full of interest in everything and everybody. She *cared*. People were drawn to her. She had no enemies. Only Tate."

Gurney wondered why Mason's relationship with his wonderful wife had ended in divorce, but that was too sharp a question for the mood of the moment.

In a softer tone he asked instead, "What was it she didn't like about your tractor?"

Mason blinked in confusion. "What?"

"You told me that Linda hated your tractor. I was wondering why."

Mason raised his hand as if to brush the question aside, then lowered it without completing the gesture. He opened his mouth, then closed it.

As Gurney watched, he could see the man's assertiveness dissolve back into a weary sadness. His voice was barely above a whisper.

"She didn't really hate the tractor."

Gurney gave him a gently questioning look.

"Sometimes things stand for other things. Do you understand?"

"What did the tractor stand for?"

Mason sighed. "Our differences. What I focused on, spent my time on. I like order, precision, proportion." He uttered a dismal little laugh. "The tyranny of perfectionism."

"The tractor stood for all that?"

"Not the thing itself, but how often I used it. Leveling areas around the edges of the field. Smoothing and re-smoothing the driveway. Grooming the trails. She saw the tractor as the part of me that stood between us."

Gurney wanted to keep him talking. "You have trails on your property?"

"Just one, in the woods on the south side of our clearing. But it connects with all the trails on Harrow Hill—miles and miles of them, on the Russell side and the Aspern side. I keep them cleared and mowed."

"Sounds like a lot of work. Why bother?"

"Because neat is better than sloppy. Order trumps disorder." Tears were welling in his eyes. "Silly, isn't it—that a marriage could fall apart over something like that?"

The tears started making wet lines down his cheeks. He gazed despairingly at the house. "I should have been with her. She was alone. With a maniac who hated her."

21

By six that evening, Gurney was ready to leave the property. He took a final walk around the edges of the spacious lawn, lingering at the trail entrance that led, according to Mason, to an intricate web of trails on Harrow Hill.

The sky's cloud cover had darkened, the path into the pine woods was uninviting, and the restless breezes had grown cooler. The broad rise of Harrow Hill itself loomed over the area—a dark presence that seemed for a moment to be the source of the chill in the air. Gurney moved on, completing his circuit of the lawn.

Barstow and her team had finished their examination of the house and barn without turning up anything that appeared inconsistent with Gurney's hypothesis of the murder. Whether that conclusion held up would depend on the analysis of the contents of their evidence vacs.

For now, it seemed a safe bet that Linda Mason's killer—presumably Billy Tate, based on the scratched symbol, method of execution, and bloody message on the wall—had gained entry to her home, knocked her unconscious in her kitchen, and dragged her to the barn, where he employed the tractor's front loader to lift her body and tilt it at a head-down angle to facilitate the draining of her blood after cutting her throat. The trace of blue paint dust on the neck wound would have come from the scalpel having been used on the front door. The fact that she'd received the blow that presumably rendered her unconscious on the *top* of her head struck Gurney as odd, since it suggested she was in a seated position at the time—not a common situation with assault victims. But there could be a simple explanation for that.

Fallow and his assistant were long gone. Morgan was likely in the midst of an angst-filled process of preparing for his press conference back at headquarters. Greg Mason had finally been persuaded to go home to his condo on the lake. The two patrol officers had been replaced by one from the night shift with instructions to maintain the site security until further notice.

Gurney decided to call it a day and set out for Walnut Crossing. He got in the Outback and followed the dirt road down through the pine-shadowed ravine. The stream next to the road reminded him that he was still thirsty. And hungry.

Realizing that his route would be taking him through the center of Larchfield, he thought he might pick up a snack for the drive home after touching base with Morgan.

When he reached the village square, he saw that Morgan's press conference was likely to be a bigger deal than he'd anticipated. Media vans, complete with rooftop satellite dishes, had made Cotswold Lane nearly impassable.

Inching his vehicle around them, he looked up the headquarters driveway and saw more vans in the parking area. Next he came to Peale's Funeral Home. A glance up that driveway revealed an emptier parking area, so he decided to use it.

Once there, however, it occurred to him that Morgan would be too much of a nervous wreck to talk to, and he didn't feel like bobbing and weaving to deflect media attention from himself. As unappetizing as it might be, he decided to head directly for the gas station mini-mart in Bastenburg. There wasn't much harm they could do to a bottle of orange juice and a granola bar.

He was about to turn his car around when another thought occurred to him. As long as he was back where it all began—the site of Tate's startling revival—why not make another visit to the embalming room, on the chance that he might see something he'd missed the first time around?

As he got out of the car, he noticed a bell at the rear door. He pressed the button and heard a faint chiming. He waited. He pressed it again, and the door opened. The perturbed expression on Danforth Peale's face faded to bland curiosity.

"Detective Gurney? What can I do for you?"

"I'd like another look at the room where Tate regained consciousness."

"Any particular reason?"

"A feeling I get sometimes—that I may have missed something. The only way I'm able to get rid of it is to take a second look around."

Peale hesitated, glancing at his watch. “Fine. But I can’t imagine what you could have missed.”

He led Gurney through the dark hallway to the windowless embalming room and switched on the lights. Gurney’s gaze moved slowly around the room. It was as he remembered it, except that the door of the cadaver storage unit, which had been open, was now closed.

“Is that being used?” he asked, pointing to it.

“No. It’s hardly a time for business as usual.”

“What I’d like to do,” said Gurney, “is step inside the storage unit—to begin where Tate began. It may be useful to follow his movements, to see things from his point of view.”

“If you think it will help, go right ahead.”

Gurney checked the operation of the emergency release lever on the inside of the door. It worked smoothly. He stepped into the unit and closed the door behind him. He tried to imagine himself lying in a closed casket, consciousness gradually returning, consciousness first of severe pain—pain in his head, neck, chest, back, arms, legs, everywhere—then the consciousness of being trapped in some sort of elongated box with no memory of how he’d gotten there. Then the inevitable panic, the stale air, the dead silence, perhaps even the dawning suspicion that the box might be a coffin. Terror. Total terror. Then the frantic battle to break out of it. The straining effort against the inside of the lid. And finally the indescribable relief of the lid breaking open. Then climbing out of the box, only to discover being in a larger box. The panic returning. The search for an exit, a seam, a crack, anything. Eventually his searching hands would come upon the lever, and the door would open.

All of this, Gurney realized as he stepped out into the light, was consistent with what he’d seen and heard on the video. He moved around the room, duplicating Tate’s progress as best he could, seeing what Tate would have seen.

“Is this doing you any good?” Peale asked.

“Putting myself in someone else’s position usually helps. How well did you know Tate?”

“No one really knew him. Certainly not me. Why would I?”

“You’re around the same age. You both grew up in this area. Maybe in elementary school? Or high school?”

The suggestion spread a look of disdain across Peale's face. "I attended Dalrymple Day School through the eighth grade, hardly the sort of place that would tolerate anyone like Billy Tate. Larchfield Academy was, by its unfortunate charter, more *inclusive*." He articulated the word as though it signified something repellent. "I believe Tate entered Larchfield a year or two before I graduated."

"So, no contact of any kind?"

"Good Lord, no."

"What can you tell me about Lori Strane?"

"She was an object of universal desire."

"Any close friends?"

"She inspired awe, envy, lust. Those are not feelings compatible with friendship."

"Was her marriage to a man fifty years older than her a shock?"

Peale shook his head. "Bit of a scandal, perhaps. Focus of intense gossip. Subject of salacious jokes. But not really a shock."

"Why not?"

"Because under all that startling beauty there was a core of selfish practicality. Her marriage to Angus Russell revealed it clearly."

"Interesting observation. What can you tell me about Selena Cursen?"

"Hard to keep up with Selena. If she didn't have so much money, she'd probably be residing in the Wiccan Weirdo Nuthouse." His little joke had the stale tone of something he'd said before.

"I understand she and Tate had a relationship."

Peale sniffed. "I've heard a rumor to that effect."

"Do you believe it?"

"It's not hard to believe that two antisocial lunatics would find common ground."

Gurney heard the rumble of a truck passing, probably on the cross street behind the building's parking area. It reminded him that Peale had mentioned that outside noise was the problem that caused him to disable the link between the room's security camera and his computer's recording function. He asked Peale if the Tate incident had motivated him to turn it back on.

"No need to, now that I know the cloud system has it covered. But whether I still have a business here to protect is doubtful at best." He sighed impatiently. "Are you finished here?"

"For now, anyway. Thank you for your patience."

Peale led him through the hallway and stepped out into the parking area with him. He gestured toward the media vehicles behind police headquarters. "Mind if I ask you . . . what's going on over there?"

"Press conference about Tate and other matters. Chief Morgan is handling it."

"I hope to God he knows what he's doing." Peale hesitated. "Might those 'other matters' be related to Mary Kane?"

"What do you know about Mary Kane?"

"There's a rumor flying around the village that she was killed. Is that true?"

"I heard the same rumor. The chief will probably address it. Keep an eye on the news."

"You don't part with information easily, do you?"

Gurney shrugged. "I just gather it. Folks up the ladder from me decide how much of it to share."

Gurney got in his Outback and headed down the driveway with Peale's unhappy gaze following him all the way.

22

The mini-mart in the Bastenburg gas station was a disheartening exemplar of its type. A shabby seller of beer, cigarettes, lottery tickets, and rewarmed pizza slices, it radiated rural malaise.

Gurney scanned the refrigerated compartments that lined the walls, finally settling on an overpriced pint of orange juice. He then searched the freestanding shelves for something to eat. Finding nothing whose labeled contents didn't take his appetite away, he went to the counter with his juice.

The young man standing by the register was enormous. His bulging cheeks had reduced his eyes to slits. He had a metal stud through his lower lip. A tabloid was open on the counter in front of him.

The headline on one page said, "Python Swallows Poodle."

The headline on the opposite page said, "Child-Porn Sting Nets Top Cop."

The young man looked up at Gurney. "Y'all set?"

"I am. Do you happen to know anything about that storefront a couple of blocks down the road? The sign in the window says 'Church of the Patriarchs.'"

The young man shook his head emphatically. "Couldn't say."

"Do you know anyone who goes to that church?"

The head shaking continued. "I'm not really from here, you know?"

"Me neither." Gurney paid for the orange juice and left.

By the time he'd put the last few scattered houses of Bastenburg in his rearview mirror, he'd finished half his juice and was beginning to feel revived.

His mind kept returning to Peale's embalming room and his efforts to imagine Tate's experience. He realized what he was lacking was a sense of the medical effects of being struck by lightning. There'd surely be a wealth of information on the internet, probably too much. Better to speak directly with someone. But whom?

Fallow would be convenient, but he might slant the facts in his own self-interest. And pathologists in general might not be the ideal experts on this situation, since they knew mainly about victims who'd died, not survived. He needed to ask someone who would at least be in a position to direct him to the right party.

Rebecca Holdenfield came to mind.

On the positive side, she was an influential psychotherapist, a respected academic, a prolific contributor to the literature on neuropsychology, and she knew *everyone*. She'd worked with Gurney on several cases, and they had a special personal chemistry. On the negative side, there were occasions when that special personal chemistry could have put his marriage at risk. However, he'd always stopped short of making a serious mistake.

At the next place on the road where the shoulder was wide enough he pulled over, took out his phone, found her number, and made the call.

She answered surprisingly quickly. "David?"

"Hey, Becca, how are you?"

"Busy, as always. What can I do for you?" The sound of her voice brought with it an image of her ironic smile, intelligent eyes, and mass of curly auburn hair.

"I'm hoping you might be able to recommend someone. I'm looking for an expert in a couple of unusual areas—survivability of lightning strikes and sudden revivals from deathlike states."

"What do you want to know?"

"It's a long story. You want me to get into the details, or save them for the expert?"

"That could be me."

"You? I didn't realize—"

"I have a long-term therapy patient who was struck by lightning—with fascinating consequences. I also happen to know something about shock-induced comas and seemingly magical resurrections. But if you'd prefer that I find someone else—"

"No need for that. If you have time now, I'll tell you what I'm dealing with."

He related the basic facts of the case, including Tate's fall from the church roof, his embalming room revival, and the evidence of his presence at the Russell, Kane, and Mason murders.

"Remarkable," said Holdenfield after a pause. "So, what do you want to know?"

"To start with, how common is it to survive a lightning strike?"

"Fairly common."

"With no ill effects?"

"I didn't say that. The effects in some cases can be catastrophic, in others superficial. The effects can be muscular or neurologic, straightforward or bizarre."

"Bizarre?"

"A pleasantly bizarre feature might be the appearance of a new talent. An ear for music that the individual didn't have before, a sudden facility with arithmetic, a greater sensitivity to colors. These benign neural realignments are extremely rare. There could also be a personality change. A new propensity for violence, for example. But that's also quite rare. Some brain damage with a variety of functional deficits would be more common. The brain is an electrochemical organ. A massive voltage surge can wreak havoc."

"Okay. Question number two. What might cause a physician to pronounce a living person dead? I've read stories of supposed 'corpses' coming to life in morgues. It does happen. But why?"

"In this case, the high-voltage effect of the lightning and the severe impact of the fall may have resulted in a profound state of shock that caused temporary suppression of respiratory and cardiac function. And there are possible issues affecting the physician—overwork, exhaustion, environmental distraction, chemical impairment. Plus the subtle factor of expectation."

"Say that again?"

"Expectation. The trauma may appear so severe—*so necessarily fatal*—that the physician's assumption of death plays an oversized role in his judgment. Research shows that expectations affect the mind's interpretation of physical data."

"That's helpful. At least it puts things in a rational context."

She laughed. "I like that. Could be a new slogan for my therapy practice."

"I have a soft spot in my heart for rationality. How are you, by the way?"

"Thriving, racing, juggling. Dodging the bullets that come with success. What are you up to? I thought you were back teaching at the academy, not out on the trail of the walking dead."

"I'm doing both."

"Glad to hear it. Busy is good. Speaking of which, I need to get to my next appointment. Nice hearing from you, David. Take care."

He reopened his container of mini-mart orange juice, finished what was left, and resumed his journey home. He was heading south now, through an area of wild meadows alternating with freshly plowed farm fields, all bathed in a strange light. There was a gap between the dense cloud cover and the western horizon, allowing the radiance of the setting sun to flood out across the landscape, creating an upside-down world in which the warm glow of the earth contrasted weirdly with the sky above it. Its strange effect on his mood was broken by his phone ringing. He glanced at the screen and saw Slovak's name.

"What's up, Brad?"

"The good news is that the forensics lab broke into Mary Kane's phone. The bad news is it doesn't lead anywhere. She never called anyone, and hardly anyone ever called her. There were only two incoming voice calls in the week before her death. We called the originating numbers. One belongs to a retired librarian in an assisted living place in Virginia. The other was from the service department of the Kia dealer in Bastenburg, letting her know she could pick up her car."

"Any texts?"

"Two, from some kind of nocturnal birding club."

"She saved the texts?"

"Yep. One was a membership renewal reminder. The other was about a website where you can listen to different owl hoots. These people are big on identifying owls by their hoots. You figure that's why she was out on her porch in the middle of the night?"

"Makes as much sense as anything else."

"So, I guess just a harmless old lady in the wrong place at the wrong time."

Gurney said nothing.

"Bottom line, her phone was a dead end. Sorry about that."

"Investigations are full of dead ends, Brad. It's the nature of the beast. How's the press conference going?"

"The conference room is packed. Department personnel had to make room for the media people and their equipment. I don't think the chief was expecting anything this big. But maybe he should have been. When a guy who's supposed to be dead pops out of a coffin and starts slicing throats, you gotta figure the press is gonna eat it up."

Slovak's view of the situation was still on Gurney's mind when, moments before arriving home, he got a call from Morgan.

"Hey, Dave. I know you don't have a TV, but could you take a look at the media websites tonight, especially RAM News?"

"What will I be looking for?"

"After I read my statement, there were questions. The RAM reporter, Kelly Tremain—her attitude gave me a bad feeling about how they'll handle the story. I'll be checking myself, but I'd appreciate your perspective."

"Sure."

"You have my cell number. Also, there's a meeting tomorrow morning at ten sharp with the village board. Lots of concerns, and they want as much of an update as we can give them."

"Should be interesting."

"More likely a total horror."

"Slow down, Mike. Linda Mason's body hanging from that front-loader was a total horror. Tomorrow's meeting won't be a total horror."

He heard Morgan sighing.

23

By the time Gurney had rounded the barn and was heading up through the low pasture to the house, it was nearly eight thirty. Dusk was beginning to decline into night. As he was parking the Outback by the side door, there was just enough light remaining for him to notice garden stakes and bright yellow string demarcating a rectangular area adjacent to the side of the chicken coop.

He got out of the car for a closer look. The marked-off area looked to be about twelve by twenty feet. Possibly, he thought with a touch of dismay, the right size for an alpaca shed.

When he went into the house, he sensed the unique silence that seemed to fill it when Madeleine was out. There was a note on the refrigerator door.

> If you haven't eaten already, there's asparagus in the fridge, shrimp defrosting on the counter by the sink, and a box of farro by the rice cooker. I should be home by 10:00 p.m.
>
> Love, Me

The note made him smile. Like most contacts with Madeleine, it nudged, at least for a moment, the rest of his life into perspective.

He went to the bathroom, washed his hands and face, kicked off his shoes in favor of a pair of slippers, did a few stretching exercises to loosen muscles that had stiffened in the car, and returned to the kitchen.

After reading the directions on the box, he put farro, water, butter, and salt in the rice cooker and turned it on. He shelled the shrimp and put a handful of asparagus spears in a bowl for the microwave. Then he went into the den and woke up his laptop.

It was 9:01 p.m. when he accessed the livestream section on the RAM News website.

The graphic pyrotechnics of the opening teasers were underway. Over a strident drumbeat soundtrack, letters were whirling in from all sides of the screen to form headlines:

—RAM NEWSBREAKER—

HORRIFYING MURDER SPREE

DID SATANIC KILLER RISE FROM THE DEAD?

Those words burst into jagged pieces, only to reform in a second series of headlines:

RURAL TOWN TERRIFIED

MAN STRUCK BY LIGHTNING BREAKS OUT OF COFFIN

VICTIMS' THROATS CUT

These words in turn flew off the screen, revealing a TV news desk under a red-white-and-blue RAM logo. A neatly groomed TV anchor was sitting at a three-quarter angle to the camera, holding a pen and gazing with concern at his clipboard. Gurney recognized him from RAM's overheated coverage of the White River murders. His anchor partner at the time was Stacey Kilbrick, a RAM star who suffered an on-screen breakdown at the gruesome finale of that case.

As the camera moved in, he lowered his clipboard, looked up, and began speaking in a voice that seemed too thin to support the gravity of his tone.

"Good evening. I'm Rory Kronck. We have a huge story for you tonight regarding the terrifying events in the once-tranquil village of Larchfield, New York. Our own Kelly Tremain is there right now. We'll get her live report in just a moment. First, I'll bring you up to speed on this mind-boggling situation."

He turned in his seat to face the camera head-on. "Our story begins on a stormy night with Billy Tate—a known practitioner of witchcraft—climbing onto the roof of his village church. As he was spray-painting a satanic symbol on the steeple, he was struck by lightning and hurled to the ground below—killed instantly, according to the county medical examiner. His body was moved to a nearby mortuary. His next of kin arrived in the wee hours of the morning and asked that the body be placed in a closed coffin, pending a decision on its final disposition. The closed and latched coffin was placed in a storage unit, where it remained throughout the day."

Kronck paused for dramatic effect. "Later that evening something bizarre occurred. Billy Tate came back to life. RAM News has obtained a copy of the video from the security camera at Peale's Funeral Home. The sounds you will hear are those of Billy Tate attempting to break out of that closed coffin. A word of warning. If you suffer from claustrophobia, you may find this extremely disturbing."

The mortuary video had been edited down to its key moments—from the first muffled sounds inside the storage unit to the eerie emergence of the hooded figure into the embalming room, his unsteady movements, his breaking into the glass case and removal of the scalpels, and his disappearance out the back door.

Gurney was wondering how RAM had gotten hold of the video—who had leaked it, with what motive—but those thoughts were interrupted by Kronck's next comments.

"That's the second time I've watched that video, and I still find it bone-chilling, especially the end, when Tate goes off into the night to begin his gruesome murder spree. It's like a scene in a horror movie, except this is real—tragically, frighteningly real." He shook his head, as if he were being forced to face the depravity at the fringes of humanity.

"Okay," he said with sudden resolve. "Let's move on to our next video—the press conference held by Larchfield's police chief."

This video opened with Morgan standing at a podium in the headquarters conference room. He was wearing a full-dress uniform with gold chief's stars on his jacket collar. He was holding a sheet of paper with both hands. His anxiety was palpable. Several rows of chairs were set up facing him. All were occupied.

He began reading, stiffly. "The Larchfield Police Department is currently investigating three local homicides: Angus Russell, age seventy-eight; Mary Kane, age seventy; and Linda Mason, age fifty-one. An APB has been issued for William 'Billy' Tate, age twenty-seven, a suspect in all three homicide cases. Tate was initially believed to have been killed in a freak accident, but new evidence suggests that he may have survived."

Morgan looked up from the paper. "If anyone has any information concerning Tate's whereabouts, please get in touch with us as soon as possible. A special phone number has been added to our website. You'll find the number at LarchfieldPDHQ.net. One important caution—these homicides were heinous and unspeakably violent acts. The suspect should be considered extremely dangerous. Do not under any circumstances approach the suspect. If you see him, or know where he is, call us immediately. Thank you."

Hands were raised. Several voices called out simultaneously. A sharp female voice cut through the others. "How does your medical examiner explain his mistake?"

Morgan was gripping the podium as if steadying the steering wheel of a bus. "We have no comment on that at this time."

The sharp voice persisted. "There's a rumor that Tate belonged to a satanic cult. Did that play a part in these killings?"

Morgan shook his head. "I'm not going to comment on hypothetical speculation."

"What about his alleged history of incest? Is that connected to these crimes?"

It was becoming clear that RAM had been given, in addition to a copy of the mortuary video, inside details of the case. Morgan responded with a deer-in-the-headlights look, and RAM chose that moment to freeze the video clip before switching back to the news desk.

"Wow, a rocky moment there for the police chief," said Kronck with a smirk. "Those probing questions came from our own Kelly Tremain. Good work, Kelly! Now, let's go live to Larchfield—to the scene of Billy Tate's supposedly fatal accident. Kelly is about to interview a controversial local preacher with a reputation for confrontation."

The scene shifted to the street in front of St. Giles Church, where a thirtysomething woman with blond hair, a red blazer, and a microphone was standing next to a compact man who appeared to be in his late fifties. He had a gray pompadour, shrewd eyes, and an oily smile. Behind them the front of the church was illuminated by a streetlight just visible at the side of the screen. The woman faced the camera with a concerned frown and raised her microphone.

"I'm just a few feet from the church where earlier this week Billy Tate was knocked from the roof by a bolt of lightning and pronounced dead at this very spot by the county medical examiner. Directly across from me, on the other side of this beautiful village square, is Peale's Funeral Home—where Tate later broke out of his locked coffin and disappeared into the night. Since then, three Larchfield residents have been killed, and the young man who some are saying actually rose from the dead is the prime suspect. I've been joined here by the Reverend Silas Gant, pastor of the Church of the Patriarchs in the neighboring town of Bastenburg."

She turned toward him. "Thank you for joining us on such short notice, Reverend. Let's get right to it. What we've been hearing is shocking beyond belief, and we're having a hard time getting public officials to confirm or deny anything. Do you have any idea what's really happening in this supposedly crime-free village?" She held the microphone in front of him.

"I do, Kelly. I absolutely do. But first let me say that I appreciate the opportunity to speak directly to folks who have the good sense to be relying on RAM News—one of the few information sources we can trust in this beleaguered nation of ours."

Kelly Tremain nodded a proud smile of agreement.

Reverend Gant continued, "The people in power aren't explaining the situation for the simple reason that they're not able to. This is so far beyond their understanding, they're paralyzed by confusion. But the fact is, what's happening is exactly what I've been predicting. Satan is loose in the land. I do not speak metaphorically. I am speaking literally of the Devil—risen up from hell, waging war on the righteous. Kelly, you and I know that this view of the world is not popular in the mainstream media—the media that's full of lies and false gods, the media that has become the shameless voice and servant of Satan. Satan residing in hell may be out of our reach, Kelly, but Satan on earth, Satan in the flesh, is a proper target for the army of the righteous. This war is ours to win. We are armed and ready for battle. And we welcome to our ranks all who are willing to take up arms in the cause of righteousness."

Tremain's smiling agreement was mixed now with a touch of uncertainty. "I must say, Reverend, your determination is . . . remarkable. Let me ask you: Do you see Billy Tate as part of the evil you're describing?"

"Kelly, Tate is dead. Struck dead in the very spot where we stand. An incestuous boy, grown into a demented man, an abettor of witchcraft. Dead as a doornail!"

Tremain's mouth was slightly open. The uncertainty in her expression was turning into confusion. "We do have a video of Tate, a video that shows—"

Gant cut her off. "That shows a hooded figure, risen from the dead. But it was not Billy Tate! It was Satan you saw in that video! Satan who is now loose in Larchfield. It is Satan who hides and creeps in the night, slaughtering the righteous. But we will find and destroy him! We will defeat all who harbor and condone him. Armageddon is upon us. Those who give succor to Satan shall taste vengeance at the hand of the Church of the Patriarchs. This attack on godliness will not go unanswered. The battle lines are drawn. We invite all the righteous to join us. In this final hour, those who are not with us are against us."

Tremain turned to the camera. "The Reverend Silas Gant, founder of the Church of the Patriarchs, speaking with me live here in Larchfield. Back to you, Rory."

The scene shifted to the news desk. Kronck was leaning back in his chair, as if blown there by a gust of wind. A balding, brown-skinned man with thick glasses was sitting next to him

"Wow," said Kronck. "Strong stuff. Now, moving along to our own RAM medical expert with a different angle on this shocking story—the strange effects of being struck by lightning. Welcome, Doctor Lou."

"Thanks, Rory. Glad to be here."

"We all know that being struck by lightning can cause terrible damage, including death. But I've heard in some cases the effects can be truly mind-boggling."

"Absolutely right, Rory. The examples are few, but they are truly amazing. The tremendous voltages involved—one hundred, two hundred, three hundred kilovolts—can totally rearrange the chemistry of the brain."

"Possibly for good? Possibly for evil?"

"Either way. Toss of the coin."

Kronck pivoted in his chair to face the doctor. "So, is it conceivable that the brain realignment caused by a lightning strike could turn an already unbalanced person into a killer?"

"I'll say this, Rory. Rewire the brain with a potentially fatal electrical jolt, and just about anything could happen."

"Wow! Thanks for coming by, Doctor Lou. You never fail to give us something to think about."

Kronck swiveled back to the camera. “In just a moment we’ll be getting another startling perspective on this remarkable case. But first, these important messages.”

“Has he lost his mind?”

Madeleine’s voice surprised Gurney. He turned from his computer screen to find her standing in the doorway. “I didn’t hear you come in.”

“Why are you watching this?”

“It’s related to the case I’m working on.”

“You’re kidding.”

“I wish I was.”

She came and stood behind his chair, watching in silence as a commercial pitchman explained the vital importance of a home security system—a necessity at a time when “our borders are crumbling, our police are under attack, and violent criminals are running loose in the land.” Immediate protection was just a phone call away.

“Yuck,” muttered Madeleine.

When the commercial ended, Kronck reappeared, the weight of his tone once again an awkward burden for his weak voice. “The sinister events in Larchfield have captured the attention of Karl Kasak, top investigative reporter on RAM’s *Crimes Beyond Reason*—the series that explores the weird, the paranormal, and the inexplicable. Karl is on his way to Larchfield as we speak. Here’s his take, recorded earlier this evening, on this developing story.”

A video came on showing a man standing next to an open car door in a parking garage. He had thick black hair brushed back from a low forehead and a gritty look of determination. A safari jacket with the sleeves rolled up created a hands-on, high-energy impression. He began speaking as the camera zoomed in.

“Karl Kasak here. I’m heading to a small rural village in upstate New York—where people claim a dead man is stalking the living—a dead man who is now the prime suspect in three ghastly killings. Can the dead come back to life? Can the dead murder the living? Those are the questions we’ll be asking. Get the shocking answers on the next edition of *Crimes Beyond Reason*.”

Madeleine seemed nonplussed. “This nonsense—this is your case?”

“Yep.”

“There’s actually a debate over whether the person walking around killing people is dead or alive?”

“Debates raise ratings. Especially absurd ones. Of course, the simple explanation is that the medical examiner was wrong. Nothing bizarre at all, just a major error."

"I still don't get it. They said your suspect broke out of a *coffin*? So it wasn't just the ME's error? The mortuary person also screwed up?"

"Apparently."

"What about heart function, lung function, brain activity, livor mortis, rigor mortis? Wasn't anyone paying attention to anything?"

"It seems to have been a perfect-storm situation. The subject was hit by lightning, fell off a roof, and evidently suffered temporary cardiac and respiratory arrest. CPR was attempted and discontinued. It was dramatically increasing blood loss, and the subject's neck and chest bones appeared to be broken. Ditto for the defib efforts. The local doctor, who's also the county's part-time ME, claimed that the absence of vitals, the failure of CPR and defib efforts, along with catastrophic traumas to the body, led to a reasonable pronouncement of death."

"What about the mortuary?"

"The funeral director claims he was just providing temporary storage for the body, pending further decisions. The subject wasn't stripped, so the presence or absence of livor mortis was never determined. As for rigor, that wouldn't have been present when the body was brought to him, and it wasn't noted when the body was transferred to a coffin several hours later. But that may have been attributed to the refrigeration in the storage unit."

"But this person was actually still alive—in a lightning-induced coma?"

"So it seems. There's a video documenting his revival and departure from the mortuary. Plus evidence of his presence at other locations later that night."

"I've never heard of an ME making that kind of mistake. Was he impaired?"

"The possibility was raised by the funeral home owner. He told us the ME smelled of alcohol. Made a pretty forceful accusation. Which the ME forcefully denied. There's no way at this point to establish the truth."

"It would explain a lot."

"Maybe, but it wouldn't make catching our killer any easier. That craziness on RAM News is no help, either. They'll have the peasants out with pitchforks, hunting for zombies."

Madeleine's expression darkened. "That's not funny. The peasants these days have assault rifles."

24

Gurney's attempts to sleep that night were repeatedly interrupted—first by wind in the thicket outside their bedroom windows, then by lashing rain. When he did finally doze off just before dawn, the sounds of the storm stirred up troubled dreams, then morphed into the sound of his alarm.

He showered, dressed, made himself a quick cup of coffee, and was about to leave a note for Madeleine when she came into the kitchen in her pajamas.

"You're heading back to that awful place?"

"I'm meeting Jack Hardwick first at Abelard's. He knows some things about Larchfield from his days with the state police."

She inserted a breakfast-blend coffee pod in the top of the coffee maker and placed her favorite mug at the bottom. "I switched the Winkler dinner to tomorrow evening. Okay?"

"Tomorrow's fine."

She peered steadily at the coffee maker as her mug was slowly filled. "You never mentioned the string."

She waited.

"Oh, yes. The yellow string rectangle off the side of the coop. I was going to ask you about that."

"I'm building an extension."

"*You* are?"

"You're obviously too busy. I think I learned enough about structure-framing when I was volunteering at Habitat."

"This extension is for . . . what exactly?"

"Could be for anything. Maybe just more chickens. It'll be an interesting challenge."

Gurney glanced up at the old regulator clock on the kitchen wall. He needed to leave if he was going to meet Hardwick on time. He suppressed an itch to ask more questions about the extension, gave Madeleine a hug and a kiss, and headed out to his car.

Abelard's, once a grungy general store in the tiny village of Dillweed, had over the past few years been gentrified into an artsy cafe through the efforts of a Brooklyn transplant by the name of Marika. The dusty displays of canned vegetables, BBQ-flavored potato chips, and two-liter bottles of off-brand colas had been replaced by imported pastas, freshly baked scones, and a remarkable variety of "artisanal" beverages. It was becoming a favorite breakfast spot for the area's clique of weekending city hipsters.

When Gurney pulled into the parking area, Hardwick's 1970 Pontiac GTO was already there. The hulking brutishness of the old muscle car, born half a century ago and in serious need of repainting, contrasted mightily with the sleek BMW and Audi roadsters next to it.

Hardwick was sitting at a small table toward the back of the place. Marika—eye-catching in blue spiked hair, scoop-neck blouse, and skintight shorts—was operating an espresso machine on a side counter. Heading for Hardwick, Gurney passed two tables occupied by slim men with expensive haircuts and neat beards.

It had been nearly a year since he'd seen Hardwick, but the man always looked the same. The compact, muscular body in black tee shirt and jeans; the hard face; the unnerving pale-blue eyes of an Alaskan sled dog. And, of course, the attitude.

"Gurney, I am so fucking impressed! First, you're an NYPD homicide hotshot. Then you move up here and show the locals how to wipe their asses. And now you're in charge of tracking down a zombie. I am in awe."

Gurney sat down at the table. "Hello, Jack."

"Is there something in the water up there in Larchfield? From what I hear, it sounds like goddamn mass psychosis."

"You've been exposed to the fanciful news reports?"

"*Fanciful?* More like fucking insane. Some Satan-loving loon got struck by lightning, then rose from the dead and murdered three people—including Angus the Scottish Scumbag? Never heard anything like it."

"The case does have peculiar aspects."

Hardwick laughed—a sound that could have been mistaken for the barking of a large dog. One of the slim bearded men glanced over in alarm.

"I saw your police chief's press conference. He looks like a nervous wreck I ran into at an interagency clusterfuck on the Piggert case. This the same guy?"

"Yes."

"That lip-biter is Larchfield's top cop?"

"Yes."

"The fuck did that happen?"

"Long story. I don't know all of it."

"How'd he rope you into this shit?"

"Another long story."

"That one I want to hear."

"First, I need some coffee." He caught Marika's eye on her way back from delivering what looked like cappuccinos to the bearded men.

She smiled her gorgeous smile. "Double espresso?"

"Good memory. It's been a long time."

"Too long." She went to the machine, put in some beans, and turned on the grinder.

Hardwick flashed his ice-glitter grin at Gurney. "So, talk. What the fuck are you doing in Larchfield?"

"I got a call from Morgan. Hadn't heard from him since he got pushed out of the department."

"For what?"

"Wrong women, wrong circumstances, wrong everything."

"No surprise. I remember at the Piggert clusterfuck he had that injured-little-boy look. Some women love it."

"Thing is, when he got pushed out, he landed on his feet. Somebody connected him to Angus Russell, and Russell picked him for the top security job at a college in Larchfield, then moved him a year later into the police chief job. Nice spot, quiet village, no real crime—until all hell broke loose a few days ago."

"That's when the vulnerable little boy called you?"

"Right. Sensational murder, turmoil in paradise, his major protector dead and gone, job on the line, self-esteem in the toilet—please help me, please help me."

"Why didn't you tell him to go fuck himself?"

"That could be awkward with a former partner who once saved my life."

Hardwick's expression didn't exactly warm up. Warmth was not a thing with him. But he did take a slow breath and nod. "A factor to be considered. So, what do you want from me?"

"Information, mainly. Larchfield being in the same state police district where you were stationed, I thought you might know something about it."

"I do. Horrible fucking place. Angus Russell was the lord, Larchfield was his manor. The local snobs ate it up. The fantasy of gentility."

"Did he have enemies?"

"Of course he did. Which is why he came to the attention of BCI to begin with. But the investigation went nowhere."

"What investigation?"

"Five, six years ago Russell got into a nasty bidding war for a prime piece of property over on Lake Champlain. Then the other bidder disappeared, and Russell got the property."

"Disappeared? Just like that?"

"Just like that. The investigation went nowhere. No proof of foul play. No law against disappearing. But the missing guy's wife hired a private detective to look into Russell's past, and he came up with something that looked interesting. A few years earlier, a developer up near Rochester was suing Russell for multimillions over a deal gone bad. He also disappeared without a trace."

"That must have gotten BCI's attention."

"Briefly. Thing is, the guy who disappeared had his own legal problems—people suing him like he was suing Russell—and there was the fact that his mistress disappeared at the same time. No evidence of forced abduction. The possibility that he decided to start a new life in a different part of the world seemed a reasonable explanation. Case closed."

"The echo of the first disappearance wasn't enough to keep the case going?"

"Against one of the state's biggest political contributors? You kidding?"

"Russell spread his money around?"

"Wherever it would buy leverage."

"Did he have any local adversaries?"

"The most visible one was Larchfield's little prick of a mayor."

"Chandler Aspern?"

"Bingo. Eyes like little round deer turds."

"Any idea what their conflict was about?"

"Bad chemistry? Type A jerks banging heads?"

"How about Billy Tate? You know anything about him?"

"Nada. Never made it onto the state police radar screen while I was there. Any problems must have been dealt with at the local or county level. But RAM News claims he's your murder suspect, so it must be true, right? Any leads?"

Gurney shook his head. "Possible sightings. An eccentric girlfriend we're staking out. But nothing that's moving the needle."

"Loners are a bitch to track down."

Marika arrived with Gurney's double espresso and a couple of her home-baked anisette cookies. "Free gift," she said. "So you remember to come by more often."

Hardwick watched as she walked away. "That woman could make a man question the wisdom of being in an exclusive relationship."

That brought to Gurney's mind an image of Esti Moreno, Hardwick's live-in girlfriend. If one were going to have an exclusive relationship, one could do a hell of a lot worse than Esti. He took a long sip of his strong coffee. "How about the Reverend Silas Gant? You know anything about him?"

"Vile son of a bitch. Figured out that religion is the perfect shield from the law. The conclusion at BCI was that he had income streams from a gun business, a conspiracy-theory website, and evangelical money-grubbing. Amazing the phony shit you can sell for real money if you call it religion. Basically, a total scumbag with bought-and-paid-for politicians in his pocket."

"Is that Church of the Patriarchs storefront in Bastenburg his headquarters?"

"Sort of. He's also got a twenty-five-acre fortified compound in the woods outside town. Registered as tax-free church property. It's really an armed-to-the-teeth loony bin—and a harem for the polygamous patriarchs."

It struck Gurney that Gant's compound must be the entity Mike Morgan's wife had been trying to shut down before she fell ill. He was trying to remember exactly what Morgan had told him when he noticed Hardwick studying him with a sardonic little tilt of his head.

"Something on your mind, Jack?"

"A few minutes ago you said what you wanted from me was *mainly* information."

"So?"

"So, that's got me wondering . . . what *else* do you want?"

Gurney saw no reason to tiptoe around the scenario lurking in the back of his mind, however remote it might be. Better to just say it. "Backup. Just in case I need it."

"You mean in case Larchfield PD isn't up to providing it?"

"Like I said, just in case."

Hardwick reacted with a cool smile. "Light or heavy artillery?"

"Too early to say. I just have an uncomfortable feeling that whatever is going on in that fancy little village might be worse than it seems."

"Worse than a zombie running around cutting people's throats?" Hardwick's smile broadened. There was a glint in the ice-blue eyes. The man had a natural hunger for a challenge.

25

During the hour-long drive to Larchfield, the rain, which had stopped shortly after dawn, began again. Gurney's thoughts wandered between the disquieting information Hardwick had given him about Angus Russell's business dealings and his own concerns about Morgan's reasons for drawing him into the case.

It was probable that Morgan's motivation was more or less as he had described it, but Gurney couldn't help wondering if the man might, in some as-yet-undisclosed way, be planning to collect on the debt incurred in the Bronx shoot-out.

Is there some aspect of the case he's expecting me to approach in a way favorable to him because of what I owe him? Am I supposed to extricate him from a tangle he's gotten himself into? Am I getting sucked into a cover-up? Or am I being as paranoid as he seems to be?

Convinced that questions about Morgan's motives were, for the present, unanswerable, he finally managed to push them aside.

By the time he arrived in Larchfield, the rain had stopped but dark clouds remained. In his dour mood, they reminded him of wads of dirty cotton.

There were two media vans in front of police headquarters. He found a third in the rear parking area, along with several private cars. Among them was Mayor Aspern's dark blue BMW.

As soon as Gurney opened the door of the Outback, a blond woman in a red blazer came hurrying toward him from the van, followed by a video tech.

"Can I ask you just one question?"

It was by her sharply distinctive voice—as much as by the blazer and mass of blond hair—that he recognized RAM's Kelly Tremain. He smiled at the "just one question" gambit. It provoked curiosity, seemed easy to deal with, and was hard to say no to.

"No," said Gurney pleasantly.

"Just one quick question, David!" she called after him as he was walking out of the parking area.

He wondered for a moment how she'd gotten his name, but it wasn't worth asking. His involvement could have been leaked by whoever had leaked the mortuary video. Or by someone else. RAM might even have rapid facial recognition software on their satellite vans. It didn't really matter. The notion that one's identity could be kept secret was, like most forms of personal privacy, a relic of a departed era.

The headquarters desk sergeant—an overweight man with a shaved head, walrus mustache, and uniform buttons strained to the popping point—directed him to Morgan's office.

A discreet brass plate on the door bore the words CHIEF OF POLICE.

Gurney knocked, and Morgan's voice replied, "Come in."

Although much smaller than the conference room, Gurney noted that the walls and furnishings were of the same lustrous mahogany. In addition to a substantial desk and several bookcases, there was a round table with six chairs encircling it. Morgan was standing behind one of them. Brad Slovak and Kyra Barstow were seated across from each other.

"Join us," said Morgan, gesturing to one of the empty chairs. "We need to review the case status before I meet with the village board. I've asked Brad and Kyra to update us. You want coffee?"

"Just had some." Gurney took a seat at the table.

"Okay. Brad, you're up."

Slovak stretched his thick neck from side to side, then ran both hands back over his bristly scalp. "First the simple stuff. Stakeout guys in the woods keeping an eye on the Cursen place reported no activity last night, then one car arriving this morning. Plate check made the registration in the name of Harold Stern. There's a Harold Stern in an Albany law firm. Garbel, Stern, Harshman, and Black. Could be she anticipates a problem, wants some on-site advice."

"Too bad," said Morgan. "Any responses to our APB?"

"Zilch. Some requests for clarification, but no leads. Opposite of the deluge of calls triggered by that RAM News thing last night, with the leaked video. People are spotting Tate everywhere, at opposite ends of the county at the same time. You know what I think is gonna happen? Crazy teenagers dripping red paint on their hoodies and trying to scare the shit out of people. Somebody's likely to get shot, the way Gant's stirring things up."

"That's all we need," muttered Morgan. "Anything from the local door-to-doors?"

"Nothing new."

He turned to Kyra. "Any forensic results?"

"Fingerprints at both the Kane and Mason homicides have been ID'd as Billy Tate's. Sneaker prints on the dusty floor of the Mason barn match the sneaker prints at the mortuary and the image of the sneaker soles in the video of Tate on the stretcher in front of the church. The message on the wall of Linda Mason's house was written in her own blood type, DNA confirmation to come. The blood appears to have been applied with a narrow, disposable sponge brush. We didn't find any similar brushes in the house or barn, so it's likely Tate came prepared."

Morgan looked across the table at Gurney. "What do you make of that?"

"An interesting combination of lunacy and logic."

Morgan nodded uneasily. "Is that it, Kyra?"

"For now."

"Dave, you have any questions?"

"I do." He turned to Slovak. "When computer forensics got into Mary Kane's phone, what did they look for?"

"Phone and text messages, sent and received. That was the point, right?"

"It might be worth checking to see if she used the phone as a recorder."

"Recording her calls?"

"I've been thinking about that nocturnal birding club that texted her."

"The owl club?"

"Right. You said one of the texts referred to a website where she could listen to birdcalls. I thought if she was interested in that sort of thing, it could be the reason why she had the phone out on the porch with her in the middle of the night—to record the calls, hoots, whatever, of owls. I doubt she was expecting an urgent call at two in the morning."

Slovak blinked in puzzlement. "You want to know if she recorded any owl hoots?"

"If she had her phone out there to record those sounds, and if that function was on when she was killed, something useful may have been recorded. It's a long shot, but easy enough to check."

"Will do."

Morgan cast a nervous glance at his watch. "Thanks, all. Let me know the instant anything significant comes up."

Realizing they'd been dismissed, Slovak and Barstow left the office.

Morgan put on a grim smile. "Now we face the village board. Expect the worst. It consists of Ron Fallow, Danforth Peale, Chandler Aspern, Hilda Russell, Harmon Gossett, Martin Carmody, and Gifford Styles. Gossett is the village attorney, sharp as a razor, with the warmth and charm of a corpse; Carmody is the retired CEO of a PR agency; Styles is an old-money idiot Angus installed on the board to give himself an extra vote. You ready for this?"

"I was told this morning that a couple of individuals who had business conflicts with Angus conveniently disappeared off the face of the earth. Is that true?"

Morgan shook his head. "The way you're saying it makes it sound terrible. There was never even the slightest evidence of Angus's involvement in anything . . . anything like the way you're making it sound. There wasn't a speck of proof that those so-called 'disappearances' were anything other than voluntary—and unrelated to Angus."

"But you are aware of these incidents."

"Yes, but not with the meaning you're implying."

"You didn't think they were worth mentioning to me?"

"To be totally honest, no. I mean, what's the relevance of a pair of wild allegations from years ago? What connection could they have to this homicidal rampage by Billy Tate?"

"I have no idea. But it's the kind of thing I like to think about."

Morgan stared at him for a moment, then looked down at his watch, cleared his throat, and said, "We better get to our meeting."

26

With these crisis inventors, these professional liars, these cable news buffoons trying to persuade the world that life in Larchfield is some kind of horror movie . . ."

Chandler Aspern was speaking as Morgan and Gurney entered the conference room. He was sitting at one end of the rectangular table, and the six other members of the village board were seated across from each other, three on each side.

Morgan and Gurney took the two empty chairs at the end of the table opposite Aspern.

"We need to get control of the public narrative," continued Aspern. "With the wild exaggerations and crazy theories promoted by the media, the image of Larchfield is going to hell in a handbasket."

Nods of agreement came from Martin Carmody and Gifford Styles.

Aspern went on. "That RAM program last night was appalling. And the headlines this morning were worse. 'The Dead Walk on Harrow Hill'—that was the top story in my news feed."

Carmody—well-fed, pink-faced, white-haired—spoke in the rich baritone of an old-time radio announcer. "Something has to be done, and quickly."

Styles, who might have been a geriatric aristocrat displeased with the progress of a polo match, shook his head. "This is intolerable. Tate isn't even from Larchfield. He's from Bastenburg. Deliberate slandering of our village. Must be stopped."

He glared across the table at Gossett. "Do something, Harmon. You're our bloody lawyer. Take action, man!"

Gossett said nothing. A thin man with thinning hair, he was as expressionless as a fish.

Peale spoke up, an acid edge to his patrician intonation. "The immediate priority should be to plug the leak! We're not going to get anywhere, if things like the Tate video are handed over to the scurrilous media. The damage is incalculable—to the town, and to me personally. Whoever gave that video to RAM wanted us to look like fools."

Although Peale was addressing Gossett, the man again remained silent and unblinking. Fallow's discomfort was obvious in the set of his mouth, but he, too, said nothing.

Aspern looked down the table at Morgan. "Finding the leaker is a job for the police."

"We're looking into it."

Gurney wondered if this was something else Morgan had failed to mention.

"Regarding the broader issue," said Aspern, "we need calm, consistent messaging to counteract the media coverage. Perhaps Martin here, with his background, can help craft that strategy?"

Carmody cleared his throat. "Happy to do what I can. But before I design the suit, I need to know the shape of the body."

Morgan blinked in confusion. "The shape of the body?"

"The raw facts of the case, especially the troublesome ones. Professional tailoring can smooth out a lot of imperfections, so long as we know what they are."

"Troublesome fact number one," snapped Peale, "is that someone who was pronounced dead is very much alive. That colossal error is the basis for these insane 'zombie' headlines and every other damn problem we're facing."

"Damned useless observation," muttered Fallow, giving Peale a black look.

Carmody was nodding attentively, as though this were any other client briefing.

"In my experience," he said, ignoring the obvious tension in the room, "there are three key ingredients in a crisis messaging strategy. Simplicity, the projection of competence, and the appearance of transparency. To begin with, it's important to explain the pronouncement of death as a reasonable diagnosis, based on the available facts. The subject's subsequent revival should be described as an uncommon but far-from-unique event. I'm sure the internet can provide examples of similar revivals. The point is to demystify it and take the air out of the supernatural speculation."

Aspern was smiling. "Simple is good. Down-to-earth. No apologies. No need to get into anything exculpatory—like our medical examiner's crushing workload with all the heroin ODs and autopsies on his plate, et cetera."

"Exactly!" said Carmody. "Basic rule number one: never offer an excuse for an error when the incident can be described in a way that makes it not an error at all, but a case of sound professional judgment misled by a deceptive set of facts."

"I like it," said Aspern. "What do you think, Harmon, from a legal point of view?"

Gossett offered an almost imperceptible nod of approval.

Styles looked like he was developing gas pains.

"Problem, Gifford?" said Aspern.

"All well and good that Fallow is off the hook. Glad, too, that all the 'resurrection' balderdash will be put to rest. But what about the witchcraft angle, the 'satanic' malarkey? Is there a plan for making that go away?"

Carmody nodded. "All part of the same cloth, Gifford. The solution depends on tone and vocabulary. The thing is, we should never use any big, fuzzy, mystical words in public. Stick to hard, small, simple terms. The suspected perp is an ex-con from a bad neighborhood, with a history of threats and assaults. The police are tracking him down. Emphasize practical procedure. The witchcraft angle should be positioned as a silly distraction, not worth discussing. Underscore the point that irrational speculation always aids the criminal. Show a high school photo of the suspect, preferably looking weak and awkward—obviously with no magic powers—a low-grade criminal whose capture is only a matter of time."

Aspern looked down the length of the table at Morgan. "You on board with this?"

Morgan cleared his throat. "No disagreement."

"How about you, Detective Gurney? Anything to say?"

"Be careful you don't minimize the danger. There's a killer on the loose. He's dangerous, clever, efficient, and cold-blooded. And probably not finished."

Aspern blinked. "What do you mean?"

"I think he has plans for more murders."

Several voices were raised at the same time. "How do you know that?"

Gurney didn't want to divulge sensitive facts in what might be a leaky environment. "I can't be specific at this point, but some evidence suggests that Tate has made preparations for additional attacks."

"My God," said Styles. "What sort of preparations? Shouldn't we be told, as a matter of personal safety?"

"Sharing what I'm referring to wouldn't be helpful in that way." He turned his attention to Aspern. "But there is something that should be added to any public information statements from your office or from the department—a request for anyone who was ever threatened by Tate to come forward."

Aspern looked alarmed. "Why do you say that?"

"Tate threatened to kill Angus Russell, and Angus Russell is dead. He threatened to kill Linda Mason, and Linda Mason is dead. His past threats should not be ignored."

Aspern's small eyes widened. "He threatened me."

"When?"

"Not too long after he got out of prison. Right after Selena Cursen bought him that orange Jeep. I caught him driving it on my trails."

"What happened?"

"I told him to get the hell off my property. He said anyone who claimed to own Harrow Hill deserved to die."

"Did you report that to the police?"

Aspern shook his head. "I assumed it was just talk."

As the meeting broke up, Carmody left with Aspern. Gurney approached Hilda Russell—who hadn't said a word at the meeting—as she was preparing to leave. A sturdy woman with short white hair clinging closely to her large head, she was wearing a plain gray suit over a black turtleneck. The suit accentuated the squareness of her physical presence.

"Reverend Russell?"

"Hello, Detective Gurney." There was intelligence in her bright blue eyes.

They smiled and shook hands. Hers was strong and surprisingly rough.

"I was wondering—" he began.

"If you could speak with me later today? Pick a time."

"Half an hour from now?"

"Here or at the parsonage?"

"The parsonage sounds more interesting."

"See you then." She walked out of the conference room, light on her feet for a woman of such solidity.

Besides Morgan and Gurney, the only other attendee still present was Dr. Ronald Fallow. He was wearing the same blue blazer he'd worn at the Kane crime scene. He was standing by his chair, swiping through a series of screens on his phone. The general resentment that had been on his face for most of the meeting had changed to an emotion Gurney couldn't readily label.

Morgan turned to Gurney. "That business about your finding evidence that Tate is planning more murders—what on earth was that all about?"

"What I found is purely suggestive. But it's nagging at me. Tate used Linda Morgan's blood to leave that Dark Angel message on the wall. That message required at the most two ounces of blood. But more than ten times that amount was drained from her body and removed from the site. It doesn't prove anything, but it does suggest a forward-looking plan of some sort."

"So you think we're just at the beginning of—"

He was interrupted by Fallow, who was approaching them, phone in hand.

"Chief, I found something that may be of interest. Something that's been bothering me ever since the Russell autopsy. The placement of the severed finger. Something about it was tugging at a memory."

He held up the phone. The screen showed a photo of a gray-haired, stone-jawed man in a courtroom witness chair, his forefinger pointing dramatically at someone or something.

"Angus," muttered Morgan, half to himself, half to Gurney.

"Yes," said Fallow. "When Billy Tate was on trial for making threats. Russell was asked by the prosecutor if he could identify the individual who had threatened him. Angus pointed directly at Tate. Do you know what happened next?"

Morgan shook his head.

"When Angus pointed at him, Tate shouted, 'How about I rip that finger off and shove it up your ass?' Interesting coincidence, is it not?"

27

Although St. Giles was just the proverbial stone's throw across the village square from police headquarters, Gurney decided to take his car. He had a notion that, after speaking with Angus Russell's bereaved sister, he might head out along Waterview Drive to Mary Kane's house. Sometimes following the route of a killer—driving where he drove, seeing what he saw—led to some unexpected insight. But first, and more concretely, he wanted to get a better reading on Hilda Russell, whose presence in the conference room had told him nothing.

As he was turning into the driveway next to St. Giles Church, he noted some work underway on the path by the corner of the building. Two men were spreading new gravel on the area where Billy Tate had landed. If the large bloodstain on Tate's hoodie were any indication, the gravel under him would have been stained as well, accounting for the cleanup underway.

Gurney followed the driveway to a parking area that separated the church from a large Victorian house, painted in muted shades of blue and gray. A neatly swept bluestone path, purple petunias planted on either side, led from the parking area to the porch steps. A mechanical twist doorbell in antique bronze was set in the center of the front door. As he was reaching for it, the door opened.

"You're right on time," said Hilda Russell, stepping back to let him in. She was still wearing the shapeless gray suit and black turtleneck. "Come this way."

She led him through a dark, wood-paneled center hall to a bright, airy room at the rear of the house. Floor-to-ceiling windows reminded Gurney of the tall windows in Angus Russell's bedroom. They looked out on a tranquil English-style garden, full of spring flowers and weeping cherry trees in blossom. A gardener was pushing a mower along a path through the flower beds.

The cherrywood desk, cabinets, and bookcases in the room were in the simple Shaker style. The brightly upholstered couch and armchairs were large and comfortable-looking. A brick fireplace had been swept clean of ashes. A crystal vase on the mantelpiece was overflowing with jonquils and daffodils.

"Very nice," said Gurney as he took it all in. "Is this your office?"

"It is, but I try to keep it as un-businesslike as possible. Please, have a seat." She gestured toward one of the armchairs by the fireplace.

She took the one that faced it. "So. How can I help you?"

"First, let me offer my condolences. I apologize for the need to bother you with questions at a time like this."

She folded her hands in her lap. "No apologies necessary. Ask whatever you wish."

"You were very quiet in that meeting this morning. I was wondering why."

"My mother's favorite saying was, 'Learn to listen, then listen to learn.' I seem to have made it my own."

He smiled. "Do you live here in the rectory?"

"I do. Upstairs. Comfortable little retreat, all to myself."

"Is that where you were when Tate fell off the church roof?"

"You mean, when Jehovah's thunderbolt struck down the evil instrument of Satan?" Her portentous tone was belied by the spark of sarcasm in her eyes. "Yes. Sound asleep, so I missed all the drama. But I shouldn't joke."

"Why do you suppose he was up there?"

"I assume to spray that symbol on the steeple—emblem of hellfire, or so I've been told."

"Does that shock you, someone doing that to your church?"

"After hearing confessions for nearly forty years, including ten as a prison chaplain, I'm not impressed by a bit of vandalism. More concerning is the way this sort of thing is used by the slick, pompadoured Silas Gants of the world for their own ends."

"How about Tate's revival after being pronounced dead? Were you impressed by that?"

"I might have been more so if it were the first time."

"Beg pardon?"

"Billy has a dark history. Sick relationships surrounded by salacious rumors, none of which am I inclined to discuss. However, as I'm sure you're aware, it's a matter of public record that his father was convicted of shooting Billy and putting him in what was believed to be a vegetative coma. Two days later he opened his eyes, asked where he was and why the hell he was connected to all those damn machines. The doctors couldn't account for it. A miracle, they called it."

"And now there's been another one."

"'Miracle' is a rather imprecise term. I came close to being expelled from the seminary for arguing that it has no real meaning at all."

"What would you call his latest revival?"

"Considering the subsequent events, I'd call it unfortunate." She paused, her gaze on the empty fireplace. "I understand you have evidence connecting him to my brother's murder."

"Does that surprise you?"

Her gaze moved from the fireplace to one of the windows looking out over the flower garden. "Billy was always unbalanced. Predictably unpredictable. Almost certainly suffered from an impulse control disorder, plus a handful of other psychiatric conditions. It's surprising he's survived as long as he has. But murder?" She shook her head. "I wouldn't have said that was likely. Especially not Mary Kane. Everyone loved her. Even Billy, I think."

"But if she recognized him the night of Angus's murder . . . well, self-preservation can be a powerful motive."

"Yes. I know."

"I was told that allegations were made in the past regarding the disappearance of individuals who were involved in conflicts with Angus."

She remained focused on some point in the garden.

"Did those allegations shock you?"

She sighed. "'Shock,' like 'miracle,' is a much-overused word."

"Did you find the accusations credible?"

"I believe that whoever was said to be missing was missing. *Why* they were missing is a different matter. Was Angus instrumental in that? I have no particular reason to believe that he was."

That, thought Gurney, was far from a wholehearted defense of her brother's innocence. He was about to pursue that point when she addressed it herself. "Angus and I were not especially close. The downside of that is the absence of the familial warmth that some siblings enjoy. The upside is objectivity, seeing people for who they are. Angus's values and ambitions were never mine. I know he could be a dangerous man if cornered. His personal desires were paramount in his life, and he had the means to achieve them. Did he have the means to arrange for his enemies to disappear? Certainly. Did he ever do so? I don't know. Perhaps I don't want to know."

Gurney got out of his chair and walked over to the nearest window. A breeze was swaying the thin branches of the weeping cherry trees. "How about Lorinda? What can you tell me about her?"

"Apart from the fact that she's an obvious symptom of Angus's greatest weakness?"

"Lust?"

"Lust was only part of it."

He turned from the window. "Part of what?"

She met his gaze and held it. "His supreme confidence in his own desires. Angus never wanted something because it was good. It was good because he wanted it—and wanting it meant he had to have it, at any cost."

"And Lorinda came at a high cost?"

"Lorinda Strane Russell is what the mindless media would call a trophy wife. She is also a vial of poison, a sociopath, and—if I may use a term from an era long past—a slut."

Gurney returned to his chair. "Meaning she had affairs outside her marriage?"

"She has that reputation."

"Affairs with whom?"

"People who might be useful to her."

"For example?"

"In the absence of proof, it would be slanderous to name names."

Gurney refrained from mentioning that the absence of proof hadn't deterred her from naming Lorinda.

Perhaps sensing the inconsistency, she added, "Sit down with her for an hour. Ask questions. Watch her. Listen to her. You'll quickly discover the kind of animal you're dealing with."

"What can you tell me about Selena Cursen?"

Russell moistened her lips and seemed to relax a bit. "Space cadet."

"That's it?"

"Involved in some Wiccan nonsense. Attracted to bad boys. Besotted with Billy. But underneath it all, an airhead. If it wasn't for the trust fund from her parents, she'd be living in a homeless shelter, staring at profound messages in a kaleidoscope."

"How about Dr. Fallow?"

"Decent enough. Too fond of his country club. Too fond of his single-malt scotches. There's an unfortunate public record of that problem, which I assume you're aware of. Bad luck, his getting caught, especially for a man in his position. So many reckless drunks get away with it again and again. Men a lot worse than Fallow. Unfairness of life."

"What can you tell me about Danforth Peale?"

"W. Danforth Peale the Third—to use the full name—is not nearly as simple as Fallow. He seemed normal enough as a small child. Then he was sent to a snobby elementary school, and the Peale gene for icy arrogance began to assert itself. It grew worse in high school. And by the time he came home from Princeton, he'd reduced his Christian name, William, into that pretentious first initial and was insisting on being addressed by his middle name. He'd also contracted the family disease of entitlement. The one positive thing to be said about him is that he doesn't seem as horrible as his late father, Elton Peale, the coldest man I've ever met. But maybe Danforth is just better at concealing it."

"Sounds charming."

"The Peales are one of the oldest New York families. They amassed a fortune in shipbuilding and slave-trading. They once owned Rolling Hills Preserve, one of the state's largest private land holdings, along with a dozen or so exclusive funeral homes and cemeteries—catering to those very special individuals who demand to be buried with people of their own class. The Peales were the equals of the Russells in wealth and close allies in greedy pursuits."

"Partners in crime?"

"Lots of dark rumors to that effect."

"So Danforth is super-wealthy?"

"Not in Larchfield terms. The Peale family lost most of its fortune and business properties to a Ponzi schemer of impeccable blue-blood provenance. Greed was the engine and destroyer of the family's wealth. Danforth inherited what was left, but has done nothing to increase it. Like many who've been given a lot, he's resentful that he wasn't given more."

"I appreciate your candor," said Gurney.

"What you mean is, you're surprised that a woman of God would speak like this behind the backs of her neighbors. The fact is that just about everything I said to you I've already said to their faces, and would gladly say again. There are many people-pleasers in this world, Detective, but I'm not one of them. I believe my creator put me on earth to tell unpleasant truths." She glanced up at an antique clock on the mantelpiece. "Any other questions?"

"Do you have an opinion of Chandler Aspern?"

She made a lemon-sucking face. "Chandler is just a poor imitation of Angus. The same greed and ruthlessness, with half the intelligence and none of the charm."

"How about Darlene Tate?"

"On the surface, a lubricious drunk. Beneath the surface, a lubricious drunk."

"I gather from your earlier comment that you have no great affection for Reverend Gant. Any particular reason for that?"

Russell unclasped her hands and, leaning forward in her chair, slowly rubbed her palms on the tops of her legs as if preparing her muscles for battle. She delivered her opinion like a battering ram.

"Silas Gant is a virus in the heart of Christianity. A walking, talking malignancy. He promotes racism, hatred, guns, and violence as though they were life's cardinal virtues. His so-called ministry is an ugly joke."

"What's in it for him?"

"Money, publicity, the thrill of stirring up an angry mob. And—if he can grow that mob big enough—a political career. He wouldn't be the first petty demagogue to rise to the heights of power on a wave of ignorant fury."

"You think that's his goal?"

"Everything he does is consistent with building a certain sort of following—resentful fundamentalists who see evil in their enemies, virtue in themselves, and the Bible as a blunt instrument for breaking heads. That constituency, led by a clever psychopath . . ."

Her voice trailed off. She shook her head in a shudder of revulsion before adding, "I'm sorry to say, Angus was one of his largest supporters."

"Really? I didn't think Angus was a particularly generous man."

She startled Gurney with a harsh laugh. "I guarantee you that nothing Angus did was even remotely connected with generosity."

She got up from her chair, which emitted a slight creak when relieved of her weight. "I hope I've been helpful."

"Perhaps we can speak again, if other questions come up?"

"I'm always here, and never too shy to share the truth."

She led Gurney through the dark center hall to the front door and opened it.

As he was about to step out onto the porch, he hesitated. "Hilda is an interesting name, one I haven't heard in a long time. Were you named after anyone in particular?"

"The seventh-century abbess of Whitby Monastery in North Yorkshire. She reputedly had a talent for turning snakes to stone." She flashed a sharp-edged smile. "I envy her."

28

Gurney emerged from the parsonage driveway onto the street that separated St. Giles from the village square. He was about to head for Waterview Drive, as he'd planned, when he noticed three figures coming out of police headquarters, wearing motorcycle leathers.

Two were hulking, bearded men—the ex-lineman types employed as bouncers in rowdy bars. The third man, walking in front of them, was clean-shaven and more compact. Gurney recognized Silas Gant's gray pompadour from his appearance on RAM News.

They went straight to three motorcycles parked in front of the headquarters building, put on their helmets, revved up their engines, and pulled away from the curb, Gant in the lead.

Deciding to postpone his trip to Mary Kane's house, Gurney drove around to the headquarters side of the square and parked in the space vacated by the trio.

He went straight to Morgan's office. He found him at his desk, looking worried as usual, phone in hand. He put it down when Gurney entered.

"I was about to call you. Gant was just here."

"I saw him leaving, with a pair of apes. What did he want?"

"To keep me informed, is what he said. He plans to hold what he called 'a gospel revelation tent meeting' tonight out at the Buckman farm. He told me that members of his Church of the Patriarchs would be providing security."

"He's expecting trouble?"

"So he says—from local Satanists and God-haters."

"What Satanists and God-haters?"

"Good question. He also wanted me to know that his security people would be conducting, in the public interest, their own search for Billy Tate and any fellow travelers supporting Tate's activities."

"And what did you say to all this?"

"I warned him not to get in the way of our official investigation, that any interference could be dangerous, and that it could result in charges of obstruction of justice."

"What did he say to that?"

"He said he would ask the good Lord to take special care of me in the tribulations of the End Days."

"Is this the same creepy character your wife was battling?"

Morgan nodded, looking down at the table as if to avoid the subject.

Slovak knocked on the jamb of the open door.

Morgan looked relieved at the interruption and waved Slovak in. "What's up, Brad?"

"We have confirmation of the time connection between the Tate sighting by Ruby-June Hooper and the murder of Mary Kane. Dave's suggestion that we check Kane's phone for audio recordings paid off."

He took a phone out of his jacket pocket, tapped the screen a few times, and laid the phone on Morgan's desk. "According to the time code, this recording was made at 2:10 a.m. the night of Angus Russell's murder—right after Tate's encounter with Hooper."

The recording began to play.

(Sound) Breezes passing through tree foliage.

(Sound) Series of shrill descending birdcall notes.

(Woman's voice) "Eastern screech owl, courtship call."

(Sound) Series of shrill descending birdcall notes.

(Sound) Breezes.

(Sound) Series of shrill descending birdcall notes.

(Woman's voice) "Courtship call from a different direction. Male moving to new perch."

(Sound) Breezes . . . approaching vehicle . . . growing louder . . . slowing . . . stopping.

(Woman's voice) "Oh my goodness! What on earth are you doing out here?"

(Sound) Vehicle door opening. Engine running softly.

(Male voice, indistinct)

(Woman's voice) "Blessed God! What happened to your face?"

(Male voice, indistinct)

(Sound) Series of shrill descending birdcall notes. Breezes. Foliage rustling.

(Woman's voice) "My God, what . . . what's wrong with you?"

(Sound) Quick footsteps.

(Male voice, guttural) "Don't move."

(Woman's voice) "Wha—"

(Sound) Rasping, gagging inhalation. Footsteps. Silence. Breezes. Series of shrill descending birdcall notes. Footsteps. Thud of a heavy object hitting the ground. Dragging of a heavy object on the ground, slowly diminishing.

That harsh, gagging gasp on the recording gave Gurney's image of the murder a vivid reality—worse in its dreadful suddenness than his memory of the woman's body lying in the drainage swale.

Slovak reached down and tapped an icon on the phone's screen. "There's an additional three-minute segment of bird and wind noises—I guess while he was dragging her body across the road—then the sound of his vehicle door being shut and him driving away. Hard to tell from the recording, but it sounds like he made that turn up toward Harrow Hill. The recording continued until the phone battery ran down, but there's nothing else on it."

Gurney turned to Morgan. "Since both women apparently recognized him, why did Ruby-June Hooper get a friendly wave and Mary Kane get her throat cut? That's the key question."

Morgan turned up his palms in an admission of bafflement.

After a moment, Slovak spoke up. "I do have other news. We managed to track down the number of the phone Tate used for the two text messages he sent from the embalming room. It's an anonymous prepaid one, but now that we have the number we can ping it for a current location."

"Is that being done?"

"We're trying it every ten minutes. So far, he's got it turned off."

"Have you found out who he was contacting?"

"Selena Cursen and Chandler Aspern."

"*Aspern?* Are you sure?"

"We have no way of knowing who actually picked up the phone, but the cell number the text was sent to is Aspern's."

"Interesting. You'll want to get copies of both texts. Service providers usually retain them for five days, so you'll need to act quickly."

"Yes, sir. Just one thing. The Jeep that Tate used is actually registered to Cursen. We added the plate number to the APB, but as far as we know, the last people to see it were those stoners the night before you discovered Linda Mason's body. But today we got three reports of churches over in Bastenburg being defaced with that weird figure eight thing, painted in blood. So maybe Tate's got another vehicle."

"Or maybe an accomplice," said Gurney. "Do we know Cursen's whereabouts?"

"I checked with our guys staking out her place. She hasn't left."

"Okay. The priority now is getting in touch with the carrier and requesting copies of the Cursen and Aspern texts."

Slovak nodded and hurried out of the office.

Morgan started rubbing his neck. "That's all we need, more church desecrations. It's the kind of crap Gant loves to shout about."

"You'll want to get the addresses of those churches and send Kyra's team out there—to find out if it's really blood, and if so, whose."

Morgan nodded vaguely. He picked up a pen from his desk, then put it back. "Dave, I want to apologize."

"For what?"

"That business about the disappearance of Angus's business rivals. I honestly didn't think it amounted to anything. But I should have told you. Total openness, right?"

"Apology accepted."

Gurney almost added, "No problem." But that wouldn't have been true. There *was* a problem—Morgan's eagerness to view Russell in a favorable light and ignore the disappearances. It was a classic example of the tendency to view facts in a way that supports one's own needs—a tendency that was always damaging and sometimes deadly.

It made Gurney wonder if Russell had installed Morgan as police chief *because* of his weaknesses, rather than in spite of them. Having an insecure police chief who depended on you could be useful. It was a point he'd need to explore, but this was not the time. There was a depth of misery in Morgan's eyes that seemed to go far beyond the issue at hand.

"Has there been any change in your wife's condition?" Gurney asked.

Morgan shook his head. "She's on hospice. Lot of drugs. Mostly sleeps." He sat up straighter, as if making a physical effort to change the subject. "What's next on your agenda?"

That reminded Gurney where he'd been heading when he was sidetracked by the sight of Gant and his apes emerging from their meeting with Morgan. "I'm going back to the Kane crime scene. Sometimes on a second visit I notice things I missed on the first."

Morgan nodded, his preoccupation obvious.

The weather was changing yet again. Dark clouds were breaking up, revealing areas of blue sky. Wind gusts were shaking the last droplets of rain from the maples on either side of Cotswold Lane. There was an herbal scent in the air. Patches of sunlight illuminated the flower beds in the village square.

Gurney got in the Outback, drove slowly around to the St. Giles side of the square, and headed for Mary Kane's house.

When he got there, he parked across the road next to the swale. The yellow police tape outlining the site had been removed, but a strip had been placed diagonally across the front door of the cottage. Gurney got out of his car and crossed the road. After debating for a minute whether to enter the cottage, he loosened the tape and opened the door.

As soon as he stepped inside, he sensed, even in the semidarkness with the blinds drawn, that something was different. As his eyes adjusted, he saw that the bird pictures that had hung above the couch were now on the floor. In their place, in dark red lettering, were the same words that had been found on the wall in Linda Mason's house.

I AM

THE DARK ANGEL

WHO ROSE

FROM THE DEAD

29

Gurney called headquarters for an evidence tech to process the scene. Kyra Barstow arrived twenty minutes later in her van.

After donning her coveralls and shoe covers and performing a preliminary luminol examination of the living room wall, she confirmed that the red substance used for the lettering was blood and appeared to have been applied with the same type of brush used on Linda Mason's upstairs wall. She then took scrapings for DNA analysis.

She and Gurney conducted a walk-through inspection of the rest of the cottage, but made no further discoveries. Everything appeared to be as it had been the previous day. They then made a similar inspection of the outside of the house and its modest grounds with a similar result. It wasn't until they had completed their circuit of the property and were standing in front of the cottage that Gurney noticed a partial tire track in the soil at the edge of the lawn.

He pointed it out to Barstow. "That wasn't there yesterday, was it?"

"Absolutely not. The body was dragged across that exact area. There's no way we could have missed a tread mark."

She took several photos with her phone, went to her van, got a ruler, laid it next to the impression for scale, and took a few more shots; then went back to the van and began preparing a special dental-stone plaster mixture to pour into the impression and create a solid model of the tread.

While she worked, Gurney went across the road for another look at the place where Mary Kane's body had been found. He made his way around the bordering row of tall bushes and stepped down into the swale. The shade from the bushes and the relative lowness of the ground had left the grass sopping from the overnight rain. Portions of the large bloodstain had been washed away or drawn down into the soil, but the coating of water made the color of the remaining stain redder.

Gurney was overcome by a sudden wave of sadness. He wondered if it was for that old woman he never knew . . . or for himself and everyone else whose final traces would eventually disappear into the wet earth. Before he could fall any deeper into the fears and regrets that come with thoughts of mortality, the ringing of his phone pulled him back.

The screen told him that it was Chandler Aspern. With some misgivings, he took the call.

"Gurney here."

"This is Mayor Aspern. We need to talk."

"You have some information you want to give me?"

"That's one way of putting it. How soon can you be in my office?"

The mayor's peremptory tone was annoying. "How vital is this information to the case?"

"How *vital*? Who the hell knows? The point is, I need to talk to you."

Gurney checked the time on his phone. It was 12:52 p.m.

"I can try to be there around one thirty."

"Fine."

On that curt note, Aspern ended the call. Gurney pocketed his phone, took a last look around the swale, and made his way up through the row of bushes.

Slovak, squinting in the sunlight, was just getting out of a black Dodge Charger, parked behind Gurney's Outback.

"Just got the news at HQ," he said, closing the car door. "Weird that Tate would take the chance of coming back here. You figure it was just to leave a creepy message?"

"If there was another reason, we haven't discovered it yet."

"If he wanted to leave us a message, why didn't he do it the night he killed her?"

"The night he killed her he was on his way to kill Russell. With that on his mind, he may not have wanted to take more time here than he had to. Fear of being discovered, maybe. Sometime yesterday or last night, his other goal may have taken over."

"Other goal?"

"He wants recognition. Common with a certain kind of killer. Ego trip. He wants the name Billy Tate up in lights."

"Man, that is so sick!"

"But possibly helpful to us. Obsession can lead to practical mistakes."

He pointed to Barstow, who was kneeling at the roadside, checking the solidity of the plaster cast. "Tate may have left that partial tire track over there. Could be a key piece of forensic evidence. You need to revisit the owners of the security cameras that captured the earlier videos of Tate's Jeep. If those cameras are still operational, you should review any vehicle or foot traffic they captured between the time the last officer left here yesterday and noon today."

"Will do. By the way, Chief Morgan just got in touch with Hilda Russell, executrix of Angus's estate, and she's providing copies of all his trust and testamentary provisions. Good to have all that, I guess—even though it doesn't seem relevant to the murder. Tate sure as hell isn't one of the beneficiaries."

"Right. But it still might be interesting. Anything else?"

"Not much. A few more idiots over in Bastenburg claiming Tate sightings, asking about a reward. Local cops are checking them out. If anything credible turns up, I'll let you know."

Slovak rubbed his scalp, got in the Charger, made a U-turn, and started driving slowly along Waterview Drive.

Gurney asked Barstow if she needed any help before he had to head back to the village for a meeting with Aspern.

"Not at the moment," she said, gently prying up the solidified cast.

The village hall was one of the three big Victorians on Cotswold Lane. Police headquarters sat in the middle, with Peale's Funeral Home on one side and the village hall on the other.

They were similar in structure, with similar front lawns and a similar profusion of lilacs in front of their porches. In the spacious entry foyer, an unsmiling receptionist, who'd evidently been told to expect him, directed Gurney along a wide center hall to the last office on the right.

The door was open. With its mahogany furniture and paneling, the office looked very much like Morgan's, just larger. Aspern was on the phone with his back to his desk. Gurney rapped sharply on the doorjamb. Aspern swiveled around, nodded, and pointed to a leather-covered chair facing his desk. He ended his call a moment later and showed his teeth in an expression that bore a distant resemblance to a smile.

"Glad you could make it."

"You said you had information."

"I do. And concerns. But first, I want you to know how much I welcome your involvement. You have a hell of a reputation." He showed his teeth again. "Experience, smarts, record of success."

He paused, as if expecting thanks for the compliment, then continued. "So, I have a question. Are you being given all the resources you need?"

"I'm not sure I understand the question." That wasn't true. He understood the question and what was likely behind it, but he wanted to hear how Aspern would explain it.

Aspern leaned back in his oversized chair and glanced at the heavy gold Rolex on his right wrist. "I'm concerned about the agenda of your old partner."

"Agenda?"

"Maybe that's not the best word. Let's call it his mindset. I worry about the mindset and priorities of a man who's been so blind to the dark side of Angus Russell. It suggests stupidity, complicity, or both."

"Tell me about Russell's dark side."

"Surely you're aware by now of the suspicious disappearances?"

"I heard there were allegations regarding two individuals—dismissed for lack of evidence."

"Three, actually. Two in the past five years, another a few years earlier. Very convenient for Angus, this tendency of his enemies to evaporate."

"You're suggesting that Angus had a super-efficient hit man who made all this happen without leaving behind any physical evidence or witnesses?"

"I'm suggesting that the facts speak for themselves. And that your former partner's attitude toward the facts fails to inspire confidence. I'm fond of facts, and my research into your background tells me that you share this fondness."

Gurney said nothing.

"You're giving me that laconic cop stare. You're wondering what my point is, right?"

"I'm sure you'll get to it."

"It's simple enough. Morgan was never the choice of the village board for police chief. He was Angus's choice. But with Angus gone, things will be different. Changes will be made. I guarantee it. The position of police chief will finally be filled the way it should have been—on the basis of experience, ability, integrity, not behind-the-scenes entanglements. A great opportunity for the right person. Something to think about, eh?"

Aspern smiled the beneficent smile of a man with the power to bestow great gifts—while his small dark eyes communicated the depth of self-interest welded to the beneficence.

If he was searching Gurney's face for a sign of gratitude or even of mild interest in what amounted to the offer of a plum job, it wasn't there to be seen. "What's on your mind, Detective?"

"Questions."

"Ask them."

"I'm thinking about Angus Russell's apparent ease in making his enemies disappear. Did you ever wonder if you were on that list?"

"I'm sure I was. I took certain precautions. I'm not without resources. I acquired some information, the publication of which would have created a significant inconvenience for Angus. I informed him of the facts I had gathered and of the instructions I had given to an unnamed law firm—to provide those facts to the media and law enforcement agencies in the event of my untimely death by any other than natural causes. It seems to have been effective."

Gurney considered the implications of that before asking his next question.

"What can you tell me about Lorinda Russell?"

Aspern uttered a harsh laugh. "Wet-dream queen of Larchfield by day, vampire bat by night. You want details, ask Morgan."

Gurney was about to pursue that further when his phone vibrated in his pocket. He took it out and glanced at the screen. It was Morgan. He decided to take the call.

"Gurney here."

The tension in the man's voice sounded more like excitement than his normal anxiety. "The carrier just provided us with copies of Tate's last two texts. The one he sent to Selena Cursen was mainly to let her know that he was alive and that she should keep it to herself. The other one—the one that went to Chandler Aspern—was more interesting."

"What does it say?"

"It's pretty slangy. But basically it reads like a proposal for some sort of cooperative arrangement. If that's what it is, it changes everything."

"I'm on my way."

Gurney ended the call and got to his feet. "Sorry. Something's come up." As he was leaving the office, he stopped and looked back at Aspern. "Regarding Billy Tate, apart from the time he threatened you, did he have any other contact with you?"

"No."

"He never accosted you on the street, at home, in your office?"

"Never."

"No phone calls, texts, emails?"

"Nothing at all. Why?"

"Just covering all the bases. Like I said, the more I know, the better. I'll be in touch."

The beneficent smile had long since disappeared from Aspern's face, but the self-interest radiating from those coal-dark eyes was as strong as ever.

30

When Gurney arrived at the doorway of Morgan's office, he found him pacing, his phone to his ear. He entered and took a seat on one of the two leather couches. The subject of the call was unclear from what Gurney could hear. It consisted mainly of Morgan's terse responses—yes, no, absolutely, absolutely not.

When the call ended, Morgan glared at the phone as if it were the source of all the pressure in his life. "That was Cam Stryker. County DA. Silas Gant is pressuring her to bundle everything that's been happening here into one big hate-crime conspiracy and take personal charge of it."

"Gant is saying the Russell, Kane, and Mason homicides were hate crimes?"

"He's pointing to the defacing of St. Giles and the three churches over in Bastenburg with those sideways figure eight symbols—calls them 'battle flags of the armies of hell'—and he claims that the killings were part of that, and it all adds up to an orchestrated attack on religion. Therefore, a vast hate-crime conspiracy."

"Did Stryker tell him he needed mental-health counseling?"

Morgan looked pained. "I doubt it. Last election was a close one for her. She can't afford to alienate anyone, especially not someone like Gant."

"What exactly is her position on this vast-conspiracy nonsense?"

"She wants it to go away. Under normal circumstances, she'd be happy to be seen as a prosecutor of religious hate crimes, defender of the God-fearing, et cetera. But these aren't normal circumstances. Not only is the logic of the thing nutty, Stryker's staff is already buried under an avalanche of heroin-fentanyl deaths, some of which appear to be opportunistic murders. Her caseload is twice what it was last year, and that's double what it was the year before."

"So what does she want from you?"

"She's desperate for us to find Tate, announce a motive for the killings that has nothing to do with religion, make sure no more figure eights appear on local churches—and get it all done before Gant can whip this mess up into a political hurricane."

"Is that all?"

Morgan sighed. "I know, I know. But I can understand the pressure she's under. Add a religious angle to a murder case, and everybody goes crazy—especially the media. All of a sudden, it's not just one more homicide in a nation that has fifteen thousand every year, plus seventy thousand drug deaths and half a million tobacco deaths. It's anti-religious terrorism! Raise an army of the righteous! Beat back the Devil! Send money to Silas Gant!"

He fell silent. The agitation in his eyes had shifted to something that looked like hatred.

A moment later, he blinked as if to erase a dangerous thought, turned to his desk, picked up two sheets of paper, and announced with a sudden change of tone, "We have copies of the texts sent from Billy Tate's phone—one to Selena Cursen, one to Chandler Aspern. Which do you want to see first?"

"The one he sent first."

"That'd be the one to Cursen," said Morgan, coming over to the couch and handing it to him. "The originals from the carrier identify Tate and Cursen only by their cell numbers. We substituted their names for sake of clarity."

Gurney read the text exchange.

Tate: lena, u there?

Cursen: ANGEL???

Tate: where am I?

Cursen: ANGEL?????????

Tate: i was on the roof, what happened?

Cursen: OMG OMG OMG

Tate: what happened?

Cursen: LIGHTNING!!!

Tate: what lightning?

Cursen: RAVEN SAID YOU DIED

Tate: died where?

Cursen: THE CHURCH WHERE THE LIGHTNING STRUCK

Tate: where did they take me?

Cursen: RAVEN SAID PEELS

Tate: peales funerals?

Cursen: ILL COME GET YOU!!! NOW???

Tate: no not now, have to think, this is big very very very big

Cursen: WHEN DO I SEE YOU???

Tate: soon, don't tell, nobody at all

Cursen: NOT EVEN RAVEN???

Tate: not yet when i see you we can decide who to tell but nobody now

Cursen: MY ANGEL

Tate: I'm the dark angel who rose from the dead—our secret, right lena?

Cursen: OUR SECRET MY ANGEL COME HOME SOON

Gurney read it a second time, then a third.

Morgan was watching him closely. "Any reaction?"

"Who's Raven?"

"She's like a younger version of Cursen. Lives at her house. A follower or apprentice. Maybe part of a threesome with Cursen and Tate."

"She was in the village square when Tate fell off the roof?"

"Apparently. I didn't see her, but that doesn't mean anything. Things were pretty crazy. She probably came to watch him spray that garbage on the steeple."

"Okay, let me see the text to Aspern."

This one was terser, but more intriguing. It was a single message with no reply.

Tate: dead man has a plan
mega score 4 u
easy peasy
c u 2nite

dont shoot

haha

B.

Gurney also read this message three times. At first, he had an urge to confront Aspern with it, since the man had just denied ever receiving any messages from Tate. Then he thought of a possible innocent explanation. Aspern could have assumed the oddball message had been sent to the wrong number and ignored it. And perhaps it was, in fact, sent to the wrong number. In any event, there was no solid basis for assuming he'd lied.

Gurney shared these thoughts with Morgan and added, "The text's intended recipient might be in doubt, but its content points to the existence of an accomplice. Or at least an intended accomplice."

Morgan nodded. "Someone Tate knew well enough to sign the text with just his initial."

"Someone," said Gurney, "who has a phone number similar to Aspern's, assuming that Tate made a one- or two-digit mistake typing it in."

As Morgan was considering this, his phone rang. He peered down at the screen. "It's Gareth Montell, the department's forensic attorney. He's meeting with Hilda Russell to go through her brother's estate documents. I should talk to him."

"Fine. I want to get back to Aspern and see what he has to say, then talk to Cursen. Can I take these copies of the texts?"

Morgan nodded and took the call from Montell.

Gurney headed next door to the village hall. As he was climbing the porch steps, he encountered Aspern on his way out.

A flash of irritation on the man's face was replaced by a cool smile.

"Something else, Detective?"

"A question. We've managed to retrieve some of Billy Tate's text messages. This one was sent to your cell number." He handed the copy to Aspern. "Do you have any recollection of receiving it?"

Aspern studied it, his nose wrinkling as if the message had an unpleasant odor.

"I remember seeing this," he said after a long moment, handing it back to Gurney. "But I had no idea it came from Tate. I assumed it was sent to me by mistake."

"Did you call the source number to ask about it?"

"Are you joking? I wouldn't waste my time on anything like that."

Aspern made a show of glancing at his Rolex. "I hope that's helpful." He flashed an empty smile and hurried past Gurney down the porch steps. He got in the passenger seat of a waiting Mercedes, which immediately pulled away.

Selena Cursen's house was located in the opposite direction from Waterview Drive, well outside the village of Larchfield—in the center of what Gurney had been told was a state-designated wilderness area where human habitation was restricted to the few widely scattered homes there at the time of the designation.

Wilderness was a good word for it, Gurney agreed as the gravel road took him through a pine forest thick enough to block out all but a few glimpses of the sky. As his GPS led him ever deeper into this dark place, he found himself with an uncomfortable sense of isolation.

He wondered how much of his uneasiness was coming from the echoes in his mind of *witchcraft* and *Satanism* and the message written in blood on the walls of the two female victims.

His GPS directed him from the gravel road onto a rougher dirt road, which terminated after another mile at a tall black-iron fence—with an opening too narrow for a car to pass through.

Each upright bar of the fence was topped with a black spearpoint shaped like an ace of spades. Beyond the opening, a stone footpath passed through an expanse of untended grass to a gray three-story Gothic Victorian.

Gurney switched off his engine and watched a flock of crows rising from the grass and settling in the tops of the pines. He took out his copy of Tate's text to Cursen and read it one more time, searching for inspiration on the best way to approach her.

As he was pondering this, he sensed some motion in front of him. A pale woman in a silky black robe appeared in the fence opening. She had straight black hair, violet eyes, black lipstick, and three silver studs in her lower lip. A polished black cameo of the horned god of witchcraft hung from a silver chain around her neck. Her fingernails were glossy black. Her feet were bare and as pale as her face. The fabric of her robe lay against the contours of her body in a way that suggested it might be all she was wearing.

Gurney restarted his car and backed slowly away from the fence to create more space between them before getting out.

She was watching him, lips slightly parted, with a look that suggested secret knowledge, a sexual fantasy, or a fried brain.

"Hello, Lena," he said gently, using the name Tate had used in his text.

There was a hint of movement in her eyes, but she said nothing.

"I saw Billy come back to life."

She moistened her lips with the tip of her tongue, its pinkness a surprise in the midst of all the black and white and silver. He thought she was about to speak, but she didn't.

"I saw Billy get out of his coffin. I saw him pick up a handful of knives and walk out into the night. He was definitely alive."

Her unblinking eyes widened. "Billy's a willow, and willows love water, and water is life, and life is love."

"And love is all there is," said Gurney, trying to match her tone.

"My Dark Angel rose from the dead," she said, more to herself than to him.

"It must be hard for you," he said, "not knowing where he is."

"He's my Dark Angel who rose from the dead," she repeated with sudden insistence, tears welling in her eyes.

The tears, more than anything else, told him what he wanted to know. After a long silence, he got his copy of Tate's text from the front seat of his car, tore off a blank part of the paper, wrote his name and cell number on it, and held it out to her. "If you want to talk to someone about Billy, you can call me."

At first, she didn't take it.

Then she did.

31

Back at headquarters, Gurney asked the desk sergeant if there was an empty office he could use. He needed to catch up on the part of the investigation process he liked the least—the paperwork involved in keeping incident reports, witness reports, and progress reports up to date. He had no problem making informal notes on his phone or in his notebook, but he had to push himself to transfer the information to the official case files.

The sergeant pointed him to a small office at the end of the central hallway. He was on his way there when Morgan intercepted him.

He motioned Gurney into his office. "How did it go with Aspern? How did he react when you confronted him with Tate's text?"

"He said that he saw it, assumed it was sent by mistake, and paid no attention to it. Too busy to be bothered. A credible enough position. No reasonable way to challenge it."

"Okay. What about Cursen?"

"My impression is that she doesn't know any more about Tate's whereabouts than we do. As for the witchcraft business, I think it may be a form of play-acting—a persona she discovered at some point and got comfortable with. Maybe a way of keeping people at a distance, feeling in control, feeling like she's connected to something profound. Or at least trying to give that impression. Bottom line, my guess is that she's a confused girl with an unfortunate attraction to bad boys."

Morgan looked disappointed. "You don't think she might be hiding Tate?"

"Not at the moment. She's obsessed with that Dark-Angel-risen-from-the-dead line in the text he sent her, but I think it's because she's afraid he might never come back to her. Underneath the weird getup and otherworldly attitude, I get the impression of sadness, loneliness, maybe fear that her fantasies are collapsing."

"Jesus, another dead end," muttered Morgan, sinking down onto one of the couches and rubbing his forehead. "A nutcase kid who was declared dead kills three people, stirs up a media tornado, flushes the image of Larchfield down the toilet, leaves the stinking mess in our laps, and disappears. And tonight Gant stages his 'revelation tent meeting,' which is bound to be a rabble-rousing horror show."

He closed his eyes. Perhaps to make it easier to think. Or not think. When he opened them, he looked pleadingly at Gurney. "We have to find that son of a bitch and put an end to this insanity!"

Gurney ignored Morgan's overwrought statement of the obvious. "Anything of interest with the lawyer from Angus's estate?"

"No surprises. The bulk of his wealth—in the neighborhood of a hundred and fifty million—goes in roughly equal thirds to Lorinda, Hilda, and Russell College. Plus half a million to Helen Stone and half a million to the Village Square Preservation Society. Montell is pursuing a more precise valuation of the real estate assets, but he's reasonably confident that the hundred and fifty number will hold up, give or take ten percent. And there's nothing in the will that benefits Billy Tate—so, whatever his motive was, it wasn't money. At least not from Angus's will."

"Have you heard anything from Brad about the Waterview Drive security cameras?"

"He'd already spoken to the homeowners and gotten the video files for the period you specified. He pulled in a couple of patrol guys to help review them, and he should have a report for us within the hour."

"Fine. I'll be updating the Russell, Kane, and Mason case files in the office at the end of the hall."

Thirty-five minutes later, as Gurney was entering the details of his brief interview with Selena Cursen, Morgan called to tell him that Slovak had arrived with the video file information.

He finished and went to Morgan's office, where he found the two men already at the conference table. Morgan gave Slovak a nod to proceed.

"We were able to access four security cameras that provide coverage of Waterview Drive. We examined video files for the period from four thirty yesterday afternoon until noon today. Fact number one, no orange Jeep. Fact number two, no driver resembling Billy Tate. Fact number three, none of the vehicles could have stopped at Mary Kane's cottage."

Gurney smiled. Maybe Slovak was smarter than he'd given him credit for.

Morgan frowned. "How on earth could you know that none of them stopped?"

Slovak looked eager to explain. "Because one of the cameras is located a mile east of the cottage, and one roughly a mile west of it. There's an analysis app that measures the speed of objects in the camera's field of view. And every vehicle that passed the first camera arrived at the second one just about when it should have at its indicated speed. If it stopped anywhere after passing the first camera, the time of its arrival at the second would have been way off."

Morgan's frown deepened. "So what are you saying? That Tate, or whoever put the damn message on the wall, came on foot through the woods?"

"Or maybe along the lakeshore, then up through the estate grounds behind the cottage."

Morgan turned to Gurney. "You agree that he must have come on foot?"

"It's possible. It's also possible that he came in the Jeep, but not along Waterview Drive. He could have driven down from Harrow Hill and come out at the intersection across from the cottage."

It was an obvious possibility, but it was also obvious from the expression on Slovak's face that he'd already dismissed it. "Nobody lives up there, except Lorinda Russell and Mayor Aspern."

"True," said Gurney, "but Greg Mason told me that Harrow Hill is crisscrossed by a network of trails that he keeps mowed and usable. In fact, one of the access points is in back of his house. So it's possible that Tate could have driven to the cottage that way—without passing any of the cameras on Waterview Drive."

Slovak rubbed the back of his neck. "But the night he killed Kane and Russell he came along Waterview Drive. Why not this time?"

"The night he killed them, no one was on the lookout for him. But at this point he'd want to minimize the chance of a patrol team spotting him."

"Sir?" Kyra Barstow was in the office doorway. "I have news from the lab. A DNA match indicates the blood used for the message on Mary Kane's wall came from Linda Mason. They also found that the blood on the wall contained microscopic traces of the polyurethane used in those little foam paint brushes."

"Fast results," said Morgan.

Slovak shifted in his seat. "What about that tire track in front of Kane's cottage? You have anything on that?"

"Soon," said Barstow.

Morgan thanked her.

She shot a quick smile at Gurney, stepped back out of the doorway, and disappeared down the hall.

Slovak shrugged. "That blood stuff was pretty much as expected."

Morgan looked at Gurney. "Any thoughts?"

"Just the obvious one. If Tate did approach the cottage via the Harrow Hill trail system, he must have gone back the same way to wherever he's hiding out. It would be a good idea to check for security cameras beyond Waterview Drive—on any other roads that might provide access to that trail network. Also, since Tate and his Jeep may be holed up somewhere in the sprawling woods of Harrow Hill itself, a feet-on-the-ground search needs to be organized."

"Wouldn't a helicopter be easier?" asked Slovak.

"For some areas, yes. But my impression of Harrow Hill is that most of it lies under a pretty thick cover of pines and hemlocks, with the exception of the area around the Russell mansion. You can check a satellite view to see if I'm right. If I am, the shoe-leather way will be the only way. You might want to download a topographic map and start designing a search grid."

Slovak glanced at Morgan, and Morgan nodded his agreement.

After Slovak left the office, Gurney suggested to Morgan that he talk to the chief over in Bastenburg, see how many men he could contribute to the effort.

"You really think we're going to need that kind of manpower?"

"Yes. Unless Tate turns himself in."

Morgan sighed, then looked at the time on his phone. "Jesus. Six thirty." He glanced uncertainly at Gurney. "Shall we get something to eat?"

Gurney's introversion would normally result in a negative response. But he was just hungry enough to say yes. He hadn't eaten anything all day—with the exception of the two anisette cookies Marika had given him that morning at Abelard's.

Morgan produced a Chinese restaurant menu from a drawer in his desk. After they made their selections and Morgan phoned them in, they sat across from each other at the table off to the side of Morgan's desk.

"Important to take time out to eat," Morgan said after an awkward silence. "We missed quite a few meals back in the day, didn't we?"

It wasn't really a question, and Gurney made no effort to reply.

"Strange," Morgan said after another silence, "how memories seem to come out of nowhere. Happens to me in the morning, when I'm still half-asleep. Vivid memories of things I hadn't thought about in years." He uttered an abrupt little laugh. "Jesus, remember Fat Frank?"

"That's who you woke up thinking about today?" Gurney's aversion to reminiscing gave his response a less-than-pleasant tone.

"No, no, I just happened to think of him now. This morning I woke up thinking about the first homicide case we worked on together. Remember that one?"

"Not immediately."

"The guy who imported jockstraps from Vietnam. George Hockenberry."

Gurney nodded. His lack of enthusiasm did nothing to dampen Morgan's.

"And the guy who supposedly shot him—the guy with all the rug stores, Kip Kleiburn. The Carpet King. Open-and-shut case against Kleiburn. Until *you* got hold of it." He nodded with a distant smile. "Those were the days, eh?"

Nostalgia was Gurney's least favorite state of mind. He pointedly changed the subject.

"What time tonight is that Silas Gant gathering?"

"Eight thirty. When it's starting to get dark. He likes fireworks."

"Fireworks?"

"You'll see."

32

The venue for Gant's "revelation tent meeting" was a rectangular, wooden-fenced field that had the scruffy look of a former pasture. Several lengths of fencing had been removed to allow vehicles to enter. Scores of cars and pickup trucks were parked around the perimeter of the field, and more were arriving. Morgan and Gurney each parked near the entry-exit opening.

The "tent" was a tarp-like canopy erected over a set of theatrical risers at the far end of the field. A podium stood on the top riser. To its left was an American flag on a gold-painted pole and to its right a gold-painted cross of equal height. On the front of the podium was a carving of two rifles with intersecting barrels.

Morgan got out of the Tahoe, and Gurney watched as he headed up behind the row of vehicles to a Larchfield patrol car and bent over to talk to the driver. Gurney went the other way, to a spot by the rear fence with a view of the whole field.

A large part of the audience, which he estimated at roughly three hundred, was already seated in informal rows of lawn chairs on either side of a central aisle that led from the rear of the field to the makeshift stage. They were universally white, mostly older, and, unlike many church congregations, mostly male. Groups of younger men stood smoking, talking, and drinking from beer cans by the parked pickups. Swarms of ragged little boys were running here and there, shouting and colliding with each other. The colors of sunset had faded away, dusk was deepening, a restless breeze was rising, and the sweet scent of mown grass was competing with the exhaust fumes of late-arriving vehicles.

Gurney was about to call Madeleine, to give her a rough idea when he'd be arriving home, when a low rumble out on the road diverted his attention. As it grew louder, the audience began looking back toward the source, and the murmur of their voices grew more excited. The rumble increased to a roar as a procession of motorcycles turned from the road into the central aisle of the seating area.

Gurney counted twelve of the heavyweight machines proceeding up the aisle toward the stage. The procession split as it reached the stage, with six machines turning right and six turning left. A thirteenth rider—this one in a shiny white leather riding suit—came slowly up the aisle and took the center position, setting off a burst of cheering from the crowd. It was Silas Gant, his gray pompadour unruffled by the breeze.

The crowd fell into an anticipatory silence. A few moments later a loud *whoosh* accompanied the fiery path of a rocket racing up into the sky, where it burst into a red-white-and-blue approximation of an American flag while the sound system blared an arena-style rendition of "God Bless America." The crowd applauded as Gant stepped up onto the risers and took his position at the podium, illuminated by a pair of spotlights.

"God bless America!" he cried, generating a reprise of the applause that had just ended.

"God save this threatened nation of ours," he continued. "That is the calling that brings us together on this beautiful night, at this critical moment in the history of our country. *Our* country! We have come together tonight to share *our* vision, to claim *our* rights, to send *our* message to the degenerates in high places conspiring to turn *our* precious homeland into a foreign garbage dump. The degenerates in the media—the corrupt, depraved media—who glorify every kind of perversion. The degenerates who laugh at our religion, our Bible, our God. The degenerates who want to strip us of our God-given, Constitution-guaranteed right to bear arms. The degenerate LGBTQ promoters who connive to turn innocent children into freaks. You know what those letters stand for? They stand for 'Leave God Behind and Turn Queer.' They are the initials of perdition! The alphabet of the demons of hell!"

He took out a large white handkerchief and wiped the sweat from his face before going on with rising intensity. "When I say the demons of hell, that's exactly what I mean. The purveyors of evil have insinuated themselves into high places. Perched like vultures on their mountains of filth, they look down on God-fearing folks like you and me. Proud in the putrefaction of their souls, they look down on us and laugh the laughter of demons!" His voice, which had risen to a sustained shout, cracked. He stepped back from the podium microphone to clear his throat.

When he spoke again, it was with less volume but no less emotion. "My fellow Americans, we come here tonight with our sacred land, our sacred rights, our sacred traditions under siege. All that we hold dear to our hearts is under assault by socialists, sodomites, and Satanists. The signs of the End Times are visible to all who have eyes to see. Look at the fires and floods ravaging the corrupt state of California, successor to Gomorrah, hotbed of every kind of anti-Christian iniquity. The Lord in his wrath is giving us a call to action. He will not purify America without our assistance. This is the word that the Lord has spoken to me. He invites us, he summons us, to join him in the great battle ahead. He calls us to enlist in his army—to be the vehicles of his word, his power, and his fire."

Gant paused, out of breath, and again wiped the sweat from his face. Then he leaned into the podium, his closeness to the microphone giving his voice a throatier intimacy. "Even as I speak, a devil stalks us—right here in our own hills and valleys—a devil in the body of a man risen from the dead. Creeping through these dark woods. Cutting throats. Defiling churches. Leaving his foul words, dripping with blood, on the walls of his victims. But with the gun and cross we will beat back the Prince of Darkness. We will bear arms into the great battle and save our country from perdition. Join us in the mighty Church of the Patriarchs. With gun and cross we stand for God and country."

After a dramatic pause, Gant pulled the microphone from the podium and strode to the edge of the top riser. "With gun and cross, we'll beat the demons down!" he cried. Then, tilting his ear toward the crowd, he asked, "What'll we do?"

The crowd responded. "With gun and cross we'll beat the demons down!"

Once again he asked, "What'll we do?"

They responded, louder this time. "With gun and cross we'll beat the demons down!"

He asked a third time, "What'll we do?"

They responded even louder. "*With gun and cross we'll beat the demons down!*"

With his white leather riding suit gleaming in the spotlights, Gant extended his arms in a triumphant embrace of the whole crowd and shouted, "God bless America!"

The crowd rose to its feet with applause that continued until the last of the thirteen motorcycles had passed down the center aisle and disappeared into the night.

33

By the time Gurney got home it was past ten thirty. Madeleine was already in bed. He drank two glasses of water while trying to decide whether to stay up or go to bed. After checking his email and finding nothing but fundraising appeals and a notice for his thirtieth college reunion, he opted for going to bed.

Although his body seemed eager for sleep, his mind was reviewing events of the day. Recurring images included the bloody Dark Angel message on Mary Kane's wall . . . the glint in Hilda Russell's eyes when she mentioned her namesake's power over snakes . . . Selena Cursen's tear-filled eyes . . . Aspern offering him Mike Morgan's job . . . the "*dead man has a plan*" message Aspern received from Tate but supposedly ignored . . . Silas Gant's promise of victory by the gun and the cross . . . the long roar of applause from his followers.

The recollected din of that cheering crowd gave Gurney a chill. Or maybe it was the breeze from the wide-open window next to the bed. As he reached down to pull up his side of the blanket, he was surprised by Madeleine's wide-awake voice.

"What are you wrestling with?"

"I don't have a firm enough grip on the situation to wrestle with it."

"Do you feel like you're making progress?"

"I'm accumulating facts, but they're not forming anything like a coherent picture."

"You want to tell me about it?"

"On one hand, there's a simple story. Billy Tate revives from near death with a desire to kill the man responsible for putting him in prison. On his way to do this, he is recognized by two women, one of whom he kills. Two nights later, he kills a woman who put him in a juvenile detention center when he was a teenager. He leaves a trail of occult symbols and messages in blood. Then he vanishes."

"Sounds awful, but somewhat coherent."

"The thing is, I'm having a hard time putting together a picture of Billy Tate. One Billy Tate is a hotheaded, impulsive kid spray-painting crazy symbols on a church steeple in the middle of a thunderstorm. The other is a cool, premeditating murderer who killed three people, each with a single, precise slash with a scalpel."

"Haven't you encountered other murderers with conflicting characteristics?"

"If it was just that, it wouldn't be bothering me so much. But there's a world of ugliness surrounding the three murders. It may be coincidental, but I don't think it is."

"Ugliness?"

"Stories about Angus Russell—allegations that he arranged for some of his enemies to 'disappear.' Mike Morgan has a complicated history with him, and he's giving off a jumpy, guilty vibe. The man's always had an anxiety problem, but this is on another level."

"Is there more?"

"Plenty more. Russell's definitely-not-grieving widow is as far from warm as a human being can be. And there's his sister, a pastor who seems to despise everyone. And Billy Tate's alcoholic stepmother, who was replaced in Billy's bed by a vulnerable young woman who's a make-believe witch. Not to mention a local mayor with financial reasons for wanting Russell dead. And I have the feeling I'm only scratching the surface of Larchfield's nastiness."

"You think all of that is connected to the three murders?"

As he considered the question, the screech of an owl in the nearby thicket pierced the silence. Another chilly breeze came through the window.

"I don't know yet what's connected to what, but I'm sure there's more to this case than a crazy kid settling scores."

Gurney closed his eyes and tried to empty his mind by concentrating on the soft rustling of the trees. Whenever the echo of Gant's words intruded, he tried to bring his attention back to the gentler sounds of the breeze.

"Maybe he has an accomplice." Madeleine's now-sleepy voice dispelled both

Gant and nature. "That could explain why you're having trouble getting a unified sense of who he is."

A few minutes later he could tell by the way she was breathing that she'd fallen asleep.

But the possibilities her comment raised kept him awake another hour. It gave a new dimension to Tate's text to Aspern. It also gave extra weight to the notion that Tate and his orange Jeep might be hiding on Harrow Hill. Aspern's casual dismissal of the text as something sent to him by mistake had been convincing, but being convincing was the basic talent of all effective liars.

The notion of a Tate-Aspern alliance seemed a stretch but not impossible. It certainly merited further exploration. That was his last conscious thought before he drifted off to sleep.

When he was awakened suddenly by Madeleine gripping his arm, it was near dawn, but the moon had moved behind a cloud bank and the room was darker.

"What was that?" There was an edge of fear in her voice.

Her tone had him fully awake.

For a long moment he heard nothing but the susurrus of the breeze in the thicket. Then he was stopped cold by a high-pitched howl. He was familiar with the howls and yips of coyotes, but this was more piercing, fading at the end into something like a demented laugh. This was no mere coyote, and the nearest wolves, even if one could produce such a sound, were over a hundred miles away in the northern Adirondacks.

He rolled out of bed and picked up the powerful LED flashlight he kept on his nightstand.

Madeleine sat up on her side of the bed. "I think it came from the low pasture."

Gurney's hearing was normal, but hers was extraordinary, and he'd learned to trust it. He went to the side of the house that looked down over the pasture, the barn, and the pond. There was enough moonlight filtering through the clouds for him to get a sense of the open parts of the landscape. He saw nothing moving. He was tempted to use his flashlight to scan the border of the woods, but decided not to. Before he announced his presence, he wanted to know what he was dealing with.

After peering out of the windows on all sides of the house, he returned to the bedroom, where he found Madeleine locking the windows. He put on a pair of jeans, sneakers, and a sweatshirt, took his 9mm Beretta from the top drawer of his nightstand, and slipped it into his sweatshirt pocket.

"What are you doing?" she asked.

"Taking a quick look around."

"Be careful!"

He left the house as quietly as he could, closing the side door gently behind him. Instead of taking the path through the pasture, he entered the narrow copse that separated the high pasture from the low one and followed it down toward the pond and barn. The moon was slowly emerging from the edge of the cloud cover. Bathed now in a silver light, the hillside seemed preternaturally quiet, focusing Gurney on the sound of each step he took.

When he reached the pond, there was a silver gleam on the black surface. The frogs, usually croaking at all hours of the night, were silent. He stood for a minute or two in the relative darkness under the drooping branches of a giant hemlock, letting his gaze move around the perimeter of the pond, then over to the end of the town road, then across to the barn.

On the wide door of the barn something caught his eye.

He removed the Beretta from his pocket and flicked off the safety. He moved cautiously from under the hemlock and approached the barn.

He was still a good fifty feet from the barn door when, in the brightening moonlight, he saw what he'd been hoping he'd never see again.

I AM

THE DARK ANGEL

WHO ROSE

FROM THE DEAD

When he reached the door, he switched on his flashlight. The painted letters were a deep red; their distinctive tackiness told him the blood had been applied very recently.

There were two doors to the barn—this large one that permitted him to move his tractor in and out, and a normal entry door. He went to that second one now, quietly turned the knob, then kicked it open, sweeping the flashlight beam across the interior, holding his Beretta in firing position.

Satisfied that the barn wasn't harboring Tate or anyone else, he stepped out, closed the door, hurried back up to the house, and made a call to police headquarters in Larchfield for the evidence team to go over the site ASAP. It was out of their jurisdiction, but involving the local police in an incident clearly tied to the Larchfield case would make no sense.

34

The morning sun, now well above the ridge in a cloudless blue sky, was illuminating the blossoms on the old apple tree by the chicken coop and turning droplets of dew on the grass into dazzling pinpoints of light.

He and Madeleine were sitting at the round pine breakfast table, each with a mug of coffee. He had opened the French doors to let in the morning air, and Madeleine had closed them. They had hardly spoken since he'd insisted that she leave the house and stay with a friend, at least for the next couple of days, or until the evident threat had been neutralized.

It was not the first time a lunatic had invaded their lives. Everything that could be said about it had been said on the previous occasion. All that remained now on Madeleine's part was a grim resignation. On Gurney's part, a sense of guilt that he'd allowed this to happen again alternated with what he considered a realistic acceptance of the nature of his career. *It is what it is*—in the words of a popular saying that struck him as both profound and inane.

His focus now was on logistics and the minimization of risk. His plan was to drive Madeleine with a suitcase of clothes and other essentials to Geraldine Mirkle's house on the other side of Walnut Crossing. She and Gerry shared the same schedule at the mental health clinic and usually drove there together. And Gerry was an extrovert who always welcomed company, especially Madeleine's—a fact confirmed by her immediate affirmative reply when Madeleine had called to ask for the favor.

Madeleine went to take a shower and pack her things, and Gurney went down to the barn to touch base with Kyra Barstow, who'd been working there for the past hour with one of her techs.

"I took a scraping for DNA," she said, pointing to the message. "And we found a couple of shoe prints in the damp ground in front of the door—I'm thinking from the same sneakers that left prints at the mortuary. No indication that he was inside the barn."

He nodded. "Are you checking for vehicle tread marks?"

"Already done." She pulled out her phone and swiped back and forth between two shots of tread marks in soft earth. "The first is from the road in front of the Kane cottage, the second is from right over there." She pointed to an area next to the barn where there was more dirt than grass. The tread marks appeared to be identical.

"Best of all," she added, "there's a double impression here, one from each side of the vehicle—which gives us the exact axle width, which with any luck may give us the make and model of the car, or at least narrow the possibilities considerably."

"Interesting," said Gurney. "He's not shy about leaving his little calling cards."

"Or his big ones." She gestured toward the bloody message on the door. "Did you hear or see anything suspicious last night?"

"Just before dawn this morning, we heard a god-awful howling—shriller, louder, more intense than any coyote or wolf. Like something out of a horror movie. Now I'm pretty sure it was him, wanting to make an impression."

"He didn't think a bloody message about rising from the dead was enough?"

Gurney smiled. "We'll ask him when we catch him."

After taking another look around the barn and finding nothing out of place, Gurney returned to the house. While he was waiting for Madeleine to finish packing, he checked the locks on all the windows, upstairs and downstairs, and the French doors.

When they finally set out, he mentioned to Madeleine that he needed to make a quick stop at Miro's Motors, their local auto repair shop, to have something looked at. It was a sign of her preoccupation that this generated no response.

Gurney wanted to make sure that whoever had left the message on the barn hadn't also affixed a GPS tracker to the Outback. The best way to examine the undercarriage was to have it raised on a lift so that all the nooks and crannies would be visible.

Miro—short for Miroslav—was an immigrant of mixed Slavic background who had taken over the Walnut Crossing auto shop around the same time the Gurneys had moved up from the city. A bone-thin man with a lined face and a sad smile, he had a penchant for a kind of sweetly pessimistic philosophizing that Madeleine found charming.

He was sweeping out one of the shop's two service bays as Gurney pulled into the parking area and lowered his window. He ambled over, broom in hand. "Your name is on the news this morning. I hear them say it, about crazy crimes up north. You're not a retired man anymore?"

Gurney wondered if the leaking of his involvement to the media had been accidental or intentional—and if intentional, with what intent. "I'm mostly retired. But not always."

Miro looked past Gurney to Madeleine. "Your husband famous guy, right? Big detective for big crimes. Like movie star, but better, because movie star only pretends to be big man."

Madeleine's expression suggested that however famous her husband might be, being driven from her home by a madman made it difficult to be thrilled by his fame.

Miro went on. "My country, no good to trust police." He looked like he was about to spit, but thought better of it. "Here much better. Police like anyone, but mostly they're not criminals." He smiled his sad smile. "So, Detective, what can I do for you?"

"I was wondering if you could take a quick look at the underside of our car. Every once in a while there's a rattle, and I'm afraid something might fall off."

Outside of undercover work, he wasn't fond of making things up. However, sharing his concern about a possible GPS tracker seemed an unnecessary complication, not to mention an extra cause of worry for Madeleine. And while Miro was searching for things that might rattle, Gurney could join him under the car and check for suspicious devices.

"Cars with things starting to fall off usually not look so good as this." He shrugged. "But pull car inside, we check."

Madeleine got out and announced she'd be in the little park adjacent to the shop.

Once the car had been raised on the hydraulic lift, Gurney and Miro engaged in their separate inspections. After another minute or two of poking around the undercarriage, Miro announced, "You got good car. Nothing falling off. Maybe vibration. Very hard to find vibration. Next time for oil change, we go out on the road, drive, listen. For now, okay."

Gurney had also come to a satisfactory conclusion regarding his own inspection. He took out his wallet. "Thank you, Miro. What do I owe you?"

"Nothing, please."

"You should be paid for your time."

"I am paid all the time. You are good customers. No charge, please."

After dropping Madeleine off, he headed north to Larchfield.

On the way, he placed a call to Morgan, got his voicemail, and left a message asking him to have the warrant for Tate's phone records expanded from the five-day text-retention window to include all calls made in the last ninety days, partly as a fishing expedition for contacts, partly to see if he'd made other calls to Aspern.

This message was the first subject Morgan raised when Gurney arrived at headquarters. "Where are you heading with this expanded warrant thing?"

"Probably nowhere. Due diligence, et cetera."

"You're not planning to pursue a warrant for Aspern's call records, too, are you?"

"Not unless Tate's records reveal texts or conversations that Aspern failed to mention."

Morgan took a labored breath. "Let's just be careful we don't jump to any conclusions." He glanced at his watch. "Speaking of the mayor, there's a one o'clock lunch meeting in the village hall. The board is having a meltdown over the media coverage of the 'Larchfield zombie'—plus the way Gant stirred up his followers out in that field last night."

"Enjoy it."

"Christ, Dave, I need you to help me navigate this. Your being in the room will calm them down."

"After what I found on my barn door this morning, I'm not in a mood to calm anyone down."

"Barstow's out there, isn't she?"

"Yes."

"Has she found anything other than the message?"

"Sneaker prints and tire tracks. Maybe they'll lead somewhere, maybe not."

"What the hell is Tate trying to do?"

"Ratchet up the panic level? Draw attention to himself? Distract us?"

"Distract us from what?"

"Maybe from the real purpose of the murders. But don't ask me what that might be."

"You really think this craziness has a purpose?"

"I think it's possible."

"Jesus." Morgan stared at Gurney in a state of obvious mental overload, then glanced again at his watch. "It's time. Let's go."

With mixed feelings, Gurney accompanied him to the village hall. The cast of characters at the conference table was the same as the previous morning, with one missing—Harmon Gossett, the village attorney. Fallow and Peale had chosen seats as far from each other as possible, as had Aspern and Hilda Russell.

A lunch buffet had been set up, along with a coffee urn. Most of the meeting attendees were focused on their sandwiches or salads. Neither Morgan nor Gurney visited the buffet. With an awkward smile, Morgan took a seat facing Aspern. Gurney sat next to Morgan.

"We should get started," said Aspern with a sour glance around the table. "Since yesterday, the situation has gotten worse. Not only do we still have a throat-slashing lunatic on the loose, we are the target of the most unfair media coverage imaginable." He looked down the table at Carmody. "Martin, I hope to God you can help us reverse the tide before the world starts thinking 'Larchfield' is the name of a horror movie."

"We're doing all we can, Chandler. Immediately after this meeting, I want to record Chief Morgan delivering a positive statement about the progress he's making. I've already written a preliminary draft. We want every internet, cable, and network news provider to have the video in hand for the next news cycle. Stern, confident, solid hand on the tiller. That's our message."

"Good," said Aspern. "Now, I want you all to see a god-awful program that ran last night on RAM-TV. By this morning it had spread to YouTube, Facebook, Twitter." He directed everyone's attention to a screen set into the conference room wall, a larger version of the one at police headquarters. "It's called *Crimes Beyond Reason*. I have our attorney looking into a possible lawsuit."

Aspern tapped an icon on his phone and the screen on the wall came to life. After a typical RAM sequence of pulsating title graphics, the program began with a doctored video of Tate on the church roof. Eerie music had been added. There were more frequent flashes in the night sky and louder claps of thunder than in the original, and when Tate was struck by the final bolt of lightning, his tumble from the roof was shown in slow motion.

When Tate hit the ground, the scene shifted to Karl Kasak in front of the church, wearing the same safari jacket Gurney remembered from the program promo on RAM News. He was speaking with the intensity of a reporter in a war zone.

"I'm Karl Kasak, here where Billy Tate, a practitioner of witchcraft, plunged to his death—a death certified by the official medical examiner. Tate's body was taken to a mortuary and placed, at the strange request of his stepmother, in a sealed coffin. Hours later, Billy Tate burst out of that coffin and began the bloody rampage people here are calling 'the zombie murders.' Did Tate experience a miraculous revival? Or has he become what investigators of the macabre call 'one of the walking dead'?"

Kasak paused to let his audience absorb that question before going on in the same dramatic tone.

"I spent today talking to area residents, learning how they feel about the nightmare that's engulfed their town—as well as to experts on the effects of lightning and to probers of the paranormal. Prepare to be shocked!"

The scene switched to a close-up of a twentysomething man with a thin mustache and big designer-frame glasses. He was identified on-screen as JASON HARKER, LARCHFIELD RESIDENT. From the background, it looked like the scene had been recorded in the village square.

Harker spoke directly to the camera. "I remember Billy from high school. The way he'd look at you sometimes . . . you'd think, whatever's on his mind, it's not good. He carried one of those knives, you flick your wrist, blade flips out. That look and that knife made you want to back away. Fast."

Kasak's next interviewee was a bullet-headed man with small eyes, a boxer's flat nose, and a purple birthmark on his shaved head. He was wearing a white tee shirt and a black leather vest. The screen identified him as ROBERT "BOB" STENGEL, PLUMBING CONTRACTOR. He had the hoarse voice of a longtime smoker.

"How do I feel? Like an animal feels before an earthquake. This kid in the coffin, you know what it makes me think of? That horror movie with the hand shooting up out of the grave. That's what's happening in the world today, evil coming up around us. Reverend Gant's got it right. Time to lock and load."

According to the identifying line at the bottom of the screen, the next interviewee was ARTHUR BUNZMAN, RETIRED EXECUTIVE. He had a narrow face, long nose, and thinning gray hair. He looked to Gurney like he'd just walked out of a photograph of the Nazis at Nuremberg.

As if responding to Robert "Bob" Stengel's call to arms, he said, "I'm ready. I've taken the steps the situation demands for my family's protection and to set an example. When the days of disorder arrive, woe betide the fool who is unprepared. There's no spot in my home where I cannot, within the space of three paces, lay my hand on a loaded firearm."

Next up was MICHAEL KRACKOWER, MALWARE CONSULTANT, a gimlet-eyed fast talker. The white lettering on his black tee shirt said TRUST NO ONE. He claimed that the events in Larchfield were the tip of a vast iceberg, that Billy Tate's return to life was linked to CIA experiments with "resurrection drugs," that artificial-intelligence life-forms were infiltrating the media, and that malignant government forces were manipulating the weather, the stock market, and the avocado industry. He said that the police department reference to three murders was an obvious lie, the truth being at least triple that.

The next three contributors described post-resurrection sightings of Tate in which his body was smoldering, he was urinating a shower of sparks, and he was speaking in tongues.

Kasak appeared again with the facade of St. Giles behind him. "Wow! What a frightening picture we're getting of Billy Tate, the Larchfield Slasher, before and after that fateful lightning bolt—which we'll hear about now from Dr. Elmer Bird, a leading researcher on the mind-blowing effects lightning can have on the human psyche."

Bird, an octogenarian in a rumpled white shirt, tilting red bow tie, and thick glasses, sat behind a desk. "You ask me about what lightning could do." He sniffled loudly and cleared his throat. "A lot, I'll say. First, it could kill you. Burn you, blind you, paralyze you. Tremendous voltage. The power to reorganize the electrochemistry of the brain, or destroy it completely. Not frequent, once in a while, this has effects we cannot imagine."

Kasak was back on the screen. "There you have it. Scientific information. We still have some big unanswered questions. We'll be taking a deep dive into those questions in the next installment of *Crimes Beyond Reason*—when we'll be joined by the controversial Mars Brothers, Clinton and Delbert, who've achieved world-wide fame as zombie hunters! Now, here's a frightening image I want to leave you with—the message Billy Tate left in the homes of two female victims. Some say the message was meant for them. Some say it was intended for all of us. Take a look . . . and pray that it doesn't give you nightmares.

The image that came into focus on the screen, accompanied by horror-movie music, was the message on Mary Kane's living room wall:

I AM

THE DARK ANGEL

WHO ROSE

FROM THE DEAD

The entire screen turned blood-red. With a succession of drumbeats, it faded to black. An announcer's voice intoned, "RAM-TV. We deliver reality."

Aspern tapped an icon on his phone, and the screen went blank. He slammed his hand down on the table. "That video of the Dark Angel claptrap on the victim's wall—I want to know who leaked that to Kasak. If we can't keep control of something like that, what *can* we control?"

Irate mutterings of agreement went around the table.

Aspern aimed his next question at Morgan. "Crime-scene photos—they're taken by people who report to you. Am I right?"

Morgan nodded.

"And they're shared on an as-needed basis with people who report to you?"

"Yes."

"Then someone who reports to you must be the damn leaker."

"I suppose that's . . . possible."

"Possible?! It sounds like an obvious conclusion!"

Morgan shifted in his chair and cleared his throat.

Gurney had an aversion to triangulating a confrontation, but a greater aversion to the bullying arrogance in Aspern's voice. He spoke up calmly. "It's not that obvious."

Aspern glared at the challenge. "What are you talking about?"

"What makes you so sure that the leaked video is the one the police took at the scene?"

"Well, who the hell else . . ." Aspern's angry tone faded, as it evidently dawned on him that the limb he was out on was fragile. "Are you saying someone else had access to the scene?"

Gurney waited patiently.

Hilda Russell leaned forward. "Chandler, for goodness' sake, isn't it obvious?"

Aspern looked like he'd regurgitated something bitter. "You're saying the leaked video may have come from Billy Tate?"

Gurney nodded. "Kyra Barstow documented the message on the wall with individual photos, not a motion video."

Aspern rechanneled his anger. "So, what the hell is Tate up to?"

"He wants attention," said Gurney. "And apparently knows how to get it."

"Speaking of attention," interjected Hilda Russell, looking down the table toward Morgan, "I'm wondering if our police department has the resources to give these multiple murders the attention they require. Are you any closer to making an arrest today than you were yesterday, or the day before, or the day before that?"

In Gurney's opinion, the honest answer to the question would be no. Instead, Morgan sidled around it like a politician. "Right now, Hilda, we're focusing on a locale where Tate may be holed up. We've got ten extra officers coming over from Bastenburg to join our guys in a major sweep of the Harrow Hill area."

Aspern leaned forward. "What do you mean by major—"

Russell cut him off. "That's fine, as far as it goes. But don't you think it might be time to bring in the state police, the sheriff's department, the DA's office? There's expertise and manpower out there that we're not taking advantage of."

Once again Morgan was looking squirmy. "There are control issues, Hilda. Once the state police come in, they run the show. They have their own priorities and couldn't care less about Larchfield's reputation."

She let out a sharp, humorless laugh. "From what I see in the news, we don't have a reputation left to worry about. What matters is having the proper resources to bring this tragedy to a proper conclusion. I say bring them in."

Morgan blinked, then sighed.

Aspern took advantage of the silence to pursue his own question to Morgan. "What do you mean by 'a major sweep'—and why the focus on Harrow Hill?"

"Some security camera videos we retrieved suggest that Tate may be using that area as a base for his movements. We believe that sealing it off and combing through it, foot by foot, is our best option at the moment."

Aspern looked troubled but said nothing.

"How long do you see this taking?" asked Russell.

Morgan turned up his palms. "Hard to say. It's a lot of ground to cover, hundreds of acres. I'm thinking at least forty-eight hours, with teams working around the clock."

"So, two more days? With no guarantee of success?" She shook her head. "I don't think it makes sense to wait that long, not with state police resources just a phone call away. Suppose Tate strikes again? Then what?"

Morgan sighed. "I hear what you're saying, Hilda, I really do. Maybe I can prevail on Bastenburg for more feet on the ground, push harder, complete the search in twenty-four to thirty-six hours. If we can wrap this up without surrendering control to an agency with no stake in—"

She cut him off. "Chandler, where do you stand on this?"

Aspern took so long to answer, he seemed not to have heard the question.

"I'm not happy about it, but giving the local department another thirty-six hours seems preferable to punting the ball to the state." He glanced around the table. "Any serious objections?"

The question was answered with shrugs. Then Martin Carmody suggested that Morgan should issue a statement to the effect that the investigation was entering a new phase, with a breakthrough expected at any time. Speaking up for the first time, Peale endorsed the idea of giving Morgan another thirty-six hours. After a short silence the meeting was adjourned.

Gurney approached Hilda Russell. "Can I speak to you for a minute?"

She led the way out of the building to a wrought iron bench in the village square park, next to a flowering crab apple tree. The afternoon sun was warm on the bench.

"So, what's on your mind?" she asked.

"I noted your eagerness to bring in the cavalry."

"Indeed."

"Does that reflect a desire to expand the investigation? Or bring it to a close?"

She shrugged. "Maybe both."

"Are you concerned that something is being overlooked?"

"Human beings tend to overlook things. A common failing, don't you think?"

"Especially when overlooking them is advantageous."

Russell smiled.

A soft breeze carried the spring scent of grass and moist earth, adding an incongruous tranquility to a conversation about murder.

Gurney mirrored her smile. "We could save some time if you'd tell me what you think is being overlooked."

"I'm not clairvoyant. I just feel that the focus of the local police may be excessively narrow."

"Are you saying your brother's murder might be more complicated than it seems?"

"I'm saying that Larchfield's flowery meadows are full of snakes. And my late brother was very much at home here."

35

Gurney's way home that afternoon passed through the east end of Walnut Crossing, coming within a quarter mile of Geraldine Mirkle's house. He decided to stop and see if Madeleine needed anything and perhaps allay some of the fear the situation would naturally be causing.

When he pulled into the driveway behind Gerry's yellow VW Beetle, he spotted them behind the house in a gazebo bedecked with baskets of petunias. The sight set off a momentary flashback to the petunias that were part of the savage conclusion of the White River murder case. He pushed that gruesome scene out of his mind and headed over to the gazebo.

They were sitting on opposite sides of a small table that supported a Scrabble board and a pitcher of iced tea. Gerry Mirkle was the first to speak.

"Good news or bad news?"

"Not much of either one." He tried for a casual smile. "I was passing by and thought I'd drop in for a minute. Who's winning?"

"Gerry, as usual," said Madeleine. "Where are you coming from?"

"Lovely Larchfield."

Her lips tightened. "Do you feel like you're getting any closer to . . . ending this?"

"There's a major manhunt underway right now, with a good chance of success."

Neither woman appeared convinced.

"Is there anything you ladies want from the village?"

Gerry shook her head.

"No," said Madeleine.

"Or from the house?"

"No. Just look in on the chickens. I think they have enough food and water, but it's worth checking. And please be careful."

"Right." He kissed the top of her head, nodded to Gerry, and returned to his car.

The route to the Gurney property out in the western hills went through the center of Walnut Crossing. It was hard to tell whether the sad condition of the upstate economy was more accurately reflected in the vacant storefronts or in those occupied by the shabby businesses that had survived—selling discount cigarettes, secondhand clothing, used furniture, lottery tickets, and junk food. The only enterprises that seemed on a solid enough footing to keep up appearances were the hospital and the funeral parlor.

Fifteen minutes later, Gurney was parked in front of his barn. The grass was in need of mowing—a reminder of how difficult he found it to balance the domestic and detective sides of his life. He decided to deal with the grass while it was on his mind. Then, as he was about to get the mower out of the barn, he was struck by the aggressive ugliness of the bloody statement on the door. The urge to do something about that first pushed the mowing plan aside.

He figured the simplest remedy would be a quick sanding and repainting of the defaced area. Barstow had already taken photographs and surface scrapings for analysis, so there was no evidence-preservation issue, and he had the materials on hand in his workshop in the barn.

Half an hour later, the job was done. His painting could have been neater, but at least the creepy message had been covered. He checked his watch. It was nearly six o'clock. He hadn't bothered to eat anything at Aspern's lunchtime meeting, and he was hungry, but he decided to inspect the barn area before it fell into the shade of the tall cherry trees.

He walked a gradually expanding spiral route around the structure, just as he'd done at countless other crime scenes. He found nothing of interest until he came to the tread marks Barstow had made impressions of that morning.

The fact that the combination of the two tread patterns and the distance between them might identify the make and model of the car had Gurney itchy for a status report. Although he was pretty sure that Barstow would notify him promptly if anything useful turned up, he called her anyway. He reached her voicemail and left a message.

Then he drove up through the low pasture to the house, intent on getting something to eat—and making sure the chickens had enough food and water.

He discovered they had plenty of both. He took a few minutes to clean off their perches, air out the coop, and put down a few handfuls of fresh straw before going into the house. After getting a pot of water boiling and adding some pasta, he took a shower and put on fresh jeans and a polo shirt. He returned to the kitchen, drained the pasta, added some butter and leftover asparagus, and carried a bowl of it to the café table outside the French doors.

The slanting rays of the early-evening sun were pleasantly warm on his back. The grass between the patio and the chicken coop was a brilliant green. The yellow strings that Madeleine had used to lay out her plan for a shed alongside the coop were swaying in a gentle breeze. Barn swallows were swooping overhead in pursuit of insects. Chipmunks were gathering seeds from under the finch feeders. The harshness of the day was fading into the background.

His sense of peace was ended by a panicky call from Morgan.

"Another episode of that damn Karl Kasak show is scheduled for ten o'clock tonight. There's a preview segment on the RAM website now. I'm trying to reach Harmon Gossett to see if we can get it killed. We've got to do something about this before it buries us."

"Good luck with Gossett."

"Right. I've got another call I need to take. Talk to you later."

After finishing his dinner and making himself a cup of coffee, Gurney went into the den, opened his laptop, and went to the RAM website. In the "Streaming Previews" section he found *Crimes Beyond Reason* and clicked on the current date.

After a two-minute commercial, Kasak appeared in front of the Gothic iron gate of a cemetery. He spoke in a tense, hushed tone.

"I'm here among the dead of Larchfield, New York—an appropriately chilling location for my meeting with Clinton and Delbert Mars, self-styled zombie hunters, drawn here by the terrifying events of the past week. You may think of zombies as creatures found only in horror movies. I asked the Mars brothers if that's true. What they told me may shock you."

The screen was filled with a close-up of two overweight, bearded men, side by side in front of a marble mausoleum. They spoke alternately, one sentence each, like twins accustomed to finishing each other's thoughts.

"The idea that the walking dead are creatures of fiction is just about the biggest lie the government wants us to swallow."

"Like telling us that UFOs are weather balloons."

"Truth is, the walking dead are real as you and me."

"As real as Billy Tate, and just as hard to kill."

"A zombie can't be killed at all, if you don't know how to do it."

"More likely, you'd be the one to get killed."

"Ninety-nine percent more likely."

"Most folks don't even know where zombies come from."

"Because they don't see it happening."

"They don't see the lightning that makes it happen."

"And mostly it happens in cemeteries."

"When lightning strikes a grave or a mausoleum."

"And brings the dead back to life."

"A kind of life that draws strength from taking the lives of others."

"The more they kill, the stronger they get."

"Like Billy Tate, they kill to stay alive."

"But we know their weakness."

"We can send them back to hell, which is where they were, before they rose up."

"By fire they rise up, by fire they fall!"

"Billy Tate, your zombie days of blood and evil are about to end!"

The scene shifted back to Kasak, standing outside the Gothic iron gate. "We're talking about a potentially fatal face-off. Gives me goose bumps just to think about it! For more about this eerie battle, tune in tonight at ten. *Crimes Beyond Reason*. On RAM-TV."

Gurney suddenly realized what Kasak's tone was reminding him of—a TV wrestling announcer. Then Kasak disappeared, and a blue logo came spinning onto a black screen.

RAM-TV

WE DELIVER REALITY

He closed his laptop—wondering if there was any limit to the market for half-witted, fearmongering nonsense—and turned his attention again to the stark reality of his barn having been visited by a probable murderer.

Although it was unlikely that anyone had seen the vehicle that left the tire marks, he felt it would be negligent not to check on it. There were only two other houses on the two-mile-long dirt-and-gravel road that led from the state route up to his barn. One was a single-wide mobile home whose onetime lawn had been displaced by skunk cabbage and thorn bushes.

In the years that the Gurneys had lived at the top end of the road, the mobile home had been sporadically occupied, and he wasn't sure about its current status. The cabin at the bottom end of the road, however, was enjoying a sudden renaissance as a getaway for city hipsters who found its overhanging hemlocks, tilting porch, ancient outhouse, gravity-fed spring, and lack of electricity charming—and the frequent howling of coyotes an exciting bonus. Or so a realtor friend of Madeleine's had told her.

Gurney got in his Outback and headed down the road. He stopped first at the deteriorating mobile home. Stepping carefully through the tangle of thorns, he reached the faded front door and knocked on it, setting off a burst of angry barking on the other side of it. A male voice shouted "Shut up!" several times before the barking stopped.

The man who opened the door was wearing only white boxer shorts and black socks. The thinning hair on his head was as black as his socks. The mass of hair on his chest and legs was gray, as was the three-day stubble on his face. He was holding a brown beer bottle by the neck, a grip suitable for using it as a club.

Gurney adjusted his stance accordingly, put on a pleasant smile, introduced himself, and added, "I'm your neighbor from up the road."

"McDermott's old farm." The man said it with an emphasis suggesting that any subsequent owner's right to be up there was doubtful.

Gurney replied blandly, "That's the place."

"You're the detective?"

"Retired."

The man switched his grip on his beer bottle and took a long, slow swig, eyeing Gurney all the while. "You're a detective. What do you do about a thief?"

"What's been stolen?"

"My compost. Gone like it wasn't ever there."

"You could report it to the Walnut Crossing Police Department."

"I told Darryl LeMoyne all about it twice, which is like talking to a groundhog."

"Does anyone live here with you?"

"Not at the current moment. My son's in prison."

"Oh?"

"Girlfriend put him there. Claimed he knocked her teeth out. Meth done that, not Emmett."

"Let me ask you something. What time did you wake up this morning?"

He shook his head. "What you want to know that for?"

"I'm wondering if you might have seen a car passing sometime before dawn this morning."

"Couldn't say. You got something stole from you, too?"

Gurney ended the conversation, thanking the man for his time and expressing the hope that his compost would be returned. He renegotiated the thorn patch, got in the Outback, and drove another mile down the road.

He pulled over behind a white Audi SUV with a double bike rack mounted on the roof. The vehicle was parked on a bed of evergreen needles at the head of the path to the cabin, which was set back from the road in a hemlock thicket.

Gurney followed the path. When he arrived at the cabin, he found a young couple wearing biking tights the color of chartreuse tennis balls, sitting on the rickety porch steps. The woman's hair was artfully disarranged. The man's hair had been wound into a bun on the top of his head, samurai-style. They were using a pail of water to wash dirt off some kind of greens. They looked up at Gurney, the woman smilingly, the man apprehensively.

"Hi," she said, brushing a few strands of hair back from her face.

"Ramps?" asked Gurney, recognizing the wet greens in her hand.

"Isn't it incredible? We were biking on a trail up in the woods this afternoon and we found a whole hillside covered with them. You know what they charge for these in Brooklyn? Do you live around here?"

"Up at the end of the road. I'm Dave Gurney."

"I'm Chloe. This is Jake. You live here, like, all the time?"

He laughed. "Yes, all the time."

"It's so absolutely gorgeous now, like a perfect spring, and the air, my God, but I can't imagine what these mountains are like in February. You have a big plow or something?"

"Pretty big. Winters can be interesting."

"Wow. I can imagine."

The friendlier she was sounding, the less friendly Jake was looking. Gurney decided it would be best to get to the point.

"I have a question—about early traffic on this road. Did either of you happen to be awake before dawn this morning?"

They glanced at each other. "Both of us, actually," she said, a little warily now.

Gurney took out his wallet and showed them his Larchfield PD credentials. "I'm working with the police department, and we need to know if there were any cars using this road between four and six this morning."

Jake spoke up. "Is there some kind of problem here?" He had worry in his eyes and pique in his voice, as though he were suspecting the cabin's rental agent of concealing something.

"Nothing that should concern you. We just need to know if anyone drove up or down the road before dawn today."

They looked at each other again.

Jake nodded reluctantly. "There was one car. We saw it leaving."

"You were out here in front of the cabin?"

"Out by our car. By the road."

"What time was this?"

"Had to be around four thirty."

"*Had to be*?"

"We were meeting an instructor down on the Willowemoc Creek at five."

"Fly fishing?"

He nodded.

"Jake fell in the creek," said Chloe with a wicked grin.

"So," said Gurney, "you saw a car at four thirty this morning. Do you remember make, model, color, style, anything specific?"

"It was super quiet," said Chloe.

"I'm pretty sure it was a BMW," said Jake. "Looked like a 5 Series."

"Did you notice the color?"

"It was too dark out to be sure. I'd guess black or dark blue?"

Gurney knew that the precise color would not have been clearly discernible in the moonlight. He just wanted to be sure the man wasn't "remembering" more than what would have been visible. He couldn't count the number of investigations that had gone awry because witnesses "recalled" details that never existed.

In this case, Jake was passing the credibility test.

"Do you remember seeing the license plate?"

He shook his head. "Now that you mention it, I think maybe the bulb was out."

"Okay. Anything else you noticed?"

He started shaking his head again, then stopped. "Oh yeah, like Chloe said, it was quiet."

"Quiet?"

"Like zero engine noise. Could've been a hybrid."

Back up at the house, Gurney went into the den and checked his phone. He found messages from Madeleine, Morgan, and Hardwick. He listened first to the one from Madeleine.

> "Hi. It's me. Obviously, I had to cancel the Winkler dinner for tonight. But when I mentioned it later to Gerry, she told me that she knows the Winklers, too. So, we're thinking about doing the dinner at her house tomorrow night. Is that okay? Talk to you soon."

Social occasions held an obvious attraction for Madeleine. The more the better, the sooner the better. They had the opposite effect on Gurney. His initial reaction to proposed get-togethers was invariably negative, although he usually ended up agreeing to attend events that were important to Madeleine. This one seemed to fall into that category.

Like a child accepting an unappealing vegetable, he called, got her voicemail, and left his message of agreement. He reminded himself that these things occasionally turned out to be more pleasant than he'd anticipated—although his past experiences with the Winklers made that outcome seem unlikely.

Morgan's message was, as usual, agitated.

> "On RAM News just now there was a video of your barn, showing that damn Dark Angel thing. They refused to give us the video files, so Gossett is getting a court order. You still think it's Tate making the videos and sending them to RAM? No chance it could be one of our own people? God, I hope not. That Rory Kronck idiot was going on about it being the Larchfield Slasher's direct challenge to you. The son of a bitch is turning you and Tate into comic-book characters! I hope to God the dragnet moving over Harrow Hill comes up with something. Tate, if we're lucky. Give me a call."

After making a mental note to check the RAM archive for the Kronck segment, Gurney listened to the third message, the one from Hardwick.

> "Last time we talked, you said you might want to enlist my services. We getting any closer to that? My hardware is cleaned, oiled, and ready for deployment. Been almost a year since I shot anybody. Speaking of which, I looked a little deeper into the Silas Gant situation. Word is that the Patriarchs are the protection and possible extortion arm of his operation, a source of fear to his enemies, and backup for business and political allies who need to show strength. Odd little factoid: the top Patriarch's name is Otis Strane, which I'm told was Lorinda Russell's maiden name. The plot thickens, Sherlock. Give me a call when you decide who needs to catch a bullet in the balls. One last thing. Check out Gant's Twitter account. He's stirring the shit like crazy."

Gurney was tempted to see what new poison Gant might be selling to his followers, but that quiet BMW Jake and Chloe saw at four thirty in the morning was occupying a more urgent spot in his mind. He decided to try Barstow again.

This time, she picked up the call on the first ring.

"David, great, I was just reaching for the phone to call you."

"Good news?"

"I got the tread and axle-matching results. They narrow the vehicle down to a single make and model group."

"BMW?"

"Yes." She sounded surprised.

"A 5 Series?"

"Yes. Any of the 5 Series sedans, starting with the 2018 model year. How come you knew that before I did?"

"Intuition."

"Like hell."

"Once in a while, we get lucky. A couple from the city happened to be in the right place at the right time."

"This means . . . what? That Tate traded in his orange Jeep for a seventy-grand Beemer?"

"Unlikely."

"So what on earth is going on?"

"Good question."

"Those sneaker impressions in the soft soil by your barn? They matched the impressions we found in the floor dust in the mortuary. And the blood on your barn door matched Linda Mason's DNA, as expected."

"So, some things are what they seem."

"Some," she said.

After hanging up, he placed a call to the central number for Larchfield police headquarters, expecting to reach the desk sergeant. Instead, Morgan answered.

"Dave? You got my message? Did you see that Rory Kronck thing?"

"I'll take a look at it. But first, do you happen to know the model and year of Aspern's BMW?"

"Why would you want to know that?" There was an instant edge on his voice.

"Just curious."

"It's a 530e, 2019."

"Does that 'e' have a particular meaning?"

"The 'e' models are hybrids." Morgan hesitated, his concern coming across loud and clear. "You sound like this is more than casual curiosity. What's going on?"

"Just one of those little echoes that seem meaningful at first, but usually end up being nothing. The thing is, there's tire-track and eyewitness evidence that the person who left the bloody message on my barn this morning was driving a BMW 5 Series hybrid."

"Jesus, don't tell me you suspect Chandler Aspern of being involved in that!"

"I realize it doesn't make much sense."

"It makes no sense at all! Chandler Aspern driving around in the middle of the night with a bucket of blood and a paintbrush?"

"Well, someone drove up to my barn in a 5 Series hybrid, got out in Billy Tate's sneakers, left that charming message, photographed it, and sent the video files to RAM News. I agree that it doesn't make sense for that person to be Chandler Aspern, nor does it make sense for Billy Tate to be driving that kind of car, unless he stole it. So, you might want to send out a theft-report inquiry for BMW sedans gone missing within the past couple of days."

"Yeah . . . okay, sure."

From the man's tone, Gurney could picture the worry lines deepening on his face.

"In the meantime," Morgan continued, "tread lightly."

"You mean, don't stomp on Aspern's toes?"

"Don't even say that! The fact that there may have been a BMW on your property and the fact that Aspern owns a BMW . . . hell, that adds up to nothing. Less than nothing. You hear what I'm saying?"

"I do." What Gurney heard was a man so focused on keeping his job that he was incapable of doing anything that might put it at risk—especially upsetting someone of importance.

After Morgan ended the call, Gurney moved from his firm desk chair to the overstuffed armchair by the den window with the broadest view of the high pasture. The sun had set, and the red and orange hues in the clouds were shifting to shades of purple. He put his feet up on the ottoman, put the open computer in his lap, silenced his phone, and let his eyes drift shut—telling himself that a restorative ten-minute nap was just what he needed before going to the RAM program archive to see Kronck's comments on the case. It had been a very long day.

A strange ringing impinged on his sleep, bringing with it the image of the alarm clock that was atop the bureau next to his bed when he was in high school—and the instant feeling of gloom that sound always brought with it. He opened his eyes and found himself still in the armchair in the now darkened den. It took another few seconds of reorientation to identify the ringing as the sound of his landline phone. He switched on the floor lamp next to the chair, made his way across the room to his desk, and picked up the phone.

"Gurney here."

"Christ, I've left three messages at your cell number. Where have you been?" Morgan's voice was a spring on the verge of snapping.

"What's the matter?"

"Selena Cursen's house was attacked. She and that girl who lives with her are in the hospital, may or may not make it."

"Who did it?"

"That's what we're trying to find out. Of course, everyone's out working the dragnet on Harrow Hill. If I call them in for this Cursen thing, that operation collapses, which we can't let happen. How soon can you get here?"

Gurney looked at the time. It was 11:20—meaning his ten-minute nap had lasted for two and a half hours.

"I can be at the Cursen place by twelve thirty."

"Ignore the speed limit."

36

The last section of the dirt road that led to the opening in Selena Cursen's iron fence had been taped off. Five official vehicles were parked outside the tape at haphazard angles—Kyra Barstow's crime-scene van, two Larchfield patrol cars, a red-and-white Chevy Suburban with a sheriff's department logo and the words FIRE INVESTIGATION UNIT across the back, and a utility van with a Larchfield Police logo on the side. Next to the van was a Toyota Camry.

Gurney figured the utility van had transported the generator he could hear humming in the background, as well as the halogen lights that were set up in the cleared area around the half-charred house. Despite having worked under those superbright lights countless times in his career, he'd never gotten used to the feeling of dislocation they created by turning night into day. Now their stark glare was giving the scene a surreal aspect. He guessed the Camry by the utility van belonged to the crime-scene photographer, whom he spotted heading into the house.

The desk sergeant from headquarters was leaning against the fender of one of the cruisers. He picked up a clipboard from the hood and stood up straighter as Gurney approached. He checked his watch and made a note on the crime-scene log.

"Hell of a thing," he said, gesturing toward the destruction. "Betcha people will say she brought it on herself."

"How?"

"All that witchery shit. Not a popular thing around here."

"Do you know if she'd received any threats?"

"I couldn't say. Some folks might have suggested she move on. Wouldn't be surprising, what with the Satanism and all that. Stirred up bad feelings."

Gurney was pretty sure those feelings were shared by the sergeant. A uniform was no antidote to the belief that unpopular victims—especially those who happened to be unconventional women—were responsible for the crimes committed against them.

His urge to dig a little deeper into the sergeant's attitude was interrupted by Barstow, calling out to him.

He called back to her over the hum of the generator. "You want me to suit up?"

"Just shoe covers. Back of my van, if you don't have your own."

He went to her van, took a pair of disposable booties from an open box, and slipped them on. He passed through the opening in the fence and headed toward Barstow through an expanse of knee-high grass that was starting to go to seed for want of mowing.

"So far we've found hundreds of these," she said, holding up a brass shell casing.

Gurney took a close look at it. "Seven point sixty-two, full metal jacket?"

She nodded appreciatively. "Fits most of the Kalashnikov-style assault rifles."

"When you said hundreds, did you mean a lot? Or literally hundreds?"

"Literally. Over three hundred so far. And still counting."

"So what happened here?"

"Hard to tell in all this grass, but my estimate from the tread marks in the dirt on the entry road is that five motorcycles came through the opening in the fence, then circled the house, firing into it. From the way some of the grass is matted down, I'd say they circled it at least three or four times. The wood siding's like Swiss cheese. Those full metal jackets ripped right through the walls, blasted everything inside the house to pieces."

He looked over at the house and saw a figure in coveralls spraying water from a garden hose through a broken window.

Barstow followed his gaze. "There's a second hose at the back of the house, and they've got a third hooked up inside. Well water. No way to get a tanker truck in here, and no pond to pump water from. The only reason the fire didn't consume everything is that it started on the leeward side of the house. If it started on this side, it would have blown through this old tinderbox in no time."

"Who reported it?"

"Ask Morgan. Far as I know, he got two or three calls from distant neighbors out in these woods. All those gunshots must have sounded like a war started."

"Morgan came out here himself?"

"Along with Sergeant Wood—the guy with the clipboard. Then he put in a call for the rest of us. Plus the EMT squad. They couldn't get the ambulance through the iron fence, so they carried Cursen and the other girl out on stretchers. That was over an hour ago. This place wasn't designed for rescue vehicles."

"Where did they find them?"

"Hiding in the basement. Wounded. Pretty badly. At least the fire hadn't gotten to them."

"Any idea what caused it?"

"Hot rounds striking combustibles in the house would be my guess. You should talk to the young man from the sheriff's department. Denzil Atkins. He's the official county fire expert. I'm sure he's bursting to reveal his expertise." She pointed toward two Tyvek-clad figures on the charred side of the house. "He's the one making notes on his iPad. Do not ask him if he was named after Denzel Washington. It's a touchy point."

"He wouldn't by any chance be one of your former forensic science students?"

There was a spark of humor in those gray eyes. "You have a talent for detection."

One of Barstow's techs walked past them, eyes to the ground, following the same type of spiral search route around the house that Gurney had followed around his barn.

"Any more?" asked Barstow.

"Five on the last rotation." Without stopping, he held up a plastic bag containing five brass casings.

"We may get to four hundred before the night is over," she said to Gurney. "You ever have a crime scene with more shots fired?"

"A few. Gang shoot-outs over drug territories. Arm the bangers with Uzis, and it's the Fourth of July. How about you?"

"Not up here. But I can recall some major fireworks down in Kingston. Drug gangs tend to be well armed."

"I better go talk to Denzil."

"See you later, boss."

Gurney made his way over to the young man with the iPad and introduced himself.

"I know who you are, sir. I'm Officer Atkins, sheriff's department. What can I do for you?" His tone was as crisp and efficient as his blond crew cut.

"Do you know yet how the fire started?"

"Yes, sir—with a reasonable degree of certitude."

Gurney recognized the witness-stand phrase. He wondered for a moment if it carried a hint of irony, but the young man didn't seem to be the ironic type.

Atkins indicated an area of the wall where the siding was partially burned through. "Ignition point was on the interior side of that wall. There's a shattered kerosene lamp on what's left of a table, approximately sixteen inches from the interior surface. Our on-site petrochemical residue test indicated kerosene combustion consistent with the lamp capacity. A bullet hole in the partly shattered lamp reservoir and in the opposite wall is consistent with a bullet trajectory beginning outside the house."

Gurney smiled at the young man's attention to detail. "You examined the whole interior?"

"Yes, sir."

"No other ignition points?"

"No, sir."

"And the wind direction is the reason that the entire house wasn't consumed?"

"That, plus a burst pipe on the second floor. The heat from the fire caused a solder joint to give way, and the water spreading over the floor and down through the wall structure acted as a partial barrier. They're off the grid here, but their generator kept working and the well pump kept pumping. If the fire got to the main breaker panel, we'd have had a different outcome. Some people are blind to the risks of a location like this."

Gurney thought about the location of his own house. "Price of privacy, I guess."

Atkins shook his head, as if to say that any clear-thinking adult would see that the price was unacceptably high.

Gurney thanked him and made his way to the porch side of the house—the side saved by a benign wind and a broken pipe.

The front door was open, and he entered a wood-paneled foyer, facing a carpeted staircase to the second floor. The acrid stink of smoke and wet ashes was much stronger here than outside. A surprising amount of light was coming in through the windows from the halogen stands surrounding the house, illuminating the smoky haze hanging in the air.

The photographer was panning with his camera around the walls of the parlor to Gurney's right, pausing at each group of bullet holes.

A woman in coveralls and gloves was using a razor knife and tweezers to probe a bullet hole in the staircase newel post. He recognized her as the hardscrabble patrol officer who'd been keeping an eye on Lorinda Russell the day after Angus's murder. She'd apparently been drafted by Barstow into helping with the massive task of bullet retrieval.

He watched as she extracted the slug, placed it in a pre-labeled envelope, then proceeded to another hole, this one in the staircase stringer board. He assumed she'd been instructed to collect as many slugs as she could, not only as pieces of evidence that could be linked ballistically to specific firearms in future legal proceedings, but as a way of determining the number of firearms used in the attack.

"Are they coming out clean?" he asked, meaning suitable for ballistics.

"Yes, sir. They're all FMJs."

There was something military in the tone of her voice that reinforced a thought he'd had at their first meeting, that she was probably one of the many police officers who found their way into law enforcement via the armed forces, having discovered a comfort zone in a world of rules, lines of command, and secure employment.

He headed up the stairs to a broad landing with a wet carpet and five open doorways leading to three partially destroyed bedrooms, a bathroom, and an enclosed staircase to the third floor. Deciding to check the third floor first, he found that it was just a large unfinished attic. The halogen light coming through the windows was weaker here, but he could see that the space was empty, apart from a gauzy lacework of cobwebs.

Returning to the second floor, he spent the next hour going through the bedrooms and bathroom. The first bedroom was the one used by Billy Tate, or at least by a male with a fondness for gray hoodies and black jeans. It exhibited a disarray familiar to him from his own son's teenage years—socks, underwear, and tee shirts on the floor, one sneaker on a chair and one under it, an open bureau drawer, a lamp with its shade askew, gum wrappers on the floor.

A heavy-metal band poster was taped to one of the walls. On another wall there were several eight-by-ten nude photographs of a woman. Looking closer, Gurney recognized the face of the black-haired beauty with three silver studs in her lower lip who he'd spoken to at the opening in the fence the day before.

"Love to my Billy forever, forever, forever, from Lena" was scrawled in girlish handwriting across the bottom of one of the photos.

On a nightstand by the unmade bed, there was a superhero comic book and a printout of the sideways figure eight symbol for sulfur and hellfire.

In the nightstand drawer, there was a flashlight, a jackknife, a box of condoms, a small plastic bag containing some pot, a pack of rolling papers, and three more comic books.

One of the room's three windows was open. Its curtain had been reduced by the fire to blackened strands of melted polyester fabric. There was ashy water on the floor and on the table under the window.

The next bedroom was more severely damaged, but enough of its contents were recognizable to identify it as Selena's. A bureau with a buckled top and scorched drawer fronts had remained intact inside—preserving an assortment of black lipsticks, black nail polishes, black panties, silky black gowns like the one he'd seen her in, and silver jewelry in the shapes of common Wiccan symbols. In the bottom drawer there were four books—*The Pagan Path to Saving the Earth*, *The Yogic Path to Beauty*, and biographies of Joan of Arc and Madonna.

In place of a closet, there was a tall armoire whose doors had been mostly burned away and whose contents were unrecognizable. The inside of the bedroom door was covered with heat-discolored photos of a young man with a smirky mouth and brooding eyes, wearing a gray hoodie and black jeans. He struck Gurney as an aging juvenile delinquent, trying to look dangerous.

The third bedroom, presumably used by the girl called Raven, had been almost entirely consumed by the fire. Apart from charred and cracked pieces of furniture and burned pieces of women's clothing, he noticed one fairly intact item—a handwritten note, stuck in the frame of a mirror that had fallen to the floor. Gurney bent over to read the message in a girlish script: "Remember the corn for the crows." It was signed, "Lena."

He went on to the last doorway on the landing, the one to the bathroom. Because of a high doorsill, the water on the floor was nearly an inch deep. Hanging on the wall next to the basin was a framed copy of "The Raven" by Edgar Allan Poe. He went quickly through the medicine cabinet and the shelving along one of the walls. He found nothing special, but that in itself was contributing to a not easily labeled feeling that had been growing from the moment he'd entered the house, a feeling that had begun the day before when he saw the tears welling in Selena Cursen's eyes. He made his way down the old-fashioned carpeted staircase and out the front door onto the porch.

Barstow was a few feet away, conferring with one of her techs. When she had sent him off with new instructions, she turned to Gurney and held up another brass casing. "New total—four hundred and one."

When he didn't answer, she looked at him more closely. "Is something wrong?"

"I wish the situation were clearer."

"What do you mean?"

"The stuff in their rooms is pretty ordinary. Nothing I saw suggests that they're devil-worshipping monsters. More like garden-variety lost kids. I've been in the homes of psychopaths, where the signs of evil are pretty obvious. That's not the case here."

"Are you saying Tate's not the murderer that all the evidence says he is?"

"I can't say anything that definitive. Sometimes the malignancy in someone is so well hidden, it's a shock to see what they're capable of. There've been mass murderers whose lives looked a lot more peaceful than Billy Tate's. I guess I was just hoping to find something here that matched the crimes we're dealing with—some clear assurance that we're on the right track."

"A psychological smoking gun?"

"Something like that."

"Maybe it got destroyed in the fire."

"Maybe. But the clearest signs of evil here right now are those bullet holes." He paused, his mouth tightening. "Sons of bitches ride in here like they're major warriors and put two helpless young women in the hospital. Jesus!"

Barstow was watching him closely, perhaps trying to understand a side of him she hadn't seen before. "I'm pretty sure we'll be able to get them. They're probably stupid enough to hold on to the weapons they used here. And unless they power-wash their bikes, soil and grass samples will link them to this site."

Gurney nodded. "It's a safe bet they were drunk or high."

She raised her eyebrows in fake surprise. “You don’t think that the idea of firing four hundred rounds into a house, roaring around it like maniacs in the middle of the night, was a sober plan?”

“What I’m thinking is that they may have been actively drinking on their way out here. Throttle in one hand, beer can in the other. Very macho.”

It took her about three seconds to grasp the implication.

“So . . . maybe I should send a couple of our people out along the entry road, have them check the brush along the edges for cans, bottles, whatever the shitheads might have tossed?”

“Sounds like a good idea.”

“Maybe something with prints the system can ID?”

“Even better.”

“Possibly the prints of a Patriarch?”

“Best of all.”

37

By the time Gurney was descending the final hill into the village of Walnut Crossing, the first blush of dawn was visible over the eastern ridge.

When he arrived at his barn fifteen minutes later, there was enough light for him to see that the door would need a second coat of paint to fully obliterate the Dark Angel message. Rather than putting it off, he decided to take care of it. He got his paint and brush from inside the barn and set to work. Applying the second coat was quicker and easier than the first. He washed out the brush in the pond's cold spring water, put it away with the remaining paint, and headed up to the house.

The morning air was cool and still. He heard the chickens moving around in the coop and went to check on their food and water. He poured more pellets into their feeding device and swept off the ramp that led into the fenced run. Then he went to the asparagus bed and cut a handful of spears to go with the scrambled eggs he was planning to have for breakfast.

Half an hour later, he was sitting at the table by the French doors, finishing a second cup of coffee. The doors were open, and the air drifting in carried a faint scent of lilacs. A flock of purple finches had arrived at the bird feeders that hung from shepherds' crooks at the edges of the patio.

He was reminded again of the stark contrasts embedded in his life. There was this peace and beauty, Madeleine's smile, the sweet air itself. And there was the ugliness of his profession. Of course, it wasn't really his profession that was ugly, it was the viciousness in human nature—the viciousness that made his profession necessary. The goal was balance. Remembering that the peace and beauty were as real as the bullet holes.

He was not a believer in the progress of the human species. Centuries of wars were proof enough of humanity's moral stagnation. But he did hang on to the notion that one could strive for moments of kindness, generosity, love, and tolerance.

The successes he had personally managed to achieve in those areas were limited, especially when it came to his animus toward the hate-mongers—the rage-merchants who ruled the echo chambers of cable news and the internet, who nurtured discontent and division, who marketed resentment for power and profit. They were, in Gurney's opinion, the scum of the earth. And the worst of the lot were the hypocrites who wrapped themselves in the banners of God and Country.

He was pulled out of this dark train of thought by the ringing of his phone.

The screen told him it was Morgan.

"Gurney here."

"Where are you?"

"At home."

"You checked out the Cursen house, right?"

"Right."

"You discover anything useful?"

"Nothing specific—just the feeling that Cursen's and Tate's evil-witch and killer-zombie reputations may be a bit exaggerated."

"What do you mean?"

"The rooms of the people living in that house did not strike me as the dens of monsters. If it turned out we were wrong about the evidence, I wouldn't be shocked."

"*What?*" Morgan's voice on the phone rose suddenly in volume and sharpness. "You're making it sound like we're sliding backward!"

"Backward may be the right direction, if we're on the wrong path."

"Great. Perfect." Morgan's tone was between petulance and panic. "I can hear myself announcing that at my next media briefing. It'll sound like I have no idea what I'm doing."

Gurney took a new tack. "How's the Harrow Hill search going?"

Morgan took a few seconds to refocus. "We've got every available pair of feet out there. Slovak figures they've covered about a third of it. The trails are a damn maze. If we don't get another downpour, within the next twenty-four hours they should find whatever—or whoever—is there to be found. But if, God forbid, we come up empty . . ."

Gurney could picture the man shaking his head in desperation.

"On top of everything else," Morgan went on, "Gant is tweeting all kinds of nonsense about Tate and Cursen, the murders, the defacing of the churches in Bastenburg, even about your barn. I'll email you the links. Let me know how you think we should respond."

"If you're thinking about accusing him of libel or inciting violence, you need to have Harmon Gossett review his statements. But Gant's probably smart enough to make sure his comments are protected by the First Amendment."

Morgan's tone turned sour. "You sound like you don't want anything to do with this."

"Mike, I'd love to see Gant in court, in prison, or worse. But there are people better equipped than I am to evaluate the legal possibilities."

"Will you at least take a look at the things he's saying?"

"Okay, sure."

Morgan breathed an audible sigh of relief. "Thank you. So . . . where do you think we need to focus our efforts now?"

"That depends on what the Harrow Hill dragnet produces."

"Let's hope it produces Billy Tate—and your doubts about him evaporate."

"Have you gotten the expanded warrant for his phone records?"

"We should have it by noon. But if this is about trying to establish a link between him and Chandler Aspern, it seems like a waste of time. Like focusing on that BMW coincidence."

"It would be nice to know where Aspern was at five o'clock yesterday morning."

"Christ, we can't interrogate the mayor like he's a suspect."

"If his phone's location feature was enabled, there could be a record of—"

"Jesus, Dave, could we please explore some other avenues first, before we create a powerful enemy in our own camp?"

Gurney said nothing.

Morgan took a deep, noisy breath. "Look, I've been working here all night. I'm running out of steam. I have to go check on Carol. Whatever news I get from the Harrow Hill sweep, I'll let you know. Take a look at the Gant video, okay?"

"Okay."

As he ended the call, Gurney noticed that he had a phone message from the night before that he hadn't listened to. A bad feeling tightened his chest as he stared at the caller's name and the time of the call.

Selena Cursen, 9:05 p.m.

He played the message.

It took him a second or two to realize he was hearing an erratic series of gunshots.

Then, combined with the gunshots, a female voice:

"It's Lena. They're shooting at us. Help! Oh, God—"

Her voice broke into a sudden scream. Then the scream was cut off, along with the sound of the gunshots, as if something had happened to the phone.

Gurney felt sick.

He listened to the message twice, to be sure he wasn't missing details that could tell him more about the attack or the attackers.

He found nothing helpful.

He just felt more pain.

And fury.

38

Gurney called the Larchfield hospital, also known as the Russell Medical Center, to learn what he could about the conditions of Selena and Raven. He was blocked by HIPAA privacy regulations.

It took ten minutes of playing the critical-need-for-information card to extract even the minimal facts that two female patients who had been admitted during the night were in the ICU and unable to receive phone calls or visitors. No, there was no exemption for police officers. No, it didn't matter that police officers had accompanied the ambulance that delivered the patients. No, it didn't matter that the patients were victims of a violent crime. HIPAA was the ultimate authority. Period.

As upsetting as the attack was, he realized there was no immediate way forward on that front—not until Barstow's people came up with an evidentiary link to one of the perps or until one of them got drunk enough on a Bastenburg barstool to brag about his daring assault on a coven of witches.

However, it wasn't in Gurney's nature to sit and wait. There were other ways he could make progress—if not on the Cursen attack, then on the larger case. He could, for example, dig deeper into what sort of person Billy Tate really was.

He checked his phone for Greg Mason's number and placed the call.

He was surprised how quickly Mason picked up and how sharp his voice sounded.

"Have you found him?"

"Not yet, sir. But we're doing everything we can. That's why I'm calling."

"What do you mean?"

"The last time we spoke, I asked you if you recalled anyone from Tate's high school years who he was close to or hung out with or had any kind of relationship with at all. You told me that everyone was afraid of him, with the exception of Lori Strane."

"Yes, so?"

"I want you to think again about that. Any sidekick, anyone with any relationship with him at all—I don't want to ignore any link that could lead us to Tate."

Mason was silent for so long, Gurney wondered if he was still there.

"Sir?"

"I'm trying to remember. But . . . he really had no friends."

Gurney detected a hint of uncertainty in Mason's voice.

"Okay. No friends. But maybe some other kind of relationship?"

Mason let out an impatient sigh. "Look, I wouldn't call it a relationship, but he may have had a connection with a local drug dealer."

"Do you recall his name?"

"Jocko."

"Was that his first or last name?"

"I have no idea. I don't even know if it was a real name. I only remember it because he spray-painted it on all the benches in the village square before he was arrested and sent away."

"Do you have any idea where Jocko is now?"

"He's probably not even alive. No great loss. One less piece of human garbage in the world."

Gurney thanked Mason and ended the call. After pondering how he might be able to track down a drug dealer who might not be alive, he decided that his arrest was the best starting point. He placed a call to Morgan.

"Jocko? Everyone in the department knows about Jocko—except now he goes by his real name, John Smith. Big turnaround. Why on earth are you asking about him?"

"Greg Mason told me there was a connection back in his drug-dealing days between him and Billy Tate."

"No surprise there."

"Do I gather Mr. Smith is living a different life now?"

"Last I heard, he was managing a sober house in Albany."

"Can you get me the name of it?"

"Hold on. I'll see."

Gurney held on for a good five minutes. He was about to end the call and try again when Morgan came back on the line.

"The place is called Free and Sober. It's a reentry program for ex-cons with substance abuse problems." He gave Gurney the address and phone number. "You think this guy is going to know something useful?"

"Probably not. But I hate ignoring possibilities."

Free and Sober occupied a neat row house, surrounded by a bleak neighborhood of semi-abandoned buildings, payday-loan outlets, liquor stores, and storefront churches. Across the street there was a pharmacy with bars on the windows. Two cars were parked in front of it, jacked up, with the wheels missing. Gurney parked his Outback down the block from them and put an OFFICIAL POLICE BUSINESS sign in his windshield. It was close to noon, but there was no one on the street.

The front door of Free and Sober was steel, painted brown. It had what looked like a reinforced peephole, but Gurney realized on closer inspection it was a shielded camera and speaker. There was a push-button bell on the brick wall next to the door. He pressed the button and heard the sound of a harsh buzzer somewhere inside the building.

The man who opened the door had the marks of a certain type of ex-con—the hard-muscled prison physique, obvious even under a loose polo shirt; the crude tattoos on his face, neck, arms, and hands; the watchful eyes that revealed nothing.

Gurney introduced himself and explained that he'd spoken with John Smith an hour earlier to arrange a meeting.

The man's expression relaxed into something just shy of welcoming. "Follow me."

He led the way along a dim-lit hallway, smelling of pine-scented floor cleaner, to the first open door and stood aside to let Gurney enter. The windowless room was furnished with a small desk, a filing cabinet, a bookcase, two chairs, a sagging couch, and a coffee table with cracked veneer. On a narrow table behind the desk there was a dated-looking computer and a framed photo of two men shaking hands. The room was lit by a single fixture in the center of the ceiling.

The man sat down in the chair behind the desk and waved his hand toward the other chair and the couch. "Take your choice."

It was then that Gurney recognized the voice of the man he'd spoken to on the phone. "Mr. Smith," he said with a smile. "I appreciate your taking the time to see me."

"No problem. But like I told you, I haven't spoken to Billy in ten years. And I don't know anything about this crazy stuff in the news. That's not the kid I remember."

"How did you happen to know him?"

"I was his dealer." Smith said this matter-of-factly, with neither the swagger nor attempt at justification that Gurney usually heard with such admissions.

"Tate was an addict?"

"More of an experimenter. He liked being on the edge. You know these pictures of people hanging off a balcony, standing next to a crocodile, that kind of shit? That was Billy."

"That's the way he was on drugs?"

"That's the way he was *without* drugs. He was crazier off them than on. Sober, he was like other guys on meth. I think he was experimenting with drugs to see what they would do for him. But the boy had a weird brain. Meth, coke, they didn't do anything for him."

"Did he try downers?"

"Sure. Oxy, heroin, tranks. They calmed him down, but Billy wasn't into calm. He was wild. Scared the shit out of people."

"Did he scare you?"

"I don't scare easy." It came across as a statement of fact, not street talk.

"Was he a bully?"

Smith didn't answer right away. "I wouldn't say he was. Bullies like to threaten little people. Billy threatened everybody. Just the way the boy's engine ran."

"Did he ever threaten you?"

Smith let out a humorless laugh. "He'd trash-talk, you know? But I never felt the need to deal with it."

"Why is that?"

"For something to be a threat, you got to feel it that way, and I never did."

"How dangerous was he?"

"Push the wrong button, everybody's dangerous. You're a cop. You know."

"How dangerous was he, compared to other people you've known?"

"Compared to the kind of gangbanger who might shoot a man because he blinked wrong, Billy wasn't that kind of animal. He had a line."

"A firm line?"

"Looked that way to me. But most people didn't see it. Billy had a way of laying down a threat on somebody with a smile—like telling them he was gonna cut their dick off and shove it up their momma's ass—like it was such a sweet idea he couldn't wait to do it."

"It was just talk?"

"Far as I know, all them men still have their dicks."

There was the sound of a vacuum starting up in a nearby room.

Smith glanced at the plastic watch on his wrist. "Cleaning time. Most residents are out at their jobs. Jobs are part of the deal here. Men that haven't found employment are assigned house maintenance." He paused. "You have any more questions?"

"You're aware that Tate is the prime suspect in three murders?"

"I saw that on TV."

"Did you find it surprising?"

"Price of being Billy is you're going to be the suspect for whatever bad shit goes down within a mile of you. But if he did them murders, then I'd say something in that boy's head must have changed."

"When you think back, can you recall any people he was close to?"

Smith shook his head. "He wasn't a *close* kind of person."

"Any idea where he might run to, if he needed to hide?"

"He used to have a thing with his stepmother. Maybe he still does."

"Anyone else?"

"Had a hard-on for Lori Strane. But so did half the county."

"Did you know her?"

"From a distance. I'd be careful around her, if I were you."

"Why is that?"

"A man of the cloth might say she has no soul."

"Did you know Angus Russell?"

"Knew *of* him. Had a rep. Not a man to fuck with. When I heard he and Lori got hooked up, I thought, holy shit, there's a match made in hell."

Gurney wasn't sure whether Smith had clarified his image of Tate or confused it further. As he was taking a final look around the office, his gaze stopped at the framed photo on the table behind Smith. He leaned forward for a closer look. "Is that you?"

"Yeah, that's me."

The other man looked familiar. "Can I see it?"

Smith handed it over.

Gurney realized why the man looked familiar. He was the state governor.

Perhaps in reaction to the surprise on Gurney's face, Smith spoke up. "We've had some success here, helping men who were incarcerated for drug-related crimes adjust to the outside world. People have no idea how hard that can be. Our program got the governor's attention early on. He dropped by with a camera crew. Gave our fundraising a big boost."

"I'm impressed."

Smith responded with the same earthbound calmness with which he seemed to address everything. "Considering where I came from, only thing that impresses me is the fact that I'm still alive."

A quarter of an hour later, Gurney was sitting in his car down the block from the Free and Sober facility, going over what John Smith had told him and deciding on his next move.

He checked his phone and found two messages that came in while he was meeting with Smith. The first was from Madeleine, letting him know that their dinner that evening with the Winklers and Gerry Mirkle would be at 7:00 p.m. The second was from Morgan, asking if he'd checked out Silas Gant's comments yet.

Though he had little appetite for it, Gurney went back to Morgan's original email and clicked on a link to a news site that had aggregated a series of tweets posted by Gant beginning at 1:05 a.m. that day.

> "The house of a self-proclaimed WITCH connected to BILLY TATE has burst into flames. FLAMES OF HELL?"

> "Servants of the DEVIL will blame my followers for the attack on that depraved house. Shame on those LIARS!"

"They spread their LIES—while SATAN, in the body
of BILLY TATE, is sharpening his knife. WANTS BLOOD!"

"The LYING MEDIA want to SILENCE AND DISARM us.
Stand with us now! We will PREVAIL!!"

There were five more in the same fiery tone, all with the core message that any implication that the Church of the Patriarchs had broken any law or fomented violence was not only a lie but a diabolical plot against the righteous. Whatever happened at that den of witches resulted from the ungodly activities of its residents.

Morgan's email included a link to a call-in interview Gant had given that morning to *RAM-Talk*, a program that thrived on outrage. He was wondering whether it would be worth listening to when his phone rang.

The screen said it was Slovak.

"Gurney here."

"Thanks for picking up." He sounded excited.

"What's up?"

"We found the orange Jeep!"

"On Harrow Hill?"

"On Aspern's side of it. About two-thirds of a mile from his house. In a thicket of pines. You were right about the helicopter problem. The Jeep would have been invisible from the air."

"Anything of interest in it?"

"Yes, sir! A bloodstained scalpel under the driver's seat. A bloodstained rag on the floor. Bloodstains on the top of the seat back—where Tate's hoodie would have rested against it."

"Any obvious prints?"

"Bloody ones on the steering wheel and the parking-brake handle. The steering wheel ones are smeared, but the ones on the brake handle look good."

"Sounds like you struck gold, Brad."

Actually, it seemed like a little too much gold, but he didn't want to say so. "Is Barstow's team there?"

"I'm going to call them right now. Wanted to fill you in ASAP."

"I appreciate that. Have you told Morgan?"

"Yes, sir, but he was on his way to see his wife. He'd gotten a call from the hospice people. I was hoping maybe you could come instead."

"I can, but I'm at least an hour away."

"No problem. We'll be here a lot longer than that. Best way in is through the trail in back of the Mason house. When you get there, call me. I'll send one of the guys down to get you."

"Have you notified Aspern?"

"I can't. I mean, the chief has a standing order that all contacts with the mayor go through him personally."

"This is different, Brad. This has nothing to do with Aspern's official role as mayor. This involves a suspect's vehicle on his property and our need to treat it as a crime scene. The evidence you observed connects it to at least one murder site, making it an extension of that scene. Since it's on his land, Aspern should be notified. But if he happens to appear at your location, he needs to be kept outside the boundaries you establish, just like any other unauthorized person. You have absolute control of that area."

The excitement had gone out of Slovak's voice. "Okay . . . if you think that's best."

Once again, Gurney found himself regretting his involvement. If he hadn't agreed to Morgan's request for assistance in the first place, the man probably would have been forced to turn the case over to the Bureau of Criminal Investigation—with all the state manpower and technical resources to handle it.

Instead, he felt an increasing weight of personal responsibility—combined with an unnerving sense that each new discovery in the case brought with it far more questions than answers.

39

An hour later Gurney was sitting in the Outback next to the trailhead behind the Mason house. After letting Slovak know he was there, he decided to use the time to take another look around the property and, if it was open, the barn where he'd found Linda Mason's body.

The first thing he noticed was that the acre or so of lawn surrounding the house had been mowed recently—probably that very day, judging from the uniform look of it, and probably by Greg Mason. It would be consistent with his fixation on orderliness—a trait likely to grow stronger when faced with the emotional chaos of murder.

The barn was locked, but the grass and plants around it had been tended to.

When Gurney made his way back to the trailhead, a Ford Explorer was waiting there. Slovak was in the driver's seat with his window open.

"I thought I should come down for you myself."

Gurney got in, and Slovak began maneuvering the Explorer up the narrow trail. "I'm glad you're here," he said after negotiating a sharp turn. "I left a message for Aspern, like you suggested, saying we found a vehicle on his property that was used in the commission of a crime. I didn't know how to describe the location, so I gave him the GPS coordinates."

"Good."

After weaving their way through the ascending labyrinth of trails, they came to a barrier of yellow police tape. Slovak parked the Explorer next to a big Sequoia SUV. There was a Russell College emblem on the door.

"Is that instead of the usual forensics van?" asked Gurney.

"Barstow was afraid she couldn't get up here without four-wheel drive." His tone seemed to question her decision.

He pulled a pair of shoe covers out of a box behind his seat and waited for Gurney to put them on. They got out of the Explorer, slipped under the tape, and followed the trail on foot.

Rounding a curve in the woods, they came upon the orange Jeep. The doors were wide open, and one of Barstow's helpers was going over the interior with an evidence vac. Barstow was on her phone, but when she saw Gurney she ended the call.

"Lots of prints, lots of blood," she said.

She began pointing out numerous chemical-stained finger- and handprints—some blue, some purple—on the Jeep's interior surfaces and the driver's-side door.

Gurney took a closer look. "Two different reagents?"

"I wasn't sure with some of the prints whether I was seeing blood or something else. I applied leucocrystal violet on those. Amido black on the others. I like the way it works on nonporous surfaces, and I figured the blue prints it produces would create a better contrast. I like the crisp look of the amido black in photographs. But I used the violet over there." She pointed to what looked like a sneaker print in the soft earth by the open driver's door. "I wasn't sure about that little spot of discoloration. It turned out to be blood."

"Everything is going to the lab for DNA?"

"Scrapings from all the prints and from the driver's seat and headrest, plus the rag and scalpel we found on the vehicle floor. Like you said yesterday, Tate isn't shy about letting us know where he's been. Be nice if he'd let us know where he is now."

"Speaking of that," said Gurney, half turning to include Slovak, "have either of you considered bringing in a K9 team?"

"Not me," said Barstow. "Chasing and capturing is Brad's department." The hint of mischief in her tone turned the fact into a challenge.

Slovak had a deer-in-the-headlights moment. "A K9 team . . . to track Tate? Can we still do that? The Jeep's been here for a while now, right? And we've had rain."

Gurney turned to Barstow. "Can you tell from the tire tracks how long it's been here?"

"I've tried to figure that out. I think the Jeep arrived, was here for maybe a day or so, then left and returned. I don't think it's been moved for the last couple of days."

"Can you tell from which direction it arrived? Or which way it left?"

She shook her head. "The only reason I can say anything at all is that the spot he chose has relatively soft soil."

Gurney turned to Slovak. "You're right about there having been rain, but it wasn't very heavy. The scent may still be followable. It's worth a shot."

"I don't think we've ever brought in a K9 team."

"All you need to do is get in touch with the NYSP regional barracks and tell them you need K9 assistance in tracking a fugitive."

Slovak's frown deepened. "The thing is, the chief's dead set against involving the state police."

"What he's dead set against is turning case jurisdiction over to BCI. This is different. The K9 unit just provides tactical support. There's no question of them taking over the case. If you call now, they may be able to have a team here tomorrow morning."

"Okay," said Slovak with lingering reluctance.

When he stepped away, Barstow gave Gurney a quizzical look. "You really think a dog can track Tate down at this point?"

"Not unless he's still in these woods. But I'd like to know what direction he took out of here. I'm also thinking about your opinion that the Jeep came here, left, and came back. I'm wondering how that pattern might fit with the other facts we have. What are you smiling at?"

"You. I can see your brain working like a 3D design program—tilting and turning the shapes to see how they join up. So, tell me how you're seeing it right now."

"Okay. Tate, after leaving Peale's mortuary, went to his parked Jeep and headed out along Waterview Drive, where he had a harmless encounter with Ruby-June Hooper and, a few minutes later, a deadly encounter with Mary Kane. He then proceeded up the Harrow Hill road to the Russell estate, broke in through the conservatory, and cut Angus's throat—after which he got back in the Jeep and drove through the trail maze to this spot. He may have stayed here himself until two evenings later—recuperating, nursing the damage to his body—at which point he could have used part of the trail system to access the back road that leads to the Mason house—the road where he was seen by a couple of local stoners."

Barstow pursed her lips. "Why didn't he just take the trail all the way down to Mason's back lawn?"

"Maybe the road was faster and safer—with all the switchbacks on the bottom half of the trail. Maybe timing was important. And there are no other houses or traffic on that final stretch, so he probably underestimated the risk of being noticed."

"Okay, what then?"

"When he arrived at the Mason house, he scratched his hellfire symbol on the front door with one of the scalpels he took from the mortuary, then waited for Linda Mason to come home. He knocked her unconscious, dragged her out to the barn, and lifted her with the loading bucket of the tractor—to simplify draining her blood. He then went back to her house, left the Dark Angel message with her blood on the upstairs wall, and drove the Jeep back here. How does that sound?"

"It's consistent with the Jeep coming, leaving, and coming back. But then what?"

"Ah, that's the question. Or maybe it isn't."

"You just lost me."

"The scenario I gave you is entirely reasonable, but it may have nothing to do with what actually happened."

"Are you always this unsure in the middle of a case?"

"Frequently."

"But you usually get to the truth, right? I mean, that award you got for clearing more homicide cases—"

Before she could finish, an irate voice interrupted.

"What the hell is all this?"

Chandler Aspern had ignored the police tape and was striding toward them, his compact frame a picture of compressed aggression.

Gurney stuck out his palm. "Hold it right there, sir. You're in a restricted area."

"Like hell I am! This is my property. No damn piece of yellow tape changes that."

"I'm afraid it does, sir. Please return to the area outside the tape, and I'll be happy to explain the situation."

"I hadn't figured you for this sort of bureaucratic nonsense." He turned and strode back the way he came, Gurney following him. They soon came to the perimeter tape, where Aspern had parked a golf cart.

"So," he demanded, "explain."

Gurney spoke with an easy calmness. "Evidence found in the vehicle back there on your trail connects it to three murders."

"Slovak left a message for me saying something like that, rather incoherently. Are you telling me that orange thing is Tate's Jeep?"

"We believe that to be the case."

"How long has it been on my property?"

"We're trying to determine that."

"When do you plan on removing it?"

"As soon as that's feasible."

"That's a meaningless answer."

"It's the only answer I can give you at this time."

"Fine." It was clear from Aspern's tone that it wasn't fine at all. He got into his golf cart, turned it around sharply on the narrow trail, and was soon out of sight.

On Gurney's way back to the Jeep, he met Slovak coming toward him, looking a little less worried.

"I got in touch with the regional barracks. They'll have a dog and handler here by ten tomorrow morning. There's going to be some paperwork, but it doesn't seem to be a big deal."

"Good. Do you know if Kyra plans to impound the Jeep?"

"Don't ask me. The woman runs her own show." His tone conveyed that the show was unpleasantly unpredictable.

Gurney was getting tired of the static in the Slovak-Barstow relationship, but that wasn't something he wanted to address—not right then, anyway. Instead, he thanked Slovak for arranging for the K9 team and continued along the trail to the Jeep.

Barstow explained she'd be completing her forensic examination of the Jeep within the hour and, yes, she intended to have it transported to the impound lot—but that wouldn't be happening until the following day, because there was a snag in getting it there. There was no key, and without one the anti-theft system would make starting the engine close to impossible, and there was no way to negotiate the trails with a tow vehicle. The nearest dealer able to provide a substitute key would have it ready for pickup in the morning. So, perhaps by tomorrow noon the Jeep would be on its way to the garage.

With little else at the moment keeping him on Harrow Hill, or anywhere else in Larchfield, Gurney's thoughts turned to Walnut Crossing and the planned dinner with the Winklers. That, in turn, reminded him of the tulips Madeleine had asked him to pick up.

An hour later, he pulled into the busy parking lot of Snook's Green World Nursery. Some customers were perusing the flower and vegetable seedlings on the outdoor tables, while others were making their way through the greenhouses. After a brief search, he located a potted tulip display, chose three pots with brightly colored varieties, paid for them, and secured them on the floor behind the front seat of the Outback.

He chose a route to Walnut Crossing that meandered through a succession of hills and valleys and wildflower meadows, but it wasn't because of the views that he chose it. It was because it was less direct and would add time to the drive. He'd accepted the need to be present at the Winkler dinner, but he had no desire to arrive early.

What he hadn't anticipated was the road-maintenance delay just outside Walnut Crossing. A pair of backhoes were deepening the drainage ditch alongside the road, and the final downhill stretch into the village that would normally take a minute to drive through took nearly twenty. It made him wonder how often lateness was a by-product of the fear of being early.

At Gerry Mirkle's driveway, he pulled in behind an eco-looking vehicle, no doubt belonging to the Winklers. He glanced at his dashboard time display and noted with relief that it was just 7:15. Arriving a quarter of an hour late could hardly be viewed as a problem.

As he was getting out of the car, Gerry opened a screen door to the driveway. She had a drink in her hand and a grin on her face.

"Welcome, traveler, we're just getting ready to eat."

He followed her through the door into a brightly lit kitchen with pictures of roosters on three of the walls. The aroma of Indian spices filled the air.

The Winklers—vegan-pale and wearing matching undyed-wool sweaters—were standing in the middle of the room, each holding a small bottled water.

Madeleine was carrying a covered casserole from the oven to a counter that separated the working part of the kitchen from a homey dining area with a pine table and captain's chairs. She set the casserole on a black-iron trivet and gestured toward the Winklers.

"You remember Deirdre and Dennis?"

Gurney walked over to Dennis with his hand extended and a smile that he hoped was sufficient to conceal his distaste for the man. "Nice to see you again."

Dennis sniffled loudly as they shook hands. Wearing a slim-cut white linen shirt, partly tucked into designer jeans, he had the curled lip of a perpetually unsatisfied connoisseur.

Deirdre offered a pale cheek to receive a welcoming kiss, which Gurney bestowed lightly.

"Oh, my . . ." she said, drawing back in dismay. "Sorry about that. You seem to have a strong negative aura. But of course you do. You're still doing police work, aren't you?"

"To some extent."

He wanted to avoid being more specific. It wasn't just his basic cop instinct for saying as little as possible about a current case. It was the fact that his last personal involvement with the Winklers involved Dennis's exposure to the frightening finale of the Peter Pan murders—a memory he didn't think anyone would want to revisit.

In an attempt to change the subject, he waved his hand toward the casserole. "Hopefully a nice dinner will get rid of my negative aura." He peered at the bottle in Dennis's hand. "What are you drinking?"

"The only absolutely pure water in America."

"Speaking of which," said Gerry to Gurney with a wink, "would you care to wet your whistle with an absolutely pure gin and tonic?"

"I would. Thank you!"

He followed Gerry to the counter, where she had the drink makings and a bucket of ice. He watched as she poured a generous shot of gin into a tall glass.

"So, how goes it?" she asked in a confidential tone.

He shrugged. "It's . . . complicated."

She glanced over toward the Winklers, as if to be sure they weren't overhearing her. "All I know is what Maddie told me, but it sounds horrendous and totally weird."

"It's all of that."

She poured some tonic over the gin, added ice cubes and a wedge of lemon, handed him the glass, then raised her voice to a more public level. "Okay, everybody, let's make our way to the table. Madeleine's put together a wonderful vegetarian biryani, and the scent of that cinnamon and cardamom is making me drool!"

While the Gurneys and Winklers were seating themselves, she went back and forth to the kitchen, bringing dishes of chutney, curried potatoes, and oven-warmed chapatis to the table.

"Wonderful stuff, Gerry," said Gurney after sampling a few items.

"Very nice," said Dennis. His flat tone suggested he'd had nicer things.

"By the way," said Deirdre, "have any of you been following what's going on up in Larchfield?"

"We don't have a TV," said Gurney quickly, having no desire to disclose his involvement. "What are they saying about it?"

"Horrible is a mild word for it," said Deirdre. "And the ironic thing is where it's happening."

"You mean Larchfield?" asked Madeleine.

"One of the classiest towns in the state! Dennis and I stayed at an inn on the lake on our tenth wedding anniversary. The inn, the lake, the homes—pure perfection! And that glorious little village square park—not one faded petal on the flowers. You could feel a sense of decorum in the air—something that's become virtually extinct in our tawdry world."

"True civilization is becoming a thing of the past," added Dennis. "The great American aristocracy has been forced to retreat into a few islands of propriety, like Larchfield. A tragedy."

From there, for the next two hours, the dinner conversation moved from one annoying topic to another, in Gurney's opinion, often involving Dennis's special occupations.

Among other things, he'd worked as a "natural-ecology arborist"—which involved a kind of matchmaking between trees and their evolutionary environments. He was also a hay-bale home builder, which he insisted was the most sensible form of residential construction. But he'd been forced to abandon that profession as a result of his hay allergy.

"And what are you doing now?" Madeleine asked, as Winkler paused to scoop the final bit of vegetable biryani from the casserole dish onto his plate.

"In addition to managing our alpaca farm, I'm now a CTB Life Guide. It's the culmination of—"

"A what?" said Gurney.

"You're not familiar with CTB? Contemporary Transcendental Buddhism. It's by far the most—"

Gerry interrupted to ask if anyone was ready for tea, regular coffee, or espresso.

Gurney opted for an espresso, Madeleine for regular tea, the Winklers for herbal tea.

Gerry began filling a teakettle with water.

"Wait a second." Dennis stood up, reached into a shoulder bag he'd hung on the back of his chair, and produced another bottle of water. "Would you mind using this for our tea?"

Gerry smiled. "No problem. Just curious—how is it different from our regular water?"

"Purity! A quality that should be built into more of the world's products."

Gurney recalled the eco-looking vehicle in the driveway. "Like your car?"

"Yes. It has *zero* emissions. Meaning it leaves the gentlest possible footprint on the world. There's a CTB saying: *Your footprint in this life forms the cradle of your next life.*"

Deirdre nodded enthusiastically. "Your actions today create what your life will be tomorrow. That's the true meaning of karma. Maybe all that horror in Larchfield is karma. Evil coming back from the dead."

Dennis offered his own summary. "Evil is done unto him who evil does."

Deirdre shuddered and crossed her arms. "That saying gives me goose bumps. But it's true, when you think about it. It's very deep."

"Well," said Gerry, standing up from the table. "It's getting dark, and I'm feeling a little chilly. Time to close the windows. Once the sun has gone behind those hills, it doesn't take long for the temperature to drop."

Everyone turned their heads to follow her gaze. The sky had faded from purple to charcoal gray. Gurney stood up to help close the windows. From somewhere in the woods behind the house there came a mournful cry.

Deirdre's eyes widened. "My God, what was that?"

Gerry shrugged. "Some kind of bird or animal. What else would be out there?"

"Oh, don't say that," cried Deirdre. "That sounds like a line in a horror movie."

"Sorry." Gerry's smile was pure innocence. "I'll check on the tea."

Madeleine spoke up cheerily. "Let's talk about alpacas."

"Oh, yes!" said Deirdre. "They're so sweet. And their wool is so gorgeous."

"Finest wool in the world," said Dennis. "Silky, durable, top-of-the-line. If someone wanted the ideal animal, the alpaca is the obvious choice."

"Kind of pricey, aren't they?" said Gurney.

"Quite the opposite, all things considered."

"What things?"

"The hidden costs of other animals. For example, cats." His intonation made cats sound about as desirable as rats. "When I met Deirdre, she had two cats, both with a preference for premium canned cat food. Two dollars a can. Four dollars a day. One thousand four hundred sixty dollars a year. And they lived for fourteen years."

"They were inseparable," said Deirdre wistfully. "Pippa died a week after Big Beau."

"Fourteen years," repeated Dennis. "At one thousand four hundred sixty dollars a year. That's twenty thousand four hundred forty dollars. Over ten thousand dollars per cat. For food. You know what an alpaca eats? Grass! And best of all—"

Gurney's phone rang. He pulled it halfway from his pocket and glanced at the screen. It was Morgan.

"Sorry," he said, "I need to take this."

A sliding glass door led to a rear deck. He stepped out into the cool night air.

"Gurney here."

"Dave! Can you hear me?" Morgan's voice was charged with excitement.

"Yes. What's happening?"

"Lorinda Russell called. She told me she just shot Billy Tate!"

"*What?*"

"She shot Billy Tate! She thinks he's dead."

"How did it happen?"

"He broke into the house. Through the conservatory, like the night he killed Angus. She heard the glass breaking and got one of Angus's guns. She went out into the conservatory, he came at her with a scalpel, and she shot him. Twice. She said he's lying there on the floor. She sounded freaked out by the blood. How fast can you get here?"

"An hour, if I leave right now. Who have you notified?"

"I sent some patrol guys over to secure the site, then I called you. I'm about to call EMS, Fallow, Slovak, Barstow. Hurry. I want you to be here when we interview Lorinda."

"When we spoke to her after Angus's death, she said she was bringing in a security company the next day to install cameras. If she did, get hold of the video files."

"Right. Will do. Wow. Tate's down! Hopefully dead. Jesus." Morgan's voice was breaking up with excitement. "I hope to God this means the case is over."

40

Gurney stood on the deck, staring out into the dark woods, trying to make sense of this strange development. There'd been unforeseen twists in cases he'd worked on over the years, but this felt different. It felt like a fundamental dislocation. It made him wonder if his previous sense of the case had any basis in reality.

What motive was he missing that would account for Tate attempting a homicidal attack on Lorinda? And from a tactical point of view, why hadn't he killed her the night he killed Angus? She was in the next bedroom, a convenient target. If he hadn't wanted to kill her then, why now?

Madeleine stepped out on the deck. "Is there a problem?"

"Morgan just told me that the 'Dark Angel' who left the message on our barn has been shot. So the case may be coming to an end, but now I'm not sure what it was all about to begin with."

"Do you have to know?"

"I'd like to."

After a silence she changed the subject. "Did you by any chance remember the tulips?"

"Actually, I did."

He retrieved the pots from the Outback and handed them to her.

"I have to leave now. Can you—"

"Explain that you've been called away on a police emergency? Of course. Be careful."

There was no traffic on the route he chose from Walnut Crossing to Larchfield, and he drove well over the speed limit. A full moon was high in a cloudless sky, giving the landscape a silvery sheen and making his headlights almost unnecessary. As he descended the long hill into Larchfield, the surface of the lake was a sheet of pewter running through the center of the valley.

Soon he was proceeding along Waterview Drive, passing a succession of lakefront mansions, coming eventually to the roadside cottage with the little porch where Mary Kane had been murdered.

Why her and not Ruby-June Hooper, who'd encountered Tate less than a mile down the road? Gurney wondered for the twentieth time. Could that little mystery be a window into the essence of the case?

Immediately after the Kane cottage, he turned up the private road that provided access to the Russell estate and the web of Harrow Hill trails. As he recalled from his experience there with Morgan, the dirt-and-gravel lane soon twisted into a series of narrow switchbacks—tricky in daylight and a real challenge at night.

He finally arrived at the estate's imposing drystone wall and stopped. Police tape had been stretched across the open gateway. A young officer with a large flashlight came to the side window of the Outback and pointed it for a moment at Gurney's face.

"Detective Gurney?"

"Right."

"You can go right on through. All vehicles are to be parked by the front portico."

"Thanks. Is he dead?"

"Oh, yeah, he's dead. I was one of the first responders, took one look, didn't need to take another. Two shots. One through the chest, one through the jaw. Blew the back of his head apart. Only thing that kept it from flying all over that greenhouse was that hoodie."

The officer lowered the tape, and Gurney drove through the open gate into the allée of tall trees that enclosed the gravel driveway on both sides. He parked the Outback next to the other vehicles by the columned portico—three Larchfield PD cruisers, Slovak's Dodge Charger, a body-transport van, Fallow's Mercedes, Morgan's Tahoe, the crime-scene photographer's Camry, and Barstow's tech van. The time on the dashboard display was 10:15 p.m. as he stepped out into the chilly night air.

As Gurney made his way around the big stone house, he passed from soft moonlight into the stark brightness of the halogen lights illuminating the area between the conservatory and the woods. He crossed paths with the photographer, who was just leaving, a bulging camera bag slung over his shoulder.

Slovak and one of the uniformed officers were examining Tate's orange Jeep, which was now at the mouth of the trail opposite the conservatory door. Two other patrol cops were using yellow tape to demarcate a wide corridor across the lawn. Through the glass-paned side of the conservatory, Gurney spotted Barstow talking to Fallow.

Morgan was standing by the open conservatory door. The emotion in his eyes was beyond anxiety.

"Thank God you're here!"

"What's the matter?"

"You'll see."

Gurney stepped inside.

What he saw at first was consistent with what he'd been envisioning, based on Morgan's phone call and the comments of the officer at the gate.

There was nothing initially surprising about the prone figure lying in the middle of the stone floor, or in the now-familiar Tate uniform of gray hoodie, black jeans, and sneakers. The body was resting on its back, legs extended toward Gurney.

Large, still tacky-looking bloodstains on the floor to the left side of the head and chest suggested that the body's original orientation had been facedown over those areas of pooled blood and that it had been rolled over by the medical examiner in the course of his preliminary in situ examination. The matching positions of the stains on the chest and neck areas of Tate's hoodie were consistent with this scenario.

When Gurney moved closer, he noted the catastrophic damage caused by the bullet that had shattered the chin and jaw before continuing on its path and apparently—according to the gate officer—blowing the rear section of the skull into the hood of the sweatshirt.

As he approached still closer and was able to get a better view of the upper part of the face, he was baffled by its transformation. It seemed to have aged in a weird way, looking nothing like the mug shot he'd seen of Tate. Certainly nothing like the photograph in Selena Cursen's bedroom.

The change was especially evident in the still-open eyes. They were smaller, darker . . .

He stopped, stared, took another step closer.

Was it possible?

He looked back at Morgan, who nodded in what looked like an ongoing state of shock.

Gurney bent over, peering intently at those small, black, dead eyes. Now he was certain.

The bloody body on the floor was Chandler Aspern's.

He stepped back, his mind racing to make sense of this bizarre development.

Barstow's voice interrupted his thoughts. "We found something interesting in his sweatshirt pocket." She held up a plastic freezer bag.

Gurney leaned forward to make sure he was seeing what he thought he was seeing.

The bag contained a severed right hand, probably male, judging from the size of it.

PART THREE

INTO THE HEART OF EVIL

41

In the forty-eight hours following the shooting, a new case narrative, complete with ample evidence, had been constructed—with Chandler Aspern, mayor of Larchfield, as its central villain.

Gurney found the new hypothesis more or less satisfactory. On the downside, it left some significant questions unanswered. On the upside, it provided credible explanations for two elements that had been troubling him—the call Tate made to Aspern's number from the mortuary and the disparity between the fates of Ruby-June Hooper and Mary Kane.

On the morning of the third day after the shooting, the Aspern-centered theory of the Larchfield murders was scheduled to be presented to the county district attorney, with the objective of securing agreement that the new narrative could be released to the media and the case could be closed.

Gurney had agreed to be present at the meeting.

At Morgan's request, he arrived at headquarters twenty minutes early for a run-through of how Morgan intended to present the evidence of Aspern's guilt.

When Morgan asked for his comments at the end of the run-through, Gurney said that it all sounded fine. In fact, he did have some lingering concerns, but he knew raising them at this point would only make Morgan more nervous.

"Have you ever met our DA?" Morgan asked.

"No."

"She's a fast-talking hotshot being groomed for bigger things by the powers that be."

"Have you had problems with her?"

"Nothing major, just the static created by the kind of person who wants everything perfect and wants it yesterday."

"You expecting significant static in this meeting?"

Before Morgan could answer, there was a knock on his open door. It was the desk sergeant.

"Stryker is here," he said, as if announcing the arrival of the IRS.

Brad Slovak and Kyra Barstow were already at the conference table. They were seated across from Martin Carmody, the PR man, and Greta Vickerz, the mechanical engineering professor who'd concluded that Tate's casket had been broken open from the inside.

An athletic-looking woman with short brown hair was standing at the end of the table, talking on her phone. She appeared to be in her late twenties, which would make her the youngest of the state's district attorneys, but there was nothing particularly youthful in her cool, hard expression.

Gurney chose a seat next to Vickerz. Morgan remained standing until Stryker ended her call and took her seat. She laid her phone in front of her, conspicuously checked the time, and said without any greeting or preamble, "Your show, Chief."

Morgan cleared his throat. "I think you know everyone in the room, Cam, except Dave Gurney—"

"I know who he is. Let's begin."

The tic at the corner of Morgan's mouth was back. "I thought we'd start at the beginning—with the videos that document Billy Tate's fall from the church roof and his subsequent revival and departure from Peale's Funeral—"

Stryker cut him off with a wave of her hand. "I've already seen them. RAM-News has been running leaked copies day and night."

"Then I'm sure you saw Tate sending two text messages from the embalming room?"

"That's what he appeared to be doing."

"Phone records show that the first was to Selena Cursen, the woman he was living with, letting her know he was alive. The second was to Chandler Aspern, suggesting a mutually beneficial opportunity and his intention to visit him later that night."

"I saw the texts in the case file. Are you assuming that after Tate left the mortuary he drove to Aspern's house?"

"Correct."

"Then what?"

"Then he spelled out for Aspern the mutual opportunity he'd referred to in his text."

"Do you know what that opportunity was?"

"We have a pretty good idea."

"You mean an unsupported speculation?" A pen had appeared in Stryker's hand, and she was tapping it lightly on the table.

Morgan's tic was accelerating. "I'd prefer to call it a reasonable conjecture, Cam—one that's supported by what happened afterward. We believe that Tate realized he was in a unique position. He was supposedly dead, and if his body was missing, the natural belief would be that it had been stolen. He could have seen that as an opportunity."

"To do what?"

"Get even with Angus Russell for having had him arrested and sent to prison. Maybe settle other scores as well. And get away with it, being officially dead."

"What's the connection to Aspern?"

"It was known that Aspern and Angus were enemies and that there was an enormous amount of money at stake. I can see Tate approaching Aspern that night with a simple question: *What would Angus's death be worth to you?* Maybe they discussed the details, maybe they didn't, but then something happened that Tate hadn't anticipated."

Stryker's pen stopped tapping. There was a spark of interest in her eyes. "Aspern turned on him?"

"Aspern killed him."

"Because he didn't trust him?" Lack of trust appeared to be a feeling she could relate to.

"Right. Why take a chance—when he could do it himself in a way that would incriminate Tate? It seems that Tate came up with the perfect crime and ended up being the victim of his own cleverness."

"So, you're suggesting that Aspern killed Tate, and then killed Angus?"

"I think Aspern killed Tate, then cut his hands off, so he could leave his prints at the crime scene. He put on Tate's clothes, took the scalpels and bone mallet that Tate stole from the mortuary, and set out for the Russell estate in Tate's Jeep. Incidentally, the fact that it was Aspern in the Jeep gave us the answer to a certain nagging question we had from the beginning." Morgan turned to Gurney, who picked up the narration.

"We were baffled by the fact that two people had encountered the Jeep and its driver on Waterview Drive that night, but only one of them was killed. Ruby-June Hooper says she recognized Billy Tate and spoke to him, with no consequences. Then, a mile down the road, Mary Kane had an encounter with him and ended up dead. But if the driver of the Jeep was Chandler Aspern, there's a logical explanation. Because of the hoodie and the only illumination being moonlight, Ruby-June Hooper assumed it was Billy and called him by name. That would have been exactly what Aspern wanted, so he drove on. But suppose Mary Kane saw the driver more clearly under that bright streetlight across from her cottage. Suppose she realized it wasn't Billy, or even recognized Aspern. That may have been what got her killed. We have a recording of the incident on her phone—which she was using to record birdcalls—that's consistent with this scenario."

Stryker nodded slowly, as though she were evaluating how the puzzle pieces were being assembled. "Why the Linda Mason murder two days later?"

"Another guess, but I'd say he wanted to add a finishing touch to his framing of Billy Tate, who was widely known to have threatened Linda Mason, just like he threatened Angus Russell."

"Aspern had nothing against the Mason woman personally?"

"We can't be sure of that, but it looks like her murder was mainly a prop to cement our focus on Tate."

"Like the hellfire symbols and the Dark Angel messages?"

"Exactly."

"Okay," said Stryker, again tapping her pen on the table and turning her attention back to Morgan. "That brings us to Aspern's ill-fated attack on Lorinda

Russell—which I'm having some trouble with. Take me through it. I want facts, not conjectures."

Morgan smiled. "We're in good shape on this final piece."

"We better be, because all we have so far is a collection of reasonable guesses."

Morgan opened the app on his phone that controlled the room's video equipment. He touched an icon, and the big screen on the wall came to life. Everyone shifted in their chairs for a better view of it. Even as he swiveled around, PR expert Martin Carmody maintained the steepled-fingers pose of a strategic thinker.

"After Angus's murder, Lorinda got in touch with a home security outfit, who got the first camera installed and running the day before Aspern's break-in. So we have a high-resolution record of his arrival on the property in Tate's Jeep and his approach to the conservatory door, wearing his Billy Tate disguise."

"In Tate's Jeep? I thought your department had taken possession of that."

"We'd found the vehicle on Aspern's property. Kyra Barstow completed her forensic examination of it on-site, but there was a delay in having it moved to the county impound lot. So Aspern had easy access to it that night."

Stryker nodded tentatively. "And, according to your new view of the case, he would have had the key?"

"Exactly. He would have taken it from Tate after he killed him." Morgan touched another icon, and the screen was filled with an image Gurney recognized as the area of lawn between the conservatory and the woods. The image definition in the moonlight was extraordinarily sharp.

"Keep your eyes on the trail opening," said Morgan.

The front of a vehicle, recognizably a Jeep even in the semidarkness, came slowly into view and stopped at the edge of the lawn.

A dark figure emerged from the Jeep into the moonlight. He seemed to be wearing the same gray hoodie, black jeans, and sneakers Tate had been wearing in the mortuary video. The figure moved quickly across the camera's field of view toward the house. Because of the angle of the camera and the size of the sweatshirt's hood, his face was hardly visible. For a second Gurney thought he could see a thick black mark on the side of his cheek.

Morgan looked down the table at Cam Stryker. "His line of movement puts him on a direct path to the conservatory."

The hooded figure passed out of the frame, and the screen went blank.

Morgan added, "Detective Gurney and I interviewed Lorinda Russell later that night, and the story she told us begins where that video left off."

"The interview was recorded?"

"It was."

"Where?"

"In a cottage on the estate."

"Why there?"

"Mrs. Russell has a phobic reaction to blood. She insisted that she couldn't stay in the main house until the body and all visible signs of blood were removed. She had the same reaction when her husband was killed."

"It's an audio recording?"

"Audio and video—already cued up in the system, ready to go."

She checked the time on her phone. "Let's do it."

The first image on the screen was of Lorinda sitting in one of the cottage's chintz-covered armchairs, wearing a cream-colored silk blouse that seemed a well-chosen counterpoint to the dark shoulder-length hair that framed her face. She managed to appear both magnetic and untouchable.

Stryker stared at the freeze-frame image. "*This* is the woman so shattered by the sight of blood that she couldn't stay in the same house with it?" She looked at Morgan. "*Really?*"

Morgan shifted in his chair. "Lorinda is . . . an unusual person."

"An unusual person whose husband was brutally murdered last week, who just came within seconds of having her own throat cut, who just shot a man dead, and she's sitting there like the queen of serenity." Stryker opened her palms as if searching for an explanation. "Is she on drugs?"

"Not that we know of," said Morgan.

After Morgan put the video in motion, the first voice heard on it was Gurney's, coming from somewhere off camera.

"As I explained, Mrs. Russell, we're recording this. Please describe in as much detail as you can everything that happened this evening—beginning with where you were and what you were doing when you got your first indication of a possible intruder."

Lorinda's unblinking eyes were gazing out of the screen at whoever might be watching the video—the result of the fact that she'd been looking not at Gurney but directly at the camera positioned next to him.

She spoke with a voice that revealed no emotion, no geographic roots.

"It was nine o'clock. I was in the downstairs office. I was about to make a call, and I saw the time on my phone."

"Who were you calling?" asked Gurney's off-camera voice.

"Danforth Peale—to let him know that the medical examiner was ready to release Angus's body, and I wanted to discuss the arrangements."

"Wasn't nine o'clock at night an odd time to be calling him about that?"

"It was when the subject occurred to me. It needed to be dealt with. I don't like putting things off."

"Did you complete the call?"

"Peale didn't pick up. It went to his voicemail."

"Did you leave a message?"

"No. That's when I heard the glass breaking. It sounded like it was in the conservatory."

"What did you do then?"

"I went to a cabinet where Angus kept one of his guns. A Glock 9. I took it out and went to the conservatory."

"Did it occur to you to call 911?"

"I don't remember."

"Or your groundskeeper? Doesn't he have an apartment over the garage?"

"He spends his nights with a woman in Bastenburg."

"Okay. So, you went to the conservatory. What then?"

"At first, nothing. There's a hallway that connects the main part of the house to the conservatory. I waited there for a minute until my eyes adjusted to the moonlight. I heard more glass breaking. Then I saw someone pushing the conservatory door open."

"How clearly did you see him?"

"Clearly enough to see that he was wearing a hooded sweatshirt and had a black mark down the side of his face. I saw something in his hand—a knife with a short blade. I raised the Glock. I stepped from the anteroom into the conservatory. I told him to stay where he was and drop the knife. He stayed perfectly still for a few seconds, then rushed at me with the knife."

"You could see the knife clearly?"

"It was shining in the moonlight—the moonlight coming through the glass roof."

"Go on."

"I pulled the trigger—twice, I think. He collapsed on the floor in front of me. I backed away. He wasn't moving. A dark spot was spreading out on the back of his sweatshirt. I couldn't look at it. The thought of it . . . I . . . I went back into the house. I called the police."

"You called Chief Morgan directly?"

"Yes."

"Rather than 911?"

"Angus always said, call the person in charge, anyone else is a waste of time."

"Did you go back into the conservatory for any reason before the police arrived?"

"No."

"Where did you go?"

"To a bench out in the entry hall near the front door."

"Did you make any other phone calls?"

"No."

"What did you do with the gun?"

"I kept it in my hand. When the first officer arrived, I gave it to him."

"Were you in the conservatory for any reason after the police came?"

"No. They told me there was a lot of blood."

"When you called Chief Morgan, you told him you'd shot Billy Tate, is that right?"

"Yes."

"What made you think it was Tate?"

"He looked exactly like Tate in the video they kept showing on TV. The hoodie. The black pants. The mark on his face. And he broke in through the same door Tate used the night he killed Angus. I'd just had the glass replaced."

"When you were told it was Chandler Aspern in Tate's clothes, what was your reaction?"

"Surprise."

"Not shock?"

"I guess you could call it shock."

"Why would Aspern attack you like that?"

"I don't know."

"When was your last contact with him?"

"We spoke on the phone that afternoon."

"What about?"

"His legal disputes with Angus. His lease on his side of Harrow Hill. Development rights. Money."

"Who called who?"

"I called him."

"Why that afternoon?"

"Why not?"

"What was the purpose of the call?"

"To see if our conflicts could be resolved."

"How did it go?"

"Not as I wished. I offered to buy back his lease. He insisted on an absurd price."

"How did the conversation end?"

"I told him what my final proposal was, and that he'd be wise to accept it. He told me I was an ignorant little bitch. I told him if he wanted to have a calm face-to-face discussion, I would be available that evening or the following day. He ended the call."

"You weren't too angry at him to make that offer—after being called an ignorant bitch?"

"Business is business. Emotions are for children and actors."

Morgan touched an icon on his phone and the video ceased, leaving just a freeze-frame of Lorinda—her dark eyes gazing from the screen at the group around the conference table.

"We also have a written statement from her," said Morgan. "It was taken later, but it's essentially identical to what you just saw."

Stryker emitted a low whistle. She was tapping her pen again. "Does the physical evidence support her story?"

"There are no obvious inconsistencies," Morgan said, adding, "The photographs taken at the scene support what she told us. Do you want to see them?"

"Definitely."

All eyes returned to the screen.

The initial images documented the site. They showed the shattered glass in the door, the botanical-garden interior, the planting beds, and the paths of yellow stone between the beds.

The next sequence focused mainly on the body, facedown, showing it from different angles. Blood had soaked through the hood and the back of the sweatshirt Aspern was wearing and had pooled on the stone floor around his head. Close-ups of these areas elicited grunts of distress from Greta Vickerz and Martin Carmody.

There were also close-ups of other parts of the body—the hands, on which Aspern wore tight nitrile gloves; the black jeans; the sneakers. Gurney was reasonably sure they were the same sneakers Tate had been wearing in the photographs taken after his fall from the church roof. The design of the uppers, the tread pattern of the soles, even the distinctive fat laces looked familiar.

Another sequence of photos showed the body after it had been rolled over on its back. Aspern's small black eyes were instantly recognizable, even though they had lost their intensity. Part of his lower chin was missing, and his jaw was shattered. A bloodstain covered the entire front of the sweatshirt, and there was a dark bullet hole in the center of the stain. In a final wide-angle photo, Gurney saw part of the big wood-framed device with overhead pulleys for moving the larger plants, which he remembered from his first visit.

Morgan touched an icon on his phone, and the screen went blank.

"Very instructive, and very convincing regarding Aspern's break-in," Stryker said. "Do we also have physical evidence linking Aspern to Tate?"

Morgan looked at Slovak. "Go through the list."

"The clothes Aspern was wearing are definitely Tate's," Slovak said. "We have DNA confirmation from blood and epithelial cells. Next to Aspern's body we found one of the scalpels Tate stole from Peale's mortuary—and the bone mallet he used to break the glass. Both of those tools had Tate's residual fingerprints on them. And when we searched Aspern's house, we found a container of Linda Mason's blood in his refrigerator."

Martin Carmody made a small sound of disgust.

Slovak continued. "We brought in a K9 team to see if we could track Tate—when we still believed he was our killer—but what they ended up finding were pieces of his body buried in the woods near Aspern's house. The flesh on the face had the burnt gash from the lightning. All the body parts have gone to the ME's office for final identification and, if we're lucky, cause-of-death determination."

Greta Vickerz wrinkled her nose, as though the odor of death had entered the room.

"Then there's the big one," said Slovak. "The severed hand we found in a plastic bag in the pocket of the sweatshirt Aspern was wearing has been identified as Tate's. We believe Aspern was carrying it so he could put Tate's prints on the conservatory door, and maybe on other surfaces in the house."

Carmody looked nauseated.

Cam Stryker's expression revealed nothing. "Has the phone call Lorinda Russell said she made to Aspern been verified?"

Morgan answered. "The carrier shows a call of approximately six minutes from her number to Aspern's number that afternoon."

"Do you have Aspern's phone?"

"Not yet. It wasn't on his body. We've checked his car—actually, all three of his cars—a BMW, a Porsche, and a Mercedes—as well as his golf cart and Tate's Jeep. We're still searching his house for it, as well as for anything else that might help us understand his motivation."

"His motivation—what's your hypothesis for that?"

Morgan wiped sweat off his forehead. "We haven't gotten very far with that. Maybe he thought that whoever would inherit Lorinda's control of the Russell half of Harrow Hill would be easier to deal with. Maybe he killed Angus in the belief that she'd be easier to deal with, then found out she wasn't."

"What's Lorinda's understanding of the motivation issue? Has she said anything other than what's in that interview video?"

"We tried to pursue that with her, but she seems to have surprisingly little interest in understanding what happened or why. She said talking about it is a waste of time."

"Does she have any close relatives?"

"One of the so-called Patriarchs in Silas Gant's church may be a cousin of hers, but she claims not to know whether he is or isn't."

Stryker uttered a one-syllable laugh. "There's something missing in that woman. What do you make of her?"

Morgan turned up his palms. "She's a mystery."

"That's all you can say?"

He shrugged. "She's the ultimate closed book."

"Okay. Moving on. Do you have the Aspern autopsy report yet?"

Morgan looked relieved to be on firmer ground. "We do. There's nothing unexpected in it. He was struck by two rounds. The one that entered through the lower jaw blew away the brain stem. The one through the sternum exploded the heart and severed the spine. Either one would have been instantly fatal."

"He was struck by both while he was upright?"

"Yes. They passed through him at essentially the same angle."

"Lorinda evidently has a steady hand and a fast trigger finger."

Morgan remained silent.

Stryker laid her pen down. With her elbows on the table she raised her hands, interlocked her fingers, and rested her forehead against them. In a different person it might have looked like a posture of prayer. In Stryker it looked like intense thought.

After a long minute she lowered her hands to the table and cleared her throat. "Okay. I think we can wrap this up. A reasonable conclusion has been reached, based on substantial physical and circumstantial evidence. *Chandler Aspern, the Larchfield murderer, was shot and killed in the course of an attack on a potential fourth victim.* Et cetera. Chief, I suggest you draft and deliver a confident statement to that effect. End of a complicated mess. End of a media circus. Justice triumphant."

Morgan sat back in his chair, a smile on his face, and looked down the table at Carmody. "Martin, I'll be calling on your expertise—to bury this monster once and for all."

Carmody rubbed his hands together. "It'll be my pleasure."

42

Later in his office, alone with Gurney, Morgan's exhilaration at the case's sudden ending was giving way to his chronic habit of worry.

"You were awfully quiet in that meeting," he said.

Gurney shrugged. "I had nothing useful to say—certainly nothing that would have gotten you the resolution you wanted from Stryker any sooner."

Morgan eyed him uneasily. "Do you have a problem with the resolution?"

"Nothing I can put my finger on."

"It makes sense."

"More or less."

"It avoids a complicated trial, legal challenges, defense attorneys picking our procedures apart, turning everything inside out."

"True."

"But you think there's a loose end somewhere?"

"I have no idea."

Morgan nodded meaninglessly.

Then Gurney asked, "How's Selena?"

"I don't know. We can check."

"Good idea."

Morgan changed the subject. "You told Barstow to check for beer cans or bottles out on the road by the Cursen place?"

"Her idea, as I recall."

"The thing is, her people found a can with a clear thumbprint belonging to a guy by the name of Randall Fleck. Long rap sheet. Drunk and disorderly, harassment, assault, et cetera. Since the can was beside a public road, and the soil traces in the tires of his motorcycle weren't unique to the Cursen property, we couldn't link him directly to the attack on the house, but we did manage to nail him with felony possession of three unregistered handguns and a fully automatic Uzi. We also confiscated a flamethrower. Hell of a thing! But they're perfectly legal, no paperwork required, so he'll eventually be able to get it back. In the meantime, I'm keeping it with his guns in our evidence locker."

"Does he have any known connection to Gant?"

"The address on his license is the address of the storefront in Bastenburg that's leased to the Church of the Patriarchs. And Gant himself bailed him out the minute the judge set the amount yesterday afternoon. Fleck was supposed to return for a court appearance this morning, but I got a message on my phone saying he didn't show up."

"Sounds like the Reverend was in a big hurry to spring him."

Morgan nodded. "Bastenburg PD's on the lookout for him. Once we've put this Aspern-Tate nightmare behind us, we can put more resources against Fleck and the Cursen thing."

Gurney felt a flash of anger. "What you're calling 'the Cursen thing' could also be described as two counts of attempted murder."

Morgan looked like he'd been slapped. "You're right—if the idiots knew the house was occupied. Otherwise, they could end up pleading out to aggravated vandalism or reckless endangerment."

Gurney restrained an urge to argue the point. He realized that he was in a combative mood—and that getting out of Morgan's office might be a good idea. In fact, getting out of Larchfield, at least for the rest of the day, might be an even better idea.

When his homeward route took him through the main street of Bastenburg, he saw a row of black motorcycles at the curb by the Church of the Patriarchs storefront. He parked a block past the storefront and walked back.

The front door was obstructed by a burly man in motorcycle leathers with weathered yellow skin and a rust-colored beard.

Gurney held up his police ID. "Detective Gurney—here to see Silas Gant. Please ask him to step out on the street."

"The Reverend is busy."

"This is police business. I need to speak to him now."

The man didn't move.

"Do you understand what I just said?"

"It's you that needs to understand."

"Step away from the door, sir."

The man stayed where he was.

Gurney moved forward at an angle, as if to get around him. The man sidestepped and began shoving him back away from the door. Gurney bent his knees to lower his center of gravity, set one foot firmly behind him, and drove his right elbow forward into the man's solar plexus, causing him to crash into the door, gasping.

The door was yanked open from the inside. Another large bearded man stepped out—with two more in the doorway behind him. He glanced back and forth between Gurney and the fellow sagging against the doorjamb. He slowly balled his hands into fists.

"What the fuck is this?"

"Police business. Step back inside. Now!"

The man stayed where he was until a soft voice behind him said, "It's okay, Deke, I'll take care of it." Then he and the others in the doorway backed away, taking their limp associate with them.

Silas Gant stepped forward, his gray pompadour as unruffled as his tone. His eyes were fixed on Gurney. He showed no emotion beyond a mild curiosity.

"Can I be of some assistance?" He sounded almost paternal.

"Gurney, Larchfield Police." He held up his ID. "I'm looking for Randall Fleck."

"He's not here, as I've already explained to the appropriate authorities. Is there anything else I can do for you?"

The question brought Gurney face-to-face with the fact that, uncharacteristically, he'd given no thought to what he wanted to accomplish. The impulse to stop there had come from another part of him, the part that had responded with pain to the attack on Selena Cursen—the part of him that was full of the equally uncharacteristic anger that had driven his elbow into the stomach of the man guarding the door.

He spoke now with a calm emphasis on every word. "You're an impressive speaker, sir. The things you say, people take them to heart. So the next time you make a speech to your congregation, you might want to include a clear condemnation of the attack on the Cursen house by a pack of ignorant, drunken slimebags."

Gant's bland expression congealed for a second into something less pleasant, which he covered with a patronizing smile. "You need to understand, Detective, that those who revel in unholy lifestyles and in the open adoration of Satan may provoke strong responses from well-meaning individuals."

"*Well-meaning individuals.* I'll bear that in mind."

"You do that."

"By the way," said Gurney, "if you run into Randall Fleck, let him know that he and his *well-meaning* friends have made the biggest mistake of their miserable lives." He paused, then winked at Gant. "You have a nice day, Reverend."

43

As Gurney was driving past his barn, he thought he saw a faint image of the Dark Angel message coming through the two coats of paint he'd applied to cover it. Then, as his angle of sight changed, the image disappeared. Hoping it had been a mere trick of the afternoon light, he continued up through the pasture to the house. He parked in his usual spot, got out, and was surprised to find Madeleine weeding the asparagus patch.

"I thought you were working at the clinic today."

"I was. Half day. Want to go for a swim in the pond? I was in a little while ago. The water is wonderful."

He tried to think of a credible reason to say no but nothing came to mind. He wasn't as fond of the chilly spring-fed pond as she was. But maybe a quick immersion was just what he needed to wash away the lingering discomfort of his confrontation with Gant.

"Okay," he said.

Half an hour later, with cool water dripping from his hair into his eyes, he stepped out of the pond onto its grassy verge. Madeleine rolled up a towel and tossed it to him from her lawn chair. After a quick wipe-down he sat in the chair next to her, shaded by a tree with glossy emerald leaves. He extended his legs out from the shade into the warmth of the sun.

"Such a lovely day," said Madeleine with a happy sigh.

"Hmm."

"Did you notice the wild irises?"

He looked around. Between the pond and the end of the road he spotted the intricate blue blossoms swaying in the breeze.

"Very nice," he said.

"The hummingbirds are back. And the orioles. And the nuthatches—the ones that hang upside down on the feeders."

"Hmm."

He reclined the back of his chair a couple of notches and closed his eyes.

A minute later she asked, "Are you napping?"

"Just . . . emptying my mind."

Their brains were wired differently in that respect. Madeleine's sense of peace in the outdoors was derived from her visual connection to it. The richness and variety of the colors transfixed her. Birds and flowers and sunsets were soothing manifestations of beauty. She seemed skeptical of Gurney's preference for the elusive scents and sensations of nature, the feeling of a light breeze, the sounds closest to silence—best experienced with his eyes shut.

"Well," she said, "in case I forget to mention it later . . . you should put another coat of paint on the barn door."

"Oh?"

"That horrible thing is starting to show through."

"Okay. I'll take care of it."

He soon discovered that his goal of letting his mind wander peacefully was not about to be realized, as the thought of the message on the barn drew him once again into wondering about its purpose.

When Billy Tate was assumed to be responsible for it, the question of motive was looser. When a perp is deemed mentally unbalanced or wildly impulsive, motivation becomes a factor hardly worth considering. But now all the evidence indicated that Chandler Aspern, not Billy Tate, was behind everything. And with Aspern it was reasonable to assume a practical motivation.

So, what was it?

The simplest would be a desire to reinforce the fiction that Billy Tate was still alive and raising hell. But the problem with that was proportionality. Did the risk/cost of the action align with the likely benefit?

In this case, how did the reinforcement of an already-accepted belief justify the risk involved in Aspern's driving up to Gurney's barn, leaving distinctive tread marks in the soil next to it, and exposing his attention-getting BMW to potential witnesses?

It was hard to see how that made sense.

"You're at work, aren't you?"

Madeleine's voice drew him back into the moment.

He smiled. "I guess so. Sorry. That barn problem is eating at me."

"The show-through?"

"No. Why the message was put there to begin with."

She raised an eyebrow.

He explained the risk-reward problem.

"Hmm. Maybe the reward was something bigger than what you're assuming?"

That struck him as an interesting possibility, but nothing tangible came to mind.

"So," she asked, "what exactly is the status of the case? When you told me about the Russell woman shooting Aspern, I got the impression it was done with."

"Technically, that's true. This morning the DA sat through a presentation of a fairly convincing point-by-point scenario—complete with physical evidence, including Billy Tate's chopped-off hand. The three murders originally attributed to Tate, as well as the murder of Tate himself, have now been attributed to Chandler Aspern. Aspern's own homicide has been accepted as a noncriminal act of self-defense. So we have five dead bodies, all neatly packaged with a narrative blessed by the DA herself. Case officially closed."

"But?"

"I have an uncomfortable feeling about it all."

44

After applying another coat of paint to the barn door and cutting back the fast-growing shoots of the forsythia next to it, Gurney spent the remainder of the afternoon on his riding mower. It had been a wetter-than-average early May, the grass was thriving, and the perimeter paths were blending into the fields they circled.

When Madeleine moved through an environment like that, it captivated her with the details of its beauty—the wildflowers dotted over the hillside, the songs of the meadow birds, the colors of the butterflies. For him, it was mainly a nonintrusive backdrop for his own thoughts. Those thoughts, as he rode the mower along the sunny border of the high pasture, were following shadowy paths through the unresolved issues of the case.

Most perplexing to him were Aspern's motives, not only for defacing his barn, but for attacking Lorinda Russell. And there was the disappearance of Randall Fleck, with its echo of the disappearances of Angus Russell's enemies. There was no apparent link between those old events and this new one. But what if there was? So his thoughts went, winding in circles, going nowhere.

That evening after dinner, he decided to give Mike Morgan a call and share his concerns.

Morgan's reaction was angry and dismissive.

"Christ, Dave, I spent two hours with Carmody this afternoon polishing our closing statement to the media. Smooth, well-reasoned, coherent. We recorded it, and he sent it out to every media outlet that's been covering the case. Now you come to me with doubts, poking holes in the logic? What the hell am I supposed to do?"

"You had this same reaction when I questioned Tate's role in the case, and again when I raised a concern about the BMW on my road. You didn't want to hear it."

"Fine. But what am I supposed to *do*? Issue a retraction?"

"I'm not suggesting you go public with anything at this point. All I'm doing is sharing the questions that are on my mind. Doesn't it bother you that we don't really know why Aspern tried to kill Lorinda, or why he chose to do it that particular night?"

"Life is full of questions I can't answer. Can't we just let this resolution alone? For God's sake, Dave, let it rest in peace!"

With Morgan on the edge of panic, Gurney ended the call. As he stood on the patio in the gathering dusk, watching the evening breeze bend the tops of the asparagus ferns, a question that had occurred to him before was nagging at him again. Had Russell installed Morgan as police chief in spite of his weaknesses . . . or because of them?

He awoke the following morning in a more pragmatic frame of mind. With Morgan determined to drop the final curtain on the case, it was obvious that his own relationship with the Larchfield PD was about to end. He decided to prepare for that possibility.

As soon as he got dressed and switched on the coffee maker, he called Slovak.

"Morning, sir, what's up?" There was a case-closed cheeriness in his voice.

"Morning, Brad. I need a copy of the Russell case file with up-to-date interview notes and verbatims, plus a USB drive with the security videos and crime-scene photos. I'll be there at nine thirty. Can you have all that ready for me by then?"

"Absolutely."

It wasn't that he intended to continue a private investigation of an officially closed case. He just wanted to make sure he hadn't missed anything. At least, that's what he told himself.

Without waking Madeleine, he set out immediately for Larchfield. The previous day's sunny weather had been replaced by an unsettled atmosphere that carried the threat of thunderstorms.

He parked on Cotswold Lane in front of police headquarters. As soon as he entered, the desk sergeant held up a bulging manila envelope.

"For you, from Slovak."

Gurney took the envelope and left immediately to minimize the chance of encountering Morgan. Back in his car, he opened the envelope to be sure it contained the requested USB drive. Then he made his way around the one-way streets bordering the village square, drove up and over the hill that separated Larchfield from Bastenburg, and headed for home.

By the time he got back to Walnut Crossing at 10:40 a.m., dark clouds were massing, and there were rumbles of thunder. As he was parking next to the asparagus patch, raindrops began splattering on the windshield. He hurried into the house and closed the French doors by the breakfast table, then brought his laptop out from the den.

When he went to the sink island to make his second coffee of the morning, he found a note from Madeleine saying she'd be working at the clinic all day.

When the coffee was ready, he brought the steaming mug to the table. He opened the manila envelope, took out the case file, and inserted the USB drive in his laptop.

Clicking on the USB icon opened a window that revealed nine more icons, one for each of five digital video files and one for each of four sets of photographs from the homicide sites. He decided to review the videos first—in chronological order, beginning with the one of Tate being knocked from the roof of St. Giles.

Having already examined it more than once, he fast-forwarded his way through most of it. He did the same with the one showing Tate's "resurrection" in Peale's mortuary.

He devoted more time to the video from Lorinda Russell's new security camera—showing Aspern, masquerading as Tate, approaching the conservatory. Despite the limited illumination provided by the moonlight, the clarity was remarkable. Visible details included the original bloodstain on the sweatshirt hood, the mallet in his hand used for breaking the glass in the conservatory door, the white laces in his sneakers, and the bulge in the sweatshirt pocket where he was carrying the bagged hand of Billy Tate.

The next video was of Lorinda responding to Gurney's questions about the shooting. Once again he was struck by the woman's glacial indifference and how little she revealed of herself. Gaining some insight into the appetites that drove the decisions inside that glossy shell might be worth some effort.

But where to begin?

He'd already heard from some locals who knew her—Helen Stone, Hilda Russell, Greg Mason, Mike Morgan—but those conversations had elicited more information about *their* feelings than hers. One exception was Greg Mason's comment that she was the only student in the high school who wasn't afraid of Billy Tate.

As he thought back over what little he'd been told about her behavior, he recalled Morgan mentioning the "inappropriate relationship" she'd reportedly had when she was fifteen with her high school principal. He wondered if now, thirteen years later, that man might be willing to talk about her.

He placed a call to Greg Mason.

Apparently noting Gurney's name on his screen, Mason began speaking in a rush of angry excitement. "I heard the news about Aspern. That evil son of a bitch! I wish I was there when Lorinda shot him. Are you sure he's dead?"

"I'm sure."

"My God, you know somebody for so many years, then you discover you didn't know him at all. I never liked him. But who would have expected this?"

"I hope his death brings you some closure."

"I don't know what 'closure' is. I'm just glad the son of a bitch is dead. Is that what you called to tell me?"

"Actually, I wanted to follow up on a subject I raised when we spoke in your office. The rumored relationship between Lorinda—Lori Strane—and Principal Bullock."

"I told you—I don't talk about rumors."

"I respect that. But when something like this pops up in the course of an investigation, it needs to be addressed. I want to speak directly to Bullock, and I was hoping you might know someone who could put me in touch with him."

"He's been gone for at least twelve years."

"He must have left a forwarding address with the school."

"I wouldn't know about that."

"But someone in the records department would know, right?"

"The only person likely to know anything would be Betty Brill."

"Does she have a title?"

"APA. Assistant Principal for Administration."

Gurney thanked him, called Larchfield Academy, and asked for Betty Brill.

When she picked up, he stated his name and police affiliation and explained that he needed to get in touch with the school's former principal.

"Hanley Bullock?" Her voice sounded dry, tight, and unhappy with the subject.

"Yes."

He heard the sound of tapping on a keyboard. Then more tapping. And more tapping.

"All I can give you is the forwarding address he provided a month after his resignation. I have no idea if it's still valid."

"Any phone number?"

"No." She sniffed and spelled out Bullock's forwarding address with a clear distaste for anything associated with the man.

Gurney entered it—36 Haze Street, Crickton, NY—into Google Maps. The app displayed an estimated drive time of an hour and nine minutes from Walnut Crossing.

The street view of the address showed the front of what looked like an old rooming house with a wide, uneven porch. Trudy's Antique Treasures was on its left side and Flacco's Deli on its right. Gurney found the deli's website and got its phone number.

A bored female voice answered on the fourth ring. "Flacco's, what can I do for you?"

Gurney explained that he was trying to get in touch with someone by the name of Hanley Bullock, who was a tenant in the building next door, and he was wondering if someone at the deli might have the name or the phone number of the building's owner.

"Hold on," she said. "You want to talk to my father."

Two minutes later a gravelly male voice said, "Who is this?"

Gurney explained who he was and what he wanted.

"That guy you're looking for isn't here anymore."

"Do you know where I can find him?"

"Died years ago."

"I see. Do you happen to know how he died?"

"Look, I don't really know who you are."

Gurney repeated his name and affiliation.

"Look, buddy, anybody can say anything on the phone. You say you're a detective. How do I know that? I got a call from somebody yesterday, said he was the IRS, and I should give him my credit card number to avoid being arrested for fraud."

"Perhaps you can just give me the name or phone number for the building's owner?"

"I'm the building's owner."

"Is it still a rooming house?"

"Not a rooming house. Never was. It's rental apartments. Very nice."

"And you are . . . ?"

"George Flacco."

"All right, George, I understand your desire to be sure who you're talking to. But let me ask you a simple question. Is there something in particular about Hanley Bullock's death that makes it a sensitive issue?"

"Maybe there is, maybe there isn't. Like I told you, I'm not saying things on the phone without some identifying corroboration."

"That's fine, George. I respect that. I'm going to drive down to Crickton later today with appropriate police identification. After you're satisfied, we can talk about your former tenant. We can do it at your place of business or at the Crickton police station, if you'd feel more comfortable there."

Never in Gurney's recollection had anyone opted for the greater comfort of a police station.

"My deli is okay," said Flacco with a resounding lack of enthusiasm. "I'm here until six. Then I'm gone."

"That's fine, George. I'll be there at five."

Most of Crickton turned out to look exactly like the street-view photo of the rooming house on Haze Street. An old river town, conspicuously ungentrified, it had numerous old redbrick buildings that once housed mills, manufacturing businesses, and implement suppliers to the mom-and-pop dairy farms that no longer existed.

On the far side of Trudy's Antique Treasures there was an abandoned nineteenth-century building whose dark brick facade was the color of smoke. A decrepit sign hanging below the boarded-up second-floor windows proclaimed, BEST FURNITURE AND COFFINS FOR ALL BUDGETS.

A bell over the deli's door produced a jangly ring as Gurney entered. The place smelled of dampness and cats. There was a white metal-and-glass case of cold cuts and salads to his right; a wall-long case of beers, sodas, and caffeine drinks to his left; four tables with chairs in the middle space; and a row of shelves across the back, full of candy and chips. There were no customers.

One of the fluorescent lights in the ceiling was buzzing. He heard a toilet flushing in a back room. A moment later a small dark-haired man—presumably George Flacco—and a heavyset redheaded woman emerged from a doorway behind the cold-cuts counter and came around it into the table area.

"You're the one that called me?" said the man.

"That's right." Gurney took out his Larchfield ID and held it up.

The redheaded woman peered at it, looking back and forth several times between Gurney's face and the picture of his face.

"You're a detective?" She made it sound like a trick question.

"Yes. For twenty-five years in New York City. Right now I'm working up in Larchfield."

"They have crime up there, do they?" She said it with a nasty sense of triumph, as though she'd caught the town in a lie.

"Yes, they do."

She folded her heavy sunburned arms and gave Gurney a challenging look. "When that Bullock fellow came here, we didn't know the first thing about him abusing that young girl up there in that fancy school."

"No way you could have," said Gurney.

"We heard the story later. After he was gone."

"I'm just interested in learning what you thought of him while he was here, what he was like, what finally happened to him."

With a small nod of satisfaction she turned to the small dark man, who seemed to take that as an okay to proceed.

"So, Detective," he said in his gravelly voice, "what do you want to know?"

"Anything at all you can remember about him. Friends? Visitors? What he talked about? How he spent his time? How he died?"

"The 'friends' part is easy. He didn't have any. Ditto for visitors."

"Until the end," corrected the redhead.

"I'm coming to that, Clarice. Don't rush me." He turned back to Gurney. "What else did you ask me?"

"What he talked about."

"Another easy one. Nothing. He didn't talk to nobody. Not a word."

"Until the end," said Clarice.

"Yeah, but not much even then. And we don't know what he said. Why do you keep interrupting me?"

She ignored the question.

He turned to Gurney. "What else?"

"How did he spend his time?"

"He watched TV."

"We don't know that," said Clarice.

"Yeah, we do. His TV was on eighteen hours a day."

"How can you be sure he was watching it, George?"

"Why else would he have the fucking thing on?"

"Some people just like it. The voices. It's company."

He turned to Gurney. "You had another question, right?"

"How did he die? He wasn't that old, was he?"

"Not really. Forty, forty-two maybe."

"Maybe forty-four, forty-five," said Clarice. "But he was a heavy drinker."

"How could you tell?" asked Gurney.

"The vodka bottles in the garbage. And the only time you'd see him on the street was coming or going to Gaffy's Liquors. The man had a problem."

"A dirty past," added George. "We found out later. A kid not even half his age. He's lucky he didn't go to prison. They don't like guys like that in prison."

"How did you find out about the problem with the girl?"

"I don't remember. I think somebody we knew might have known somebody in Larchfield. Right, Clarice?" When she didn't answer, he continued. "Anyway, the story got passed along. And we heard the name. Hanley Bullock. Figured there couldn't be two Hanley Bullocks around. So that was it. But that was after he died."

"And that happened . . . how, exactly?"

"Now we get into the funny part."

"Funny weird," said Clarice.

"This guy showed up one day. A big guy on a black motorcycle, asking up and down the street if anyone knew Hanley Bullock."

"This was before we heard about the problem in Larchfield," said Clarice.

"He said he was Hanley's cousin, and he knew Hanley lived in Crickton, and he thought he'd drop by and say hello on his way through. So we gave him the apartment number."

"As I recall," said Clarice, "it was Trudy down the block gave him the apartment number."

"Whoever the hell gave it to him, he got the number and went to the apartment. Pretty soon the radio came on. Country music. Stayed on for hours. And we could hear the big guy's voice. Had a loud laugh."

"You folks have an apartment in the same building?"

"Yeah, it's our building. Pluses and minuses to that, I can tell you. So we hear a lot, want to or not. Mostly we'd rather not."

"Did you get the big guy's name?"

"I don't recall it. You, Clarice?"

She made a constipated kind of face, as if trying to remember were a physical strain. "Country-music kind of name," she announced finally. "What it was I couldn't tell you. We're talking ten years ago."

"Okay," said Gurney, turning back to George. "So you heard them in Bullock's apartment, playing music and laughing?"

"The music, yeah, and the big guy letting out a loud laugh every so often. I don't believe I ever heard Hanley laugh—not then, not ever."

"This went on how long?"

"All that afternoon and into the night. In the morning, it was real quiet. Round about midday, a fancy car pulled up in front of the building. I could see it right out this front window. A fancy little man got out of the car with one of them little black doctor's bags and went into the building. I thought, what kind of trouble we got now? And I followed him in, caught up with him at the foot of the stairs. He said he was a doctor and he'd gotten a call about a Mr. Bullock. I gave him the number of the apartment, and up he went. Half hour later he came down, came into the deli here, asked what my relationship was to Mr. Bullock. I told him it wasn't any kind of relationship, Mr. Bullock was just our tenant. He said he regretted to inform me that Mr. Bullock had suffered two massive heart attacks and had passed away. Since he'd been present when the second one occurred, he was able to sign a death certificate without hesitation. And since Mr. Bullock's cousin was present and willing to be responsible for the removal of the body, there would be no problem or inconvenience for me. In fact, he said, a call had already been made and a removal vehicle was on the way. That's what he called it. A removal vehicle."

"How did they bring the body down the stairs?" asked Gurney.

"You recall, Clarice?"

"One of them body bags like you see on TV, with handles on it. The two of them carried it down—the big guy and the doctor. Someone else had arrived in a hearse—what the doctor called the removal vehicle. They loaded the body in it, and off they went. The big guy on his motorcycle, the doctor in his shiny black car, and Mr. Bullock's body in the hearse."

"You mentioned a couple of minutes ago there was something weird about the situation. What was it?"

"I guess the way it felt." Clarice looked at her husband. "What would you say it was?"

"How fast it all happened. One day he was fine, next morning he was dead, and an hour later he was heading out of town in the back of a hearse. And that was that. The end. We never heard another word. No obituary notices, no nothing. One day he's our tenant in apartment 2A, next day it's like he never existed."

Clarice was nodding. "It was way too fast. Everyone was in a hurry. I told the big guy with the beard, the one who said he was his cousin, I told him that Bullock was a month behind in his rent. He asked me how much he owed, took out his wallet, and gave me the money in cash. Didn't even ask for a receipt. I wasn't worried about it at the time. I'm being totally honest here, it doesn't sound nice, but I just wanted the damn body out of that apartment. But I got to thinking about it afterward—what the heck was the big rush?"

"Interesting. So, there were three people involved in the removal—the guy with the beard, the doctor, and the hearse driver. I know it was a long time ago, but I'd like you to try to picture them. As best you can. Any details you can remember—anything at all, no matter how trivial it might seem."

They looked at each other. Clarice spoke first. "The big guy was like six three, six four, black leather jacket, big beard, dull eyes. The hearse driver . . ." She hesitated. "I think he was kinda thin, balding. In his forties, I'd guess. Maybe around the same age as Mr. Bullock. Anything come to your mind, George?"

He shook his head.

"What about the doctor?" asked Gurney.

She closed her eyes tightly, as if straining again to visualize something. "My own height, I think, because I sort of recall being even with him, not looking up or down. I remember him being neatly dressed, maybe in a dark suit? And sunglasses. He was wearing sunglasses, so I didn't see his eyes. I don't remember anything else, except his hair."

"What about his hair?"

"It was perfect," said Clarice.

"Too perfect," said George.

"What color was it?"

"Gray," said George.

"Silver," said Clarice.

45

At 6:07 p.m. by his dashboard clock, about halfway home, Gurney pulled over on the weedy shoulder of the road to make some calls. The first, to Madeleine, which went to voicemail, was to apologize for not being there to get dinner ready and to let her know that he'd be arriving around 6:45.

His next call, to Hardwick, also went to voicemail. He left a message.

"I'm hoping we can get together tomorrow. The Larchfield situation may be wrapped up. But it feels a little off-center. I just discovered something that could be an unexploded bomb. I can be at Abelard's by eleven. If you can't make it, call me. Otherwise, I'll see you there."

His third call was to Slovak, who picked up on the first ring.

"Yes, sir?"

"Hi, Brad. I was wondering if you had any luck yet with your search for Aspern's phone."

"No, not really."

"*Not really?*"

"I mean, we didn't find it, but we weren't looking very long. The chief pulled everyone off the case. He said it's done and over with, and he reassigned everyone to normal duties." He paused. "You think that's a problem?"

"I have no idea." Gurney was thinking it might very well turn out to be a problem, but there was no point in putting Slovak between a rock and a hard place.

"I was wondering . . . are you still interested in knowing about stuff related to the case?"

"Why do you ask?"

"Well . . . an odd thing happened about an hour ago. I got a call from Harold Storm, who owns the liquor store in town. He'd heard about Aspern committing the murders that had been blamed on Tate and then getting shot at the Russell estate."

"And?"

"He said Aspern had been in the store earlier that evening, and that he'd bought a bottle of wine."

"So?"

"It was a three-hundred-dollar bottle."

"What was his point in telling you this?"

"He said since it was Aspern, and since he was in the store just a few hours before he got shot, he thought he should let us know. You think it means anything?"

"Hard to say," said Gurney. "But you sound like you've been giving it some thought."

"Actually, I have. And I figured maybe the wine was to celebrate—you know, later that night."

"Celebrate what?"

"Getting rid of Lorinda."

"You figure he was planning to cut her throat, pop the cork, and celebrate his victory?"

"Can't you just see it?"

Not really, thought Gurney, but he didn't say so.

For the rest of his drive to Walnut Crossing, his mind was leaping from case to case, from Aspern back to Bullock, from ten years ago to the present. He was trying not to give too much weight to what the Flaccos told him. Ten years after the events, the "facts" in their memories were simply not reliable. He reminded himself of the lessons he taught at the academy regarding the fallibility of eyewitnesses and the overeagerness of investigators to believe them.

When he finally got home, it was nearly seven. The dishes in the sink revealed that Madeleine had already eaten, as did the sound of her cello coming from the upstairs room where she practiced after dinner. He went to the wok on the stove and found a still-warm mixture of rice, scallops, and bok choy. He went to the foot of the stairs and called up to Madeleine.

"I'm home."

"Good," she called back without interrupting her melodic bowing. "Dinner's in the wok."

"Sorry I'm so late. Something came up."

There was no answer but the music.

After eating, he cleared the table and opened his laptop. He knew that the best antidote to useless speculation was a deep dive into a sea of facts.

He reinserted the USB drive with all the videos and crime-scene photos. He reviewed every item, every detail, until he could no longer keep his eyes open.

Morning came with a clap of thunder, followed by the downpour that had seemed imminent the previous day.

As Gurney steered the Outback into Abelard's parking area, Hardwick's growling GTO was pulling in from the other side. They emerged from their cars at the same time. The rain had finally let up, leaving large puddles on the saturated ground and a cool, clean scent in the air. They went inside and sat at their usual table.

Marika came over holding a small pad and pencil. The hair that was blue a few days before was now platinum blond. Her lipstick was retro red.

"Hey, boys, what's it gonna be today?" She seemed to be doing a riff on a diner waitress in an old movie.

Hardwick ordered regular coffee, black. Gurney ordered a double espresso. Hardwick then turned to Gurney.

"I saw your friend Morgan on TV last night. Quite the fucking story."

"What did you think of it?"

"You mean, what do I think of the little creep with the deer-turd eyes turning out to be the bad guy? Hey, Larchfield's a creepy shithole, so the idea that the shithole mayor is a multiple murderer didn't exactly knock me off my feet." He paused and gave Gurney an appraising look. "But that phone message you left for me sounded like you're not on board with the happy resolution."

Gurney shrugged. "There are always unresolved issues when the people you'd most like to interview are all dead."

"Issues like the 'unexploded bomb' you mentioned in your message? The fuck is that about?"

It was about what George and Clarice Flacco had told Gurney during his visit to Crickton. He filled Hardwick in on the background events—Hanley Bullock's rumored "affair" with the underage Lori Strane, his subsequent resignation from Larchfield Academy, his relocation to Crickton, and his embrace of vodka.

"The same Lori Strane who later became Mrs. Angus Russell?"

"The very one." Gurney then related in detail the Flaccos' account of what had happened the day of Bullock's death and who was present for it.

Hardwick reacted with his routine skepticism. "So when Bullock croaked, a bearded guy and a gray-haired guy were there. That's it?"

"A big bearded guy who arrived on a black motorcycle and a neat little guy with silver-gray hair."

"So you've decided that the big guy must have been one of Gant's Patriarchs and the little guy was Gant himself—and that they were sent there by Angus Russell to ice Bullock?"

"That thought did occur to me."

"The motive being what?"

"Angus wanting to flex his muscles? Show Lorinda what he had the power to do? Possibly give her a subtle warning? Maybe he liked the idea of making Bullock pay for what he did with a fifteen-year-old. Or maybe Bullock discovered something damaging about Angus, tried to take advantage of it, and didn't realize who he was dealing with."

"How far out on that branch do you want to get before it breaks and dumps you in the shitter? Sure, what you're saying is *possible*. But it's equally possible that the big guy really was Bullock's cousin, the gray-haired guy really was a doctor, and Bullock really did die of a heart attack. And it's *very* possible that the Flaccos' recollections of what happened on one high-stress day ten years ago are totally screwed up. And no matter what the truth is, at this point who the hell cares? More to the fucking point, why do *you* care?"

"If Angus was behind it and Gant was involved, it would be evidence of a long-standing criminal relationship between the Russells and the Patriarchs, and it would suggest that they may have cooperated in those unsolved 'disappearances' of Angus's enemies. Hilda Russell told me that Angus gave a lot of money to Gant's church. That could have been a way of paying him for services rendered—and even getting a tax deduction for it."

"Christ, you're actually thinking that the Reverend is a hit man?"

"I'm thinking he *could* be. Interestingly, he bailed out one of his Patriarchs—who could have proved to be a dangerous embarrassment—and the guy hasn't been seen since."

"Which means he's holed up somewhere with half a dozen hookers on meth."

"Always possible. But I'd bet on a terminal disappearance."

"Because he knew too much?"

"Because he could link Gant's Patriarchs to an armed attack on a local eccentric."

Marika arrived with their coffees. It took Hardwick a moment to refocus. "You've shared these thoughts with Morgan?"

Gurney shook his head. "Morgan doesn't want complications. He's committed to a simple message: evil has been vanquished, peace has been restored. No doubts. No questions. No static."

Hardwick made a sucking noise through his teeth. "Look, I'm not saying this Bullock thing is worth pursuing, but if it were, where would you start?"

Gurney smiled. "I'd ask someone with a PI license who knows his way around the block to find out if Bullock ever had a big bearded motorcycle-riding cousin."

"Basic footwork like that too boring for a genius like you?"

"My credentials are from Larchfield PD. Someone could call to check me out. I don't want Morgan to know I'm still poking at the edges of a closed case."

Hardwick gave him a major you're-going-to-owe-me look before asking, "Did the Flaccos get the doctor's name?"

"They couldn't remember."

"Or the name of the guy who said he was Bullock's cousin?"

"Bullock's ex-wife might be a good place to start."

"Naturally, you'll give me her name and contact information?"

"That would take the fun out of it."

Hardwick stared down into his coffee mug. "I'm missing something here. What's Bullock's demise got to do with Angus getting his throat cut ten years later?"

"Maybe nothing. But the likely involvement of Gant in the Bullock thing is just one of the oddities troubling my sleep."

"How many fucking oddities you talking about?"

"Aspern's phone hasn't been found. And Morgan's case-closed fixation means no one is allowed to look for it."

"That's the kind of shit keeping you awake at night?"

"Not just that. Aspern drives a 530e BMW. A few nights ago a message was painted on my barn in the blood of one of the victims. A guy at the end of my road saw someone coming down from my property in a BMW. He was pretty sure it was a 530e. And there were tread marks in the soil by my barn that have been ID'd as belonging to a 5 Series BMW."

"So you're thinking this was Aspern?"

"That's what it looks like."

"So what's the problem?"

"The risk-reward ratio. Aspern was no fool. So why expose himself like that, carrying the blood of one of the victims in his car, leaving his tire tracks on my property? For what? To make me think Billy Tate did it? I don't get the point of that. That's not enough of a payoff to take the chance of being caught."

"Maybe Aspern was crazier than you think."

Gurney sighed, unconvinced. "Madeleine said I might not be seeing what his goal really was. Maybe it was something that was worth the big risk after all."

"And Morgan—"

"Morgan doesn't want to hear a word about it."

Hardwick's expression turned sour. "You think the fucker is bent?"

"I never thought so before. I still don't want to. But his determination to shut things down is so damn rigid . . . it's becoming another sleep disturber."

After a silence during which they both paid attention to their coffees, Hardwick developed a puzzled look. "This Bullock thing—what sent you off looking for him to begin with?"

"Curiosity about Lorinda. Apart from a few obvious characteristics, she baffles me. I wanted to find someone who might know her better than the people I've talked to so far."

By the time Gurney got back to Walnut Crossing, the weather had changed again. The sky was clear, the grass was drying in the midday sun, and the chickens were pecking energetically at the cracked corn that Madeleine had tossed into the fenced run before she left for work. Swallows were swerving through the air over the low pasture.

He brought his laptop out to the little table on the patio and began yet another review of the security camera videos and homicide scene photos—searching for anything odd, anything unexpected, anything inconsistent.

He spent an hour going through all the visual files in chronological order. He then went back and replayed the video of Tate emerging from the cadaver-storage cabinet and making his way around the embalming room. Next he examined the video of Aspern in Tate's clothes approaching the conservatory.

He was struck by Aspern's attention to the details of the deception, even to the extent of mimicking Tate's halting stride and the forward hunch of his shoulders—which he'd probably observed in the leaked video on the RAM-TV website. His attention was also drawn to the floppy white laces on Tate's sneakers—worn by Tate himself in the first video and by Aspern disguised as Tate in the second. The bow loops appeared noticeably smaller in the second, but that was perhaps too small a point for even the detail-focused Aspern to have bothered to get right.

Next he viewed the still photos of Aspern's body on the conservatory floor in Tate's now blood-soaked clothes—twelve in its facedown position and another twelve taken after the body had been turned over by the ME for an in situ exam and pronouncement of death.

He noticed that the bow loops visible in these photos were larger than they had seemed in at least one of the two preceding videos. He replayed the videos to be sure, and what he found puzzled him. The bows in the still photos of Aspern's body on the floor were larger than the ones in the video of his approach to the house.

That made no sense—unless Aspern had retied his laces in the time between his walking across the lawn and his breaking into the conservatory. But why would he do that? This was a man on his way to cut a woman's throat. A man carrying another man's severed hand in his sweatshirt pocket. Would he stop in the midst of this grotesque mission to retie his shoelaces?

But he either retied them or he didn't. And if he didn't, who did? And why?

The ringing of his phone interrupted his train of thought.

It was Slovak.

"Sorry to bother you, sir. I just wanted to make sure you knew about Carol Morgan. She passed, sir, early this morning."

"Jesus. How's Mike doing?"

"I don't really know. I think he's at home."

"Okay. Thanks for letting me know."

Gurney laid his phone down next to his laptop on the table and sat gazing out over the pasture. As a homicide detective, death was part of his life. Approaching it objectively was the essence of his job. But this sort of death was different. It came at him from an angle that bypassed his professionalism. It touched that mostly hidden part of him that responded to the world with emotion rather than analysis.

He picked up his phone and placed a call to Morgan.

"Yeah?" His voice was ragged.

"Mike, I just heard about Carol. I'm so sorry."

"Who is this?"

"Dave Gurney."

"Oh."

"Are you all right?"

"What? No. No. Not really."

"Is there anything I can do for you? Anything you need?"

"No."

"Are you sure?"

He didn't answer.

"Mike?"

There was a sound that might have been a stifled sob. Or a cough.

Gurney waited.

"She didn't know who I was, Dave. I was there, standing next to the bed. She was awake, looking right at me. 'Who are you?' That's what she said, looking right at me. I said, 'It's Mike. Your husband. It's me. Mike.' She said, 'I don't have a husband.' I didn't know what to say. I tried to hold her hand. She pulled it away. Then she closed her eyes. That was it. She stopped breathing. That was the end."

Gurney heard that stifled sound again. This time he was certain it was a sob.

46

Gurney wasn't sure how long he'd been sitting there on the patio. The phone call with Mike Morgan had broken his sense of time.

Finding himself gazing blankly at the rectangle of yellow string Madeleine had set up next to the chicken coop, he got up and walked over for a closer look.

Picturing as best he could the alpaca shelter diagram she'd gotten from Dennis Winkler, he paced along the edges of the rectangle to get an idea of the dimensions. He went back to his laptop and spent the next half hour figuring out the lumber and hardware needs and putting together a materials list. Having done that, he felt less adrift. Over the years he'd come to rely on the grounding effect of small practical actions.

Now, in the hope of maintaining that effect and perhaps solving the shoelace conundrum, he returned to his examination of the photo and video files. An attentive pass through all the material took another hour. He was in the middle of a second pass at five thirty when Madeleine called to tell him that she and Gerry were going to dinner in Oneonta and then to a movie, so she wouldn't be home until sometime after ten.

He brought his laptop inside to the table by the French doors and once again gave his attention to all the pictures documenting the movements of Billy Tate and Chandler Aspern. He was convinced that in one of the images he would find an explanation for the inconsistent sizes of the bow loops on the sneakers.

Three hours later he still had not succeeded. He suspected the answer was staring him in the face and he just wasn't recognizing it. Perhaps he should take a break. His need for sleep was undeniable, and he knew that pushing himself any further at that point would not be productive. He decided to lie down without setting his alarm, letting his brain determine how much rest it required.

Too tired to fall into a natural sleep, he slipped into a state of uneasy, semi-wakeful dreaming. Even that was interrupted—by Madeleine's arriving home and opening the bedroom windows, then by a cramp in his leg, and still later by the yipping of coyotes in the high pasture.

A little after four in the morning he gave up hope of sleeping comfortably—the result of a fretful dream that featured Tate with his spray can, applying figure eight hellfire symbols on the church steeple. The dream kept repeating, with the variation that Tate sometimes held the spray can in his right hand and sometimes in his left hand.

Gurney was made so restless by the contradictory images that he felt a need to resolve the confusion then and there. He got up and went out to the table where he'd left his laptop and opened the two video files.

What he saw on the screen provided the resolution, but at the cost of more confusion. On the church roof Tate sprayed the symbol on the steeple with his left hand, but in the embalming room he scraped it on the wall with his right.

He then opened the video of Aspern approaching the conservatory in his Tate disguise. He was holding the mallet in his right hand. But Gurney recalled Aspern being left-handed.

"Do you realize what time it is?"

He was startled at the closeness of Madeleine's voice. She was standing in the kitchen just a few feet away. It was 4:25, at least a half hour before dawn.

"I was having trouble sleeping," he said.

"Are you coming back to bed?"

Her tone made it sound more like an invitation than a question.

He followed her into the bedroom. One thing led to another, and he finally sank into a real sleep.

He awoke around eight when Madeleine left for the clinic, drifted back to sleep, and awoke again suddenly at nine thirty with his phone ringing on the night table. He blinked, squinting at the screen. It was Jack Hardwick.

"Wake up, you fucker. You sound drunk."

"You have news?"

"Yeah, I have news. The kiddie-banger had two cousins. One's a nun, the other died of AIDS twenty years ago. No relatives with a beard or a big bad motorcycle."

"You got this from his ex-wife?"

"No. The ex-wife wouldn't say a word about him. Still hates the ground he walked on. But she did give me the name and address of his brother. The brother didn't like him, either. Referred to him as a drunken sleaze who deserved to be dead. Had less than no interest in the circumstances of his death. Said if Hanley got iced he'd shake the hand of the iceman. But at least he was willing to give me the cousin data."

"So the guy who claimed to be Bullock's cousin was lying."

"Fact that he wasn't Bullock's cousin doesn't make him a Patriarch."

"But it does make it more likely."

"*More likely* don't mean shit. But for the sake of argument, let's imagine you're right. What's your hotshot scenario for how it all went down?"

Gurney sat up on the edge of the bed and took a few moments to organize the sequence in his mind.

"The way I see it, it all starts when Angus Russell, for whatever reason, decides he wants Hanley Bullock dead. He makes his desire known to Silas Gant. Gant sends one of his trusted Patriarchs down to Crickton to deal with it in a way that creates the fewest possible waves. Maybe the guy invents a story that gets him invited into the apartment. Or maybe he just knocks on the door and blackjacks him as soon as he opens it. Once he's inside he finishes Bullock off quietly, probably by strangling him. He spends the night there—playing music, laughing, making whatever sounds the Flaccos say they heard. In the morning Gant shows up—the neat little 'doctor' with the silver-gray hair. After spending some time in the apartment, he comes out and gives George and Clarice the sad news about Mr. Bullock's fatal heart attack. A little while later an accomplice shows up in a hearse, the body is bagged and removed from the premises, and everybody disappears over the horizon. No obvious evidence of any crime. Bullock had no one in his life who cared enough to look into the situation. The perfect crime, right down to the hearse."

"What do you mean?"

"Even if it got stopped for a traffic violation and the cop found the body in it, there wouldn't have been a problem. It's a hearse. There's supposed to be a body in it."

"Very smooth. Assuming it's true. But all it means, at the most, is that Angus had a criminal relationship with Gant—ten years ago. You're trying to link a possible old Angus-Gant relationship to the current craziness with Aspern. The hell kind of link could there be?"

"Maybe none. But the more I learn about Larchfield, the more it seems that everything is wired together."

"Maybe it's time for dynamite. Just blow the fucking place off the face of the earth."

"Always an option. But I'd like to get answers to a few bothersome questions first."

"Like what?"

"Hold on for a minute."

Gurney went to the bathroom and splashed some cold water on his face, then slipped on a pair of jeans and a tee shirt before returning to the phone. "You still there?"

"Waiting patiently for your questions."

"Okay. On the roof of St. Giles Billy Tate was using his left hand. In the mortuary video he was using his right hand. How would you explain that?"

"He fell off the fucking roof. Maybe he broke his left hand."

"Okay. How about Aspern? In the video of him approaching the Russell house, he's carrying a mallet in his right hand. But when I met with him in his office I'd swear he was left-handed."

"So he was ambidextrous. Lot of people are. Or maybe his left hand was occupied with something the video didn't catch. What else is bothering you?"

"The tire marks next to my barn—forensically ID'd as belonging to the same BMW model that Aspern drives, one that's extremely rare around Walnut Crossing. In fact, in my five years here I've never seen a single one. So it seems he took a very large risk, compared to very little reward. What does that tell us?"

"You're the one that keeps thinking about it. What does it tell you?"

"That we may need to reevaluate our suppositions."

"Shit, Gurney, try using smaller words for us mortals."

"I thought originally the risk was that the unusual car would be observed and linked to Aspern—which is exactly what happened. But suppose I've been looking at it upside down."

"Meaning what?"

"I've been assuming that the risk was that the car might be ID'd. But maybe that was the objective. What I thought was an effort by Aspern to further incriminate Billy Tate could just as easily have been an effort by a third party to incriminate Aspern. The distinctive tread marks left in the soft earth by my barn may have been left there on purpose."

Hardwick grunted. He sounded unconvinced. "So, if it wasn't Aspern, your 'third party' just happened to own the same kind of car? That's a big fucking coincidence."

"The car may have been rented. There are elite rental outfits that specialize in vehicles like that. I know it seems like one more complication in a case that's already mired in complications, but I have a feeling I'm onto something."

"I have a feeling, too. Like I'm in the land of make-believe."

"What you need to clear your mind is a practical assignment, Jack. Something along the lines of identifying rental agencies dealing in relatively new BMWs and discovering if any of them recently provided a customer with a 530e. Sound like something you'd be willing to sink your teeth into?"

"Fuck you, Sherlock."

Gurney assumed that was a yes.

47

Giving voice to his car theory seemed to give it greater credibility. However, Gurney was wary of the temptation to embrace any new idea too tightly. One of the most dangerous traps in an investigation was the trick of the mind that turned possibility into probability and probability into certainty. The antidotes were patience and more facts. Gurney was hoping that Hardwick's efforts would contribute significantly to the second part of that.

His revised view of the barn incident raised new questions. Making Aspern the target of a clever deception potentially changed him from a perp to a victim. Did that mean he was innocent of the murders of Angus Russell, Mary Kane, Linda Mason, and Billy Tate?

If the barn incident was a deliberate attempt to cast suspicion on Aspern, a question remained concerning its motivation. Was Aspern an innocent man being framed for the Larchfield murders? Or was someone who knew Aspern was guilty trying to bring him to the attention of law enforcement?

Gurney saw problems with both interpretations. If Aspern were guilty, why had the unknown individual chosen such an elaborate approach, when he or she could have accomplished the same thing with an anonymous call or text that spelled out whatever incriminating information they had? But if Aspern were innocent, how could one explain his bizarre attempt on Lorinda Russell's life?

Gurney made himself an extra-strong mug of coffee, opened the French doors to let in the cool morning air, and settled down at the breakfast table to wrestle with the possibilities. Once again he was interrupted by the ringing of his phone.

The number on the screen was faintly familiar.

"Detective?"

"Yes?"

"I remembered his name."

"Sorry, who is this?"

"Clarice. Clarice Flacco. You said to call if I remembered anything else. It was Otis. The one with the motorcycle. His name was Otis."

"He told you that?"

"No, that's why I didn't remember. He didn't tell me his name. It was tattooed on the knuckles of his right hand, one letter on each knuckle. I didn't see it at first because he was wearing gloves. When he was about to leave, he took out his wallet to pay for Mr. Bullock's back rent. Did I tell you about that?"

"You did."

"Anyway," said Clarice, "he took off his gloves, to get the money out of his wallet. That's when I saw the name. Otis."

"Did you happen to see the knuckles of his other hand?"

"I don't think so."

"Okay, Clarice, that's very helpful. By the way, did anyone ever call or come to see you about Mr. Bullock's possessions? Whatever was left in the apartment?"

"He didn't have hardly anything." There was a defensiveness in her tone now. "No personal items, credit cards, checks, phone. Definitely no cash. The cousin must have took all that. I don't know if Mr. Bullock ever had a computer. I forget what happened about the clothes and furniture. We probably gave whatever there was to the Salvation Army."

Gurney had his doubts about that, but saw no point in pursuing it. He thanked her for getting in touch with him and encouraged her to call again if new memories surfaced.

Then he called Hardwick and left a message:

"Regarding the Crickton thing, the big guy's name was Otis. As in Otis Strane. As far as I'm concerned, that seals the deal on Gant-Patriarch involvement in Bullock's death. The question is, what might that have to do with the present situation? Maybe nothing, right? On the other hand, maybe everything. Let's talk."

Next, he called Slovak.

As usual, he picked up immediately. "Yes, sir?"

"Morning, Brad. I wanted to follow up with you on a few loose ends. That call you told me you got from the liquor store owner, about Aspern buying a three-hundred-dollar bottle of wine. Did you ever find the bottle?"

"No, sir. Like I told you, once the DA gave the word to close the case, Chief Morgan shut everything down."

"So, the bottle of wine might still be in Aspern's house?"

"I guess, but . . ."

"I know the chief doesn't want to allocate resources to a cleared case, but this wouldn't fall in that category. No expenditures involved, and hardly any time—just a final check of the victim's residence. I bet you and a couple of your people could handle it in less than an hour. A bottle of wine shouldn't be too hard to spot."

"Yeah, I guess. Okay. I'll let you know if I find anything."

"Have you heard from the chief this morning?"

"No, sir. I left a message, but he hasn't gotten back to me."

"And there's no command structure between you and him, is that right?"

"Right. We've always been a small department, pretty informal, with the sergeants reporting directly to the chief. We never had layers of lieutenants and captains. I guess that's good and bad."

"Okay, Brad, let me know how the wine search turns out. And keep an eye open for Aspern's missing phone."

"Yes, sir."

Next, Gurney turned his attention to the question he'd raised with Hardwick. If someone wanted Aspern to appear responsible for the message on the barn and, by extension, for the Larchfield murders . . . were they trying to frame an innocent man or focus attention on a guilty one?

Neither possibility made much sense. He couldn't recall a single instance of anyone engaging in an act of criminal mischief in order to draw law enforcement attention to a real evildoer. On the other hand, Aspern's attack on Lorinda made it difficult to view him as the innocent victim of a frame job.

Gurney concluded that he was missing something—something that could be the key to a completely different understanding of the murders. And that brought back the feeling he might have overlooked something crucial in the videos. He decided to make his way through them one final time. He opened his laptop and began the familiar process.

The video of Tate on the roof of St. Giles yielded no new information. It just reinforced the impression Gurney had of Tate's recklessness. There were no "Aha!" moments in the mortuary video, either. His attention was drawn mainly to the splintering sound of the casket bursting open. The sound conjured an image of a gasping, wild-eyed Billy Tate—panic and confusion mixed with a surge of relief at breaking out of a confinement he could not at that moment have understood.

He recalled that Dr. Vickerz's analysis of the torn wood fibers around the latch had focused on the direction from which the force had been applied to break open the casket lid, not on how *much* force had been required. In a practical sense it might not matter. Whatever the amount of force, it had been sufficient, and Tate was reputed to have been unusually strong. Still, it remained an unknown, and Gurney was hungry for facts.

He didn't have a number for Vickerz, so he called Barstow and left a message asking that Vickerz perform an additional experiment to determine how much upward force would have been needed against the inside of the casket lid to tear the wood apart from the metal latch. He was hoping that Barstow would pass the request along without challenging the appropriateness of conducting another test in the context of a closed case, and that Vickerz's scientific curiosity would carry the ball from there.

Going through the rest of the videos, he saw nothing he hadn't seen before. He was still made uneasy by the fact that Aspern was carrying the mallet in his right hand as he approached the conservatory, and even more uneasy by the discrepancy between the size of the shoelace bows in that video of Aspern's approach and their size in the post-shooting photos of his body.

These oddities brought to mind a digital video issue frequently in the news—deepfake manipulation. Although that technology appeared to have no application to these videos, other forms of manipulation were possible.

He placed another call to Barstow. This time she picked up.

"Sorry I missed your first call. Greta's on the job. She's obsessive, so you're sure to get a precise answer. Obsession can be a good thing, don't you think?"

"It depends."

"I agree. Anything else?"

"Can your computer lab test the integrity of video files?"

"There are some basic diagnostics. You have a worry?"

"With all the digital fakery going on these days, it seems worth checking. I'm talking about the videos that were shown in the meeting with Cam Stryker."

"I'll call you as soon as we have something."

He thanked her and ended the call.

As he was about to close down his laptop, a document title in the Recent Activity window caught his eye—"Materials List for Alpaca Shed"—reminding him that there were other areas of his life that needed his attention.

He decided to make a start on the project.

48

The following morning was the Platonic ideal of spring in the Catskills. The early sunlight slanting across the hillsides illuminated countless shades of green. The low pasture was dotted with patches of purple clover. The sun was warm, the breeze was cool, and the scent of lilacs sweetened the air.

He was sitting with Madeleine at the patio table, sharing a breakfast of blueberry pancakes. Every once in a while Madeleine glanced with a smile at the start he'd made the previous afternoon on the shed. The necessary lumber was piled neatly next to the chicken coop. The holes for the corner posts had been dug—no small achievement in the rocky soil—and two of the posts had been set and braced.

"I can help with the next steps," she said happily. "We can work on it together this weekend."

Oddly, it was at times like this—when he'd acted like a real husband instead of like a detective who was sharing the house—that he felt his marital shortcomings most acutely.

She was gazing at him as though she were reading his mind. She got up from the table, came around behind him, and kissed him on the back of the neck.

At exactly ten o'clock that morning, he received the first of the phone calls he'd been hoping for.

"Good morning, Detective. This is Greta Vickerz. I have the information for you. You want me to give you first the number of pounds force required, or the method of testing?"

"Good morning, Dr. Vickerz. In whatever order you wish."

"Method first is more logical, followed by results. First, we reinstalled the metal latch in an undamaged area of the wood. Second, we drilled a small hole in the casket lid and inserted a narrow cable with a bracket on the inside of the lid to hold it in place. Third, we closed the lid and engaged the latch. Fourth, we attached the cable to the laboratory's spring scale and ratcheted it up until breaking force was achieved, providing force measurement in pounds. You understand?"

"I think so."

"Then we repeated the procedure, again reinstalling the latch in a second undamaged area. This was to provide a second reading. There was less than ten percent variance in the necessary breaking force, so the results have a good confidence level. You want numbers now?"

"Please."

"First test, breaking force one hundred fourteen pounds. Second test, one hundred six pounds. Average one hundred ten pounds."

"So, you're saying that the original breaking force exerted on the inside of that lid in the mortuary would have been in that neighborhood?"

"I would say with ninety percent confidence that the force would have been between ninety and one hundred thirty pounds."

"This is helpful. Thank you."

"All very interesting. If you want, I can investigate further an oddity."

"Sorry?"

"For testing, we removed the lining from the casket. In the bottom, we observed a hole, seven millimeters in diameter."

"Part of the original structure of the casket?"

"Drilled later."

"Any obvious function?"

"No."

"Too small for an air hole, I would think."

"Too small, wrong place. Also an air hole in a casket would be . . . hard to understand."

Like everything else in this case, thought Gurney.

He asked if she could imagine any possible purpose for it. She said no, but she could develop a technical study proposal with a cost estimate. That struck him as a process more likely to raise red flags than produce useful results. The little hole was intriguing, but its relevance was questionable. He thanked her again and ended the call.

He spent some time thinking about the force that Tate had to apply to break open the casket. Considering his damaged physical condition, even the lower end of the range seemed challenging. But his constricted position, an apparent limitation, could have been an advantage, since it was similar to a weight lifter's bench-press posture. Bottom line, Vickerz's testing was instructive without resolving anything.

Gurney couldn't help wondering about that seven-millimeter hole in the bottom of the casket, but his wondering was truncated by another phone call—this one from Hardwick.

"Hey, Sherlock, definitely some odd shit connected to that BMW. I found an outfit down in Montville—calls itself Eleganza Luxury Rentals—specializing in everything from Beemers and Audis up to Bentleys and Lamborghinis. Funny thing happened. I called them last night and told the guy who answered that I was looking to rent a 5 Series BMW, preferably a 530e. He said I was in luck. They had that exact car in dark blue—just returned yesterday after being out for three or four days."

"That has to be the one. Were you able to get the renter's name?"

"Good news and bad news. The guy I spoke to was the service manager, not the agent who rented the car. They were just closing, and the agent was gone for the day. So I called back this morning. Got the agent. Totally different story. Very vague. And get this. He claims there was a glitch in the system, and the information on the renter was accidentally deleted. And naturally the agent's description of him is useless. Normal height, normal weight, ordinary voice, wore a hat, wore sunglasses. Could even have been a woman."

"Interesting."

"So, the bad news is we don't know who rented the car. The good news is the slimebag agent was apparently motivated to fuck up the record system, which suggests that the renter bribed him to hide his identity, which suggests you may be right about the car being used for a shady purpose."

"Nice to discover I'm moving in the right direction."

"So the evidence would *suggest*. But be careful where you step, Davey boy. Pride goeth before the fall. And I'd hate to see you trip into a pile of shit."

"I'll be in touch."

As soon as he ended the call he placed one to Slovak.

"Brad, I need a favor. Remember those three churches over in Bastenburg that had the Dark Angel message scrawled on their doors?"

"Absolutely. We had the uniforms out canvassing for anyone who might've seen Tate's orange Jeep in the neighborhood."

"We need to go back and ask about a dark blue BMW—and whether anyone can recall anything about the driver. I know these things get hazy fast, but it's worth a try."

"This is ringing a bell. Hold on a second, let me bring up the interview reports on the computer."

A minute or two later, Slovak was back. "I knew it sounded familiar. The manager of an all-night laundromat down the block from one of the churches said there was, quote, 'one of them fancy BMWs' in his parking lot the night in question. He noticed it because, 'Ain't nobody in Bastenburg got the spare cash for a ride like that.' We didn't follow up because we were just looking for people who saw Tate's Jeep."

"I need you to pay him a visit and find out if he saw the driver. But keep that between you and me for now."

"Will do."

Gurney gave his next call some thought before placing it. He was reluctant to disturb Morgan, but even more reluctant to withhold information that could upend the case conclusion presented to the public.

Morgan picked up on the fourth ring.

"Yeah?" His voice sounded dull as lead.

"Mike? This is Dave Gurney."

"I know."

"I'm sorry to be bothering you, Mike, but there are some developments in the Russell case that you need to be aware of."

Morgan didn't reply.

"Would it be all right if I came to see you?"

"Yeah."

He asked Morgan for his home address, entered it in his GPS, and set out.

The splendid May morning was largely wasted on him, preoccupied as he was by Morgan's emotional state, which sounded darker than normal grief.

He'd once told Gurney that his home was in the wilderness outside Larchfield—an apt description, Gurney discovered, as his GPS led him off the county route onto a rutted road that wound its way through several miles of boggy woodland before arriving at a log home in the middle of a small clearing. The lawn needed mowing. Beds of wilted pansies and daffodils separated the lawn from the house.

Gurney pulled up next to Morgan's Tahoe in front of a covered porch and got out. There were four Adirondack chairs on the porch. Morgan was sitting in one of them. His hair was uncombed, he needed a shave, and his shirt had the wrinkled look of having been slept in.

Gurney sat in the chair nearest him. "How are you doing, Mike?"

Morgan smiled in a way that conveyed only depression. "The case is messed up, right? That what you came to tell me?"

"There's evidence that suggests it may be more complicated than we thought."

"More complicated?"

"There are problems with the version given to Cam Stryker."

"Problems?"

"Serious doubts."

"Christ." He shook his head slowly. "It never ends. It just gets worse. Worse and worse."

Gurney noted a half-empty bottle of bourbon by the leg of Morgan's chair. He wondered if the man were drunk as well as depressed and grieving.

Morgan coughed weakly, his body shaking. "You heard about Peale suing Fallow? Alleging gross incompetence. Failure to conduct appropriate tests to justify the pronouncement of death. Causing irreparable harm to his funeral home and personal reputation."

He picked up the bourbon bottle, looked at it, moistened his lips, then put it back. He turned to Gurney. "You suggesting that Aspern isn't our perp after all?"

"All we know at the moment is that someone seems to have gone to considerable trouble to incriminate him."

"What about that bloody mess at Lorinda's? Wasn't he trying to kill her?"

"The situation may not be what it seems to be."

Morgan's eyes widened slowly. "I don't understand."

"I'm not sure I do, either. I do know that Aspern got a call from Lorinda a few hours before she shot him, and his phone is missing. I'm thinking he might have recorded the call, and that's the reason it's missing."

"Lorinda? You're saying . . . what? That she set Aspern up? That she . . . murdered him?"

"I'm saying it's possible. With an accomplice. She couldn't have done it alone."

Morgan picked up his bottle again. This time he opened it and took a long wincing swallow before putting it back. "You have any idea who this accomplice could be?"

"Nothing solid. But I did make an interesting discovery. It looks like Hanley Bullock, the principal who was involved with fifteen-year-old Lorinda, was murdered ten years ago—I suspect at the request of either Angus Russell or Lorinda herself. It was right around the time of their marriage."

Morgan looked like he was trying to see through a fog. "What's that . . . got to do with . . . anything?"

"The hit man was either Otis Strane or Silas Gant. I believe they were both present, and there's reason to believe there was a long-standing relationship between the Russells and Gant."

There was a panicky edge on Morgan's voice. "I don't . . . I mean . . . so what?"

"You asked me who Lorinda's accomplice might be."

"*Silas Gant?*"

"If he provided that kind of service before, why not again?"

Morgan picked up his bottle and held it on the arm of his chair without opening it. He appeared to be gazing into it as if it might hold the answer to a question. He cleared his throat. "You think Lorinda could be . . . that deeply involved . . . with Gant?"

"Why not? It could be a mutually beneficial relationship. She'd get an iceman to remove inconvenient people from her world, and he'd get sex, money, or whatever else she might be willing to offer."

A long minute passed before Morgan spoke again. Gurney had the strange sense that something inside the man was collapsing.

"You know all about the mess I created in the NYPD. Maybe Carol knew, too. I'm not sure. Even if she did, she was still willing to come up to Larchfield with me.

Let the past be the past. New life. Everything was good. Then, about a year ago . . . the addiction came back. The obsession. Full force. Crazier than ever."

"Crazier in what way?"

"The woman I got involved with. The choice I made. A god-awful choice. The worst. Absolutely the worst."

"Lorinda Russell?"

Morgan's jaw went slack. He stared at Gurney. "How did you know?"

"Just a guess."

"Now you're telling me she's in bed with Silas Gant, and they murdered Aspern."

"I can't prove that, Mike. I'm just filling you in on how it looks."

"Gant is the evil piece of shit Carol was at war with."

Gurney said nothing.

"You always get to the ugly truth. You dig it up and drag it into the daylight."

Gurney waited a moment, then asked, "Who initiated the affair?"

Morgan blinked, refocusing. "I thought I did. Now I don't know."

"What do you think she wanted from you?"

He managed a weak shrug. "I thought it was about sex."

"But now you're not so sure?"

"I'm not sure of anything."

"What else might she have wanted from you?"

"I have no idea," said Morgan, a bit too quickly.

"I'll put it another way. Did she ever talk to you about wanting anything in her life to be different from the way it was?"

Morgan stared into his bottle of half-finished bourbon as if looking for any answer other than the one that he couldn't evade. "Yes," he finally said, almost inaudibly. "She talked about how much brighter things would be . . . if it weren't for Angus."

Gurney let Morgan sit with the echo and implication of his own words.

"You think she was asking me . . . to make that happen?"

"What do *you* think?"

49

As Gurney drove home to Walnut Crossing, he pondered the likely result of Lorinda's view of what would make her life brighter—namely, that she'd finally found someone more willing than Morgan to grasp what she was asking for and to make it happen.

Someone like Silas Gant.

Gurney recognized that he was on dangerous ground with this idea—in no small part because of his eagerness to embrace it. He *wanted* the multiple murderer to be Gant. It was time to sit down again with Jack Hardwick, ultimate skeptic.

The man answered his call and agreed to meet him at Abelard's in forty-five minutes.

Along the way Gurney called Slovak to find out if Aspern's phone or his three-hundred-dollar bottle of wine had been located. Slovak reported that they hadn't, despite a careful search of Aspern's house, garage, and three cars. Although Gurney knew their absence proved nothing, it was encouragingly consistent with the case narrative coming together in his mind.

When he arrived at Abelard's, Hardwick was sitting at their regular table and had already secured a large black coffee for himself and a double espresso for Gurney.

"Thanks, Jack. I appreciate your coming."

"Did I correctly intuit from what you said on the phone that the status of Mayor Turd-Eyes has been officially changed from villain to victim?"

"Not officially. Not yet. But I'm envisioning a whole new storyline for the case, and I wanted to get your opinion."

"I can't bear the fucking suspense."

Gurney took a sip of his espresso and gathered his thoughts.

"Okay, here goes. It's the same as the official version up to the point where Billy Tate walks out of the mortuary—but instead of taking his proposal for killing Angus to Chandler Aspern, he takes it to Lorinda Russell. She loves the idea, but she has an even better one. She calls in a hit man to kill Tate, and then kill Angus—using Tate's fingerprints and the scalpels he stole from the mortuary to create crime-scene confusion and all the 'walking dead' nonsense. The hit man, wearing Tate's clothes and driving his Jeep, also kills Mary Kane and Linda Mason, for the reasons we assumed they were killed. Then, with his help, Lorinda adds the brilliant twist of setting up Aspern for what would appear to be a self-defense killing—in order to end the police investigation of the other three murders and get rid of an aggressive legal antagonist at the same time."

Hardwick's acid-reflux expression was intense.

"You have a problem with this scenario?" asked Gurney.

"Too fucking clever, too fucking complicated, too many fucking spots where the train could've gone off the tracks."

"You want to explain that?"

"First, tell me how you think they set up that self-defense ruse at the end."

"Lorinda told us she called Aspern to discuss their dispute over his lease, and that the discussion ended badly. We know from the carrier's records that she did make the call, but we have no way of verifying her version of the conversation. In fact, it may have been a lot friendlier than she claimed. She may have extended an offer he couldn't refuse. *Now that Angus is out of the picture, I'm sure we can work this out in an amicable way*, et cetera. I suspect she might have emphasized the amicability angle by inviting him to have dinner with her. Aspern may have recorded the call, but his phone seems to have evaporated. Interestingly, he bought a very special bottle of wine later that afternoon, and I'm thinking it was to bring to Lorinda's. You with this so far?"

"So far, it's the fucking definition of hypothetical. But keep going."

"Aspern arrives for dinner around seven o'clock. He and Lorinda have a few drinks. Maybe they open his fancy wine. At some point when he's nice and relaxed, her hit-man accomplice—same one who killed Tate—comes into the room behind Aspern and renders him unconscious, probably with a blow to the base of the skull. Then—wearing Tate's hoodie, jeans, and sneakers—he drives the vehicle Aspern arrived in back to Aspern's house, gets Tate's Jeep from its place in the woods, and drives to the point where the trail opens into the lawn by the conservatory. You following this so far?"

"What happens if Aspern wakes up while the accomplice is gone?"

"A forceful enough blow to the base of the skull would have kept him immobile for quite a while, if not paralyzed him. And he might have been tied up."

"Okay, so the accomplice is in the Jeep at the trail opening. What now?"

"Now is where the security camera video takes over. We see a hooded figure emerge from the Jeep and walk across the lawn toward the house, holding a mallet. He passes out of the camera's range, breaks the glass panel in the conservatory door, and enters the house. While he's taking off his hoodie, jeans, and sneakers, Lorinda is stripping Aspern. Then they put Tate's clothes on him and drag him into the conservatory."

"But he must have been shot standing up, for the bullet trajectories to turn out the way they did. How'd they manage that?"

"That had me stumped. Then I remembered seeing a device in the conservatory for moving heavy tropical plants—a hoist with ratcheted pulleys."

"You figure they used that to stand him up and shoot him?"

"It's a possibility. It's also interesting that the shooter placed one of the shots through Aspern's lower jaw—creating a rear exit wound that would destroy any evidence of an earlier blow to the base of the skull."

Hardwick's acid reflux expression had shifted to his more common skeptical frown. "So, after he was shot twice, they dumped him on the floor, facedown, like he'd been coming at Lorinda when she shot him and his momentum carried him forward?"

"That's the way it looks. The accomplice leaves. Lorinda gets rid of evidence of Aspern's earlier presence in the house—for example, the wine bottle that disappeared along with his phone. She calls Mike Morgan and announces that she just shot Billy Tate. And everyone later swallows that as an understandable misidentification as a result of Aspern being in Tate's clothes, limited moonlight visibility, and the body ending up facedown on the floor."

"Clever as hell," said Hardwick. "Almost too fucking clever. But it's conceivable. Not goddamn likely, but more conceivable than the first part of the story—where

Tate supposedly goes to Lorinda with an unsolicited offer to kill her husband, and she immediately calls in her friendly neighborhood hit man, who grabs a handful of scalpels and starts slicing throats. That strikes me as fucking nuts."

"The logistics of that do seem tangled, but I think the basic thrust is valid."

"The thrust being what exactly?"

"Originally, we thought Tate was the killer. Then we thought Aspern was the killer, trying to make it look like it was Tate. Now I'm pretty sure it was a third individual, trying to make it look like it was Aspern."

"This third guy being Lorinda's hit-man accomplice?"

"Yes."

"And the winner's name is . . . ?

"My guess is Silas Gant."

"Based on what? A ten-year-old story about Hanley Bullock dying while being visited by a neat guy with gray hair and a rough guy with 'OTIS' tattooed on his knuckles?"

"That, and the fact that Gant's church was getting major donations from Angus Russell—more likely for services rendered than from the goodness of his heart."

"Fucking hell, Gurney, you're not just doing a dance out at the end of a fragile branch, there's no goddamn branch at all!" Hardwick picked up his coffee mug and took a large swallow.

Gurney shrugged. "I may have the logistics wrong. The truth may be simpler than I'm making it out to be. But I'm convinced there's an evil relationship at the heart of what's been happening in Larchfield. And I'd like to prove it."

"Laudable goal, Sherlock. Any clue on how to make it happen?"

Gurney finished his double espresso before answering in a lowered voice. "Blackmail might be an interesting approach."

Hardwick leaned back in his creaky chair, apparently giving the suggestion serious thought. "Could be a profitable approach, considering the resources at the disposal of the wealthy widow."

Gurney sometimes found it difficult to know when Hardwick was joking. "Putting aside the major felony of actual blackmail, I think a pretense of blackmail could provide an interesting window into Lorinda's guilt or innocence."

"Sounds to me like you're putting aside a pot-of-gold opportunity that the good Lord has placed before us. But so be it. Tell me more."

"I'm thinking we could send a text message to Lorinda from an anonymous prepaid phone. A message that sounds like it's coming from someone who's secretly been keeping an eye on her—and who not only saw what happened to Chandler Aspern in the greenhouse, but has photographs of it. The message could conclude with a request for a personal meeting at the Russell house—say tomorrow evening at eight o'clock—along with a demand for ten thousand dollars."

Hardwick smiled. "Nasty. How do you think she'll react?"

"If she's telling the truth about the Aspern shooting, her natural reaction would be to call the police and report receiving a baseless extortion threat. If she's lying about the shooting, I suspect she'll bring in some private muscle to deal with her greedy pen pal."

"You're imagining the private muscle will be Silas Gant?"

"Or Cousin Otis."

Hardwick sucked at his teeth. "So, who gets to stand under the portico with his dick in his hand, pretending to be the blackmailer, while Reverend Silas and Cousin Otis lock and load?"

"Nobody. That's the beauty of it. There's no actual confrontation involved. A confrontation would be a disaster. The goal is just to discover which option Lorinda chooses—police or private muscle. And if she chooses the latter, it'll be interesting to see who shows up to help solve her problem."

"So we're just observing?"

"Right."

"From where? The top of a fucking tree?"

"We're in the twenty-first century, Jack. Ever hear of a device called a drone?"

"Shit, Gurney, the kind of drone you need for serious remote surveillance is no goddamn toy. It's got to be silent, super-stable, GPS-guidable, with hi-res video transmission, and at least a half hour to an hour flight time. You happen to have one of those in your glove compartment?"

"I don't, but I'm thinking you could arrange an emergency overnight loan from your friends at the NYSP."

"Fuck."

"I knew I could rely on you."

Hardwick gulped down the rest of his coffee.

50

On his way to Walnut Crossing, Gurney stopped at a mom-and-pop electronics shop in a roadside mall and made a cash purchase of a prepaid phone with a bundle of minutes.

As soon as he got home, he got a pad from the den and wrote out a rough draft of the message, along the lines of what he'd described at Abelard's. Then he put the draft aside, intending to come back to it later with fresh eyes and make final adjustments to the wording before texting it to Lorinda's cell number.

In the meantime, he got out the copy of the case file he'd received from Slovak and went to the section that dealt with the details of the security camera video from the night of the Aspern shooting. He was hoping it contained contact information for the company that installed the camera.

It did. It even included a Larchfield-area phone number, which he called.

After providing his name and the badge number on his LPD credentials, he was transferred to the company's installation manager.

Yes, he was familiar with the details of the Russell job.

Yes, only one camera had been installed.

Yes, that was unusual on a house of that size.

Yes, additional cameras had been recommended, but Mrs. Russell insisted on proceeding gradually.

Yes, Mrs. Russell had chosen the location for the first installation. In fact, she'd even specified the camera's angle and field of view.

Gurney emphasized that these inquiries were confidential aspects of an ongoing investigation and thanked the manager for his help.

Like the disappearance of the phone and the bottle of wine, the installation information by itself proved nothing. Lorinda's evident manipulation of the situation could be rendered meaningless by a defense attorney. However, it provided support for his growing suspicion and additional justification for the sting-like operation he was about to set in motion.

Rarely had he been so sure of anyone's complicity in a murder, with so little hard evidence. He was certain that Lorinda would fail to call the police. About Gant's personal involvement in Aspern's death, he was less certain. He was hoping the following night's surveillance would add some clarity.

Gurney's next call was to Slovak.

"Brad, I need to examine Aspern's house. Can you send someone out there tomorrow morning to unlock it?"

"Do you think we missed something?"

"Nothing specific. In fact, I have no idea what I'm looking for. It's just an itch I sometimes get—to walk through the world of a victim or a perp and see whatever I can see."

"Okay, I'll make sure the place is unlocked. If you want help with your walk-through, let me know."

Gurney's "walk-through" itch was real enough. But he also wanted to use the Aspern property as the control site for the drone. It was isolated, yet not too far from the Russell property, so if some malfunction caused the drone to come down in the intervening woods, he could easily retrieve it. And what he'd told Slovak would serve as a useful cover story in the event that he was seen there.

With that taken care of, he returned to his rough draft of the message to Lorinda. He read it over several times and made a few small changes. Then he entered it as a text on the anonymous phone and sent it to Lorinda's cell number.

A simple action—with the potential for game-changing consequences.

He intended to pay a visit to Morgan the following morning to fill him in on the operation. Despite Morgan's emotional state, letting him know about a major investigative initiative remained a formal necessity.

But that was a task for tomorrow. Seeing the case demanded nothing else of him for the remainder of the afternoon, he turned his attention to the alpaca shed.

By the time Madeleine got home from the clinic, he'd cut the lumber to the right sizes for the stud walls, rafters, and door framing and he'd restacked it, ready for use—without, however, proceeding with the actual construction, which he knew she wanted to be involved in.

His accomplishment left him feeling relaxed and pleasantly virtuous. Their dinner together was happy and stress-free, with frequent bursts of laughter. They headed for bed that evening earlier than usual.

He also woke up earlier than usual, well before dawn.

The euphoria of the previous evening had been replaced by the uncertainties of the Larchfield murders. He knew that trying to get back to sleep with that tangle of questions on his mind was pointless.

He showered and dressed and made himself a cup of coffee.

At daybreak he was on the patio with a second cup, imagining how Morgan might react to the explanation of the trap being set for Lorinda—and how Lorinda might react to the text he'd sent her.

At sunrise he heard his phone ringing in the house. He hurried inside to get to it before it woke Madeleine. He was surprised to see Kyra Barstow's name on the screen.

"What's up?"

"I asked Keith Boron, one of our computer techs, to analyze those video files you asked about. He told me this morning that he's confident of the integrity of ninety-nine percent of the digital content, but there's one percent that bothers him."

"Bothers him how?"

"He says there's a three-second sonic anomaly in the mortuary video."

"What kind of sonic anomaly?"

"He said that the sound of the casket breaking open—the sound of the wood splintering—created a peculiar audio-frequency footprint."

"What might that mean?"

"He's performing additional tests to get to the bottom of it. I just wanted you to know that he found something odd, since you asked for the analysis. I'll call as soon as I hear more."

The chance of returning to bed at that point for anything resembling sweet dreams was zero. Apart from the jarring effect of one more oddity being added to a case already bursting with them, he'd promised Madeleine that he'd spend the morning working with her on the shed.

The challenge would be to stay in the moment—to keep his mind on leveling and squaring, screwing and hammering—rather than slipping off into the world of murderers and sonic anomalies.

When noon finally arrived, he concluded that he'd reached his goal of remaining focused on his physical efforts about half the time; even that was quite an achievement. He wished he could pay as close attention to domestic activities as he did to crime scenes, but his brain just wasn't built that way.

In any event, the shed had now grown into a recognizable structure, needing only exterior siding and waterproof roofing to be complete. Madeleine was clearly happy with their joint endeavor—a mood that carried over into their lunch together.

As he was getting into the Outback at three that afternoon to set out for Larchfield, she was making a list of flowers she wanted to plant around the old henhouse and the new shed.

She came over to his car door. "I'm thinking mainly cornflowers and hollyhocks on the sunny sides and begonias on the shady sides. What do you think?"

"Sounds good."

"Do you even know what they look like?"

"I'm picturing . . . something colorful."

She sighed, leaned into the car, and kissed him.

"Be careful," she said with sudden seriousness.

51

Number one on Gurney's mental list of things to do in Larchfield was the visit to Morgan. On his way there he stopped for gas and called Morgan's cell number. The call went to voicemail, and he left a message saying he was en route. He couldn't help wondering what condition Morgan would be in. None of the likely possibilities were good, and the man's failure to answer the phone was not encouraging.

With an ominous feeling, he drove on.

The spring weather was in the midst of another reversal, and by the time he reached Morgan's house the blue skies of the morning had given way to dismal clouds. In the gloom the wilted daffodils in front of the porch looked like dead weeds.

There was no response to his knocking on the door. He knocked again, harder.

"Mike, it's Dave Gurney!"

The door opened, and Morgan stared out at him—still unshaven, his hair uncombed, his gaze emotionless. He was wearing a food-stained tee shirt, jeans with the fly open, and one blue sock. He smelled of alcohol and sweat.

Gurney tried to smile. "Hello, Mike. Did you get my message?"

Morgan blinked and shook his head.

"Can I come in? Or would you rather come out?"

"Come out. Get some air." He stepped out on the porch, took a deep breath, and sat down heavily in the nearest Adirondack chair. Gurney took the one next to it.

"I'm sorry to be bothering you like this, Mike, but I want you to be aware of a specific effort I'm making to verify the suspicions I have about the case."

Morgan closed his eyes, then opened them. "Suspicions about Lorinda and Gant?"

"Yes. And anyone else who may have been involved in the murders."

"You're sure about Lorinda." It was mostly a statement, with the hint of a question.

"Apart from Hilda Russell, she's the only person alive who benefits from Angus's death. And if Aspern's death was set up the way I think it was, she was part of that, too."

"That's what you came to tell me?"

"I came to tell you that I have a way of testing her to see if I'm right."

Morgan raised his head in a show of interest, and Gurney explained his plan for evaluating Lorinda's reaction to a would-be blackmailer.

Morgan nodded slowly. "You want to see who she brings in . . . to handle the problem?"

"That, but mainly I wanted to see if she'd call the police when she received the text, as an innocent person would—which she still hasn't done, even though I sent it to her yesterday." He took a printed-out copy of the text from his pocket and handed it to Morgan.

He read it and reread it, then lowered it into his lap. "You think she'll bring in Gant?"

"Yes, if I'm right about him being the family hit man. Or someone else, if I'm not. Either way, I'll end up knowing more than I do now."

Morgan nodded and looked away. His gaze settled for a while on the bed of withered daffodils. Then he picked up the copy of the text to Lorinda from his lap and read it again.

"It's a horror show," he said softly. "Everything. Life. A horror show."

After a long silence, Gurney made an open-ended offer of help, to which Morgan had no reaction. So he said goodbye and left.

When he reached the end of the dirt road that connected Morgan's property to the county road, he stopped and entered the address of Aspern's Harrow Hill house in his GPS.

As he was about to set out again, his phone rang. It was Hardwick.

"Yes, Jack?"

"Where am I supposed to bring this thing?"

"You're referring to the drone?"

"No, my giant dick. The fuck do you think I'm referring to?"

52

The route to the north side of Harrow Hill, the Aspern side, took Gurney through a landscape darker, wilder, less inhabited than the Waterview Drive approach to the Russell side. It had—like the vast, forested rise of Harrow Hill itself—a lonely, forbidding quality.

It was a feeling that only grew stronger as he followed Aspern's mile-long driveway up through the dense evergreen woods and into the sunless clearing that surrounded the house—a large, muddy-brown, shingle-style structure with a distinctly joyless personality.

After walking around it and locating an open porch that appeared suitable for launching and controlling the drone, he decided to go inside. The front door was, as requested, unlocked.

The interior was upscale and impersonal, more like a hotel than a home. Open desk and bureau drawers, as well as open cabinets and closets, were evidence of Slovak's search for Aspern's phone and bottle of wine. The place told Gurney relatively little about its late occupant—beyond his being conventionally expensive in his tastes, with no apparent interest in art, music, or literature. There were no decorative objects, no photographs, nothing frivolous or quirky. There was a stillness about the place, outside and inside—not the stillness of ordinary repose, but the stillness of a cemetery.

Gurney continued his exploration of the house until he heard the unmistakable growl of Hardwick's GTO.

They met on the open porch.

Hardwick opened a large aluminum anti-shock carrying case and gingerly removed a serious-looking quadcopter drone, a controller, a tablet computer, a battery charger, three batteries, and a manual.

"This little mother is a twelve-grand piece of equipment. Carbon fiber construction. Hasselblad lenses. GPS and GLONASS satellite guidance. Retractable landing gear. Sixty-minute flight time. External monitor feed."

"Should we start studying that manual, or did your contact give you instructions?"

"He did. Good thing, because the fucking manual is incomprehensible. If I can manage to remember what he said, there's at least a fifty-fifty chance I won't crash the damn thing."

Hardwick plugged the controller and the drone batteries into the multiple-input charger and the charger into the outlet on the porch.

Gurney checked his watch. It was 5:10 p.m.

"How long does it take?"

"The man told me an hour. Hopefully he wasn't full of shit."

At 6:05 p.m. the red light on the charger turned green.

Hardwick set up the tablet as a supplementary monitor with a live video feed, inserted a charged battery into the drone, then moved the drone out onto the lawn. "What time you want to start surveilling the Russell place?"

"Seven fifteen should be good. Based on the text I sent her, Lorinda will be expecting the blackmailer at eight. If she's bringing in help, there's a good chance they'll be arriving somewhere in that forty-five-minute window. Between now and then, you might want to do a practice run, get a feel for the equipment."

Resting the supplementary tablet monitor on the wide porch railing, Hardwick manipulated the buttons and levers on the controller. The four drone propellers began turning. With a muted whirring sound, the drone rose slowly into the air until it was well over the height of the tallest trees in the area. With Gurney and Hardwick observing its progress on the monitor, it proceeded to the preset GPS coordinates of a location with a wide-angle view of the front and one side of the Russell house, the allée, and the open entry gate.

Gurney suggested that there was more than enough clearance above the treetops to allow the drone's altitude to be lowered in order to see under the portico.

Hardwick made it happen. After experimenting with a number of alternate angles and zoom settings, the device was given a return-to-base command, and three minutes later it descended gently to the lawn.

At 7:10 p.m., responding to Hardwick's controller inputs, the drone rose again into the overcast sky and flew to its intended position.

The transmitting video was remarkably sharp. The low light level from the dense overcast had no effect on the vibrancy of the image. Even the darker area beneath the portico was clearly detailed.

For the next half hour, nothing happened. That changed at 7:41.

A black motorcycle bearing a leather-clad rider with a black helmet passed through the gate into the allée and proceeded slowly toward the portico. It was followed by another, then another, until a total of seven had entered the estate grounds. They continued in single file under the portico and around the front corner of the house.

Hardwick was giving the tablet screen a squinty look. "You figure one of those fuckheads is Gant?"

"That would be my guess. The helmets make it hard to tell."

Again in single file, but this time on foot, they came back around to the front of the house and up the wide marble steps while removing their helmets—six burly men with backwoods beards, followed by a smaller, clean-shaven man with a silvery pompadour.

The front door opened. As they went into the house, Gurney caught a glimpse of Lorinda in the foyer light, wearing a cream-colored jacket.

Again, all was peaceful on the tablet screen. A few birds flew by, heading for their evening roosts.

"Okay, Sherlock, I guess that's it. You see what you wanted to see?"

"I think so. Lorinda was threatened with blackmail by someone who claimed to have incriminating photos of Aspern's death, and she called Gant instead of the police. And Gant arrived with muscle to spare."

"You figure that means she and Gant killed Aspern?"

"I'd say there's an awfully good chance. You don't think so?"

"Suppose she doesn't trust cops. Just wants to handle the situation her own way. Keep control of the outcome. Attitude like that is fucking genetic, you know what I mean?"

"I do. But I think we can agree that what we saw on that screen was not a major indicator of innocence."

Hardwick spit over the railing of the porch. "Fine. Can we get out of here now? I'm getting eaten alive by the goddamn gnats."

Gurney nodded. "Bring the drone down, pack it up, and we're done."

Hardwick picked up the controller, checked the settings, and—

"Whoa!" cried Gurney, pointing at the tablet.

Hardwick leaned closer to the screen. "What the fuck?"

A dark vehicle, barely visible through the trees, had just come to a stop at the open entry gate.

"Can you reposition the drone for a better view?" asked Gurney.

Keeping an eye on the screen, Hardwick began adjusting the levers and dials on the controller. As the drone moved, its field of view changed, but none of the new perspectives offered a clearer view of the vehicle.

"Who the hell is that?" said Hardwick.

A dark figure emerged from the vehicle and started to move through the allée toward the house. Although the allée trees were in the way, the view here was less obstructed, and when the figure emerged into the open area beneath the portico, there was no obstruction at all. The screen showed an individual in a black, hooded, ankle-length poncho, standing perfectly still, approximately twenty feet from the steps leading up to the front door. Gurney was reminded of the Grim Reaper—this figure lacked only the scythe.

The door opened, and a big man in black leathers came out onto the steps, followed by another, and another, until six in all had arrayed themselves in a wide semicircle facing the motionless figure in the poncho. All six were carrying assault rifles. A seventh man then emerged and stood in front of the open doorway. A warm glow from the foyer behind him highlighted his silver-gray hair.

"It's Gant, no doubt about it," said Hardwick, "but what the fuck's going on?"

Gurney had a sinking feeling about what was going on. A disaster that he'd failed to anticipate.

Gant appeared to be speaking—almost certainly to the figure in the poncho. Because of the hood, it was impossible to see if there was any response.

Gant spoke again, and his six companions began to raise their weapons.

There was a sudden movement under the poncho as the individual crouched, swiveling rapidly from left to right and back again, the poncho vibrating along with the movement, as one after another of the big men were knocked backward onto the marble steps.

Gurney heard the sound of an automatic weapon firing steadily for four or five seconds, the sound coming not via the drone, which wasn't equipped for audio transmission, but directly through the half mile of forest that separated the Russell house from Aspern's.

On the screen, Gant was now returning fire with a pistol.

The figure in the poncho staggered sideways—dropping what looked to Gurney like an Uzi with an extended magazine—and sank to his knees.

Gant took a step forward, raising his pistol slowly in a two-handed grip. As he was leveling it on his kneeling target, the side of the poncho flew up, revealing something that looked like a narrow-tubed leaf-blower. A stream of flame shot out of it, reaching Gant and instantly engulfing him.

Gant staggered backward, dropping the pistol, waving his arms wildly, falling through the open doorway behind him, pursued by that stream of flame, now reaching into the center hall of the house.

The wounded figure in the poncho struggled to an upright position. Stumbling forward, he turned the blast of fire on each of the men sprawled on the steps, then collapsed backward like a felled tree. The weapon was now pointing straight up, its long tongue of flame igniting the underside of the portico roof and cascading back down on the immobile figure in the poncho.

Seven burning bodies lay outside the Russell mansion. Inside, the fire was rapidly taking hold.

"Holy shit," muttered Hardwick, staring openmouthed at the screen. "Who the fuck is the crazy motherfucker with the Uzi and the flamethrower?"

Gurney felt sick. He wished he didn't know the answer.

"Mike Morgan."

53

Gurney had to think fast. He could imagine the pointed second-guessing and blame-assigning that would go on at various official levels, including the DA's office, regarding what was intended to be a safe investigatory ploy. But he realized if the drone element were removed from the equation . . . and if Morgan were to bear posthumous responsibility, as he surely should, for what happened . . . then there might still be a way of extracting persuasive evidence of Lorinda's guilt from the hideous debacle.

He called Larchfield PD and spoke to the night-shift desk sergeant.

"This is Dave Gurney. I'm at the Aspern house on Harrow Hill. I'm calling to report gunfire in the area. My guess is a single automatic weapon with a large magazine. The sound came from the direction of the Russell house. I'm heading over there now through the woods."

Hardwick meanwhile had retrieved the drone and was packing it in its carrying case, along with its accessories. Gurney told him to make a separate copy of the stored video, in the event that it might someday be needed, then delete the original file along with any related GPS data. "Then get out of here before the troops start swarming the area. I'll meet them at the Russell place and make sure they come to the right conclusions about what happened there, based on the evidence on the ground."

Hardwick left without another word.

Gurney brought up an off-road navigation app on his phone, entered the GPS coordinates for the Russell house, and hurried off in the direction it indicated. A few minutes later he called Larchfield PD again. He reported seeing an orange glow in the low clouds ahead, a likely sign of a major fire, and directed that all available fire and rescue equipment be dispatched ASAP.

Ten minutes later, when he emerged onto the back lawn of the Russell mansion, the fire had become a monster. Its shifting red and orange glare shone through all the windows Gurney could see. It sounded like a high wind through a thicket, its crackling like the snapping of branches. Flames were blowing out through an open rear window over a bed of tulips, already withered from the heat.

He ran around to the front of the house. The acrid smoke there carried the odor of gasoline and burnt flesh.

He counted six smoldering bodies splayed out in a loose arc across the marble steps and one on the ground under the charred portico. Near that seventh body there was an Uzi with a large aftermarket magazine. The body was Mike Morgan's—not that it was easy to tell, since his head and upper body were burned to the point of no longer appearing human. His left hand, however, had escaped the burning gasoline that had descended on him from the geyser his flamethrower had produced in its final vertical position; its stubby fingertips, nails bitten to the quick, were all too recognizable.

With no protective clothing, Gurney was finding the heat from the open doorway of the burning house unbearable, and he retreated to the allée. Further now from the fire's roar, he could hear the sirens of the slowly approaching emergency vehicles.

Seeing that Morgan's Tahoe was blocking the gateway to the grounds, Gurney hurried over to move it, only to discover that Morgan had taken the key. No matter, he realized; one of the fire trucks could push it out of the way.

Then another thought occurred to him. Since Morgan was responsible for turning an information-gathering effort into this multiple-homicide apocalypse, it would simplify the investigation to place the initiating text in the hands of the investigators, ensuring that they would understand the preamble to the carnage. He took the anonymous phone out of his pocket—the phone from which the "blackmail" text had been sent to Lorinda—wiped off his fingerprints, and dropped it on the ground near the Tahoe. If anyone misconstrued the text to mean that Morgan had actual blackmail in mind, Gurney was sure he could persuade them otherwise.

The first arrivals were two Larchfield PD cruisers with two uniformed cops in each, followed by Slovak in his Dodge Charger. Leaving their vehicles at the entry gate behind the Tahoe, all five entered the grounds with their weapons drawn.

Gurney stood still, hands open and away from his body, until Slovak recognized him and came running over.

"Jesus, Dave, what the hell's happening?"

"Looks like there was a shoot-out between Chief Morgan and half a dozen of Gant's Patriarchs. One of Morgan's hands is still wrapped around a flamethrower, which probably started the fire. Everyone out here is dead."

Slovak looked around in wide-eyed amazement, horror, and excitement. "Is there anyone in the house?"

"We should assume Lorinda, until we find out otherwise. Also, I counted seven motorcycles in back of the house, but only six bodies on the ground, in addition to Morgan's. So the seventh rider may be in the house. Beyond that, I have no idea. I looked for a way in, but the ground floor access points are all blocked by the fire."

Slovak now was staring openmouthed at the bodies, repeating "Jesus" to himself and rubbing his scalp with both hands.

Gurney put a steadying hand on Slovak's shoulder. "Look, Brad, you're the ranking officer here. You need to take charge of the scene. If all those sirens I hear are any indication, this place is going to be an operational madhouse in a few minutes. I suggest you cordon off the area around the bodies and keep the fire engines to either side. Be sure to station one of your guys at the gate to keep a record of who enters and leaves. You've got a huge crime scene here and you can't let it get out of control."

"Right. Okay. Right. But . . . Chief Morgan? In a shoot-out? With Gant's Patriarchs?"

"That's the way it looks. I was over in Aspern's house when I heard gunfire coming from this direction. I called headquarters, then got over here as fast as I could. What I saw when I arrived is what you see now."

"He had a flamethrower?"

"Yes. Maybe the one confiscated from Randall Fleck."

Soon the other vehicles began arriving, sirens blaring—Bastenburg, state police, and sheriff's department cruisers; two EMT ambulances; another Larchfield cruiser; and finally a thousand-gallon pumper truck from the Larchfield Fire Department and another from Bastenburg.

Gurney remained at the periphery of the action, occasionally making sure that Slovak's grasp of the situation was entirely consistent with the facts conveyed by the drone, without including anything beyond what could be seen or inferred from the evidence in front of them. It was a tricky balancing act.

He was pleased to see that one of the officers had found the phone on the ground and brought it to the attention of Slovak—who then mentioned it to Gurney, who agreed that it could be important.

Gurney was starting to ask if Barstow's forensic team had been called in yet when he was stopped dead by a wavering scream piercing through the roar of the fire. He turned toward the house just as a second-floor casement window came flying open.

Lorinda Russell, the fire at her back and the sleeves of her cream-white jacket in flames, was trying to climb through the opening. She had one leg out when her hair went up in a sudden blaze. With a strangled screech of pain, she toppled back into the burning room. That final, dying cry was so dreadful—so razor-sharp in its agony—he feared he would never be free of it.

54

The unnatural May weather went overnight from merely dismal to raw and blustery.

"It's more like winter than spring," muttered Gurney, gazing out through the tightly shut French doors toward the old apple tree, whose few remaining blossoms were disintegrating in the wind.

Madeleine was looking at him over the rim of her coffee mug, which she was holding in both hands to warm them. "You want to talk about it?"

"The weather?"

"Last night's insanity. Isn't that what's on your mind?"

It was, of course, very much on his mind, as it had been all through a restless night and into the morning.

"I'm not sure where to begin."

She lowered her mug to the table. "With what's bothering you the most."

He took a moment to collect his thoughts. "I had a bright idea for discovering how Lorinda Russell would react to an extortion attempt by someone claiming to know that the shooting of Chandler Aspern wasn't what it appeared to be. My idea turned into a nightmare."

"I know. You told me all about it at two o'clock this morning."

"I just can't get it out of my head that I concocted this plan, and nine people ended up dead."

"Was that your goal?"

"Of course not."

"Was it something you imagined could happen?"

"No."

"Why *did* it happen?"

"Morgan hijacked the plan for his own purpose."

"What purpose was that?"

Gurney looked back out at the swaying branches of the apple tree. "My guess is that he wanted to make up for his own selfish behavior, his own mistakes, by killing the bad guys and going out in a blaze of glory. Or maybe he was feeling trapped and angry at himself and wanted to commit suicide in the most destructive way possible. Who the hell knows?"

"Do you feel responsible for his actions?"

"No."

"Then what part of it can't you let go of?"

He lifted his coffee mug, then put it down.

"Maybe I'm uncomfortable with the way I'm finessing the facts. At the scene last night, I avoided disclosing that I set up the trap. I shifted responsibility for the idea to Morgan by dropping the phone I used for my text to Lorinda near his vehicle. I told myself that raising my hand and claiming credit for the idea would only suck me into the murderous mess Morgan created—without my admission adding any clarity to the investigation."

"And that has you tied up in knots?"

"Yes."

"For his own selfish, erratic, suicidal reasons Morgan subverted your plan into a flaming disaster, and you're bothered by the fact that you're not broadcasting your ownership of the original version of the idea?"

Gurney sighed uncomfortably. "Yes."

"Why does it bother you that you're not accepting responsibility for something that is, in point of fact, not your responsibility?"

"Maybe because I'm being less than truthful, less than open about my part in it."

She stared at him. "My God, do you have any idea how absurd that is?"

He didn't reply.

"Perfection is a direction, not a goal. And *perfectionism* is a vice, not a virtue.

You're a human being, doing the best he can. And by the way, your 'best' is head and shoulders over most people's. But you keep thinking it's not good enough. Do you honestly believe that you should stand up and shout, *Hey, it was my idea that this nutcase took advantage of in his own twisted way*? Would that add a single speck of useful truth to anyone's understanding of the whole Larchfield horror story? It wouldn't. It would be nothing but a distraction. You know that. For God's sake, accept it!"

They sat in silence until Madeleine added in a brighter tone, "Apart from the time you're setting aside for self-flagellation, what's on your schedule today?"

"There's a noon meeting in Larchfield. I expect the DA will be taking control of the investigation herself or referring it to the state police."

"It sounds like the people they'd want to talk to are all dead."

It occurred to Gurney that he'd had the same thought after Aspern's death.

The predictably huge media presence on Cotswold Lane, as well as in the police headquarters parking area, made getting from his Outback into the building a bit of a challenge. The sketchiness of what had leaked to the media overnight gave the questions shouted at him a wild scattershot quality.

"Is it true that a local pastor was burned to death?"

"Is this being treated as a hate crime?"

"Is there a connection to the zombie murders?"

"Is it true the attackers were armed with flamethrowers?"

"Are you exploring the Satanism angle?"

"Are you bringing in the FBI?"

"Is it true the police chief was involved in the shooting?"

"Is this connected to the murder of Angus Russell?"

"How many people were killed?"

"Was there a political motive?"

"Dave, can I ask you just one question?"

Gurney recognized the sharp voice, blond hair, and red blazer of Kelly Tremain of RAM News. It was the same just-one-question ploy she'd tried on him a week earlier. It hadn't worked then, and it didn't work now. He hurried past her into the big Victorian.

"Meeting's in the conference room," said the desk sergeant.

Gurney started down the hall, but stopped when his phone rang. He saw Hardwick's name on the screen. He checked the time—11:54 a.m.—and decided to take the call.

"Gurney here."

"Bad news, Sherlock. Gant's not your man."

"How do you know?"

"I have an app that tracks the latest news items mentioning any name I enter. On the night Aspern was killed, Gant was the featured speaker at a rally in West Virginia—sponsored by the Armed Ministers Movement. So Lorinda must have had a different helper."

"Thanks. I'll talk to you later. I need to go into a meeting. By the way, did you—"

"Did I return the borrowed device, without incident, scrubbed of all video and location data? Affirmative."

Gurney ended the call and went into the conference room.

Cam Stryker was standing at the end of the long table, just finishing a call of her own. Hilda Russell was sitting across from Dr. Ronald Fallow. Brad Slovak was sitting across from Kyra Barstow. Gurney sat next to Slovak.

Stryker sat down, tapped a few icons on her phone, and laid it in front of her on the table. She began by asking Slovak to present a summary of the previous night's Harrow Hill mayhem.

He stretched his neck, as if trying to loosen a cramp. "Fortunately, ma'am, we recovered a text message we believe Chief Morgan sent to Lorinda Russell the day before the mayhem. It gave us an insight into what happened, so maybe we should start with that?"

"Let's see it."

Slovak slid a printed copy over to her and passed others around the table.

As her eyes moved down the page, her expression, not pleasant to begin with, hardened. She read it again, slowly, then dropped it on the table as though the paper itself had become offensive.

"Proceed," she said.

Slovak described a chain of events that matched in all significant details what Gurney had observed on the drone monitor—including Morgan's dispatching of the Patriarchs with an Uzi, his use of the flamethrower on Gant and the fallen Patriarchs, and his own immolation.

He went on to list the names of the dead, and Gurney noted without surprise that Otis Strane was among them. He concluded with the fact that the burned bodies of Lorinda Russell and Silas Gant had been found in the house.

Stryker asked Fallow if he had any pre-autopsy comments on the bodies.

He declined to offer any.

Stryker asked Barstow if she had anything to add.

Based on the petrochemical residues, she offered her opinion that the overall fire, as well as the direct burns on the bodies of the Patriarchs, Gant, and Morgan, were caused by the gasoline-fueled flamethrower held by Morgan. She said that a more detailed report would be coming from Denzil Atkins, the county's forensic fire expert.

"There was one unusual thing," she added. "The phone found at the scene had no fingerprints on it. Odd for a phone."

Apart from a momentary frown, Stryker showed little interest in the absence of prints. "Any other forensic developments I should be aware of?"

"We're double-checking the video files from the mortuary camera. Our tech found a tiny audio blip, which may be nothing, but we want to be sure."

Stryker turned to Hilda Russell.

"Anything to add?"

She responded with a priestly smile. "Not at the moment."

Finally, Stryker turned to Gurney. She pointed at the text. "According to that, your old NYPD partner decided to try his hand at extortion. You have any thoughts about that?"

"Considering what happened last night, it's difficult to read that as an actual extortion attempt. By way of background, Morgan told me a couple of days ago he had serious doubts about Lorinda's version of how and why she shot Aspern. He'd found a discrepancy in the visual evidence."

Stryker leaned forward. "What sort of discrepancy?"

"Aspern's shoelaces in the approach video were tied differently from the shoelaces in the postmortem photos of his body on the conservatory floor."

"Did you confirm that?"

"I did."

"What does it mean to you?"

"Either Aspern's body was tampered with after the shooting, or the individual in the approach video was someone other than Aspern. Either way, it suggests that Lorinda's story was either incomplete or a complete fabrication."

"Did Morgan confront her?"

"He said he wanted to test his idea first."

"How?"

"He didn't say. But the text that Brad just showed us may be the answer."

Stryker picked up her copy and read it again.

Gurney could see in her eyes a rapid weighing of the possibilities.

"He sent this threat to . . . evaluate her response?"

Gurney paused before answering. It was important to get this just right—to ensure that attributing certain discoveries and conclusions to Morgan rather than to himself didn't distort the underlying reality of the situation.

"Morgan was a troubled man. He suffered from anxiety and self-hatred, conditions that worsened considerably with his wife's illness and death. In his state of mind, it's inconceivable that he'd concoct a money-making scheme. I think this was a grandiose, suicidal confrontation with evil. You don't bring a flamethrower to a discussion of your blackmail demands. I can see a Glock. Even the Uzi. But not a flamethrower."

Stryker was silent for a long moment, keeping her gaze on Gurney.

"If the text was an effort to evaluate Lorinda Russell's response, how would you explain what actually went down?"

"I think it's clear that Morgan interpreted her failure to report the blackmail demand to the police as a sign of her guilt. So he came prepared for a confrontation."

"Knowing that she'd probably make her own preparations and that he might be killed?"

"Yes. But he was determined to take the opposition down with him."

Stryker steepled her fingers. "You sound very sure of all this."

Gurney nodded. "I have a history with Morgan. What he did is consistent with what I know about him."

"We'll come back to that. First, I want to address a structural issue. In losing Chief Morgan, the department has lost what little command structure it had. Last night's carnage obviously demands a thorough investigation with manpower resources that simply do not exist in Larchfield at this time. The best solution I see is for my office to assume overall responsibility for the investigation."

She gestured toward Slovak and Barstow. "This doesn't reflect in any way on your handling of the case. I want your good work to continue. Tomorrow morning, Detective Lieutenant Derek Hapsburg from my staff will step into a supervisory role and bring in whatever additional resources the case requires. When he arrives, we'll sit down with you for a briefing on the facts. At that time, be ready to provide him with copies of the case files, along with the pertinent videos, et cetera. Any questions?"

Slovak raised his hand. "What about the media mob outside?"

"Give them no information. And I mean *none.* Refer them to Sergeant Pat Lemon, my media liaison. She'll deal with them."

Stryker looked at Barstow.

She shook her head. "No questions."

"Reverend Russell?"

She produced one of her mild clerical smiles. "The additional resources you mentioned will certainly be welcome."

"I should have asked—in your new role as acting mayor, would you prefer to be addressed that way, or shall we stay with *Reverend*?"

"*Hilda* would be entirely adequate."

Stryker produced a cool smile of her own, then stood up from the table, indicating the meeting was over.

As the others rose to leave, she motioned to Gurney to stay.

When they were alone, she closed the conference room door and sat down across from him. "You seemed quite certain that your friend Morgan couldn't be a blackmailer but could be a homicidal-suicidal maniac. Did I understand that correctly?"

"More or less."

"What's the 'less' part?"

"You referred to him as my friend. That's a bit of an exaggeration."

"Okay. What makes you so sure about the motives of this non-friend?"

"Apart from simple logic and the evidence on the ground?"

"Apart from that."

After considering the pluses and minuses of revealing the event at the heart of his relationship with Mike Morgan, he decided to go ahead and tell Stryker the story of the apartment house shoot-out.

She paid close attention and at the end nodded slightly, as if she might be agreeing that it was relevant in understanding Morgan's motives. Then she changed the subject.

"I've been in two meetings with you now, and both times I've gotten the impression that you know more than you're saying. Is that true?"

"It's not anything I *know*. It's just a feeling."

"What kind of feeling?"

"That it's all too complicated."

"What do you mean?"

"What we have here is a series of winding narratives that turn one way, then another way, but never seem to straighten out. When you get to the heart of it, there's a straight line in every crime. But the straight line in what's happening here is eluding me."

"Maybe fourteen dead bodies can't be lined up that neatly."

Gurney didn't reply.

"Do you share the doubts Morgan had about Chandler Aspern's death?"

"I do."

"Do you believe Lorinda Russell was involved?"

"I do. Along with an accomplice."

"And who might that be?"

"We suspected Silas Gant, but it couldn't have been him. He was addressing a religious gun rally hundreds of miles away the night of Aspern's death."

Stryker began tapping her pen lightly on the table.

"So, you're telling me we still have a murderer on the loose?"

"It would seem so."

55

After sharing with Stryker his other thoughts on the peculiarities of the case—which he still viewed as a single entity, convinced as he was that all the fatalities were connected by a single underlying cause—Gurney headed back to Walnut Crossing.

During the drive, he thought of little else but the open question of Lorinda's accomplice in the murder of Aspern. If the individual approaching the conservatory wearing Billy Tate's clothes in the security camera video wasn't Aspern and wasn't Gant, it had to be someone else of roughly the same size.

Someone else.

That simple phrase had an odd resonance in Gurney's mind, the feeling of an elusive recollection that only became more so the harder he tried to identify it. When he turned his attention away from it, the feeling grew stronger. When he pursued it, it faded. It was frustrating—that stubborn trait of memory that refuses to be coerced, allowing access only when one stops beating on the door.

And so it was this time.

As Gurney was parking, his eyes on the half-finished alpaca shed, he recalled for no discernible reason something Clarice Flacco had said about the removal of Hanley Bullock's body from his apartment. After describing how the "cousin" and the "doctor" had carried the body down the stairs, she had said, "Someone else had arrived in a hearse."

He was surprised that someone's use of a phrase as innocuous as "someone else" would create an echo to his own use of the same phrase days later. But what mattered to him now was not the phrase itself, but the far more interesting memory it led to—Clarice Flacco's description of that individual. To be sure he was recalling it accurately, he took out his phone and checked the note he'd made about it after they spoke.

Thin, balding, forties. About the same age as Bullock.

In his forties, ten years ago.

The implications burst on Gurney like the flood of light from the halogens at a crime scene. He sat perfectly still in the Outback, as if any movement might shatter the picture of the Larchfield murders forming in his mind.

He began to see the straight line he'd been searching for.

It was the line that connected everything—from the ME's hurried pronouncement of Tate's death to Peale's jacked-up Lexus behind the funeral home, from Lorinda's promiscuity to Morgan's blaze-of-glory suicide, from the shoelace discrepancy to everything Hilda Russell had told him about the prominent citizens of Larchfield, from the audio anomaly in the embalming room video to Peale's rage at Fallow.

He grinned at the realization that the only person everyone said was wrong was the only one who was right. And the one who stood to lose the most was the one with the most to gain.

He was elated at finally grasping the simple truth at the root of it all, embarrassed by how easily he'd been deceived by the sequential narrative presented by Kyra Barstow and Greta Vickerz, and doubly embarrassed by having fallen into one of the classic traps he'd warned his academy class against. Worst of all, he'd ignored the investigation axiom tattooed on the arm of his crusty NYPD mentor:

Believe nothing. Trust no one. Question everything.

The excitement of clarity soon pushed his embarrassment aside. However, he realized that all his excitement had little practical value. He was sure of what had happened, but he had no proof. And acquiring that proof would not be easy, since almost everyone involved in the case was now dead.

With little time to waste, he decided to proceed immediately along one of the few still-open pathways. The first thing he did after hurrying into the house was call Slovak.

"Yes, sir, what can I do for you?"

"The first day I came to Larchfield I saw Peale's Lexus jacked up in back of the funeral home. He later told me he'd borrowed the jack from a neighbor. Do you know who that might be?"

"My bet would be Hugh Stanhope. Man owns five Ferraris. Richer than God, but likes to get his hands dirty. Once he offered to soup up our Dodge Chargers. Why?"

"Do you think you could get the brand and model number of that jack from him—the one he lent to Peale?"

"I guess so. Sure. But—"

"It's a long story, Brad. But I'm in a time crunch. I'll explain later."

"I'll give him a call and get right back to you."

Next he called Barstow and got her voicemail.

"Hi, Kyra. I have a question for you to pass along to that tech in your computer forensics department, the one who found the sonic anomaly in the mortuary video. Ask him if it could have been caused by that segment of the audio having been recorded twice. I just want a simple answer, no technical explanation required. And, yes, of course it's urgent. Thanks."

Realizing he was hungry, he opened a loaf of whole wheat bread and made himself a sandwich of cheese and pickles. Then he turned on the coffee machine and washed one of the mugs in the sink. As he was drying it, his phone rang.

It was Slovak with the jack information he'd asked for.

Gurney thanked him and went immediately to his laptop and the manufacturer's website. He found the information he was looking for deep in the device's technical specs. Like some of his other discoveries, by itself it proved nothing, but it encouraged him to take the next step.

He called Slovak again.

"Brad, we need to talk to Peale ASAP. I want you to locate him and let him know that, without realizing it, he may have some critical, time-sensitive information related to the case. Do it face-to-face."

"Should I have him come in to headquarters?"

"That would be ideal. But if there's some reason he can't or won't do that, just stay with him and let him know I'm on my way. Then call me and tell me where you are."

"Will do." Slovak hesitated. "Should we let Stryker know?"

"Not yet. I want to nail down a few facts first."

That was certainly the truth. He could have added that he wanted to handle the situation in his own way without the possibility of interference, but that would only have given Slovak something else to worry about.

Gurney spent the next twenty-five minutes on his sandwich, his coffee, and his thoughts on how best to approach Peale.

Those thoughts, along with his preparation of a second cup of coffee, ended abruptly when Slovak called back with panic in his voice.

"Dave?"

"Yes?"

"I'm at Peale's house. It's been broken into. I think he's been murdered."

56

The stately stone residence of W. Danforth Peale III was located at the end of a white gravel driveway bordered by neatly trimmed boxwood hedges. The drive widened into a spacious oval in front of the house, an area now occupied by Slovak's Charger, three patrol cars, Barstow's van, an unmarked black Explorer, and the photographer's Camry. Gurney parked next to the Camry.

To the left of the oval was a three-car garage. Its open doors revealed one small off-road utility vehicle, one antique British sports car, and one empty bay. Yellow police tape had been strung up around the garage, the house, and a wide swath of the surrounding lawn. A Larchfield cop with a clipboard was manning an opening in the tape.

He recognized Gurney, made a notation on the site's access log, and pointed to the open back of Barstow's van. "Gloves and shoe covers over there. Crime scene's at the rear of the house."

With gloves and booties on, Gurney headed around to the area behind the house, which was approximately half lawn and half stone patio. A corridor of sorts had been cordoned off with additional yellow tape, beginning at the back door of the house and extending across the patio onto the lawn. The rest of the lawn had been gridded with white string into a standard geometric search pattern. One of Barstow's techs was proceeding slowly through it, his attention on the ground in front of him. A wide-eyed Slovak hurried over to Gurney.

"It looks like someone broke in through the back door and got into a scuffle with Peale, killed him, and dragged his body outside. There are tire marks on the grass—like they brought a car around to take the body away. Peale's Lexus is gone, so that may be the vehicle that left the marks. The gas stove in the kitchen was still on, like Peale had been cooking something, but it was all just a blackened mess, the pot even had a hole burned through it. The house stinks from the smoke, lucky the whole place didn't go up in a blaze."

"Any estimate of the time this happened?"

"The blood is still tacky in a few spots, so I'm guessing sometime this morning?"

"What are you focused on right now?"

"I just sent two of our patrol guys around the neighborhood to find out if anyone noticed anyone coming or going around this house. And I issued an APB on Peale's Lexus. What's next, I'm not sure." He lowered his voice. "DA Stryker has taken over the scene. She tells us to do one thing, then another thing. I don't know if she knows what she's doing herself."

On cue, Stryker appeared inside the open back door and summoned Gurney over with a peremptory wave of her hand.

"Take a look in here. I want your interpretation of this." Her voice had the rigid edge that often comes with an effort to project self-confidence.

When Gurney reached the taped corridor leading out from the back door, he noted the reddish-brown drag marks on the patio. He stepped gingerly around them and followed Stryker into the rear hall of the house. As he passed the door, he saw that the glass panel nearest the knob had been broken. Some of the glass pieces were on the hall floor and some were outside the doorway on the patio, seemingly where they had been dragged. Those had the same brownish-red traces on them as the hall floor and the patio stones.

Stryker pointed along the hallway. "Actual crime scene is in the kitchen."

There was blood all over the floor, mainly, but also on the kitchen tabletop and chair back, where a handprint, perhaps of the staggering victim, had smeared it. There were scuff marks on the floor, a spoon, and the pieces of a broken bowl. There was an open oatmeal container and a measuring cup on a countertop next to the stove. The blackened, warped remnant of a pot sat on one of the burners. The tile wall behind the stove and the exhaust fan above it were covered with soot.

Gurney looked more closely at the central bloodstain on the floor. It appeared that a body or other substantial object had rested in it, then been dragged out of the kitchen, through the hall, and out the back door. He followed the smeared bloodstains out onto the patio and through the taped corridor onto the lawn, where they stopped. The portly photographer was taking multiple shots of that area, with Barstow and Slovak both directing him to places in the grass they wanted him to focus on.

Stryker had followed Gurney out of the house and was standing behind him.

"Well?"

Gurney ignored the question. He was estimating the distance from the last bloodstain in the grass to the indentations caused by a vehicle's tires.

"Looks like this is where he dumped the body in the trunk," said Slovak, stretching his thick neck from side to side.

Gurney noticed a plastic evidence bag in Barstow's hand with something dark inside it. He asked what she'd found.

She held it up so he could see it more clearly. "Peale's wallet. It was tossed on the grass over there." She pointed to a spot a few feet from where they were standing. "Driver's license, Lexus registration, credit cards were all missing, along with any cash he might have been carrying. Other items were still in it—golf club membership card, Mensa membership, hunting club membership, medical insurance cards." A damp, gusty wind was blowing her hair sideways, but she seemed not to notice.

"Whoever did it just took the essentials," added Slovak, unnecessarily.

"Well, Detective?" The edge in Stryker's voice had become more insistent.

He turned to her. "Yes?"

"I'm waiting for your reaction."

"So far, I have nothing to add to what's obvious."

"What would you say is obvious?"

"There's a lot of blood in the kitchen. Some of it seems to have been dragged out here. And a vehicle of some sort was recently driven across the lawn."

"That's all your famous power of deduction tells you?"

"I'm afraid so."

After staring at him for a moment in disbelief, she turned to Slovak. "How about you? How would you explain what we're seeing here?"

He swallowed, in obvious between-a-rock-and-a-hard-place discomfort. "Well, ma'am . . . I guess . . . I mean . . . it seems that Dan Peale's been murdered. By someone who broke in, struggled with him, and killed him. They probably used a knife . . . or scalpel . . . considering the amount of blood. Then they dragged his body out of the house, took his car keys, took the essential stuff out of his wallet, got his Lexus out of the garage, loaded his body in the trunk, and drove off."

Stryker nodded encouragingly. "Anything else?"

"Peale was waiting for his oatmeal to cook when the killer broke in."

"How do you know he wasn't eating it?"

"The spoon and plate pieces we found on the floor are clean."

She nodded again. "Very good. Any ideas about who the killer might be?"

After casting a nervous glance at Gurney, he cleared his throat. "Just one, but there's no proof, it's just an idea."

"Ideas are exactly what we need at this point."

He took a deep breath. "Dr. Ronald Fallow."

Stryker blinked in surprise, then urged him to go on.

"Peale was suing him. He was telling everyone that since the false death pronouncement had destroyed his funeral business, he wanted Fallow's medical license taken away, and he was suing him for, like, a hundred million dollars. And he kept bad-mouthing Fallow around town—like, nonstop. I figure Fallow got to the point where he just snapped."

Stryker turned to Gurney, a glint of triumph in her eyes. "So, what do you think of that?"

"I'd have to give it some thought."

"Good plan." Her phone rang. She looked at the screen and, before stepping away to take the call, added pointedly, "Before you leave, I want to speak to you."

Slovak looked at Gurney with a kind of questioning hopefulness. "I hope what I said was all right. She asked what I thought, and that was what I was thinking."

Gurney smiled. "Ideas solve cases. Better to share them than keep them to yourself."

Slovak seemed satisfied with that and headed for the house.

Barstow went back to conferring with the photographer over the tire tracks in the grass.

While Stryker was involved in her phone call, Gurney decided to take a walk around the exterior of Peale's house. It appeared to be meticulously maintained, no doubt by hired gardeners. Peale didn't strike him as the sort of man who'd want to muddy his knees weeding a flower bed.

He made a complete circuit of the place and found himself back at the yellow-tape entry point. The gray-haired cop with the clipboard gestured toward the house.

"Not bad for a caretaker's cottage, eh?"

"Caretaker's cottage?"

"Not now, of course, but that's what it used to be. For the big Peale estate. Most of that got sold off years ago, when the current Mr. Peale was just a kid. All that's left of it now is this 'cottage' and a few acres around it. Tell you what—I wouldn't mind coming down in the world, if this was what I got to come down to. Everything's relative, right?"

"Gurney!" Stryker was calling to him from a spot on the back lawn, away from the others working the scene.

He headed over, in no great rush, prepared for what he guessed would be her first question.

He was right.

"I'm curious about something. You told Slovak to find Peale. Why?"

"I wanted to speak to him—face-to-face, not on the phone."

"Why?"

"A computer forensics tech found an anomaly in the security video of Tate's resurrection in the mortuary. I wanted to question him about it."

"What sort of anomaly?"

"That's not clear, but even a slight possibility of there being anything misleading in that video would definitely need to be pursued."

"So you diverted Slovak from the assignment I'd given him, in order to pursue this *anomaly*?"

Gurney was tempted to point out that the anomaly could end up being of far greater import than any assignment Slovak might have been diverted from, but he thought it better to let that obvious fact simply hang in the air between them.

And so it did, until Stryker moved on in an equally aggressive tone to her next topic.

"I've read the terms of your agreement with the Larchfield Police Department. The arrangement is loosely defined, to say the least. As part of regularizing the reporting structure here, we need to deal with that. For the duration of your activity on this case, you'll be reporting to my Detective Lieutenant Hapsburg. That will be effective starting—"

Gurney cut her off. "You've misunderstood the nature of my involvement."

Stryker blinked. "*Misunderstood*?"

"At Mike Morgan's request, I volunteered to take a look at the case and offer my suggestions to him, to Brad Slovak, and to Kyra Barstow. I don't *report to* anyone."

"That's neither professional nor appropriate. This is a law-enforcement operation. Accountability is a requirement, not an option."

"I understand."

"Good. Then, as of tomorrow morning, you'll be reporting—"

He cut her off again. "What I understand is that the terms of my agreement are no longer acceptable—meaning that you're not willing to have me involved in the only way that I'm willing to be involved. If you should happen to change your mind, the department has my number. In the meantime, good luck and be careful."

She stared at him.

He nodded pleasantly, walked to the Outback, and headed for Walnut Crossing.

57

In the course of the trip home, Gurney received two calls. The first was from Slovak.

"I hope I'm not interrupting anything."

"Not at all."

"Is it true that you're off the case?"

"Officially, yes. The DA wants to organize the investigation in her own way."

"Jeez, that sounds like a big mistake."

"It's her right."

"I know, but she doesn't inspire a lot of confidence. Would it be okay if I stayed in touch with you?"

"Sure."

"Do you have any advice for me?"

"Relax. Do your job. And try to keep an open mind about Stryker."

"Do you think I should be following up on my idea about Fallow being Peale's murderer? Maybe I should see if he can account for his whereabouts this morning?"

"If I were you, I'd back up a little. Instead of rushing to answer the question of who killed Peale, ask yourself first, why was his body removed?"

"Do you already know why?"

"Not yet. But I think it's the key question."

After ending the call with Slovak, Gurney discovered a new voicemail message from Barstow.

"To your notion of a double recording being embedded in the mortuary audio, our tech says yes, it could explain the odd sonic footprint. Hope that's what you wanted to hear. By the way, I heard you had a falling-out with Stryker. No shock to me. Someday that lady's gonna bleed on her own sharp edge. Stay in touch. I like the way you think."

Pleased but not surprised by the tech's confirmation of his suspicion, he refocused on the matter at hand, specifically on the question he'd left with Slovak. Why was the body removed?

The normal answer didn't apply. In every case he could recall that involved a missing body, it had been removed as part of an effort to conceal the fact that a homicide had taken place. But that could hardly be the reason in a situation where no effort had been made to clean up the blood and the evidence of a struggle.

When he arrived home at four thirty, he was no closer to an answer but even more convinced that it would hold the key to understanding what had happened in Peale's kitchen that morning and why. When Madeleine got home a little after five, he tried to put that conundrum aside and shift his attention to a brighter subject.

Before he could settle on one, she presented one of her own.

"I heard we're supposed to get thunderstorms later, so how about we eat early, then work on the shed till it gets dark?"

He agreed, making an effort to exhibit an appropriate level of enthusiasm, and after a simple dinner of salmon, rice, and asparagus, they set to work on the job of sheathing and roofing.

Both tasks involved trimming sheets of exterior plywood to the right size. Madeleine insisted on being the one to operate the handheld circular saw while he steadied the sheets on the supporting sawhorses. Since she'd never used a circular saw before, he spent some time showing her how to guide the spinning blade through the wood, how to avoid any kickback, and how the safety guard should be positioned. As he often did in these kinds of situations, he spent too much time explaining how to use the tool and warning of its dangers, and she grew impatient.

For the rest of the evening, however, all went well. The shed was successfully sided and roofed, and all that remained for another day was the installation of the door. As the dusk deepened and the wind rose, they left their tools in the nearly finished structure and went back into the house, sharing smiles of satisfaction. Madeleine was obviously happy with what she had done, and he was happy that she was happy.

Still in that mood later that night, they went to bed, made love, and drifted toward an untroubled sleep.

To Gurney, this state of mind and spirit amounted to a sense that all the bits and pieces of the world, however chaotic they might seem, were somehow in their proper places, and all was well. All was calm, timeless, and still.

Into this idyll of peace the sound intruded like a dagger.

It was the same ferocious, high-pitched howl he'd heard the night the Dark Angel message had appeared in blood on the barn door. But this time it was coming from somewhere closer to the house. Much closer.

"David, wake up!"

"I'm awake."

"What are we going to do? Shall I turn on the light?"

"No. No lights."

He rolled out of bed and dressed quickly in the dark. He took his Beretta from the night table drawer and stuck it in the back pocket of his jeans.

"What are you doing?" whispered Madeleine.

He didn't answer.

He checked the time on his phone. It was just one minute after midnight. There was a distant flash of lightning, followed several seconds later by a rumble of thunder. The air from the open window was cool and damp.

He placed a call to Hardwick.

The voice that that answered was rough and sleepy. "Yeah?"

"Sorry to wake you, Jack. I've got a visitor."

"You have a plan?"

"Catch him. ID him. Arrest him. Question him."

"That's not a plan." Hardwick cleared his throat with disgusting thoroughness. "That's a procedure-manual fantasy."

"You have a better idea?"

"Put a bullet in his head, rocks in his pockets, and dump him in your pond."

"Always a possibility. Drop by if you can."

"On my way, Sherlock, locked and loaded."

Gurney slipped the phone in his pocket. There was another flash of lightning and another rumble of thunder. The storm was getting closer.

Madeleine was sitting on the edge of the bed. "You called Hardwick."

"Yes."

"Why not 911?"

"He'll get here quicker."

"Quicker than the cops down in Walnut Crossing?"

"After ten o'clock there are no cops in Walnut Crossing. Everything gets redirected to the sheriff's department in Bounderville."

"So what will—" She stopped, staring out the window. "What's that?"

Gurney looked out in the direction she was pointing. There was an almost imperceptible orange glow on the foliage of a tree by the corner of the house. The glow was faint and unsteady, like the reflection of a small fire. He moved closer to the window for a broader view. There was no fire visible on that side of the house.

He ran to the kitchen and saw it immediately through the French doors—the beginning of a fire at the point where the new shed and the chicken coop were joined together. Madeleine followed him and was heading for the doors.

He put out his arm to stop her. "Stay back! The son of a bitch is waiting for us to come out."

"But we have to stop the fire!"

"We will. But not this way. That's what he wants. I'm going out the back way."

He ran to the bedroom, put on his sneakers, and slipped out through the window next to the bed. Landing on an uneven spot in the moist grass, he twisted his ankle sharply, the stab of pain diluted by adrenaline. He pulled the Beretta from his rear pocket and eased off the safety.

A triple flash of lightning illuminated the thicket behind the house. He saw no one. He made his way in the dark to the nearest corner of the house, then around that to the end of the side that faced the chicken coop. Crouching, he peered slowly around the corner drainpipe.

The fire was larger now, its glow clearly illuminating the area between the coop and the house. The area behind the coop and on Gurney's side of it were left in darkness, seemingly deeper now in contrast with the blaze.

Still seeing no one, he crept out from the house as far as the asparagus bed, whose foot-high enclosure of four-by-fours offered partial shelter, and waited there to see what the next lightning flash might reveal.

The flash came a second later. What it revealed was both predictable and shocking.

Beyond the end of the coop, at the corner of the new shed, stood a perfect image of Billy Tate—the Billy Tate he'd seen in the video of the crazy night on the roof of St. Giles—Billy Tate in a gray hoodie and black jeans. But instead of a spray can for graffiti, this Billy Tate was carrying an AK-47. As suddenly as it had illuminated him, the flash died, and the hooded figure disappeared in the darkness, followed by a deafening crash of thunder.

The idea of calling out, "Police! Drop the gun! Now!" would satisfy a procedural guideline, but it would materially diminish the chances of survival—his own and Madeleine's. And survival was now the imperative.

With one knee on the ground, Gurney raised his Beretta in a solid two-handed firing grip and waited again for the lightning. When the flash came, his view of the corner of the shed was partially blocked by the asparagus ferns bending and swaying in the wind. But he caught a glimpse of the assault rifle and the gray sweatshirt, and he fired off three quick rounds.

There was a yelp of pain, a curse, followed a moment later in the pitch darkness by half a dozen return rounds, two of which Gurney heard strike the low wall of the planting bed he was using as a shield.

Since there was no longer any downside in doing so, he shouted out the standard police warning. Twice. When there was no reply, he fired off another three rounds in the direction of the shed, then retreated around to the back of the house, feeling his way to the far side, from which he'd have a clear, direct line of fire to the hidden side of the shed.

Aided now by multiple lightning flashes, he ran toward that ideal position. Just as he arrived there, he stepped on the edge of a rock, turning the same ankle he'd injured on his way out the bedroom window. Feeling something in the joint snap, he stumbled out uncontrollably from behind the house into firelight and fell to the ground.

The hooded figure at the side of the shed whirled around, firing wildly in the direction of the sound. Gurney heard the sharp *crack-crack-crack* of the bullets hitting the house and still others ripping through the thick shrubs at the edge of the patio. From his prone position, he fired back—eight or nine rounds, he wasn't sure which.

In the next lightning flash there was no sign of the hooded figure. Gurney forced himself to his feet, thinking that he would make his way back to the bedroom window and into the house for his shotgun. But when he tried to walk, he found that he couldn't. His mind was racing for an alternative when the gray figure slowly emerged from the darkness by the shed into the light of the fire.

Gurney raised the Beretta, pulled the trigger, and heard the worst possible sound—the metallic click of the hammer on an empty chamber.

The gray figure moved a few steps forward, the AK-47 leveled at Gurney's chest. The lack of any discernible features beneath the hood made the rasping laugh that came out of it seem hardly human.

"Time to take out the garbage," said the voice. Neither identifiably male nor female, it sounded like something being extruded from a rusted machine.

Having been on the front line of hundreds of homicide investigations in the city, this was not the first time Gurney had found himself at a potentially fatal disadvantage with a killer. The crucial objective was to create a delay. The longer he could keep that trigger from being pulled, the better his chance of preventing it entirely.

His experience told him that most killers, unless driven by uncontrollable rages, could be tempted into pausing in situations like this in order to find out what the intended victim or the police might know about them or their crimes. The key was to reveal a sequence of facts, gradually drawing out the narrative without the real goal—delay—becoming obvious. This demanded a delicate balance. Details that carried an emotional charge were the best obscurers of delay, but they carried the risk of igniting a deadly reaction.

Gurney began with a simple question.

"Was she worth it?"

A jagged lightning strike punctuated the question, and for a startling second its flash was reflected in the malevolent eyes fixed on Gurney.

He continued, speaking softly, insinuatingly. "The high school goddess. Irresistible and untouchable. Except by Billy Tate. It must have been nearly unbearable that a scruffy delinquent like Tate could have what you couldn't. And then, even worse, she sold herself to that disgusting old man on Harrow Hill. I can imagine your envy, the acid eating away your life, year after year. And then, the miracle. She spoke to you. Showed interest in you. My God, what a rush that must have been! Your chance at last. I wonder how long it took before she started telling you how unhappy she was with her married life, how she longed to be free of it. Perhaps she claimed to have certain feelings about you, maybe that she always felt you two had something in common. Maybe that was all the direction and encouragement you needed. Or maybe she was more specific about that terrible old Angus being the sole obstacle to her happiness—a happiness that she'd be inclined to share with you. Perhaps she gave you an advance taste of that happiness. You understood what she wanted you to do. You just weren't sure how to proceed. So much at stake. Such a desirable prize. Such a terrible risk. But then the great opportunity fell into your lap."

The chickens were squawking wildly now, no doubt sensing the growing conflagration on the outside of their coop.

When Gurney glanced in that direction, he noticed a dark figure moving along the edge of the firelit area and disappearing behind the coop.

He tried to maintain the calm flow of his narrative.

"The stars were aligned as never before. You knew you had to act immediately, or you never would. You explained the situation—the unique opportunity—to Lorinda. You told her it was now or never. She agreed. You stitched together a plan. And you pulled it off. Beautifully. At least the parts of the plan you could control. The hidden wild card was Mike Morgan. Anxious, guilt-ridden, womanizing Mike Morgan. Did Lorinda mention that you weren't the first man she tried to interest in getting rid of Angus? No, I don't suppose she did. Nobody wants to be second choice."

The AK-47, which had been slightly lowered, was raised. Gurney heard a sound like a simmering growl emanating from the darkness under the hood. He had no alternative now but to press forward.

"But Morgan hadn't gotten the message. He'd thought his relationship with Lorinda was just about casual sex, like all his other relationships. When Lorinda realized that he wasn't going to take the next step, the only step that mattered to her, she moved on. To you."

Gurney was wondering how much longer he could stretch this out. He hardly noticed that it had started to rain, and little rivulets of water were running down his face. "You know, I thought I had everything figured out. Then I walked into that kitchen, saw all that blood, saw the drag marks leading out to the tire impressions in the grass—and I was baffled all over again. I kept asking myself what seemed like the obvious question. *Why was the body removed?* But that was the wrong question, wasn't it?"

A flash of lightning revealed teeth in what appeared to be a grin in the shadow of the hood.

"Goodbye, Detective." The harshness, the raspiness, the effort at disguising the voice had ceased. It was clear, icy, and quite identifiable.

As the muzzle of the AK-47 was aimed at the center of Gurney's breastbone, a shrill metallic whine arose behind the hooded figure, whose sudden effort to turn toward it ended in a horrific shriek as Madeleine thrust the circular saw forward and the teeth of the spinning blade tore through one of the hands holding the weapon.

A spray of blood whipped across Gurney's face as a convulsive jerk of his attacker's arm sent the AK-47 clattering across the patio.

The hooded figure staggered backward.

Madeleine attacked again.

Another shriek, longer and wilder than the first.

This time the spray of blood fell in a line across the patio, a severed hand fell on the grass at Gurney's feet, and the hooded figure ran with a gagging scream into the darkness of the low pasture.

Madeleine was breathing hard, with a rigid grip on the still-whining saw.

"It's okay," said Gurney. "You can put it down."

The meaning of his words seemed not to register.

It wasn't until she noticed blood dripping from the blade housing onto her knuckles that she tossed the tool away from her. The sharp clang when it hit the stone patio seemed to bring her back from wherever the intensity of the experience had taken her. Tears welled in her eyes. Gurney tried to step toward her, but the pain that instantly shot up through his leg stopped him. She came to him, and they embraced for a long minute.

Gurney heard the sound of a car starting down by the barn and driving off into the night in a spray of gravel. He figured it was the missing Lexus.

"We have to put out the fire," she said.

"Turn on the garden hose."

The spigot was next to the back door. She switched on the patio floodlights, then turned on the spigot, unreeled the hose, and aimed it at the burning siding. The combination of water from the hose and the now-heavy rain extinguished the flames, converting the whole front of the coop and half of the shed siding into a smoldering black wall.

Gurney took out his phone. "Time to call 911."

"I already did. Before I came out."

The sound of a distant crash came from somewhere on the town road that led from their barn down the long hill to the county route.

"Help me to the Outback," he said. "I need to get down to whatever just happened."

She turned off the hose. "I'm going with you."

A mile down the road, they came upon the collision. In the headlights of the Outback, it appeared that a silver-gray Lexus had smashed at high speed into the front of a red Pontiac GTO. Jack Hardwick was standing next to the Lexus. His head and face were covered with blood. It was mixing with the rain and running down onto his tee shirt. His nose looked broken.

Gurney struggled out of his car, putting all his weight on one leg and using the open door as a support. "Jack?"

Hardwick pointed at the driver's-side window of the Lexus. "That bastard in the hoodie better be dead. Who the fuck is he, anyway?"

Gurney was 95 percent sure, about as sure as he ever was about anything.

"William Danforth Peale the Third."

58

The Walnut Crossing hospital was a modest one-story structure whose services were limited to diagnostic imaging, lab analyses, and crisis medicine. Their emergency room was large for a small town and had recently been updated.

In a roomy private bay with a sliding glass door, Hardwick was propped up into a semi-sitting position on an ER bed. He was wearing a green hospital gown. His head and nose were bandaged, an IV tube ran from a clear plastic bag on a pole down into his forearm, and a set of wires connected him to a device with a vital-signs screen next to the bed.

Gurney, also in a hospital gown, was sitting in a wheelchair a few feet away. The lower half of his left leg was encased in a fiberglass cast. Madeleine was sitting next to him, dressed in the same black slacks and sweatshirt she'd worn in her attack on Peale.

With her back to the closed glass door, Cam Stryker, in a blue business suit, was sitting where she could face them all. She'd lowered one of the ER's rolling tray tables to desk height in front of her. On it were an attaché case, an iPad, a phone, and a notebook. Detective Lieutenant Derek Hapsburg was standing near her, a small man with thin lips and a stony expression. His arms were folded.

A digital clock on the wall behind Hardwick's bed said it was 4:05 a.m.

Stryker activated her iPad. After announcing the time, the fact that the meeting was being recorded, and the names of the people present, she asked Gurney to recount the events of the night in detail, from the moment he suspected the presence of a trespasser on his property up to his arrival at the fatal collision site.

He went through it all—beginning with Madeleine's initial glimpse of the flickering orange glow, and proceeding in vivid detail through the exchange of gunfire, at which point Stryker interrupted to ask if he'd identified himself as a police officer. He said that he had, loud and clear, and that his announcement was ignored. All true enough. He went on to describe the injury that had rendered him helpless, Madeleine's weaponizing of the battery-driven circular saw, the mutilation of Peale, and his shrieking flight into the night—the "escape" that ended in a fatal collision a mile down the road.

Stryker asked why he'd called Hardwick at the outset rather than 911. He gave her the same answer he'd given Madeleine. She frowned but said nothing.

She asked Madeleine to describe her thoughts, movements, reason for choosing the saw, what options she had considered, and what her intention was as she approached Peale.

Madeleine stared at her in disbelief. "A homicidal lunatic with an assault rifle was about to kill my husband. My intention was to save his life. I did what occurred to me. There was no time for *options*. If I'd stopped to consider *options*, my husband would be dead."

Stryker nodded without conveying an iota of sympathy. She turned her attention back to Gurney.

"I understand that you told Jack Hardwick that the man who had just fled from your property and crashed into him was Danforth Peale. How did you know that?"

"I wasn't absolutely certain until the very end—when he pointed that damn AK-47 at my heart and was about to pull the trigger. At that moment he abandoned the effort to disguise his voice. I recognized it. His intonations were quite distinctive."

"You say that's when you were *absolutely* certain. Does that mean at some earlier point you were *moderately* certain?"

Gurney wondered whether she was making a special effort to be grating, or if it was a natural gift. Either way, he decided to ignore the tone and respond to the content of the question.

"By yesterday morning I'd seen enough arrows pointing toward Peale to convince me that they weren't all coincidental and that he was, in fact, Lorinda's accomplice. But then—"

Stryker interrupted him.

"Why on earth did you keep this to yourself? You were right there with me at Peale's house, but you didn't say a single word. I'd like to know why."

"What I thought I knew was rendered meaningless by what appeared to be Peale's murder. It suddenly seemed more likely that Lorinda's accomplice was someone else, and Peale was just his latest victim."

Stryker began tapping her pen on the table. "And this confusion didn't get cleared up until the moment you recognized his voice?"

"It started getting cleared up before that. My confusion when I saw that bloody kitchen and the drag marks outside was caused by my asking myself why the body had been removed. That stymied me. But when I asked instead why it was *missing*, the answer occurred to me. It was missing for the simple reason that it didn't exist. There was no body—because there was no murder."

Stryker's pen stopped moving. "Then whose blood was it? Who got dragged out to the car?"

"The whole scene was a setup. Peale probably used his own blood. You'll know for sure when you get the DNA results. As for the drag marks, he could have made those with anything. I suspect the moment he heard what had happened on Harrow Hill he realized his grand plan had collapsed and it was time to get the hell out of Larchfield. The 'murder' scene was an effort to cover his tracks."

"Grand plan? What grand plan?"

"The plan he'd worked out with Lorinda from day one."

"*Day one*? Are you suggesting that he killed *everyone*—Angus Russell, Mary Kane, Linda Mason, Chandler Aspern, Billy Tate?"

"Russell, Kane, Mason, Aspern—all of those, but not Tate. Definitely not Tate."

"Then who—"

He cut her off. "There are some things you need to know about Larchfield. Some are a matter of public record, some I got from Hilda Russell, and some through my own investigation."

Stryker laid her pen down, steepled her fingers, and gave Gurney her expressionless attention.

He told her about the past disappearances of people in conflict with Angus,

Angus's financial relationship with Silas Gant, Lorinda's blood relationship with Otis Strane, and—according to Hilda—the existence of a long-standing shady relationship between the Russell and Peale families. He then described the suggestive circumstances of Hanley Bullock's death, and how that death seemed to involve those relationships. Surely the neat man with the silver-gray pompadour was Gant and the man with "OTIS" tattooed on his knuckles was Otis Strane.

"I can't prove it," Gurney continued, "but I'd be willing to bet my pension that the hearse driver in Crickton that day, the man who drove off with Bullock's body, was Danforth Peale's father, who Hilda Russell described as the coldest man she'd ever met—a man whose ownership of hearses and cemeteries would put him in an ideal position for getting rid of bodies."

Stryker opened her palms in a gesture of impatience. "That was ten years ago. What's it got to do with—"

He cut her off again. "I got to thinking about the people Lorinda might be relying on. The first one who came to mind was Gant. But the night Aspern was killed, Gant was speaking at that gun rally in West Virginia. So it had to be someone else. And that's when Peale came to mind, along with a simple thought: like father, like son."

Stryker screwed up her face in disbelief. "*Like father, like son*? That's it? That was your basis for zeroing in on Peale?"

Detective Lieutenant Hapsburg uttered a small snort of derision.

Hardwick eyed him as though he might be measuring him for a body bag.

"It wasn't just that," said Gurney mildly. "There was also that oddity in the audio portion of the mortuary video that I've already mentioned to you. The idea that something in that video might have been tampered with struck me as a red flag. And it turns out part of the audio may have been faked. In fact, I'm now sure that Peale's security camera was recording a prerecorded sound of the casket being broken open, rather than the actual event."

Stryker folded her arms. "Anything else?"

"Yes. One of the lab experts discovered a small hole that had been drilled in the bottom of the casket—which made no sense to me, until I remembered seeing Peale with an automobile jack. When I checked the specs on that model, they were consistent with my suspicion that Peale had been Lorinda's accomplice from the beginning. They also explained how the first big trick in the case was pulled off."

Stryker unfolded her arms, then folded them again. "You're saying Peale was involved from the beginning, but you said a minute ago that he's not the one who killed Tate. If he didn't, who did?"

"That was the simplest piece of the puzzle," said Gurney. "It was right in front of our faces all the time. In fact, we'd been told what the answer was. If only we'd been willing to believe it. If only—"

The detective lieutenant interrupted him. "We don't need the big lead-in. How about you just answer the question."

Gurney smiled. "Billy Tate was killed by a combination of a direct lightning strike and a devastating fall. Dr. Ronald Fallow declared him dead, correctly so. Fallow, the one person everyone came to believe was wrong, was the only one who was right. Tate was dead. But the circumstances surrounding his death very quickly captivated Danforth Peale. In fact, those circumstances were the irresistible gift placed in his hands—the golden opportunity of a lifetime."

"Opportunity to do what?"

"What Lorinda Russell had made clear she wanted him to do: get rid of her husband. And now he had the perfect way to do it. The body that had been rolled into his mortuary that night belonged to a young man who had publicly threatened Angus Russell, who was known to be interested in witchcraft and Satanism—a loose cannon if there ever was one. And best of all, no one wanted the body. His stepmother wanted absolutely nothing of his; wouldn't even touch his phone or car keys; wanted no memorial service, no visiting hours, nothing. All she asked was for Peale to store the body until she could decide how to dispose of it."

"But the video . . ." began Stryker.

"The video was Peale's stroke of genius. He was close enough to Tate's size that he could fit into his clothes. He had mortician's makeup he could use to make his face look convincingly burned and disfigured, at least from a distance. And he borrowed that auto jack from his neighbor as a way of breaking open the casket from the inside. I mentioned a minute ago that I checked the specs on that model. What I discovered was that it was electric and could be operated with a remote. That hole Peale drilled in the bottom of the casket was just right for the power cord. He put the jack in the casket, closed and latched the lid, then used the jack to push it open from the inside, ripping the latches out of the wood. He recorded that ripping, breaking sound. That evening, before the security camera was automatically switched on, he pushed the casket into the cadaver storage unit and stayed in there with it, with the door closed.

"Later, with the camera activated, he made all the sounds we heard on the video, building up to the moment when he played back the sound of the casket being broken open. You saw all the rest on the video—him emerging in Tate's clothes, stumbling around the room, using Tate's phone to send those texts to Selena Cursen and Aspern."

Stryker was leaning forward now. "Why Aspern?"

"Framing Aspern was an option from the beginning, and sending him that text laid the groundwork."

"What did he do with Tate's body?"

"Cut off the hands to leave Tate's fingerprints in the storage unit and wherever else they might be useful, took some blood to leave at Angus's for DNA identification, then cut the rest of the body into pieces and buried them in the woods near Aspern's house."

"My God," muttered Stryker. In her eyes Gurney could see her mind racing through everything she knew about the case, testing the credibility of what she'd just been told.

A nurse with a friendly face gave a perfunctory knock on the glass door behind Stryker and slid it open. "Sorry to interrupt, I need to look in on my patients." She checked the numbers on the screen next to Hardwick's bed and the fluid level in his plastic IV bag.

"I think you'll live. We'll keep you here for twenty-four hours, and if all your levels are stable at that point, we'll turn you loose. One of our aftercare recommendations will be that you try to avoid major head-on collisions. At least for a while." She smiled and turned to Gurney.

"Any pain?"

"Not really."

"Good. As far as I know, you're all set to go." She smiled again and departed, sliding the glass door shut behind her.

Stryker was frowning, as though her review of the facts had hit a sticking point.

"According to your scenario, Peale went through that elaborate charade of Tate's revival in the mortuary specifically to create the misleading security camera video. Is that right?"

"Yes."

"But I read in the interview notes that he claimed at first there was no video. Why would he do that?"

"I wondered about that myself—until a computer forensics expert told me that cloud-based backups are so common these days it's the first thing they'd look for. If Peale was aware of that, he would have known that the video would come to light—and his professed ignorance of its existence would only add to its credibility."

"You have a high opinion of Mr. Peale's talent for deception."

"I do."

"One more question. If he set up that bloody scene at his house as part of his disappearing act—a way of escaping without anyone thinking he was still alive—why would he take time out to kill you?"

Gurney shrugged. "It doesn't seem very practical, does it?"

"No, it doesn't."

"I'll have to give that some thought."

Hardwick spoke up. "I'll tell you why. Once Sherlock here latches on to something, the son of a bitch never lets go. Peale was not stupid. Maybe he figured the only way to be sure this guy wouldn't come knocking on his door a year down the road was to ice him now."

After a long silence, Stryker nodded.

"That's enough for now. We'll be in touch."

Since Gurney and Madeleine had ridden together to the hospital in the local EMS ambulance, they had no vehicle there, and an off-duty security guard offered to drive them home.

When they arrived at the point between the barn and the pond, where the town road dead-ended into their property, Madeleine asked that they be let out. It took Gurney a minute to manage his exit from the car and get upright on the crutches the hospital had provided. After the guard had refused Madeleine's offer of payment for the ride and had headed back down the road, she suggested sitting for a while in the pair of lawn chairs by the pond.

With Gurney being new to crutches, it took some time to get there. When they were finally settled in, Madeleine explained that she was purposely delaying the sight of the burned henhouse and the terrifying memories it would evoke. She felt all that would be easier to face if she could wrap herself first in the beauty of the morning.

The rising sun was visible above the eastern ridge. The earlier thunderstorm was long gone, the sky was clear, the air was pleasantly cool, the water droplets on the grass were glimmering points of light. Swirls of tiny insects were rising and falling over the surface of the pond. Redwing blackbirds were building nests in the reeds. The night's rain seemed to have intensified the blue of the wild irises by the road.

He reached out and held her hand.

"I was thinking," she said, "that maybe we should go ahead and get a pair of alpacas."

"Oh?"

"Yes. I mean, I feel like we've been given a sign. Sort of, anyway."

"How's that?"

"If we hadn't been talking about alpacas, we probably wouldn't have thought of building the shed extension on the henhouse. And if we hadn't built the shed, the saw wouldn't have been out there, and I wouldn't have known how to use it. So, in a way, talking about alpacas ended up saving your life."

"Hmm."

"So, what do you think?"

EPILOGUE

Martin Carmody's best PR efforts were no match for the sheer number of homicides now associated with Larchfield. The media continued to befoul the reputation of the place in a way that seemed irreversible. The nadir was a RAM-TV special, *Village of the Dead*.

From legal and tax points of view, Silas Gant's Church of the Patriarchs turned out to be unusually complex. From a practical point of view, it simply fell apart. In the absence of their well-connected leader and protector, the remaining Patriarchs faded back into the motorcycle-gang netherworld from which they had come. The frightened, emotionally damaged young women who had been kept at Gant's fortified compound were taken under the wing of a state social service agency, where they were offered all the forms of transitional help and direction that the "caring professions" are empowered to provide.

Discovered among Danforth Peale's assets were three upstate New York cemeteries. In one mausoleum several unidentified bodies were discovered in advanced stages of decomposition, along with a new one, easily recognizable as Randall Fleck.

—

Selena Cursen and Raven (née Lulu Rubin) were released from the hospital, put the property with the burned and bullet-ridden house up for sale, and moved into a holistic community for trauma victims in California.

Mary Kane's body remained for six weeks at the morgue. No relatives could be located. The Nocturnal Bird Club, to which she'd left her meager estate, finally assumed responsibility for her burial.

Angus and Lorinda Russell were both cremated with no one in attendance. Hilda Russell directed that their ashes be disposed of as medical waste.

Silas Gant was given a high-profile funeral by the Armed Ministers Movement. He was eulogized as a true Crusader, ready to stand his ground for God against the rising tide of atheists, socialists, and queers. His killing was condemned as a terrorist attack on Christianity.

Linda Mason's sister had her body transported to the tiny upstate town of Vorlandville, where she was born. She was buried in the Gate of Angels cemetery next to the graves of her parents.

Billy Tate's body parts—which had been removed from the places where Peale had buried them near Chandler Aspern's house and sent to the ME's office for forensic identification—were unclaimed. Despite Darlene Tate's request that they be fed to sewer rats, they were disposed of in the manner prescribed by New York State Department of Health regulations.

Minute flecks of Chandler Aspern's blood were found on the ropes of the conservatory plant hoist, confirming Gurney's suspicion that the device had been used to facilitate shooting him in an upright position.

—

William Danforth Peale III was interred, according to the instructions in his will, in the Peale family's mausoleum in the most exclusive of the three Peale cemeteries. There was a minimal media presence at the event. No family members or friends could be located.

Aided by Madeleine's dependable instinct for the truth, Gurney made an assessment of the mistakes he'd made in the course of the investigation: the faith he'd originally placed in the integrity of the mortuary video, the excessive fondness for a coherent narrative that led to his unquestioning acceptance of Barstow's and Vickerz's description of Tate's putative "escape" from the casket, the credulity with which he'd swallowed Peale's pretense of rage against Fallow. That particular failure of judgment revealed something in himself he hadn't previously been aware of—his tendency to ascribe greater authenticity to expressions of hatred than expressions of love. Rage seemed real, affection questionable. Perhaps someday he'd get to the root of that. In the meantime, he decided to incorporate an unsparing description of his errors into his next academy lecture. He knew that nothing captured a student's attention more effectively than a teacher's admitted screwups.

From time to time—usually in the wee hours of the morning—he would relive the night of carnage at the Russell mansion and question once again the wisdom of his original plan, his fateful decision to reveal it to Morgan, and the way he chose to handle the fallout. On these occasions he would try to embrace Madeleine's perspective. His recollection of her comments brought him a degree of peace.

In her capacity as acting mayor, Hilda Russell called Gurney one bright morning in July and offered him the position of Larchfield Chief of Police. He politely declined. He thanked her again for all that she'd told him about Larchfield's prominent citizens the day they met at the parsonage, and especially for her mention of the long, dark relationship that existed between the Russells and the Peales—without which he might never have gotten to the heart of the case.

Both Lorinda Russell and Chandler Aspern had died intestate. Their substantial assets, including their Harrow Hill properties, were destined to be tied up in legal knots for years to come.

On the gray day of Gurney's last drive through Larchfield, the vast, uninhabited expanse of Harrow Hill was looming over the dead-still water of the lake in a way that gave him an eerie chill.

ACKNOWLEDGMENTS

The Dave Gurney series continues to benefit from the care, energy, and insight of extraordinary people.

First, my thanks to the publishing professionals at Counterpoint, all so good at what they do—especially my superb editor, Dan Smetanka, whose unerring sense of tone and pace I rely on without reservation.

My thanks also to my wonderfully supportive agents, Molly Friedrich, Lucy Carson, and Hannah Brattesani. I can't imagine having smarter, nicer, more effective champions in my corner.

My special thanks to the loyal readers of the Dave Gurney series, whose enthusiasm for its central characters and twisty plots are such a big part of my motivation in creating these stories.

And my thanks to my wife for all the encouragement she gives me, for her remarkable patience with my long periods of silent immersion in devising the bizarre crimes for Gurney to unravel, and, most of all, for giving me a wonderful life.

© Naomi Fisch

JOHN VERDON is the author of the Dave Gurney series of thrillers, international bestsellers published in more than two dozen languages: *Think of a Number*, *Shut Your Eyes Tight*, *Let the Devil Sleep*, *Peter Pan Must Die*, *Wolf Lake*, and *White River Burning*. Before becoming a crime fiction writer, Verdon had two previous careers: as an advertising creative director and a custom furniture maker. He currently lives with his wife, Naomi, in upstate New York. Find out more at johnverdon.net.